# Also by Terry Spear

# HEART
## OF THE
# WOLF

# TERRY
# SPEAR

sourcebooks
casablanca

Published by Sourcebooks Casablanca, an imprint of Sourcebooks, Inc.
P.O. Box 4410, Naperville, Illinois 60567-4410
(630) 961-3900
Fax: (630) 961-2168
sourcebooks.com

Printed and bound in the United States of America.
OPM 10 9 8 7 6 5 4 3 2 1

*To my late mother, my daughter, and my son with all my love for their unwavering encouragement in my story writing for all these years.*

# Letter to Readers

The joy of writing the Heart of the Wolf series and the "Heart of the Jaguars" for me is creating believable shifter characters based on the real animal. Besides reading biologists' studies on wolves and jaguars in the wild—including viewing scenes from videotaped captures of wolves and jaguars in their native environments as they play, hunt, and court—I've visited several wolf reserves and zoos to observe the captive species.

Some would say the animals shouldn't be caged, that they should be free. It's true: in a perfect world, they should live free. But we don't live in a perfect world, and even when the wolves and jaguars are protected, some hunters will illegally hunt them. In some cases, their habitats are being destroyed.

My hat is off to those who educate people about the beauty of wolves and jaguars. One of the stories I learned while visiting a wolf reserve was about a man who raised sheep, but was faced with a dilemma. A she-wolf had lost a leg in an animal leg-trap. She'd also lost her mate and was trying to raise a litter of pups. The only prey she could take down were the farmer's sheep, and she was teaching her pups to do the same. He could have killed her and had a right to do so. But he tranquilized her and turned her and her pups over to one of the wolf reserves that serves as an educational center. There, she had the longest life of any wolf they'd ever cared for.

I had the honor of visiting a wolf reserve in New Mexico where a gray wolf and an Arctic wolf were brought to see us at the sole cabin at the reserve. Zoerro, the gray wolf, had been used in promotional work for the TV-show *Game of Thrones*. He and Sabine, the Arctic wolf, served as ambassador wolves to teach people about wolves and conservation of the environment.

Thanks for reading my books! You never know when you'll be reading something that is truly about a real wolf, or jaguar, in the wild.

Terry Spear

# Prologue

*1850*
*Colorado*

AS SOON AS HE STRIPPED NAKED, HE'D BE HERS.

Unbraiding her hair, Bella Wilder's blood heated with desire while she observed the dark-haired boy. He looked about eighteen, two years older than she. He yanked off one boot, then another, at the lake's edge. It wasn't the first time she'd watched him peel out of his clothes, but it *was* the first time she'd join him. If he had a taste of her, wouldn't he crave her? Hunger to be like her? Wild and free?

She swallowed hard, longing to be Devlyn Greystoke's mate—rather than some human's—but it would never be. Lifting her chin, she resolved to make the human hers. She untied her ankle-high boots, then slipped them off her feet.

The human boy's pet gray wolf rested at the shoreline, his ears perked up as he watched her. But the boy didn't see her—he was unobservant, as most humans were.

However, a boy who cared for his wolf such as he did would care for her, too, wouldn't he? He'd studied her when she swam here before, naked, splashing lazily across the water's surface, attempting to draw him to her. Though he'd tried to conceal himself in the woods, she'd seen him. And heard him with her sensitive hearing when he stepped on dried oak leaves and pine needles to draw closer, to see her more clearly. She'd smelled his heady man scent on the breeze. He'd desired her then, setting her belly afire; he'd desire her now.

Tilting her nose up, she breathed in his masculinity. Masculine but not as wild as her own kind—*lupus garou*. A human who treated a woman with kindness, that's what she desired.

She tugged her pale-blue dress over her head, struggling to shed her clothes as quickly as she could now. Wanting to get her plan into motion, before she changed her mind, or one of the pack tried to change it for her.

Adopted by the gray pack, she wasn't even a gray wolf. So why should it matter if she left them and chose the human boy for her own? Volan, the gray alpha pack leader, wanted her, that's why. Her stomach clenched with the thought that the man who'd nearly raped her would have her if she couldn't find a way out of the nightmare.

The human pulled off his breeches. A boy, still not well muscled, but well on his way. A survivor, living on his own—that's what intrigued her so much about him. A loner, like a rogue wolf, determined to endure.

Only in her heart, she desired the gray who'd saved her life when they were younger—Devlyn. Even now she had difficulty not comparing his rangy, taller body with this boy's. They had the same dark hair and eyes, which maybe explained why the human had attracted her. She wanted Devlyn with all her heart, but craving his attention would only result in Volan killing him.

Best to leave the pack and mate with a human, cut her ties with the grays, and start her own pack.

She'd watched the human ride, run, hunt with his rifle, but she admired him most when he swam. Her gaze dropped lower to the patch of dark hair resting above his legs and...

She raised her brows. A thrill of expectation of having his manhood buried deep inside her sent a tingling of gooseflesh across her skin. If her drawers hadn't been crotchless, they'd have been wet in anticipation. She smiled at the sight of him. He'd produce fine offspring.

He dove into the water with a splash. With powerful strokes he glided across the placid surface of the small, summer-warmed lake. She slipped out of her last petticoat, then her drawers. Without a stitch of clothes on, she stood on the opposite shore, waiting for him to catch sight of her. Wouldn't he yearn for her like her own kind did?

She had to entice him to make love to her. Then she'd change into the wolf and bite him. And transfer the beauty of the wolf to him in the ancient way.

Running her fingers through her cinnamon curls, she fanned them over her shoulders, down to her hips.

They'd live together in his log cabin, taking jaunts through the woods in their wolf states under the bright moon forever. His mother, father, and little sister had died during the winter, and none of his kind lived within a fifteen-mile radius. He'd want her—he had to. Like her wolf pack, most humankind desired companionship.

She stepped into the water.

Then he caught sight of her.

His dark eyes widened and his mouth dropped open. But he didn't swim toward her as she expected. He didn't come for her, ravish her as she wanted. His eyes inspected every bit of her, but then he turned and swam away from her, back to the shore and his clothes. What was wrong with him?

Her mind warred between anger and confusion. Didn't he find her appealing?

She swam toward him, trying to reach the shore before he dressed and headed back to his cabin. But by the time she reached the lake halfway, he'd jerked on his breeches and boots, not even bothering with his shirt or vest, and vanished into the woods with his wolf at his heel.

In disbelief, she stared after him.

"Bella!" the leader of her pack hollered, his voice forbidding and warlike.

She snapped her head around. Her heart nearly stopped when she saw the gray leader.

Volan stood like a predator waiting for the right time to go after his prey. His ebony hair was bound tight, and his black eyes narrowed. As a wolf, he was heavyset, broad shouldered, and thick necked, the leader by virtue of his size, powerful jaws, and wicked killer canines. But now he stood as a man, his thoughts darker than night, his face menacing as he considered her swimming naked in the lake.

Did the boy get away in time, before Volan caught sight of him? How could she be so naive as to think that Volan would let her have a human male?

She paddled in place and glared at him. "What do you

want, Volan?" she growled back, unable to hold a civil tongue whenever he stood near.

"Come out at once!"

He turned his head toward the woods.

Had he smelled the human? Her heart rate quickened. She swam back to her clothes, determined to draw his attention away from the boy.

Then she spied Devlyn, watching, half hidden in the shadows of the forest, as if he and the pack leader were maneuvering in for the kill. A pang of regret sliced through her that Devlyn might have seen her lusting after a human. Three years older than she, he still vied for his place within the pack. A strap of leather tied back his coffee-colored, shoulder-length hair, and she fought the urge to set it free, to soften his harsh look. His equally dark-brown eyes glowered at her, while his sturdy jaw clenched.

He stepped closer, not menacingly, but as if he stalked a deer and feared scaring away his prey. She raised a brow. This time, he seemed to have Volan's permission to draw close.

She growled. "Stay away." Wading out of the water, she distracted Volan from considering the woods or who might have disappeared into them. Devlyn, too, eyed her with far too much interest.

She hurried to slip into her clothes, irritated to have the wrong audience. Still, the way Devlyn closed in on her, only keeping a few feet from her until she was dressed, while Volan remained a hundred yards away, sent a trickle of dread through her.

Volan never allowed males to get close to her when she was naked, and normally she wouldn't have permitted it either. So what were they up to? She left her wet hair loose, then Volan nodded.

As soon as he signaled to Devlyn, her heart skipped a beat, but she didn't react quickly enough. Devlyn surged forward and grabbed her wrist. In the same instant, Volan charged in the direction of the woods where the young man had disappeared.

"Volan!" she screamed.

He intended to murder the boy. Only she had really killed him, as surely as if she'd ripped out his throat herself. Wanting to save him, she struggled to free herself from Devlyn. "Let me go!"

He gripped her wrist tighter and hurried her toward their village.

"He didn't do anything!"

Devlyn glared at her, his eyes unforgiving, blacker than she'd ever seen them. Anger smoldered in the depths. An anger she couldn't understand.

"Please," she pleaded, trying to soften his heart.

She tried to break free, and he wrenched her back to his side. "You're a fool, Bella."

"I won't be Volan's mate!"

For an instant, Devlyn's grasp on her arm lessened. Then he tightened his grip again. "You have no choice. And after what you've done here, he won't wait any longer."

Was there regret in his voice? God, how she wanted him to save her from Volan...to be her mate.

A howl sounded in the distance, and she sank to her knees. Volan had murdered the young man and shouted his actions to the world with great pleasure.

Devlyn yanked her from the ground and hurried her on their way.

"You won't ever leave the pack, Devlyn. You'll always be nothing but a follower!" She hadn't meant to say the hurtful words, but the anger she harbored simmered red hot, like molten lava beneath the surface. "Why can't you run with me? Why can't you take me for your own somewhere far from here?"

He glared at her. "They're my family. They'll always be my family. Something you don't comprehend, apparently."

"I—I thought you felt something for me."

Devlyn pulled her to a stop and grabbed her shoulders. "It can never be between us! Volan would hunt us down, both of us. What kind of a life would that be? He'd kill our offspring, too. Is that what you want? Maybe if I'd been older, stronger, but now he won't wait to have you." He shook his head. "Dammit, Bella, as far as the human was concerned, he wouldn't have wanted you! Can't you see that? If he'd seen you changed, he would have been repulsed. If he could have discovered a way, he'd have killed you." He held her tightly, staring into her eyes with a mixture of anger and hunger. "You know what I want from you."

He was hard and smelled of sex. She sensed that his hormones raged, urging him to mount her. Her breath came quickly as she desired his attentions, but feared them, too. Feared them because of what Volan would do to Devlyn if Volan caught him lusting after her. She'd never seen Devlyn so outwardly angry, so filled with venom—so sexually alive.

"You could smell his putrid fear, woman!" He pulled her against his body and kissed her hard on the mouth, no teasing or waiting for her approval—just pure lust, conquering and decisive. And she loved him, every bit of the dangerous and feral *lupus garou* that he was.

Her body melted to his touch, but Volan's musky, bloody scent drifted to her on the breeze. Panic sliced through her. Volan would claim her now. But if he caught Devlyn touching her...

Volan appeared in a couple of bounds in his ebony-pelted wolf form, his eyes narrowed with hate. He growled, and immediately Devlyn released her. She stepped back, assuming Volan would kill Devlyn for his actions, the thought wrenching at her gut.

Devlyn stood his ground. "I tried to convince her how stupid she was for feeling anything for the human."

Volan turned to Bella. He'd show her how a male wolf took a mate. The moisture from her throat evaporated. The image of him trying to take her when she was much younger still fed her nightmares. A streak of shudders racked her body.

Volan turned his attention back to Devlyn. The hair stood on end from the nape of his neck to the tip of his tail. He advanced aggressively, then stopped.

Torn between giving herself to Volan to protect Devlyn and fighting Volan herself, she knew neither would work. Devlyn would hate her either way—damn his male wolf pride.

Volan growled again. Devlyn yanked off his shirt. His muscles flexed as he tugged at his belt, his golden skin shimmering with sweat in the summer sun. Any other day, she loved to see every bit of his handsome physique—his muscled thighs, the dark patch of curly hair between his legs, and the erection she'd encouraged. But not now, not with Volan threatening to rip him to shreds.

As soon as Devlyn stood naked, he began to change, his body twisting into the form of a wolf, his snout elongated. A thick brown pelt as rich as a mink's covered his long legs and torso. He howled as the change took place. Volan waited patiently before he lunged.

She couldn't watch him rip Devlyn apart. She couldn't stomach seeing the bully hurt any other wolf of the pack. But certainly not Devlyn, with whom she'd played as a pup, not Devlyn who'd rescued her from the wildfire that took her red wolf pack's lives. She couldn't save him now…only maybe herself. Yet when Volan lunged for Devlyn, she dashed between them to protect him. Volan clamped his teeth down on her arm, having the ability to crush the bone with his powerful canines. She cried out when a streak of pain shot up her arm and blood dripped from the wound. Though his eyes reflected remorse at once and he released her, he growled at her to stay out of the way. And so did Devlyn.

Maybe if she ran, Volan would come after her. Maybe she could save Devlyn that way. But she would never return to the pack.

She bolted, with her legs stretched far out, her heart pounding, her breath steady, but her mind frantic—her only chance was to toss her clothes and run like the wolf.

# Chapter 1

ONE HUNDRED AND FIFTY YEARS LATER—AGING ONE YEAR for every thirty that passed once a *lupus garou* reached puberty—Bella was the equivalent of a human twenty-one-year-old. She longed more than ever to have Devlyn for her mate, wishing she hadn't had to hide from the pack all these years. The burning desire for him flooded her veins whenever she came into the wolf's heat. Her body craved his touch, but her mind had given up hoping to ever have him for her own. If she could find a strong, agreeable human mate, she could change him into a *lupus garou,* and he would keep her safe from Volan.

She shook her head, trying to rid herself of the image of the brutish fiend, and continued to pack her overnight bag. Any man would be better than he—a good mate who would help her establish her own pack.

She turned to look at Devlyn's photo sitting on the bedside table, the most recent one that Argos, the old, retired pack leader, had sent her. Taking a deep breath, she threw another pair of jeans into her bag, determined to get her mind off Devlyn.

Knowing she couldn't put off mating much longer, she realized that one's second choice far outweighed living alone; even the sound of a dog's howl on the night's breeze triggered the gnawing craving to be with a pack.

She stalked into her office and left an email message for Argos, a routine she'd adopted because he insisted she keep him posted whenever she went into the woods. As a loner, she'd have no backup.

> Off to the cabin for the weekend again, Argos.
> Give the pack my love, in secret. Yours always,
> love, Bella

She didn't have to tell him to keep her correspondence a secret; he knew what would happen if Volan learned where she was…

Turning off her computer, she picked up her phone and called her next-door neighbor—a woman who had partially eased Bella's loneliness after losing her twin sister in a fire so many years ago. "Chrissie, I'm going to my cabin for the weekend again. Can you keep an eye on my place?"

"Sure thing, Bella. Pick up your mail on Saturday, too, if you'd like. And I'll water your greenhouse plants. Hey, I don't want to hold you up, but did you hear about the latest killing?"

"Yeah, the police have got to catch the bastard soon."

That was one of the reasons she was going to her cabin, to get away, to consider the facts of the murders, to search for clues in the woods. He had to be from Portland or the surrounding area, since it was there he'd killed all the women. And he had to take a jaunt in a forest from time to time. The call of the wild was too strong in them. She hadn't expected to smell red *lupus garou* in the place where she ran, as far away as it was from the city. For three years she hadn't smelled a hint of them. Not until last weekend. Was one of them the killer? She had to know.

Bella tossed a pink sweatshirt into the bag.

"You be careful, honey. The victims are all redheads in their twenties. And the last was killed not far from here."

"Don't worry, Chrissie. I've got a gun for protection." Well, two: one at her cabin, and one at home, but who was counting? Silver bullets, too; Bella had them made for Volan. It wasn't the *lupus garou* way, but she had no other way to fight him. She would never be his.

"A...a gun? Do you know how to shoot it?"

Yep, she'd learned how to shoot a gun a good century and a half ago, ever since the early days when she had lived in the wilderness, trying to survive in the lands west of Colorado.

"Yeah, don't worry. Give your kids hugs for me, will you? Tell Mary I want to see the painting she did for art class, and tell Jimmy that I want to see his science project when I return."

Chrissie sighed. "I'll tell them. You be careful up there all by yourself. That is, if you're going all by yourself."

Always checking. Chrissie was looking for husband number two, and she assumed Bella rendezvoused with some mountain man every time she returned to her cabin.

"See you Monday."

"Be careful, Bella. You never know where that maniac will end up."

"I'll be cautious. Got to go."

Bella hung up the phone and zipped her suitcase. Before it turned dark she had every intention of searching the woods for further clues concerning the red *lupus garou*—not a wild dog, a mixed wolf-dog breed, or as some thought, a pit bull that some bastard had trained to kill his victims—that might be killing the women.

Why had she caught the scent of red *lupus garou* in the area near her cabin now, when the woods had been free of their kind for the last three years? She envisioned a lone female wouldn't stand a chance at remaining that way. Her stomach curdled with the idea that she'd have to give up her cabin and find a new place to run. Just one more concern to add to her growing list of worries.

---

Later that day, when Bella arrived at her cabin, the waning moon called to her though it was still fairly light out. She tilted her nose up to the breeze, standing on the porch of her cedar home in the woods, the building now a faded gray. It served as her hideaway on the weekends when she lived on the wild side, away from the hustle and bustle of the city of Portland. She would be the right age to be Volan's mate, if he ever found her. Smiling at how clever she had been to avoid him, the smile faded as a coyote howled. She wasn't meant to be a rogue wolf, living alone without a pack. Some were naturally geared that way. Not her.

More than that, Devlyn still held her heart hostage, *damn him*. She could still feel the way his strong fingers had gripped her shoulders with possessiveness, smell his feral craving to have her, feel his heart thundering when he crushed her against him. Why couldn't he have run with her?

She shook her head, trying to clear her thoughts of the one who'd possessed her soul since the beginning.

It wasn't that she didn't care for the gray wolf pack, the *lupus garou* family who had taken her in. It was the unfathomable notion that she'd have been Volan's mate that fired her soul to the depths of hell. Stronger than the rest, he wasn't brighter, nor caring in the least bit. Just a bully, such as in ancient times when the strongest men ruled. Why couldn't she find a mate who would treat her as…as…an equal?

Somewhere, such a male had to exist.

Taking a deep breath, she pulled off her sweater, turtleneck, denims, and hiking boots, and dropped them on a porch chair. Standing naked, she shivered, then breathed in the heavenly scent of pine needles, the smell once again triggering the memory of Devlyn kissing her. No man since had kissed her like he had.

She gritted her teeth and swallowed hard. He stirred primal longings in her too strong to quench. The desire to feel him deep inside her, filling her with his seed, producing their offspring, their family—sharing a life-time commitment as mates forever—overwhelmed her. But he wasn't the leader of the pack. Even if she wanted Devlyn for her mate, she didn't think he'd ever be strong enough to have her. Yet, she couldn't help but keep in touch with Argos, the old former leader of the pack. Knowing Devlyn was alive and well...

She growled with exasperation. For now she had to hunt like a wolf, and in the interim, search for a different prey—the feral predator that stalked human redheaded females and murdered them like a rabid wolf.

Stretching again, her lean body began to take the form of the wolf. The painless transformation always occurred quickly and filled her with a sense of urgency—to hunt, to run wild among the other creatures of the forest.

A thick, cinnamon-red pelt covered her skin as her nose elongated into a snout, and her teeth grew ready for the hunt. She straightened her back, howled with the change, then dropped to her paws. Her nails extended into sharp claws, itching to dig into the pine needle–cushioned earth.

Though she preferred venison to rabbit, she hunted the latter. Killing deer out of season constituted a crime. If anyone found the leftovers of such a kill, an investigation would follow. Soon word would spread that a wolf was killing deer in the area. A wolf that might next go after ranchers' sheep or cattle, or household pets, or children. A wolf thought to be extinct in these parts.

Leaping off the porch, her long legs carried her with graceful bounds through the wilderness. She traveled through several hundreds of acres before spying another cabin—quiet, vacated. Since it was winter and no longer hunting season, except for the end of dusky Canadian goose season, she shouldn't glimpse another human being.

She thought she caught a whiff of something familiar. Pausing, she sniffed the air, and recognized the distinctive smell of *lupus garou*—red *lupus garou*.

Loping toward the origin of the scent, she darted past pines and firs, ducked beneath low-hanging branches, jumped a moss-covered log in her path…then halted.

A patch of red fur clung to the bark of an oak. Definitely red wolf; and because none existed here, it had to be a red *lupus garou*'s.

She contemplated returning to her human form and taking the evidence back to her cabin, but she was miles from there, and as cold as it was, her human counterpart probably wouldn't make it.

The breeze shifted. She smelled the red's scent stronger now. He'd just urinated somewhere nearby, marking his territory. She hesitated. If he were looking for a mate, she'd be a prime target; and if he were an alpha male, she wouldn't be strong enough to fight him if he decided to force a mating.

Leaves rustled. A twig snapped underfoot a short distance away. A chill raced all the way down her spine to the tip of her taut tail. An eerie feeling she was being watched froze her in place.

What if he was the killer? What if he was hunting *her* now? But what if she could lure him into the open, play his game, and turn him over to whatever pack happened to live in the area? Even if he were a loner, the pack in the territory would condemn him to die. Killing humans put every *lupus garou* at risk. Keeping their secret hidden was the only way for them to survive.

Then again, he might just be a pack member hunting

for fresh meat—enjoying the freedom of the change like she was—who had come across her, a loner *lupus garou* violating the pack's territory. Unless...unless their reds had a shortage of females like the Colorado grays did, and...

*Damn*, why hadn't she considered that before now?

She stared into the shadowy woods where bugs cricketed in a raucous chorus and a breeze ruffled the pine needles in a whispered hush. If there was a severe shortage of female *lupus garou*, was the killer trying to turn a human female in the ancient way? To make her his mate?

*Not* good.

She dashed to where he'd left his mark. No sign of him. But the urine was fresh. Too fresh. He had to be close by, but if he were stalking her he couldn't be an alpha male. An alpha male would have already approached her and let her know he wanted her, if he needed a mate. He had to smell how ripe she was and know she was ready, too. Was that why he went after female humans, because they were easier to take than a *lupus garou*? Maybe he was afraid to advance on a loner who was more feral, warier, more unpredictable.

She caught the scent of another. Also male. Except for twitching her ears back and forth and withdrawing her panting tongue, she listened and sniffed the air but stood in place.

She smelled...water.

Swallowing, she felt parched, and loped toward the sound of Wolf Creek, the water bubbling nearby. At the fringe of the forest she hesitated, not liking the way

the stream's banks were so exposed. For several minutes she stood watching, listening for signs of danger—
human danger.

Nothing.

The water beckoned to her. She swallowed again,
stared at the rush of the stream, then walked cautiously
across the pebble bank.

Unable to shake the feeling that someone watched
her, she waited like a rabbit cornered by a wolf,
cemented in place.

Ice-cold water from melting snow off the mountains
dove over rounded rock. She dipped her tongue into the
water and lapped it up; the liquid cooled and soothed
her dry throat.

She couldn't help wishing she were back in Colorado,
running with Devlyn like they'd done when they were
younger—chasing through the woods, nipping at each
other's hindquarters, feeling the wind ruffle their fur.
God, how she wished he'd mated with her.

Water trickled and gurgled at her feet, birds chirped
overhead, and sugar-drained oak leaves rustled in the
breeze all around her. But then a flash of red fur caught
her attention, and she turned.

The glitter of the sun's fading reflection off a wolf's
amber eyes captured her, held her hostage, but her gaze
held him captive, too. But only for a moment. His head
whipped to the side. Another flash of fur, and another
male appeared. Then, the wave of a wolf's tail as the
*lupus garou* made a hasty retreat. She should have
heeded the instinctual warning. Instead, she gauged the
remaining wolf's posture, the way he turned his attention

back to her, closed his mouth, and almost seemed to smile before dashing after his companion.

The crashing through the underbrush couldn't hide the most dangerous sound known to wildlife—a trigger clicking on a rifle. Nothing could disguise the sound of death.

Immediately her tail stood upright, and the hair on her back and neck stood on end.

A chill hurtled down her spine and she dashed through the creek, her heart thundering. Her ears twisted back and forth, trying to identify where the hunter stood.

The sound of a crack rang across the woods and open area, and a sharp pain stabbed her in the left flank. She stumbled…then attempted to dash off again, her leg numbed with paralysis.

The hunter shouted, "He's still going! I've never seen a red wolf that big! Shoot him again!"

*Idiots*. They couldn't kill her with normal bullets.

Running for several yards, she reached the edge of the forest, but the guarded relief she felt withered when the men splashed across the creek in hot pursuit of her. She sprinted north toward her cabin, miles away. Except going this way meant she had to cross the river. Then again, she could ford it, while she doubted they could.

"Hurry!" one of the men shouted, his voice rife with enthusiasm, but shadowed with a hint of concern.

She would have clenched her teeth in anger, but she was panting too hard. Her movements slowed. Even her brain fuzzed, and her eyesight blurred. Ripping out their throats came to mind, if they got close enough. The

primal instinct for self-preservation voided out the ruling
drummed into her that her kind didn't kill humans; keeping their existence a secret outweighed the importance
of the life of any single *lupus garou*.

"Tag him before he reaches the river! We don't want
him drowning!" the same man shouted.

Another crack. Another stab of pain. This time her
right flank. Her back legs gave out and she stumbled.
What had they shot her with? She panted, her heart
racing as she tried to keep her wits.

The men crashed through the brush toward her. Their
boots impacting with the earth radiated outward and the
tremor centered in her pads. She struggled to run. Her
heart rate slowed.

"Man oh man, I told you, didn't I, Thompson? He's
beautiful," a tall man said, wearing camouflaged gear, his
dark hair chopped short, the bill of a camouflaged baseball
cap shading his eyes. He approached her with caution.

She gave him a feral look that meant danger and
dragged her back legs. *Work, damn you! Work!* But no
matter how much she willed her legs to push her forward, she couldn't manage. She sat, panic driving her to
run, but unable to oblige as a strange numbness slipped
through her body. No longer able to sit up, she rolled
over onto her side. And watched the hunters approach
with murder in her eyes.

"Damn! He's the biggest red wolf I've ever seen,
Joe," Thompson said as both drew closer...cautiously...
the smell of fear cloaking them. He was dressed like the
other, only his blue eyes were wide with excitement.

She lifted her head, snarled, and snapped her teeth,

but the futile effort cost her precious energy. Exhausted, she dropped her head back to the forest floor, the bed of pine needles tickling her nose.

Joe crouched at her back, then pulled something from her hip. A dart, not bullets. *Damn*. Her heart beat so slowly she thought she'd die.

"You sure as hell were right that a red wolf prowled these parts. But they've been extinct for years. How in the hell did he get here? I mean, he couldn't have traveled all the way from the Great Smoky Mountains National Park." Joe smelled of sweat and sex and a musky deodorant that wasn't holding up under the pressure; nor was his flowery cologne hiding the body odor.

Thompson, a blond-haired, bearded man, smelled just as sweaty and virile, but he wore no artificial sweeteners to attract the female variety. She could hear his heart hammering against his ribs when he raised her back leg.

Unable to lift her head, she snarled, but the sound, muffled in sleep, didn't have the threat she intended.

"He's a she. Damn. How'd a female ever grow this big?"

She growled, priding herself in being a red wolf, and small. Sure, for a real wolf she appeared big, but as a *lupus garou*...

He ran his hand over her hind leg. If she hadn't seen him do it, she'd never have realized it, as numb as her leg was. "Long legs, best looking red pelt I've ever seen on a feral wolf." He looked over at the dark-haired man. "She's in heat, Joe. We'll have to find her a mate."

Mate? Great. If they locked her in a room with a real

red wolf…ohmigod, they couldn't be planning on taking her to a *zoo*!

"That'd be the ticket." Joe lifted a cell phone to his ear. "Hey, we got her! Yeah, the wolf's a she, not a he as I'd assumed. No shit! I told you I'd seen her running through here last weekend."

Why hadn't she seen these men? Smelled their pungent odors? Heard them?

She had let down her guard, and now she would pay.

"Yeah, she's a big one." Joe nodded. "We figured one dart would be enough…took two." He ran his hand over her side. She attempted her most terrifying growl, but it sounded more like a sickly, low moan. "Maybe 110 pounds, more the size of a gray." He chuckled. "I know, I know, I told you she's big. No, not fat. Lean as they come, just longer legged and longer bodied, and she has the prettiest red pelt you ever did see."

He ran his hand over her back. "Okay, we'll pack her out of here. Be there in about three hours; longer, if she comes to. The tranquilizers each were set for a forty-pound wolf, not one as big as she is. But we didn't want to overdo it. And let 'em know Big Red can have a mate now. No need for the Brevard Zoo to send us a loaner. Unless she's been mating with coyotes, she's about due for a hunk of a red wolf."

He laughed, undoubtedly amused by the response to his comment on the other end of the line.

She groaned inwardly.

"All right, out here." He turned to the blond. "Seems a shame if she's doing so well in these woods that we have to put her into captivity, Thompson."

"Hey, like you said, she won't find any of her kind around here. We're doing her a favor."

Inwardly, she fumed, and if she hadn't been so doped up, she'd have bitten both of them.

---

Three days later, Bella paced across her new zoo home—nice, flat boulders for her to rest on, tree-shaded areas, and an indoor exhibit where humans gawked at her through fingerprint-smudged windows.

Furious with the hunters, and even more so with herself, a growl rumbled in her throat. How could she have been so lax in her run not to have noticed them before this?

She paused and took a deep breath, then glanced up at the top of the pen. No way to climb up above. Even if she changed into her human form, she'd never make it, given the way the cliff arched back over the top, providing shade on a sunny day.

She wandered over to the water trough. When she dipped her tongue into the water, Big Red slinked in behind her. She growled. He backed off. The poor old horny red wolf was dying to mate with her. She smelled perfectly ripe, the precise mating time for a wolf, so what was wrong with her, she was sure he wondered.

She shuddered. Mating with a pure wolf...the very thought.

She resumed her pacing, but when the familiar scent of *lupus garou* caught her off guard, she stopped. Two men, both around five foot ten, leaned over the wrought iron railing across the moat. The breeze carried their scent to her, musky and wild. But she recognized the scent of one of them from the Cascades when she went on her run. Ohmigod, they'd followed her all the way here? Unless they lived in Portland or the surrounding area...*not good*.

She studied them closer. Both men wore their brown hair—tinged with a slight reddish cast—short and watched her with intrigue. But they both had small chins, not a nice square manly jaw like Devlyn had, and both were scrawny compared to the taller, sturdier built grays.

*Red lupus garou*. Her heart took a dive. She hadn't seen her kind in human form since she lost her own people when she turned six.

They smiled as she observed them, and tilted their noses up slightly, smelling the breeze when it shifted.

"Hello, sweetheart," the older man said, who appeared to be in his late twenties. "Where have you been all of my life?"

She looked over at the other, probably closer to her age. He grinned like he advertised teeth whitener. "Yeah, Alfred, she's one of us all right. Understands every word we say. The right mating age, too."

"Yeah, and in heat, too." Alfred rubbed his smooth chin. "Got yourself in kind of a bind, eh?" He glanced around, and seeing no other visitors nearby, turned back to her and winked. "We'll risk getting you out, but on one condition."

She bared her teeth at him, and he burst out laughing. His friend joined in on the chorus.

"Maybe she'd rather have *me*," the other man said,

poking his thumb at his chest. "She surely can't want *him*." He pointed at Big Red. Folding his arms, he said, "She's the one from the woods, don't you think?"

Alfred nodded, the smile on his lips not reaching his dark eyes. "From all accounts, she's the one." He grabbed his companion's shoulder. "Make sure nobody's coming."

His friend turned around and served as lookout as Alfred unzipped his pants. He obviously planned to rescue her and make her his mate. The wolf urge to mark his territory overwhelmed his better human judgment. After he urinated along the bottom edge of the fence, he zipped his pants and smiled. "We'll be back later, sweet thing."

*God help me.*

The keeper's door creaked opened, and she turned when Thompson walked in with the dark-haired man. Thompson folded his arms as she stared at him. "So what have they been feeding her, Joe?"

"They fast 'em once a week. Feed 'em bone or muscle meat once a week. Two-thirds canine maintenance, one-third frozen feline diet the remainder of the week. She's eating well. Don't know what seems to be the problem. She won't let him near her to breed."

*You'd better believe it, Joe.*

She strolled off, found a protected area in the sun near the entrance to their faux cave, lay down, and rested her head on her paws.

"We've thought of sending her to another zoo. Several are interested in pairing her up with a male to provide some more offspring. They're trying to introduce some

more red wolves into the Smokies, but they need to be
feral. She'd certainly do if they could find her a mate as
wild as she is."

She raised her head and looked back at them. If she
could have glared at them, she would have.

Thompson smiled. "Seems that might interest her.
But unsettling her again might do more harm than good.
Let her grow used to him for a couple of more weeks.
Then if she's still not ready, we'll move her."

Joe pushed his baseball cap back off his forehead.
"You don't think she's too young."

"No, she's ready. She's just a little shy."

*Hmpf. Shy, that'd be the day.* Then she had an idea.
Maybe Thompson would make a good mate. He looked
strong enough to take Volan on, and he did like wolves.
Maybe he could be the one, if she could get over the fact
that he had shot her and stuck her in a zoo with a horny,
big red wolf. She laid her head back on her legs.

But then a horrible thought dawned on her. When
would the moon fade from the sky? *Damn.* The waning
crescent would pass shortly. Then it would be the new
moon again. Jumping up, she began to pace.

She had to make her escape before that happened,
before she became a human with no chance to remain
a wolf, not until the return of the moon. It would be
seven days until the new moon from the beginning of the
waning crescent. But three days had passed and when
she took her fatal run she'd already observed the waning
crescent for...

She couldn't remember. Two days? Three?
*Damn.*

"There's been some unusual recent interest in her," Thompson said.

She stopped pacing and turned to listen.

Thompson placed his hands on his hips. "Now isn't it interesting how she listens to our conversation?"

"She seems to sometimes. She's really gentle."

*You should see me on a bad day.*

Thompson shook his head. "A wolf is a wolf, still wild at heart. Anyway, a man was interested in transferring her to another zoo. But…" He looked at his feet. "I don't know. I didn't trust him. He seemed to have something else in mind."

When he looked up, his blue eyes widened, and he straightened his back. He motioned with his head toward the railing. "In fact, there's the man, right there."

She turned to look at the railing, and her heart nearly stopped.

"See what I mean? It's like she understands everything we say."

Staring at Devlyn, she couldn't unlock her gaze from him. So many lonely years, dreaming of his hard embrace, and now he stood across the moat from her in the flesh. Her heart beat so hard it was sure to bruise her ribs. Adrenaline coursed through her body at breakneck speeds, the thought that he'd come to free her giving her hope. What she wouldn't give to nip him in the neck, to tackle him and force him to the ground. To have his heated kisses, his firm touch embracing her with wanton desire.

She took a steadying breath. She couldn't deny he still held her heart captive.

Like before, a strap tied his shoulder-length, dark-brown hair back. A black leather jacket fitted over his broad shoulders, and denims stretched comfortably down his long, muscular legs to his well-worn western boots. He was every bit as handsome as she remembered him, only much taller and more imposing and real than the photos Argos had sent her.

She focused on Devlyn's mouth. How many women had he kissed since he'd kissed her? Her veins turned to ice as an uncontrollable jealousy washed over her.

Was he already mated? Her gut tightened with the idea. She shifted her gaze back to his eyes. His dark-brown eyes turned into black quartz, angry with a hint of concern.

Did he recognize her? Sure he did. If she caught him in his wolf suit, she'd know him any day. But how had he found her?

Unless...unless...somehow the fact that a red wolf was living in the Cascades, when none should, got big-time media. *Great*. That's how he'd found her. He must realize the predicament she faced and the danger to all of them. That's why he'd tried to move her from the zoo. If she turned into a human by the new moon, she could be used to prove legendary werewolves truly exist.

Did he have a plan? He moved his hands over the black wrought iron posts, up and down. His actions hypnotized her. What was his plan?

"What's he doing?" Thompson asked.

"I don't know, but he sure has her attention. You think maybe she belonged to him once?"

"Hmm, now that sounds like a distinct possibility.

And he wants her back so he can release her to the wild again. I want him checked out and watched. He's probably one of those crazy animal rights activists. Doesn't he realize she's safer here, with a good diet, and no one to hunt her down? Besides, where can she find a male red to mate? She'd be stuck with scrawny coyotes."

Joe laughed. "Guess it wouldn't matter to her, as long as the deed is done."

She emitted a low growl.

"Don't think she likes your suggestion," Thompson joked.

She turned her attention back to Devlyn. He looked kissable. He'd filled out into a man-size hunk, but his eyes remained dark and foreboding—even more so now.

Devlyn tilted his chin up as if taunting her to tell him what she thought of him, but he continued to stroke the bars. She realized then he smelled she was in heat. The urge to mate with her would be as natural to him as breathing the air or blinking an eye.

Her gaze met his, the depths of his eyes smoldering with lust. Then he scowled and turned away. He strode off, his long gait taking him away from her within seconds. She wanted to scream at him to set her free. But in the worst way she wanted him to mate with her, to fulfill the unquenchable craving that the sight of him sparked, to take her for his own, his mate forever.

"She knows him, all right, don't you think, Joe?"

"Yeah, like a dog knows his owner."

She whipped her head around too fast in anger, a growl rumbling in her throat.

Both Thompson's and Joe's mouths dropped open.

Thompson said, "My God, I swear she thought you'd insulted her."

She loped back to her den, a cement home, hidden from everyone's view. Insult was right. *A dog*. And Devlyn her master? She growled again.

Then she thought what if she changed and, damn... as a woman, albeit naked, she could open the door to the wolf's den. Unless they locked it. Why would they lock it? The wolves couldn't just leave.

Big Red crept closer to the entrance of the den. She growled so ferociously, he immediately backed off.

The two men laughed. Thompson studied the den. "You can see who wears the pants in the family."

Settled down on the floor, she rested her head on her paws. But wouldn't they lock the doors to keep others out? Sure. To protect idiot visitors who wanted to pet the nice wolves.

Bella lifted her snout and howled. She howled for the loss of freedom, for the loss of her red wolf family, for missing the affection of the grays who had taken her in, and for the love she felt for Devlyn—a hopeless, pitiful fondness for a *lupus garou* she could never have as a mate.

"She's howling for him, don't you think?" Joe asked.

"If I didn't know better, yeah, I'd think so." Thompson folded his arms, his blue eyes studying her with sympathy.

"Hey, Thompson," a new male voice said, "there's some guy named Volan Smith on the phone who says he's got transfer papers to take our new little lady out of here."

Bella's ears perked up. Her heartbeat increased so

rapidly she feared she was having an early heart attack. *Volan* had arranged for Devlyn to come for her. Damn the both of them. She growled low with hatred.

Thompson shook his head. "Rosa's not leaving here without some verification that this man has legitimate papers to move her. I've heard nothing about this."

To Bella's profound relief, the men left the pen, and she closed her eyes. When the zoo shut for the night and all of the personnel had gone home, she'd change into her human form and escape across the moat, hopefully, before anyone could turn her over to Volan.

She couldn't believe after all these years that she'd been safe from him, one mistake in the woods could cost her much more than her freedom. Life as Volan's mate would be a living hell.

She suspected Devlyn would return to her under the cover of night. She had to flee before then.

For some time, she slept quietly, allowing the darkness to come. But in that darkness, nightmares that had plagued her forever returned—the searing heat, the white-hot flames, the choking smoke, the fire that killed her entire red *lupus garou* family. Then Devlyn, a lanky immature youngster of a gray werewolf pack, nearly twice her size, arrived at the stony river's edge. Without hesitation, he grabbed her by the scuff of the neck and swam across the river to save her.

For a moment, she felt a sense of peace.

Then, instinctively, something awakened her in the wolves' pen. A low, menacing growl? A padded footstep creeping toward her?

She opened her eyes as Big Red took a step toward

her. She'd been so keyed up, so tired, and now still so groggy, she hadn't realized what had happened right away. She stared at her changed form. No longer did she have the warm pelt of a red wolf, nor four legs, or an elongated snout. Now lying on the icy cement floor, she was a woman, cold, naked, and facing a snarling Big Red.

Hell, she hadn't correctly calculated the days of the waning crescent of the moon. The new moon had arrived and, except for a sprinkling of stars across the black satin night, no sphere lighted the way.

This time Big Red growled at her, exposing his canines and a few front teeth. His tail stood erect, and so did the hair on the nape of his neck and back. She rose slowly from her prone position, but could only crouch because of the low ceiling in the den.

She needed to stand, to spread her arms, to make him think she was bigger and more powerful. But it was too cramped. She stared him down, intimidating him like he attempted to do to her now.

In her present form, she hated to advance on him. She had to move slowly so as not to frighten him more. He could kill her and what a mess that would be.

How could she explain how a woman entered the wolves' den and survived a vicious attack if he decided to bite, and she survived. How could she explain why she was naked? And how could she explain how Rosa had vanished into thin air? Further, how quickly could she heal if he injured her?

Would the legendary werewolf come to mind?

# Chapter 2

DEVLYN STARED AT THE INKY SKY FROM THE BALCONY OF his hotel room, his heart pounding furiously as he considered how Bella had been locked up in the zoo. He never thought he'd see her again, but she was even more beautiful than before, if that was possible. He recognized the longing in her whiskey-colored eyes. *Save me,* they pleaded. And the smell of her—wild and ripe for the picking.

God, how he wanted to claim her heart and body for his own.

He gritted his teeth and fisted his hands. How many times did he have to rescue the woman before she recognized how...

He shook his head. It didn't matter how he felt. She could never be his. Even if Volan didn't lead the pack, it wouldn't matter—Bella was so hell-bent on having a human for a mate. His neck muscles grew taut.

The door adjoining his room squeaked open. He turned.

Gray-haired, wiry Argos nodded. Once the leader of the pack, he had stepped down when he'd grown too old. "Are you sure she'll come to me?"

"She trusts you."

Argos winced. The old leader didn't like the idea of returning her to Volan any more than Devlyn did, but she wouldn't be safe on her own. Worse, she threatened the secrecy of their kind with her rash decisions. She belonged to their pack for safe keeping, period.

"You were like a father to her. She was happy with us until Volan took over," Devlyn continued. "She'll come to you."

"I know what you want, but you can't have her."

"Nobody can have her. Not while she's got this insane notion of finding a human to love. Why does Volan want her so badly? She'll make a lousy alpha female mate when she despises him so. He can't lock her up or force her to mate with him."

Argos raised his brows, but remained silent.

Devlyn rubbed his temple, trying to massage away the tension that collected there. "He wouldn't, would he?"

"He's the pack leader. Once he gets hold of her, she'll obey him or pay the consequences. He's driven to have her as much as she's driven to avoid him and find the perfect human mate. So what drives you, Devlyn?"

Hatred of male humans. Procreation of his kind, if he could ever find a suitable mate. But none of the other females in their pack were an acceptable age that he wanted. Only Bella. And searching for another of his kind—well, of the red wolf variety, as that's what he had his heart set on—proved unachievable.

It was like looking for red wolves in the wild in the States. Nearly impossible to find. And no other kind of wolf would do. The red wolf in her had to be what drew him to her.

"I've heard rumors he killed his own brother," Devlyn said, avoiding Argos's question.

"Which one?"

In disbelief, Devlyn stared at him. "There was more than one?"

"Two, both died before you joined the pack. But no, they were accidents. A mountain lion killed his youngest triplet when he was a juvenile. He'd roamed away from the pack on a hunt and the others couldn't reach him in time. His eldest brother died in a raging flood. Tree was uprooted, smashed into his skull. The healers said he was dead before the river pulled him under. But Volan learned his bullying from that brother, the meanest, most crotchety wolf known to *lupus garou*. Just surviving his browbeating made Volan as strong as he is today."

Devlyn made a disgruntled throaty sound. He'd always wondered why Volan was so aggressive and controlling, but as far as he was concerned, it didn't excuse his behavior. "Are the others ready?"

"Yes."

"Volan's not coming for her later, is he?" Devlyn jerked his leather jacket on.

"No. He's the leader, not stupid."

"Some of us would argue that point."

Volan sent Devlyn to retrieve Bella because he wanted to emphasize the point that Devlyn would reclaim her, but she belonged to Volan. The thought curdled Devlyn's supper, a couple of hastily eaten half-raw burgers, resting like a greasy lump in the pit of his stomach.

Once they'd seen the newsflash concerning her, they had to be sure it was her, though. Finding a red wolf in the Cascades was unheard of, and to top that off, she was larger than normal. The pack knew the red wolf could only be a *lupus garou,* and Argos knew it had to be Bella or she would have been with a pack.

But Devlyn had to make sure. She could have been any one of a number of lone red *lupus garou* females all across the States. Or not. Because such a shortage existed, he sure as hell hoped Argos was right—that she was their stubborn Bella.

When Devlyn saw her in the pen at the zoo, he knew. He couldn't be angry with her for having run away—but for her to risk proving to the world that *lupus garous* existed? That was irresponsible and unforgivable. At least that's what he told himself, though his heart ached to hold her close again, only this time to claim her for his own.

Devlyn stalked toward the door of his hotel suite. "All right. Let's break our little red wolf out of jail." The notion that she was theirs, though, struck a chord. She wasn't theirs. She belonged to Volan. Fire burned in Devlyn's veins with the thought. Ever since Devlyn had rescued her near the river, the wildfire in hot pursuit of her, Volan had wanted her, too.

For years Devlyn had pinned her to the ground in their wolf states, avoiding her retaliatory bites, playing with her as young wolves frolicked. He still wanted to tackle her to the ground, to force her reaction, to have her pay attention to him. But the burning desire to have her for his mate drove away any notion of having another female.

He hurried his four younger male cousins out to the SUV with Argos at his side in the freezing drizzle. The black-haired, amber-eyed quadruplets, twenty-two years of age, all itched for a fight as they clenched their fists and steeled their square jaws.

Devlyn slammed his door. "If we wait much longer, she'll have changed and be half frozen in this weather." He'd rescue her again. He had to. Not for Volan, but for his own greedy desires. But what to do with her afterwards? He knew what he wanted to do with her. Make her his...forever...his mate for life.

But with Volan still living, how could Devlyn hope to take her for his own? That question had plagued him every minute of the day since he'd learned she still lived.

---

Backed into the confines of the wolf den, Bella spread her arms out, slowly, in her crouched position, to make herself appear larger. "Back off, Big Red."

He continued to snarl. She took a step forward, and shivered, but it wasn't the chill in the air that made her tremble. The notion that the zoo staff would catch her in the wolves' den in human form forced concern to worm its way into every pore.

Big Red held his ground.

She took another step in his direction. Her eyes remained locked onto his. He didn't back down.

Wrinkling her nose, she bared her not-very-scary human teeth. Anything to show him she wasn't intimidated by his posturing.

After what seemed like an eternity of an old western gunfight showdown, he turned, and trotted out of the den. She took a deep breath, then quickly followed him out. The icy drizzle coated her skin. Hoping to make her escape easily, she crossed the pen to the keeper's door.

*Locked.*

Her stomach muscles tightened with irritation. Heading for the water trough, she thought to use it as a step in the moat. But it was filled to the brim with water, and she couldn't budge it. Her frustration level mounted, but her body temperature dropped rapidly with the chilly wet breeze swirling about her.

What she wouldn't have given for her wolf's thick undercoat—the dense second coat of fur virtually waterproof, a thermal insulator so effective even snow falling on her back wouldn't melt.

She hurried to the edge of the moat and considered the height of the wall across from the pen. Big Red watched her from a corner of the pen, but never made a menacing move toward her. She'd probably confused the hell out of him. She smelled like a wolf in heat, the same one he wanted to mate, but she didn't look like one in the least bit now. *Poor fellow.*

She sat on the edge of the concrete, the substance icy and rough on her bare bottom. After twisting around, she clung to the edge with frigid fingers, then dropped into the moat. It was about a six-and-a-half-foot drop and, with her five-four height, easy to make. But when she turned to consider the other side her heart filled with alarm.

Whether the wall rose eight feet or ten...didn't matter. She didn't see any way to climb the rough concrete without foot or hand holds. She turned back to the other side. Her heart fell. She wouldn't be able to climb out that way, either.

The cold had already affected her mind, slowing her ability to think. The shock at turning into her human form earlier than she'd planned had compelled her to panic.

*Great. Just great.* The next morning, the zookeepers would find a half-frozen, naked woman in the moat. She jumped at the shorter side, but couldn't reach the top edge.

After several tries, she did what went against every instinct for survival—she gave up and yelled for help.

For an hour she screamed and hollered. *Some night watchman.* She imagined her lips were blue from the cold. Her fingers and toes grew numb. And her voice was reduced to a croak.

Attempting to conserve her body heat, she crouched against the wall, her arms around her knees, her long hair dripping, with icicles dangling about her.

Boots running on pavement in her direction barely registered in her mind.

"The woman's screams came from this direction, Randolph," a deep male voice shouted, nearly out of breath.

She shivered so hard her knees knocked together and her teeth chattered. "Here," she attempted to shout, but her word barely reached her own ears.

"Miss, where are you?" another male voice shouted, older and rustier. Their footsteps stopped at the pen next door. "She sounded desperate, Mack."

The only thought she could focus on was that the news media would have a field day when they learned a crazy, naked woman slipped into the wolves' pen.

She attempted to stand, but the bitter cold froze her joints, locking them in place.

"I know we weren't hearing things. She had to be close to here," Randolph said.

"Maybe she's injured or unconscious."

"Here," she said, the word merely an angry whisper. Furious with herself for being so needy, furious that her voice gave out on her when she needed it most, she had lived for many years as a lone *lupus garou*. Self-sufficient. She didn't need anyone. Only the image of Devlyn kissing her overran that thought. Damn him for making it impossible to find someone else for her to love.

"One of the predators in these pens could have torn her up," Randolph said.

They flashed their lights into the pen beside hers where two lions prowled.

"Call in some more of the staff."

The flashlight's beam poked into the darkness of her pen, angled toward Big Red. "What are you doing out here, big fellow? Little lady won't let you snuggle yet?"

"Hey, Randolph, what's that?"

The iron fence rattled as they leaned over it and poured their beams of light into the moat.

Bella closed her eyes as the light touched her face. Her long red hair covered her naked body like Lady Godiva on her famous ride. She stopped breathing while her heart nearly leapt out of her chest to know they'd found her, and would take her someplace warm.

"There!" the older man said.

"What the hell?"

———~~~———

"Are you sure she'll go with me?" Argos asked Devlyn again, worry evident in his voice as they climbed into the SUV.

"She only saw *me* at the zoo. She doesn't know Volan still rules the pack and wants her."

Argos shook his head. "I can't believe she got herself locked up in a zoo."

Devlyn gave an evil smile, the notion he'd have to rescue her from a *real* wolf's attentions amusing him. "The big red wolf they tried to mate her with sure looked disappointed, hungry, and dissatisfied."

Devlyn's cousins and Argos chuckled.

"I can just imagine how mad she is over that." Argos stared out the window. "I've always wondered if we shouldn't have tried to find a red wolf pack for her to mix with. Maybe she would have found a mate with one of her own kind."

Devlyn started the ignition with a jerk. "*We're* her family," he said abruptly, not in the mood for hiding his feelings for her. "Besides, I doubt Volan would have stood for it."

Intent on freeing her before she turned into her human form, Devlyn sped down the road. With the temperature dropping to thirty degrees and a wind-chilled rain making it even worse, she'd be in real trouble soon.

He thought back to Volan and his desire to have Bella. Although Devlyn had warred with him over her so many times in the past when he was an immature *lupus garou*, he'd never had a chance to best him. Thinking she no longer lived, he had long ago ended his quarrel with Volan, concentrating instead on making his leather goods factory a success. But now, could he fight the leader and have the female he wanted most?

His hands fisted on the steering wheel, he shook his head. The notion that she loved humans gnawed at him as much as he fought not wanting to care. There was no sense in wanting what he couldn't have.

A police siren wailed behind him, shattering the otherwise quiet, and forced a shard of anger to rip through him.

Everyone turned around to see what was wrong. Frowning, Devlyn pulled the vehicle to the shoulder, spitting gravel out of its path.

"Speeding a little, Devlyn?" Argos asked, his voice amused.

*Speeding a lot.* Devlyn tightened his grip on the steering wheel, not wanting to leave Bella in the zoo's pen one more minute. He glanced at the rearview mirror to see a policeman approaching. If Devlyn tore off now, he could probably lose the cop. The officer would never guess Devlyn would hightail it to the zoo.

He slipped his foot off the brake.

---

Bella had been so intent on fleeing confinement that, when the night watchmen discovered her hiding in the moat, she didn't realize how chilled she'd become. In her wolf form, the March temperature didn't bother her. But, as a naked human, she was frozen to the bone.

"Jesus, Randolph, she's...she's naked," the younger

male voice said, as he hung over the railing where zoo patrons normally observed the animals in the pen.

"Yeah, Mack. Call for backup. We don't know yet how badly she's hurt." He tugged off his jacket and dropped it on top of her. "Miss, we'll reach you as soon as we can. Are you injured?"

Her mind was fuzzy and disoriented. Hurt? Tired. Sleepy.

"She's probably hypothermic." He ran toward the entrance to the wolf's pen.

His companion relayed the messages into a phone, his footsteps running behind the other. "We have a naked woman in Big Red's pen, down in the moat. Yeah, yeah!" he hollered. "I'm serious. She's naked. We don't know if she's injured or not. Randolph says she's got to be hypothermic as cold as it is. All right." He snapped the phone shut. "The boss is making all of the calls. We're not to move her if she's hurt, just try to keep her warm. But how in the hell did..." His voice faded, then the metal door squeaked open to the building housing the inside part of the wolves' exhibit. They disappeared inside the building, then the door creaked open to the outer portion of the pen.

Numb and stiff, Bella couldn't even move to put on the jacket that the man had tossed to her. Still, the fleece helped warm her.

The men ran across the pen to the moat from the shorter concrete wall on the opposite side. "Watch my back, Randolph, in case Big Red or Rosa get any ideas. If either injured the woman, they may still feel threatened."

"Rosa must be sleeping in her den. Big Red's sitting in the corner watching us."

"Keep an eye on him. I'll lift the woman to you."

He sat at the edge of the moat, turned, and eased himself down. When his feet hit the ground, he whipped around and ran to her. "Are you hurt?"

Trembling so hard that her teeth chattered, she couldn't croak a word.

He ran his flashlight over her and then helped her into his jacket. "She doesn't appear to be injured, but she's half frozen." He covered her lap with the other jacket. Lifting her off the rough pavement, he carried her to the older man, who was leaning down with his arms outstretched.

With the two men's heavy jackets covering her, her body warmed some, yet she still shivered uncontrollably, craved sleep, and could barely focus.

Vaguely, she worried about being caught, about freeing herself from her current predicament, about hiding before Volan found her.

Suddenly, more shouts erupted and running footsteps headed toward the patron's safety railing across the moat.

"Is she injured?" Thompson hollered from the iron fence.

"It appears she's just hypothermic," Mack shouted back. "Her pulse is awfully slow. She has some scratches but doesn't appear to have been bitten or to have broken any bones."

Mack rubbed her hand while Randolph wrapped his coat around her legs. The door squeaked open, and she turned her head slightly when blond-bearded Thompson dashed into the pen, his blue eyes worried.

Yanking off his coat, he laid it over her. He touched her cheek with clinical concern. "Who are you, and how did you get in here?"

She stared at him, hearing the question and vaguely remembering that he'd shot her with a tranquilizer and incarcerated her here. *That's* how she'd gotten in here. The men's faces wavered in front of her, and she blinked her eyes slowly, trying to focus.

"What's your name?" He turned to Mack. "Has she spoken at all?"

"We heard her screaming and yelling. By the time we located her, she was crouched against the wall of the moat and hasn't said a word. She's barely conscious."

"The ambulance is on its way," Thompson said. "What about the wolves?"

"Big Red's sitting over there watching. Rosa must be sleeping in the den," Randolph said.

Thompson crouched down in front of her and touched her wrist. "Miss, what's your name? What happened?"

More flashlights wavered in the night. More men were shouting, issuing directions to the wolves' pen. Bella blinked as two uniformed policemen hurried into the pen, then closed her eyes, wondering how she was going to extract herself from this mess.

"What happened here, Mr. Thompson?" one of the policemen asked.

Thompson explained all he knew and then reached over and held Bella's hand. "She's ice cold."

The men piled two more coats on top of her.

"Most bizarre thing I've ever seen in the fifteen years I've been a night watchman," Randolph said.

"Damn," Mack said, tightening his grip on Bella's other hand. "Here come the media."

<center>~~~</center>

Before Devlyn could step on the gas and leave the cop behind in the dust, Argos grabbed his arm. "Wait."

The policeman spoke into his radio. "You've got what?" Then he leaned into the open SUV window and said to Devlyn, "Got another call. Slow it down, will you, bud?"

"Yes, sir," Devlyn said, as amicably as he could. His hands still clutched the steering wheel with a death grip.

The policeman nodded and then hurried back to his car, shouting to the other officer, "Problem at the zoo. You're never going to believe this."

Devlyn glanced at Argos, whose tanned face had turned gray.

When Devlyn finally reached the zoo's main entrance, he shut off his headlights and drove into the zoo's lower parking lot. But the sight of the police cars' and an ambulance's flashing lights washing the area near the zoo's entrance in a prism of color sent a splinter of ice into his heart. She would live. The cold or some animal's injury—if minor enough—wouldn't kill her, but how in the hell was he to secret her away?

"When the ambulance leaves, follow them to the hospital," Argos said, as if reading Devlyn's mind. "We can more easily slip her out of there than we could have here."

Sitting in the dark, like when the pack went on a hunt, they waited quietly for their prey to appear. The thought of hunting Bella sent a surge of heat through his system, a longing he had no business feeling, a lustful desire for her he could never fulfill.

The paramedics rolled her out to the ambulance; her red hair spilled over the stretcher, the blankets burying her under the covers. Devlyn could only imagine how close to death she'd come. His anger boiled deep inside. How could she be so foolish as to leave the pack like she did? This is the kind of trouble she'd get in for it. She needed a pack leader to keep her in line. No, not the pack leader...*him*.

Despite the knowledge that she didn't want him, or any of his kind, she was tied to him—bound together not only by the fire that killed her family, but by something deeper, more primal. He sought to rise above the darkness that filled him with wanting—with the soul-wrenching yearning for the little red wolf. But part of him wouldn't submit.

Argos cleared his gravelly throat. "We'll all go into the hospital and try to create some distraction so that we can remove her. Until then, I'll let you discover where she is and how serious her injuries are. If she's too bad off, we may have to let her stay overnight and take her out sometime after that."

Still brooding over the circumstances of her captivity, Devlyn had every intention of moving her tonight. Their own healers could take care of her much better than the human doctors could because of the many years they'd practiced medicine. Devlyn and his packmates had to remove her before anyone discovered too much about her. But it was more than that. He wanted to hold her tightly in his grasp again, to reassure himself that she was safe in his care. He wouldn't wait a second longer than necessary.

They followed the string of police cars escorting the ambulance to the hospital, their blue and red lights flashing against the blackness. The drive seemed interminable. But finally the ambulance pulled into the brightly illuminated emergency entrance, and Devlyn veered away from the circus of police cars following in the ambulance's wake. Seeing the main entrance, he parked near the doors; the lot was fairly empty because of the lateness of the hour.

Before he could jerk his door open, Devlyn spied Henry Thompson headed for the emergency room doors, his stride quick and determined.

"Damn it to hell," Devlyn swore under his breath.

He hated for any man or *lupus garou* to get close to Bella, but especially some idiot who was in love with wolves. Would Bella mistake Thompson's wanting to help wolves with desiring to have her?

Devlyn shook his head and fisted his hands, still unable to understand what she could see in human males. Yet he had every intention of making her realize how lame a human male he was, how weak and fearful, and, worse, how dangerous they could be.

"What's wrong?" Argos asked, his voice harsh with worry.

Devlyn motioned with his head toward zoo man Thompson. "He's the one I talked to about removing

Rosa from the zoo. He's going to wonder what the hell I'm doing here."

Argos watched Thompson disappear inside the hospital and then let out his breath. "Then you can stay in the vehicle."

Devlyn jerked his door open. "Like hell I am."

# Chapter 3

THE SMELL OF ANTISEPTICS WAFTED IN THE ROOM, AND the air conditioner poured out of the vents, intent on putting patients into a deep freeze, Bella was certain. Feigning sleep, she lay quietly in the hospital bed, the highly starched sheets scratchy against her exposed backside where the gown opened up. The white woolen blankets, piled four or five high fresh out of a blanket warmer, buried her, raising her internal temperature. But the knowledge that she wasn't safe yet chilled her all over again.

The room remained quiet, all except for the sound of hearts beating nearby. Once she was hooked up to the IV, the medicine whooshing through her veins, heating her blood, the nurse left the room. But Thompson and the doctor stood silently watching her.

"Does she have any injuries, Doctor?" Thompson finally asked.

"Just hypothermia. As low as her temperature was, it's a good thing your staff found her when they did. Another couple of degrees drop and she wouldn't have survived. You can speak with her when she comes to, but not for long. She needs to rest. However, most likely she'll be incoherent at first—effects of prolonged hypothermia."

"Thanks, Doctor. I'll only speak to her for a moment."

She didn't believe him for an instant. The way

Thompson had hunted her in the woods was reminiscent of a bull dog: determined, dependable to a fault, not someone easily thwarted.

Footfalls sounded, moving across the room and out the door. The doctor?

His pungent cologne preceding him, Thompson moved closer to the bed. Why did human males wear such gaudy-smelling perfumes? Their own musky scent smelled so much more enticing.

Taking a deep breath, she was glad her kind's unique DNA structure shifted with the change—perfectly normal wolf DNA when they wore the wolf coat, and human DNA when they turned back into their *homo sapiens* form. Thompson touched her hair, sending a curl of warmth through her. The toasty, thin blankets helped, but his touch caused a different kind of heat, the kind that stirred her longing to mate.

"Miss." Thompson's voice was deep, rugged, and concerned. He reminded her of a mountain man she'd once met, caring the same for nature's habitat, the same aura of wildness surrounding him, except that the mountain man wanted to be left alone with no human contact. Thompson was different.

"Miss," he said again.

She didn't respond. This wasn't the time or place to seduce him. Later she'd work her charms on him. He cared for Rosa. Wouldn't he care for the human side of her, too?

His fingers touched her cheek and she craved opening her eyes to see the expression in his gaze. Was it longing? Lustful? Did she intrigue him a little?

"Can you tell me what happened to you?"

The sound of boots tromping toward the room caught her attention. Two men entered. She concentrated on the smell of them, different colognes, just as heavy, just as nauseating.

"Officers," Thompson said.

Her heart rate shifted to higher gear.

"Mr. Thompson," one of the policemen said. "Has she come to?"

"Not yet. The doctor said it might be a while."

A chair slid over to the bed.

*Great*. She had a whole mess of observers, like at the zoo.

"What do you think happened?" one of the policemen asked.

"No telling, but I'm not leaving until I know. Thanks, by the way, for keeping the media out of it for the moment," Thompson said.

"You're welcome. We might have an attempted rape or even an attempted murder case here. Don't need the media involved quite yet. On the other hand, she might be mentally ill."

She fought making a face at them.

"I considered that." Thompson grasped her wrist, the strength of his touch spiraling through her like a gigantic heated wave. "Pulse is…well, a little rapid, but definitely better than nearly nonexistent. I thought she was too far gone there for a while."

A cell phone jingled in close proximity to Thompson. She held her breath, fearful that his staff would inform him someone had stolen Rosa from the wolves' pen.

"Thompson here," he said.

Too much silence followed. The seconds lingered like minutes, yet Thompson didn't speak a word. The suspense was killing her. When no one conversed further, she opened her eyes. Thompson stared at her with raw disbelief.

She swallowed hard, the moisture in her throat all but gone.

"Yeah," he said into the phone. "The little lady just came to. I'll ask her where Rosa is."

The hardness in his face and the grim set of his mouth and jaw indicated losing Rosa had angered him. *Good.* Then if he wanted her back, he could promise his undying love to her and—

"Call you right back when I have some answers." He ended the call and then furrowed his brow. "What were you doing in the wolves' pen?"

Gone were the kid gloves.

What the hell was she supposed to say? Her mind was slightly muddled still and any fabrications she might have conjured up weren't coming to her readily.

Wondering what the police officers' take was on the situation and wanting to avoid Thompson's steely-eyed glower, she glanced over at them. Both were in their midthirties, one taller than the other with questioning green eyes, both with dark-brown hair.

The green-eyed cop's phone rang and he lifted it to his ear. "Sgt. Stevenson… *What?* Detain him. I'll be right down." He shoved his phone into the pouch attached to his belt. "Man at the front desk is asking about a woman brought in half frozen from hypothermia."

"The media?" Thompson asked, steeling his back, his voice concerned.

"Yeah, suspect so. We don't need a media circus here. I'll head him off." He turned to his partner. "You stay here. Call you in a minute."

The other man nodded, and in five quick strides, Sgt. Stevenson disappeared from the room.

Thompson turned his attention back to Bella. *More interrogation.* Didn't the doctor tell the zoo man to take it easy on her? At least that's what she thought he'd said.

She closed her eyes. How in the hell was she going to get herself out of this predicament now?

Thompson cleared his throat. "Now listen, miss, if you're some kind of animal rights activist and wanted to free the wolf…" He paused and then continued. "Okay, let me tell you a little tale. Last year we had a similar scenario. The wolf was someone's pet, but the owner decided he couldn't manage the animal when his wife had a new baby. So what did he do? Afraid the wolf might attack his child, he released the wolf into the wild. Sure, wolves are feral, but this one had been domesticated, too. She kept returning to Portland neighborhoods, looking for the home life she was used to, and finally killed someone's toy poodle—not out of viciousness, but because she was starving. So the dog owner shot and killed her. If she'd been brought to the zoo, she would have been safe, protected, well fed, and content."

*And mated with Big Red.*

Saddened that the dog owner had destroyed the wolf and that his beloved pet had to die, Bella hid her feelings and still didn't say anything.

"Several have asked to transfer Rosa to other zoos. It wouldn't have been you and some of your cohorts, would it?" Thompson added.

The cop said, "If you suspect her of wrongdoing, she needs to be read her rights and—"

Thompson interrupted him and directed his comments to Bella. "Listen, we only want to protect Rosa. I know you and your friends do, too. If you hand her over to us, we'll drop the charges."

Was he bluffing to make her tell him the truth? No, she believed he'd honor his word.

"Okay, let's start off all over again. My name is Henry Thompson, one of the biggest contributors to the zoo. I oversee some of the more endangered species, including red wolves. I've worked with other zoos for years, trying to return a select number to the wild, but we can't set Rosa loose out here. No red wolves exist in the Cascades for her to mate. She'd end up mating with coyotes, and the result wouldn't be pure red wolf, which is what has happened in Texas, nearly obliterating the original red wolf species until more recently."

When she wouldn't respond, the cop said, "We have to know what you were doing in the wolves' pen, miss."

She looked back at the blankets covering her, considered the IV attached to her arm, and wondered which floor of the hospital her room was located on.

Thompson sat in the chair beside her. "I'm not leaving until I have some answers."

Maybe not, but perhaps he'd grow sleepy, or take a bathroom break, or...

The cop's phone rang. "Yeah? I'll be right down." He hung up and then said, "The media man vanished. I'm going to help my partner look for the news van. The lady at the front desk gave out the wrong room number for wolf lady here."

She couldn't help but cast him a sardonic smile at the name he called her.

"You won't be smiling when we put you in jail for this little stunt you've just pulled," Thompson said, his tone harsh.

Wouldn't that be ironic? If she sat in jail long enough, she could turn back into the wolf. Then the charges would be dropped against Bella, and she'd be returned to the wolf pen as Rosa.

"You might want to stay with her in the event some-one locates her anyway," the cop said. "Be back in a little while."

"I'll be here."

The cop hurried out of the room and shut the door behind him with a click.

Fleeing seemed much more plausible now with Thompson all alone with her in the room. He leaned closer to the bed and tapped his fingers on the mattress, his eyes pinning her with authority. "We might not be able to make the charges of wolf-napping stick against you, but we can get you for trespassing."

She closed her eyes.

He grunted. "You're as stubborn as my ex-wife. When she'd made up her mind not to say something, there wasn't anything I could do to convince her to open up."

Bella wanted to ask why they were divorced, but she figured she was better off keeping quiet.

The door opened, and Bella opened her eyes. The nurse poked her head in. "The doctor said you have ten more minutes and then the patient needs to rest. Visitors aren't normally allowed in the rooms at this hour."

"But—"

The nurse raised her hand. "Doctor's orders."

Before she shut the door, another scent filtered into the room—Devlyn's aromatic male scent.

Hell, he was coming for her, the traitor, and he'd return her to Volan posthaste.

"Get me out of here now, and I'll tell you where Rosa is." Bella's voice was still little more than a whisper, which probably saved her butt or Devlyn would have heard her.

Thompson folded his arms and leaned back in the chair. "No. You're too weak. Not until the doctor says—"

She glanced at the IV in her arm and then yanked it out. To stop the bleeding, she clamped her hand over the tape that had held the IV in place.

"Wait, miss—"

Jerking her blankets to the floor, she stumbled out of bed. What she wouldn't have given for some swift wolf's legs about now. Although she could run long and hard as a human, too, a nice warm wolf pelt would have been preferable in the cold winter weather to a human's naked body.

Thompson jumped up from the chair and headed for her.

Her head swam, and she grabbed the mattress. The idea that she had completely recovered was a delusion.

Thompson skirted around the bed to help her. "I'm—I'm sorry. You need to return to bed, miss. I didn't mean to upset you."

She rushed past him into the bathroom. With only a flimsy hospital gown tied at the back and nothing else to clothe her body, she was out of luck. She locked the bathroom door and then looked at the window. *No way to open it.* No escape. She hurried out of the bathroom.

Thompson hit the nurse's call button, his tanned face now pale. "I'll get a nurse to put the IV back—"

Desperate to escape Devlyn, Bella ran out of the room. She dashed for the nearest exit sign down the long corridor.

"Miss!" Thompson shouted after her.

She slammed into the fire stairs door, glancing back to see Devlyn at the nurses' station and Thompson tearing out of the room.

Thompson looked back at Devlyn, evidently to see what caught her eye. Both men stared at each other for a moment. She didn't wait to see what happened next.

After charging down two flights of stairs, she bolted onto the first floor. One man's boots tromped down the stairwell in hasty pursuit of her. She dove undetected into a hospital room. Thank God an elderly patient snored in his sleep in one of the beds. Heart pounding, she slid under the unoccupied bed.

The door to the room opened. She scarcely breathed. Boots stood in the doorway but then moved away and the door closed.

Hurrying out from underneath the bed, she searched through the man's wall closet.

After tossing the hospital gown, she slipped on his large, collared, button-down shirt that reached midthigh. She pulled a bulky sweater over this. His baggy trousers and canoe-size shoes were way too big. Grabbing his corduroy jacket, she shoved her arms into the sleeves. Barefooted and barelegged, she ran to the door and peeked out.

The hallway remained empty, but Thompson, the police, and Devlyn had to be nearby. She leaned against the doorframe, dizzy—not yet herself. Her head fuzzed and her heart beat way out of control.

When her head cleared, she dashed for the front door that she envisioned lay beyond the bend in the hall, centered in the middle of the building.

Devlyn suddenly walked out of a room down the hall and into her path, his back to her. Her breath caught in her throat. Bolting, she tried to dash past him, but he jumped to block her. She slammed against his body instead, and he wrapped his arms around her in a secure vise.

Panic filled her. His touch forced her to want more from him—a searing embrace, another kiss, full of passion. *Madness*. He'd turn her over to the pack leader, damn him.

Devlyn pulled her into the room. To her horror, Thompson and the two cops lay still as death on the floor, forcing a gasp from her lips. "What—"

His eyes burning with anger, he held a finger to her lips. Then he took her hand and whispered harshly, "We're leaving through the front door, quietly." When she tried to jerk free, he gripped her hand tighter. "Quietly, damn it, Bella. Behave for once."

Straightening her shoulders, she narrowed her eyes. She'd slipped away from the pack before. She could do it again. And, for now, Devlyn seemed her only chance to flee the hospital. Yet, God, how she hungered for more than his hand gripping hers. It was mating season, she reminded herself, nothing more, and she would lust after any male that…hell, who was she trying to kid? The way he looked at her bare legs, even while they stood in imminent danger of being discovered, the way he touched her—he craved her as much as she did him.

He walked her back into the hall toward the center of the building, his stride long and indomitable, his arm wrapped tightly around her waist. His touch should have warmed her…well, hell, it did. But for all of the wrong reasons. She craved more of his touch, at the same time resenting the implication. He was her captor, her new zookeeper; her blood sizzled.

When they walked past the nurses' station, a woman wearing polka-dot scrubs spoke on the phone, her eyes wide. "The patient is missing?"

His jaw tight, Devlyn hurried Bella toward the door past the station.

The woman said, "Wait! Sir! Miss!"

He hit the door with his shoulder and yanked Bella outside into the crisp, cold air. Grabbing her up in his arms, he ran for the black SUV parked curbside.

Gray-haired Argos tugged the door open.

"Argos," she said under her breath, the pleasure at seeing him overshadowed by the realization that the pack was returning her to Volan. She clenched her teeth.

He gave her a warm smile. "We've missed you."

"Volan has missed me."

Argos's smile faded.

"Hurry." Tanner, Devlyn's cousin, pointed out the window. "A security guard is headed this way."

Devlyn jumped into the driver's seat while Tanner and his brother Heath wedged Bella between them in the middle seat. Devlyn gunned the engine. "We'll split up. Give the police clues that Bella and I have headed in other directions."

Bella was squished between Devlyn's cousins, who sat too close for comfort. "Give me some more room," she growled.

Tanner chuckled. "Spicy vinegar, just like the old days, eh, Bella?"

"Volan won't like it if we split up," Argos warned, glancing over the seat at her.

She shoved at Tanner to move his leg, uncomfortably wedged against her thigh, but he wouldn't budge. His brother patted her bare thigh. "About time you returned to the pack. Sure missed having you around."

She slapped his hand.

"They'll catch all of us if we don't split up," Devlyn countered, shifting his attention from the road to his rearview mirror, and gave his cousins a dangerous glare.

Murmured objections filtered forward, but by pack rules, Devlyn was older, and since Argos, though the eldest, had stepped down from pack leadership, Devlyn made the decisions.

"Bella stays with me. Everyone else takes whatever route they need to, to make it back to Colorado," Devlyn clarified.

Argos took a deep breath. "And the two of you?"

"We'll have a time with Thompson." Devlyn shook his head at Bella. "You sure have confused him."

She jerked Tanner's fingers free from a coil of her hair. "Touch me again and you'll lose your fingers."

The cousins all laughed, but Devlyn gave them a look like he'd be the one to follow through with Bella's threat if they didn't behave.

When they arrived at the hotel, the time approached one in the morning. With obvious disdain, Devlyn's cousins reluctantly drove off into the dark in separate vehicles. Argos gave Bella a warm embrace in the parking area of the five-story hotel. He'd been the father she'd lost so long ago, and her heart sank with the knowledge that she might never see him again.

"Welcome back to the pack, Bella. We'll see you soon."

Instantly, he stoked her ire. She was never returning to Volan, ever. "It's good to see you again, Argos. You take care."

He'd always been kind to her, protecting her when the overly rambunctious males had overextended their boundaries with her during her teens, keeping in touch with her all of these years. She loved seeing him again, even briefly. But she knew she'd never be able to correspond with him again for fear Volan would discover her.

Argos nodded as if he knew her thoughts and acknowledged she would make Devlyn's life hell if he contemplated returning her home.

He shook Devlyn's hand. "Keep her safe and bring her home."

"Will do."

Argos quickly disappeared into the blackness, too.

Instantly, being alone with Devlyn sent a spark of concern through her. All male, he was the right age to crave mating with a female in heat. Would he make a move on her while Volan remained out of the way?

Secretly, the urge to mate with Devlyn wreaked havoc with her feelings. She couldn't encourage his attentions, or both would suffer Volan's wrath. But still the desire to have Devlyn's kiss again—

Devlyn grabbed her arm and pulled her into the cement stairwell, their footsteps echoing all the way up to the second floor. Down a long, carpeted, dusty-smelling hall, he hastened her to his room.

"You're barely able to stay on your feet and your eyes look soggy, half-drugged. We'll sleep here for a couple of hours and then move." He shoved the keycard into the slot and then opened the door into a living area furnished with a sofa and a couple of chairs.

At once, the idea that he'd take her back to the pack leader stirred her blood all over again. "You're not taking me back to Volan." She didn't have to say it, but she wanted to state the facts up front, to let Devlyn know that, even if he thought he was the boss of the situation, she had other plans.

He walked her across the living room and then pulled her into the bedroom. "Whatever you say, Bella." While blocking her escape path through the doorway, he yanked off his leather jacket.

The black shirt he wore fit over shoulders that had broadened since the last time she'd seen him. Were his pecs as hard and well sculpted as she imagined them? She was dying to see. On the other hand, she couldn't let him know how much she desired him.

She folded her arms. "You're not staying in here with me."

He crossed the floor to her, pulled the way-too-big jacket from her shoulders, and then dropped it on the floor. "You're not sleeping by yourself so you can give me the slip. We'll have enough running to do. That Thompson fellow is like a bloodhound. He won't be satisfied until he gets you back."

"You mean the wolf back."

"Yeah, and that means you."

Her eyes remained riveted on his buttons while he worked to remove his shirt. When he pulled it off and dropped it on the floor, she stared at his dark-haired chest and chiseled abs. She sighed at the sight of his well-toned body. Already her hormones were set in high gear. She would be attracted to any male, she reminded herself, as much as she desired to mate. But she couldn't help the feeling that this one stirred her like no other.

Her nipples tightened and her breasts swelled in anticipation of his touch. She was sure the short curls between her legs were drenched with expectation, as much as she ached for him. Damn being in heat.

She folded her arms again and hoped to both stop what she figured he had in mind and still leave herself a chance of escaping him. "Volan won't like it if you share a bed with me."

"He doesn't *have* to like it."

She raised her brows to hear his defiant words. "So,

does that mean you've finally grown some balls?" If he were ready to fight Volan—

"Don't, Bella. Don't make anything more out of this than a bad case of necessity. You'll run if I don't stay with you. That's all. You're going home to the pack where you belong."

She curbed the anger that simmered beneath the surface. He didn't want her after all. He only used her to get in good with the leader of the pack. "Why didn't you have Argos stay with me instead?"

"He'd have let you have your own way."

She didn't believe Devlyn for an instant. Sure, Argos had always been good to her, but she was certain he felt she'd be safer at home with the pack and wouldn't have let her off that easily.

"And your cousins?"

"Any one of them would have tried to have their way with you. They're immature and would lose their heads over the thought of you naked in bed with them." He reached over to touch her belly. "As ripe as you are, your smell is an aphrodisiac."

She slapped his hand away. His intimation that her alluring scent was the only reason the other males wanted her forced a chill of irritation across her skin. But hell, maybe he was right. Maybe Volan was the only one who really desired her for a permanent mate. Her stomach rolled with nausea at the idea.

Devlyn walked over to the bedroom door and shut it. With a click, he locked it. But it wasn't half as secure as the zoo cell. She smiled inwardly but glowered outwardly. He returned to the bed, sat, and pulled off his boots.

Considering his words again, she observed his actions. "But *you* won't lose your head over me?"

"I have a bit more control than that."

*Right.*

She walked over to the bed and jerked the solid green comforter back. "Good for you, though I'm not removing anything more anyway."

Crossing the floor in a flash, he pulled her around to face him. His unbridled actions signaled danger. She sensed he was close to losing control. He'd done it before when he kissed her, and the fire burned and the anger smoldered in his dark eyes now like that day long ago. His gaze dropped to her lips as her heart sent the blood rushing to her ears. He wasn't as immune to her as he pretended. Why couldn't she meet a human male who aroused her like he did? But Devlyn could never be her mate. He would always be Volan's lackey.

She tried to pull away, but he shoved her back on the bed, making her sit. Glaring at him, she folded her arms.

He yanked off the cardigan sweater and then unbuttoned her shirt. Once he'd pulled it from her shoulders and dropped it on the floor, he said, "I won't sleep with something that smells like a human male."

His gaze dropped from hers to enjoy her nudity. He smiled appreciatively.

"You've seen me naked before." She slid into bed and then yanked the covers over her.

"It's been a good long while and you're a bit more mature now." His eyes sparkled with intrigue and his lips still smiled.

She assumed he wouldn't try to make love to her.

But then he dropped his pants and she saw his erection. He was one gorgeous hunk of a gray *lupus garou*. She hadn't remembered him being that big. She wasn't sure he could hold back and not attempt to mate with her. On the other hand, she wasn't sure she wanted him to stop himself, either.

He yanked the covers off her. "Slide over."

"Go around to the other side of the bed," she growled.

"You're on my side. But if you prefer to sleep here, too…" Letting his words trail off, he climbed on top of her and pinned her to the mattress.

Clenching her teeth, she tried to wriggle out from underneath his hard, naked body, but his hands seized her wrists and he spread his legs on either side of her, boxing her in. His thick arousal pressed hard against her mound and liquid heat pooled between her legs.

"Like it here still?" he asked, licking her cheek.

Lost in the feel of him, his heart beating rapidly against her chest, his skin hot, his body hard, and his smell wild, out-of-doors, and musk, she fought parting her legs for him; the ache to have him penetrate her feminine folds was overwhelming.

His erection stirred and he swept his lips over the sensitive skin at her throat.

Was he having a difficult time maintaining his subservient position in the pack?

"Get off me," she growled, although she wanted to encourage his actions.

"I gave you ample opportunity to move and you wouldn't listen." His voice sounded drenched with lust. His mouth caressed the line of her jaw, making her skin tingle in heady expectation. "When you're in a pack, there are rules."

Unable to control her body's reaction, her heated core ached for him to follow through. "Yes, and one of them is not to seduce the pack leader's intended bitch," she said, meaning to sound irritated and put him off, but her voice seemed sexually frustrated instead.

Devlyn cast her an evil smile. "I'm not seducing you. You're still suffering from the effects of hypothermia. I'm merely providing necessary medical attention."

Again she tried to squirm free, to show him he couldn't control her, but every wiggle only made her more aware of how ready his body was to take hers. She swore she heard him muffle a groan.

"Yeah, right, Devlyn. Volan would really believe that line as much as I do."

He ran his fingers through her hair and touched his lips to hers, softly this time.

She couldn't help but respond, desperately needy for a mate's touch...Devlyn's touch. The doubts she had about Volan, Devlyn, or wanting a human male all faded from her thoughts in an instant. She licked his lips and then nipped the lower one.

He issued a deep-throated growl.

She paused. What the hell was she doing? He said he could control himself, but not the way he touched her. His erection throbbed against her waist as the sweet ache between her legs intensified. She didn't want him to stop. What was wrong with her? She couldn't encourage him. Volan would kill him for certain.

When she stilled beneath him, Devlyn took a long,

ragged breath and then rolled off her. "Get some sleep, Bella. We'll have several long days ahead of us."

She turned away from him, hurt, confused, angry. She wanted him to be her mate forever and didn't want to wait for that day.

Wrapping his arm around her waist, he pulled her against his arousal, her backside bared to him, and she wanted him to take her like a wolf would in the wild.

"To ensure you don't get any ideas of slipping away in the night," he said, his face nuzzling her hair.

She attempted to jerk away from him.

He tightened his iron hold on her. "It's hard enough for me to...well, just lie still, Bella."

But she couldn't sleep, let alone think; the ache between her legs begged for satisfaction. She rubbed her bottom against him, offering herself to him, and he growled in response, the kind of growl that meant he was losing control.

# Chapter 4

BELLA STROKED HER BOTTOM AGAINST DEVLYN'S raging arousal, triggering an undeniable lust for the woman he'd coveted endlessly.

"Damn it, Bella, stop it." To still her actions, he tightened his hold on her waist, the insatiable urge to take her filling him with feral aggression.

"I can't help it. Your scent and your touch are driving me nuts," she growled.

"You only say that because you want me to let you go, but I don't trust you."

Ignoring him, she pressed herself hard against him, challenging him to mate.

No human or *lupus garou* bitch boasted the same alluring scent as Bella. Taking a deep breath, he drank in her wild fragrance, a heady aphrodisiac compelling him to mate with her against all common sense. He nuzzled his face in her silky red hair, making the attraction stronger, not controlling his behavior as he should.

Devlyn ran his hand over Bella's side, down the gentle curve of her hip, to her inner thigh. She parted her legs for him, and he groaned with insatiable lust. Sliding his hand up her belly, he reached her breast and squeezed the full soft mound.

She moaned and pressed against his heavy loins again.

"Be still," he whispered into her hair.

"You don't want me to be still," she growled. "Not if you're going to keep touching me."

Hungering to mate with her, he lifted her leg over his. She stiffened her back.

"Nothing that will get us into too much trouble, Bella. Just going to relieve some of your tension."

As soon as he slipped his fingers between her legs, into the hot, wet, swollen folds, she trembled. Stroking her, he whispered next to her ear, "How does that feel?"

"Harder, faster," she managed to get out.

The thrill of having her tight against his body, naked as he had imagined for so many years, filled him with primal need. "Breathe, Bella. I don't want you passing out."

Squirming against him, she prodded him to quit talking and do more.

Reveling in the sweet musky scent that was all Bella, he stroked in and out and then touched her nub again. She placed her hand on his, pressing his fingers harder against her, forcing him to rub faster. Arching her back, she groaned. His arousal stretched out to her like a pike readied to enter her virgin territory, touching her between the folds, but not penetrating. Her moans of ecstasy and writhing lithe body undid him. With Bella's body squirming against him, his erection sliding against her folds, he fought losing control.

Her body shuddered, she cried out, her inner muscles contracting with her climax, and he quickly pulled away before he finished what he'd started.

She gazed at him with darker amber eyes. "Are you okay?"

His hormones raged out of control, his arousal ached

for release, and she had to ask if he was all right? In a husky voice, he motioned to the bathroom and said, "Why don't you wash up, Bella."

"Right." She crossed the floor to the bathroom, her silky skin covered in a fine sheen of perspiration, her red hair in tangles as though she'd been well loved.

God, how he wanted to make her his mate for real.

He was a fool to have touched her, knowing how she turned him on, but even when he'd played with her when they were young, there was always the need to conquer her, to make her his own. Pacing across the room, he tried to get his wolf instincts under control, when instead he wanted to join her in the shower and lick and nip every inch of her delectable skin and penetrate her slick folds.

The shower ran for a short while and then shut off, and she walked out of the bathroom—the towel wrapped around her head, the rest of her naked, her rosy nipples extended, willing him to touch them with his tongue. He took a ragged breath and stalked toward the bathroom. "I'll wash up." A dip in the icy stream back home would cool him down nicely about now. He paused at the door, scowling at her while she slipped into bed. "Don't leave, Bella."

A sly smile curved her lips, stirring his libido all over again. "Why would I do that when you can relieve my... *tension*, so well?"

He growled. "Don't mention it."

"We didn't mate," she said softly, pulling the cover to her breast. "Don't give it another thought."

As if that could ever happen. He'd think of every

stroke, every moan of ecstasy she'd made, the feel of her soft wet folds, her musky sweet scent, every bit of her forever. Just as he couldn't get out of his mind the kiss he'd given her so long ago.

Not trusting her to stay put, he hesitated. She watched him, her expression curious as he pondered what to do. Then he gathered their discarded clothes that were piled on the floor. He didn't think she'd try to run without them.

She cast him an annoyed look. He gave her a tight smile and hurried into the bathroom, leaving the door open. A quick shower with the curtain pulled aside would have to suffice, as he didn't trust Bella to not run off.

After he finished showering, he towel dried and then strode into the dark room. His blood heated when he saw only pillows stacked together where she'd lain down.

He yanked the pillow away and stared at the vixen. Bella was sleeping soundly, as innocent as an angel.

*Innocent, my ass.* There was no innocence in the way she tasted, smelled, or felt.

He walked around to the other side of the bed and slid between the coarse bleached sheets. As soon as he wrapped his arm around her waist and pulled her tight against his body, she hummed. "What took you so long? And why didn't you make me move over for you this time, Devlyn?"

He grunted. "I thought you were asleep. Guess you were only pretending."

"Nearly asleep," she said, her voice soft, alluring, tempting him.

He ran his fingers through her silky, damp hair. "Why haven't you found this human mate of yours yet?" He wasn't sure what got into him to ask—maybe the annoyance he felt that she wanted one, maybe the concern she'd come close to finding one. But afterward he wondered if he should have brought the subject up or kept it buried, like so many other things he didn't ever want to discuss with her.

She tensed in his arms. "Haven't had the time. I have to be selective, you know. One chance for the mate of a lifetime."

"You've had a lot of years to find one. You're lucky we don't age as fast as humans or you'd be dead and gone by now."

"All the more reason to find the right one. Besides, because I haven't been around our kind, this was the first wolf heat I've ever come into since I left the pack. Not sure why it happened this time, unless it's my human age catching up with me. Haven't had much of an urge to find a mate…until now." She paused. "What about you? Why have you never mated?"

"Maybe I have."

She grew quiet.

Maybe she wasn't so determined to find a human for companionship after all. "I've never chosen a mate. Seems I can't find the right one either."

She let out her breath. "Why have you never left the pack? I thought you would years ago."

"I did, a few times." He wasn't about to tell how long and hard he'd searched for her. "But I always longed to be back with my own kind. When Argos took me in—"

"What?"

"I thought you knew."

"Argos's wolf pack wasn't your own?"

Nuzzling his mouth against her ear, he nibbled at the lobe. "No. They took me and my cousins in like they did you."

"I thought you were part of the family." Her fingertips caressed his arm with featherlight strokes.

His body hardened in response, but he fought giving into his baser instincts. "I was…am. They're my family. And, as much as I don't care for Volan, he's the pack leader. For the most part, he rules well and keeps the pack safe. I'm not a lone wolf kind of guy. I like being a member of a family."

"So your cousins who came with you aren't really your cousins?"

"They are. In a manner of speaking, you're a distant cousin, too, if you want to get right down to it."

"Thank you, no."

"Don't think you're good enough to be a cousin to a gray?"

A sensual chuckle issued from her belly, warming him several degrees.

Ringing her nipple with the tip of his finger, he enticed it to harden. The sensation shot a spark of interest straight to his groin. He could never get enough of touching her to make up for the time lost. Yet, in the back of his mind, he knew she didn't want him, that it was only her wolf's heat that made her crave him. "Argos wondered if we did you a disservice by not finding a red *lupus garou* pack to return you to, if maybe you would have settled down with your own kind."

"I'm afraid I've been with the bigger grays for so long that the reds look puny."

He stilled his hands. "You've been in touch with some, Bella?"

"At...at the zoo."

"What?"

"Two men. About our age. They said they'd break me out. One urinated along the fence line. Didn't you catch his odor?"

*Hell and damnation.* Fisting his hands in her hair, he knew damn well what the red intended with his actions. "The breeze must have shifted." Damn his bad luck. Not only would the reds frown on another male *lupus garou* trespassing, but a gray trying to take a red to another wolves' territory wouldn't set well with them. "You should have told me."

"You're not worried about them, are you? We left the zoo and then ended up at the hospital and now here. They won't be able to follow me."

"The news will carry the story about your hospital stay and subsequent disappearance. The mystery woman found in the wolf's pen, without clothes, the disappearance of the red wolf, and most likely my description, too. If the red who targeted you is a pack leader, no one would cross him. So he'd know I was from out of town, not a member of his pack."

"He was young, your age...early twenties, small. He wouldn't be a leader."

"Reds are smaller." He wasn't dismissing the fact

that they could have more trouble than they bargained for—first zoo man Thompson, then the cops, and now a pack of red wolves.

"Besides, Devlyn, *I* am selecting my mate."

"That's what this is all about? You want to choose instead of a male choosing you?" His voice sounded as incredulous as he felt.

"This is all about *not* wanting to be Volan's mate. Don't you see?"

"He's the leader. You should be proud a leader wants you. He'll always safeguard you. Besides, I thought you and he shared a connection." He couldn't help sounding peeved. But, in truth, besides the fact she wanted a human mate and the way she denied wanting to be with Volan, he felt otherwise.

She didn't respond.

"Bella?"

"Leave it," she snapped.

"Why do you despise him so? It's not because he killed the boy at the lake. You hated Volan long before this, although I recall a time when that wasn't the case." The instance when Volan had encouraged her to eat after the death of her best friend—yet she'd bitten Devlyn when he'd tried to console her—hadn't faded from his memory. The image of Volan's arms snug around her and Bella's head pressed against his chest still burned hot in Devlyn's mind.

She abruptly changed the subject. "What happened between you and Volan the day I ran? I didn't think you'd survive."

"Disappointed?" He knew there was something more to the story with Volan, damn it.

She tried to wriggle out of his arms. "Don't be an idiot. Of course I didn't want him hurting you. I didn't want him hurting the human boy either."

Attempting to squash the hard knot in the pit of his stomach when the image of her lusting after the human in the lake came to mind, he redirected the conversation. "Volan was angry with me for kissing you."

"Some kiss."

The way she said it, dreamily and with intrigue, diminished his annoyance with her over the human boy. "Did you like it?"

"It was all right," she responded too nonchalantly, as if she were playing a role in a movie but overplaying her part a bit.

"You've had better?" he asked, his tone mocking.

Silence greeted him.

Inwardly, he chuckled. "Thought not."

"I'm not going to tell you about all of the guys I've kissed." She tried to squirm free, but he tightened his grip. Sighing heavily, she quit her struggles. "What happened between you and Volan?"

"He planned to tear me to shreds until you ran off. Then Volan hesitated. He wasn't sure whether to kill me or chase you. After scrapping with me for a couple of minutes to make a point, he took after you."

"Were you badly injured?"

"Nothing that wouldn't heal in a couple of days. When Volan returned home two days later without you, he was hell to live with. After I healed, I left the pack."

"In search of me?"

He couldn't reveal that a feminine red *lupus garou* had brought a big gray to his knees. And he didn't want to tell her that not only could he not win against Volan, but he couldn't locate one little runaway female red wolf. This time *he* didn't answer her.

When he didn't respond, she lifted his hand to her lips and kissed it, warming him thoroughly. "Did you see a newscast about me?"

"Yeah, Argos said it was you right away."

She shrugged and muttered under her breath, "Could have been another."

"Nope, had your trademark all over it."

"I've *never* been caught and stuck in a zoo before."

He nudged her neck with his cheek. "No, but you've needed rescuing before. So, how was Big Red?"

She slugged him in the shoulder, forcing him to laugh out loud. Playing with her again felt good, but he wanted more. Resenting that he couldn't take her for his own, the powerful need to renew the good memories of their youth and to form new ones as mates strangled him. But it wasn't his business to want the pack leader's intended bitch and, worse, one who wanted a human companion.

With the need for sleep tantamount, both grew quiet; his arms securely wrapped around her, and they slept soundly for a couple of hours.

Something woke Devlyn. He sat up in bed, his heightened wolf senses taking hold. The smell of men's cologne, the sound of a keycard sliding into a slot, and the hush of men's voices in the hallway of their hotel suite triggered adrenaline to course through his blood at racetrack speed.

He jerked the covers aside, jumped off the mattress, and seized Bella's wrist. Clasping his hand over her mouth, he spoke against her ear in a hushed voice; her heart beat hard and her eyes were wild with fear. "Police, I think, trying to enter the living area of the hotel suite. Get dressed."

He shoved her clothes to her and pushed the queen-sized bed against the door. Throwing on his clothes, he turned to see Bella, already dressed in the oversized men's garments, sliding the patio door open and running onto the balcony. Before he could reach her, she climbed over the patio railing. For a moment, she hung from the concrete patio like a monkey, swinging in the cold city jungle, a drizzle coating everything in icy wetness.

He touched her hand. "Can you make it all right?"

"Yes," she whispered, her amber eyes darkening.

She dropped to the grassy ground shimmering with water droplets. Devlyn jumped down next to her and grabbed her hand. When he started to lift her, she objected.

"You're not wearing shoes, Bella. Let me do this my way."

"All right, boss, do it."

Black as night, Devlyn's eyes studied her for a moment. "It's about time you said so." His voice was hushed but different than Bella had ever heard it. Before she could further consider the change in his mood, he lifted her in his arms and ran across a road, the feel of his virile strength feeding her own. Skirting to the backside of an apartment complex, he headed for an SUV.

"I hope it's yours."

"Rental. We had several, figuring we'd give the

police a good chase with all of us going in different directions. We kept this one here in case anyone discovered us at the hotel."

Releasing her, he unlocked the vehicle's doors with the click of the button. "I have a change of clothes for you in the backseat. Put them on while I get us out of here."

After she slipped into the back, he took the wheel and drove out of the parking area. Unzipping the bag, she pulled out the contents—a scrappy pair of red lace panties, a bra the same color, a pair of pale-blue running pants, a sweatshirt, socks, and sneakers, trimmed with hearts.

"Who picked out the red scraps of lace?"

"Tanner."

She laughed at the thought of Devlyn's cousin, always playing the bad boy role. "Figures. He always did have a thing for red."

"If you don't like the color, you don't have to put them on."

"Go without?"

He glanced at the rearview mirror, his eyes smoldering.

She clicked the bra closed in front and frowned. "It's a pushup bra."

"Didn't need anything pushed up," he said, his voice ragged. "But it suits you."

"Watch your driving."

"Can't help the distraction," he growled.

Horny and frustrated, he acted like Big Red at the zoo. She pulled the rest of the clothes on and climbed into the front seat. "I can't believe I didn't pick up on those cops at the front door."

"You were still recovering from your harrowing experience at the zoo. How do you feel?"

"Like I'll have to take another nap later on."

"Want to crawl in the back and sleep for a while?"

"I couldn't right now. My skin's still prickling from nearly getting caught." She ran her hands over the running pants, wiping off the clamminess.

"What's bothering you, Bella?"

"Nothing."

"Don't tell me nothing. I can tell from the tension in your voice you're worried, and about more than the cops almost catching us."

She turned away from him and stared out the window; a light mist drizzled down the pane. "It's nothing."

"If you're considering not going home with me, think again. You're not safe on your own. *Lupus garous* have to stick together to survive. Loners get themselves killed. And no matter what, you can't expose our kind."

She glanced at him and opened her mouth to tell him off.

Tightening his grip on the steering wheel, Devlyn cursed under his breath. "Ah, hell. Trouble, straight ahead."

# Chapter 5

A *ROADBLOCK*. TWO POLICE CRUISERS SAT DEAD AHEAD on the shoulder of the road. While one policeman spoke to the driver of a compact, another eyed Devlyn and Bella's approaching SUV.

Despite the car's heater running on high, a chill ran down Bella's spine, and she involuntarily shuddered. "Maybe they're just looking for drunk drivers."

Devlyn shook his head. "We can't risk that they aren't looking for us."

"They'll recognize us, won't they, if they get a good look at us?"

"Yeah, I imagine so. Thompson probably gave them a rough description. That long, red hair of yours will be a dead giveaway." Devlyn turned down a side street before they reached the checkpoint and switched off his headlights. "Hold on tight. Someone will probably check us out because we avoided the roadblock."

She swallowed hard, not liking the situation at all. "See the carport in front of those apartments? Pull into a vacant slot. A police helicopter searching from above won't see the SUV then."

"I'm more concerned about the ones looking from the ground."

"Do it, Devlyn."

He grunted. "What happened to *my* being the boss?"

"You can be the boss later, stud."

He turned to look at her, his eyes darker than usual, his expression surprised. She sensed her new nickname for him pleased him in a sensual sort of way, and her own body responded as the ache returned between her legs.

"Let's try to find an apartment where no one's home and get some more sleep," she suggested.

"I hope you're right about this." He turned into the two-story apartment complex and parked underneath the metal carport.

"We probably couldn't outrun them. But if they didn't see us pull in here, they'll probably keep driving and—"

A police car approached and Bella and Devlyn ducked down.

Seconds passed. The vehicle continued down the road, its engine rumbling slightly.

Devlyn peered out the windshield. "They're still going. If they come back to check the parking lots, they may find the SUV, especially if they caught sight of the license plate before we turned down the street perpendicular to the one where the roadblock was set up."

She climbed out of the vehicle, glad the police hadn't noticed the wet drizzle on the vehicle when the ones parked next to it were dry as the desert. "You don't have to come."

"You're not running away from me again." He slammed his door shut.

"Oh?" She darted across the parking area in the thickening mist, and he dashed after her, catching her wrist with a viselike grip. She would have loved his possessiveness if he'd wanted her for his own. But no, he was keeping her from running away so he could turn her over to Volan. The bastard.

"When did I ever run away from you?" Dropping down behind a razor-toothed holly shrub, she listened for sounds in the apartment.

"When you left Colorado," he said, his harsh tone hushed while he crouched beside her.

"I slipped away from Volan, not you," she whispered in retort.

He clamped his mouth shut.

She stared at him. He'd only kissed her so long ago to prove he was more virile than the human boy, nothing more. Hell, he'd never even searched for her, or Argos would have said. "Devlyn, you can't mean you want me. Volan would kill you."

"Like hell he would."

The image of the last wolf Volan had killed flashed through her mind, and, with Devlyn not giving an inch, she tried to clear her thoughts of the vicious memory. She darted past an apartment window, dragging Devlyn with her. She listened again. "A man snoring."

She ran past the apartment and Devlyn gave her a dark look. A dog barked in the next one. Shaking her head, she moved to the next window. A distinctive odor of death and something more caught her attention—the smell of a red male *lupus garou*. Instantly, she made the connection between the rogue she'd caught a whiff of in the woods and the one who had been here. Her skin chilled. She was used to the hunt, but this was something else, something purely evil.

Intending to investigate and sure that Devlyn would not agree, she twisted her arm free of him and ran up the steps to the front door.

Dashing after her, Devlyn grabbed her wrist. "No," he whispered harshly. "You stay here and I'll check it out."

Grateful he would, she asked, "Do you smell it, too?"

A look of feral hostility flashed across his face.

"Maybe we can…help." But she doubted they could. She yanked at his leather jacket. "You have a lock pick, don't you?"

"Standard *lupus garou* toolkit. Where's yours?" He pulled out a leather kit and slid a tool out.

"I never sneaked into human's homes like you and your cousins did for fun, remember?"

"Only because you were too shy."

She snorted.

Jiggling the pick in the lock, he sprang the mechanism open. He shoved the door aside and walked into the room. "The air is foul," he whispered.

"Someone's died," she whispered back, her skin damp and crawling.

"A few days ago. Decay's already set in despite the place being ice cold. Air conditioner's running on high even though the temperature is barely above freezing outside."

"Natural causes. Let it be by natural causes." But she knew it wasn't, knew it had to be the killer she'd tried to track in the Cascades. She recognized his scent right before zoo man Thompson had caught her on her jaunt through the woods. Was it one of the two wolves she saw watching her at the stream? She couldn't be sure. The breeze had shifted and it might have disguised which of them it was. Or it might have been another, one she hadn't seen, hidden in the woods.

The sound of shattering glass in a room down the hall incited Devlyn to surge forward, but as an afterthought, he turned to her. "Stay here…and don't leave."

She nodded, realizing he wanted to keep her safe, but her blood heated that he'd think she'd run out on him when their situation only grew bleaker by the moment.

The strong odor of incense filling the living area overwhelmed the faint odor of blood emanating from what she assumed must be the bedroom.

Everything in the place appeared immaculately clean, as though a maid had just tidied up, except for a patch of…

She drew closer to the pale-blue sofa. Coarse brown hair, reddish at the tips, clung to the back. She reached out to collect it.

Devlyn rushed out of the bedroom. "Let's go, Bella." His stern face allowed no argument. He seized her wrist and jerked her toward the door. "Now, Bella, now!"

"What happened?"

After pulling her from the apartment, he slammed the door. "A woman around your age, murdered in bed." He rushed Bella back to the SUV. "We have to risk driving. We can't be caught here."

"How was she killed?"

He banged her door shut and ran to the other side of the vehicle. As soon as he started the ignition, he turned to her. "A wild animal ripped out her throat."

"*Lupus garou*," she whispered. "They'll think it's us."

"They'll think it's a wild animal. Werewolves are fanciful legends concocted by our human ancestors, remember? But it fits. He killed her before the waning moon completely faded."

"But the sound of the glass shattering—"

"He must have been living here for the last couple of days. By breaking into the place, we startled him, and he busted the window and took off. The window must have been stuck tight." Devlyn sped out of the parking lot.

"They'll think the killer is Rosa, the freed wolf...me, because she'd be the only wild wolf loose in the city."

He pursed his lips and pinched his brows in a frown. "Possibly. If zoo man Thompson gets hold of this news, he may think the woman had something to do with freeing Rosa, that she kept her in the apartment, or maybe they'll think it's another wild wolf."

"We have to stop him."

He glanced at her, his dark brows lifted. "I have only one mission and that's returning you to Colorado and the pack."

She shook her head. "He's one of mine."

Devlyn stared at her like she'd lost her mind.

"He's a red." She raised the clump of hair she'd hastily plucked from the couch. "We have to stop him before he exposes the legend for what it really is—fact."

"No. Humans are already hunting us."

"You didn't...didn't kill Thompson or the cops, did you?"

The look Devlyn gave her made her wish she had

never spoken the cutting words. Deep-seated hurt flashed across his eyes. He clenched his jaw and turned to watch his driving. "We're being hunted because you and I freed a little red wolf from the zoo and because I liberated you from the hospital, knocking some officials out in the process. I'm sure they consider me armed and dangerous. I'm not sure what they think of you, considering you were naked and nearly frozen."

"I'm sorry, Devlyn. This whole thing's kind of gotten to me. *Lupus garous* don't kill humans without good reason."

"This one did."

"Yes, and we have to make sure he doesn't again."

"Not us. His own pack, Bella."

"Then we have to make them aware that he's doing this." She wouldn't stand by and let it continue, though her own investigation hadn't turned up much. But the scent of the one in the apartment definitely matched the smell she had caught a whiff of in the woods. Was he one of the ones she saw at the zoo? She'd been only able to catch the smell of one of them because of the way the breeze shifted at random. She couldn't have identified which one the scent had belonged to. But at least one was in the clear.

Concentrating on his driving, Devlyn didn't say anything for a moment. "No, Bella, we're not contacting the reds."

Taking an exasperated breath, she reached over and touched his hand. "We have to."

"Damn it, Bella, you're going to get us both caught and in a hell of a lot more trouble."

She folded her arms. "We have to," she growled.
"We owe it to our kind."

Again, a shimmer of something elusive crossed his
face. For several more minutes, he remained quiet, and
she knew he was coming to a decision. He finally let out
his breath. "All right."

Relief shadowed with worry skittered across her skin.
"Thank you."

"I hope we don't live to regret this," he groused, "but
it's about time you realized where you belonged."

For a second, she didn't respond, wondering where
the hell that came from. Then the realization struck
her—she'd given up *lupus garou* to live with humans
and now wanted to help her own kind. *That's* why he
agreed. Hoping what? She'd give up the notion of finding a human male to mate?

Figuring he had made a concession and might change
his mind if she ticked him off, she bit her tongue before
she made a hasty retort. "Did he urinate in the apartment?" she asked instead.

Devlyn studied her for a moment, took a long breath,
and nodded.

"His territory. Do you think he wanted her, and she
grew terrified when he changed into the wolf?"

"Maybe."

"Maybe not? Does he just want to kill humans?"

Devlyn gripped the steering wheel tightly.

"Devlyn?"

Through clenched teeth, he said, "She was a redhead,
Bella. He's a red *lupus garou* looking for a mate. There
must be a shortage of eligible females in the area."

Bella's throat felt parched as if she'd crossed the Badlands without a lick of water.

Devlyn continued, "He must have convinced her he loved her and then risked changing to turn her. Only she would have been terrified. Humans can't deal with what we are, Bella. Can't you understand that?"

This wasn't about the woman. She figured this was about her wanting a human male.

"You see now why I didn't want you involved?" he asked. "If he catches sight of you…"

He shook his head.

Rubbing her temple, she tried to figure out a way to alert the killer's pack. "The two men at the zoo are probably related to the killer's pack. We have to send word to them. Find them somehow."

"How do you propose to do that when we're on the run?"

"Take us to Tigard; it's south of Portland. That's where I live, and we can use it as our base for the time being."

He scowled at her. "The things I do for you."

"Yeah," she said huskily, "like relieving my… tension."

He glanced at her, granting her a wicked, wolfish smile that said he wanted to eat her all up, and she wondered then if he'd want to do more to relieve her tension the next time. But a police cruiser passed them by, and she shrank in her seat, remembering the danger they were still in.

---

Thirty minutes later, they reached Bella's house without incident, thank the stars. But until they'd hidden the rental SUV, she still didn't feel safe. And if her neighbor saw her coming home in a different vehicle than the one she'd left in, the questioning would begin in earnest.

Good-natured Chrissie was truly a friend, but she was also too curious for her own good.

At four in the morning, the area remained blanketed in black, except for two security lights illuminating the entryway of the peach stone two-bedroom house.

"Your outside lamps are on," Devlyn said, his voice worried.

"Security. They automatically come on when it grows dark. Park around back. We can hide the SUV in the garage, but we'll have to open it from inside. I don't have my garage door controller with me."

"Your vehicle is still in the Cascades?"

"Yeah. Next to the cabin I own there."

They shut the vehicle's doors as quietly as they could, and then he hurried with her to the front door. "Let me go inside first."

Slipping a key from a vine-covered trellis, she handed it to him, appreciating his concern. "Be my guest."

As soon as he opened the door, he took a step inside, lifted his chin, and sniffed the air.

"Smell anything?" she whispered.

A slow smile crept across his face. "Yeah, you, Bella honey."

She pushed him into the house and locked the door. "You're supposed to be keeping your mind on business. Let's move the SUV into the garage; then we can plan our next—"

"Sleep. We haven't had enough sleep to keep us going."

She noticed the dark skin beneath his eyes. "All right." She motioned to the kitchen. "Door to the garage is that way."

"Be right back. Undress and I'll meet you in bed." He waited for her to agree.

"Still worried I might bolt?" She folded her arms and lifted a brow.

"No. Not now that you want to catch the killer." He sounded annoyed.

"Then you can sleep on the couch."

"In your dreams."

She chuckled and intended to go to the bedroom when she noticed how wilted her houseplants were and made a detour to the kitchen. She swore that as soon as she gave water to the ficus trees and the winding ivy, they perked up right away. Then she entered her bedroom and glanced out the window at her greenhouse. Chrissie would have made sure everything was well watered, she was certain. It seemed like eons since she'd been here last, not just a few days.

Sighing deeply, Bella felt safe for the moment and overjoyed to be in her own home again. She yanked off her sneakers, determined to climb into bed and fall asleep before the big gray wolf returned and gave her other notions. Then she formulated a plan.

After crossing the room, she dug in her linen closet and pulled out a spare set of sheets and a pillow. Dashing back down the hall, she hurried to the floral sofa. She laid the sheets and pillow on one end and strode back to her bedroom.

Once she removed the rest of her clothes, she heard

the garage door grumble shut, and then the kitchen door leading to the garage opened and closed. She climbed into bed, pulled the green velvet spread under her chin, and closed her eyes.

For several minutes, she lay still, listening for Devlyn, but when he didn't come to the bedroom, her heart sank. Playing games with him when they were young inspired her interest in him. Didn't he realize she was teasing him about sleeping on the couch?

She was too tired to care.

After another couple of minutes, she tossed onto her side and growled.

The shattering of glass on the tile kitchen floor sent a spike of adrenaline racing through her veins. She bolted from the bed, tugged on the sweatshirt, and ran down the hall. All she could think of was protecting Devlyn, yet when she approached the kitchen, she realized she had forgotten the gun, even though the silver bullets were meant for Volan, should he ever find her.

She peered around the cabinets to see into the kitchen.

Standing in front of the refrigerator, Devlyn stared at the collage of pictures hanging from the door. Broken glass rested at his feet.

"Devlyn," she said under her breath, her heartbeat thundering.

He looked at her. "Who sent the pictures of us to you?"

Holding her breath, she rubbed her arms as a chill fluttered across her skin. She didn't like the accusation in the tone of his voice or the anger in his eyes.

"Who, Bella?"

Without answering him, she turned to a cupboard, but before she could grab the broom and dustpan, he crossed the floor and seized her arm. Pulling her to face him, he asked again, "Who, Bella? Who in the pack knew where you were and for how long?"

"Let go of me," she growled and tried to free herself from his iron hold.

He pressed her back against the cupboard and gripped her shoulders. "You didn't really leave the pack permanently, did you? You kept in touch. Someone sent you our photos. The colored pictures more recently, black and white for some years earlier, sepia before this. Who's been corresponding with you about us?"

Tears rolled down her cheeks. If she hadn't been so tired, if one of her own kind hadn't killed a woman, if she hadn't been incarcerated in the zoo, she could have handled Devlyn's harsh accusations better. She missed them terribly, nearly every one of the members of the pack…her family. But she wouldn't be Volan's. And if she returned, she'd have no choice.

"Bella," Devlyn said, his voice gentler as he lifted her in his arms and carried her to the bedroom, "you cared about us, didn't you? Even though you have more pictures of me than any of the others in the pack."

She wiped her eyes, attempting to avoid the implication. "He sent more of them to me."

"Who?" He laid her down in the bed and then unbuttoned his shirt. "You have mine more prominently displayed."

"There were more of them. I already said so." Her voice was sterner than she meant it to be.

His penetrating gaze clouded with lust and he yanked off his shirt.

She tugged her sweatshirt off and tossed it on the floor and then pulled the covers up.

A smile tugged at the corners of his lips. He unfastened his belt and pulled his zipper down. His gaze took in her furnishings, but before he could look at her nightstand, she grabbed the picture off it and shoved it under her pillow. No sense in giving him the wrong idea.

But he caught her in the act and his eyes turned black. "A secret admirer? A human male?" His voice was couched in anger. He sat down next to her on the edge of the bed. After pulling off his boots, he stood and removed his trousers, dropping them on the floor.

Her gaze shifted to the dark, curly hair between his legs and his prominent erection. He was ready to mate if she were willing, and the overwhelming animal urge instantly prepped her for his penetration.

"Who sent the photos to you?" His tone turned lighter, more conversational rather than demanding.

She glared at him, still annoyed with his earlier bullying. "It's none of your business."

He hit the bed with his fist, shocking her at seeing his temper flare so quickly. She jumped, irritated with herself for reacting instead of remaining calm, unflinching.

"Damn it, Bella. I've searched on and off for you for years."

Her eyes grew big as her heart leapt. Then she realized he'd followed pack orders—Volan's command to have her returned to him. She narrowed her eyes and crossed her arms. "Yeah, so you could return me to Volan."

His brows knit tightly, but he didn't say anything. He jammed his hand underneath her pillow and yanked out the cherry wood picture frame. A smile simmered on his lips.

Her cheeks burned with embarrassment, and she tried to think of a reason for having his photo next to her bed. Unable to come up with a plausible explanation, she turned her back to him and closed her eyes. "Good night, Devlyn. Pleasant dreams."

He jerked the covers aside. She turned and glowered at him.

Smiling appreciably as he gazed at her naked body, he took in a deep breath. "Feral like the redwoods, sweet as wild roses."

She covered herself again.

He wiggled his dark brows. "It's a picture of me." He glanced back at the photo he'd set upright on her nightstand. "Great image, too. One of my better pictures."

"What of it? It was too big to fit on the fridge. I told him not to send any more that size because they're too big."

Devlyn pulled the back of the frame open, and she knew he'd discover the truth.

"You've had this one enlarged. Gives a photo ID on the back, a local Oregon printer. You had a smaller version of the same photo on the fridge, probably the one he sent you." He cast her an elusive smile.

She pursed her lips.

Pulling the covers back down, he exposed her breasts to the cool air in the bedroom. Instantly, the nipples turned into pert red peaks. He leaned over and kissed one and then the other, making them throb with need.

But she couldn't mate with him, as much as her body readied itself to accept his virile strength. She'd endanger him too much if she gave into her primal instincts, her deep-seated cravings for the gray. She touched his whiskery cheek. "You were supposed to sleep on the couch."

"You've been keeping my image close to your bed. Now you can keep the flesh and blood me *in* your bed." He climbed into bed next to her and touched her cheek. "Tell me how much you love me, Bella. Tell me how many times you wrote to whoever it was, asking about me."

"He didn't tell me you searched for me."

"*Who* didn't tell you?"

She sensed the tightness in his voice, the way he barely curbed his anger. "It's late. We need to sleep."

He ran his tongue down her belly, forcing a quiver of anticipation. "I won't quit asking until you tell me. Who was it?"

Giving up the guarded secret, she sighed heavily and admitted, "Argos."

Devlyn stilled his actions and growled, irritated that the old wolf hadn't told him the truth. How he had longed to know what had become of Bella all those years. When he'd spoken to Argos, the sly old wolf had assured him she'd be all right. He should have known Argos knew what had happened to her. "Damn him."

"I shouldn't have told you. I wrote to let him know I was safe after I ran away. I couldn't let him think I'd died. From then on, we corresponded."

"No wonder he knew it was you in that news report. I figured he had some kind of a sixth sense. But all along he knew you lived in the area." He studied her eyes, tired and wary. The annoyance he felt that Argos had kept the secret about Bella faded into wry amusement. "You wanted to know about me, about how I fared."

"Don't be so conceited."

Knowing she disguised the truth, his lips curved up. His intense craving to mate with her filled him with an ache he longed to fulfill. He threaded his fingers through her satiny hair and licked her throat. She moaned. His erection pulsed with renewed gusto. His instincts were right concerning her. She wanted him as much as he lusted after her.

He pressed his arousal against her soft body. "You know how much I desire to have you, Bella. Tell me you want me, too."

Shaking her head, her eyes misted.

He growled at her stubbornness. Then he nuzzled his cheek against hers, enjoying the delicate ivory fragrance she'd washed with, hoping she'd succumb to his advances. He ran his finger over her firm nipple. "I won't let Volan have you. We'll return to the pack and then—"

"No. He'll kill you. I don't want you for a mate. Don't you understand?" She tried to pull away from him, her voice heated with anger. "I don't want you."

But he recognized from her words and actions that it wasn't true; he'd use every trick he knew to convince her to tell the truth.

# Chapter 6

BELLA RECLINED AGAINST HER BED AND SNIFFLED, HER tears undoing Devlyn. "I just wanted to know about the family, that's all, Devlyn. That's why I wrote to Argos."

Wanting to force the truth from her, he knew she loved him, even if she denied it. "We're both tired." He pulled her hair away from her face and kissed her wet, salty cheek. "Let's sleep." Having every intention of making her see his way once they were well rested, he gathered her against him and inhaled the essence of her. "I want you, Bella."

"You can't," she sniffled again.

"Sorry, from the moment I rescued you from the wildfire, I'd claimed you. Now you just have to agree to be my mate." Yet the question still nagging him slipped out again: "Why do you hate Volan so?"

---

Early the next morning, Devlyn stretched out on the mattress, annoyed that Bella had tensed and turned away from him the night before, avoiding his question about Volan, even though he'd forced her to curl up with him anyway. No way could he sleep next to the wolf siren and not touch her. Now his fingers itched to have Bella in their grasp, but not locating her, his eyes shot open. Tearing the covers aside, he dashed out of the room and down the hall.

Unable to curb how furious he was that she'd run off, he stormed into the kitchen, his blood on fire. She'd cleaned up the broken glass, but otherwise there was no sign of her.

"Damn it, Bella!" he roared. How could he have trusted the vixen? He should have realized she wouldn't have stayed put.

Suspecting the worst, he yanked open the kitchen door to the garage. The SUV was gone and the garage was empty except for cardboard boxes stacked up in a corner.

He rubbed his stubbled chin, formulating his next plan of action. But where in the hell would she have disappeared to?

The SUV's engine suddenly purred in the driveway, his skin grew sweaty with anticipation, and the garage door rumbled open.

He still couldn't curb his irritation that she would have left him, even for a short while. What if she'd been seen?

When she had parked the car, Bella smiled at him from the driver's seat, a devilish glint in her eyes. The image of her naked in bed with him came instantly to mind. Folding his arms, he frowned at her until the woman sitting on the passenger's side caught his attention. Her mouth dropped wide open and her eyes grew as round as the full moon while she gaped at him. Well, not at him exactly, but at a particular lower part of his anatomy that, on seeing Bella return, had already risen to greet her.

Slamming the door on his rapid retreat into the kitchen, he cursed all of the way back to the bedroom, the fire burning in his veins. How could he have thought

Bella would run? Because she would, when the time was right. Who the hell was that other woman? They needed to use secrecy.

He yanked his jeans on.

*Secrecy*. Hell, he'd been the one caught stark naked, making a permanent impression on that shocked woman's mind.

Light footsteps hurried down the hall. He turned.

Bella leaned against the doorjamb, her posture relaxed, an impish smile tugging at her mouth. "My next-door neighbor went home and skipped having a cup of coffee with me." She wet her lips in a slow sensual sweep and then crossed her arms beneath her breasts. "Hmm, you sure gave Chrissie something to dream about, though I don't think I've ever seen her quite that speechless before." Her smile spread across her face.

He stalked toward Bella, backed her against the wall, and placed his hands on either side of her head, caging her in. "I thought you'd left me." His voice was husky and more desperate than he wanted it to sound.

"Her car's in the shop, and she needed milk for her kids." Bella's gaze shifted from his eyes to his lips.

"Hell, her kids were in the car?" he asked, his voice darkening with concern.

"No, they're at school." Running her finger down his stomach, she sent a surge of electricity straight to his groin.

He let out his breath, her touch wreaking havoc with his need to control. "Really, Bella, you have to be more careful. We can't afford to get caught."

She tilted her head to the side and scanned his whole

body with a naughty look. "It seems you made more of an impression on her than I did on anyone this morning."

Growling, he plundered her mouth, dominating, conquering, not willing to let her fight him, if she had any notion to do so.

She squeezed his denim-covered butt, tangled her tongue with his, and pressed her heavenly breasts against his bare chest. "She wanted to know who the iron man hunk was standing naked in my kitchen entryway."

"I didn't expect you to bring company home with you. In fact, I didn't expect you to return home at all," he growled, only it came out more like a wolfish groan. He tangled his fingers in her hair.

"She was glad to have the opportunity to meet you. Said something about maybe having a barbecue."

"No."

She stroked his shoulder blades, the muscles taut. "It's okay, Devlyn. I told her you were all mine. A friend from my youth, renewing an old friendship. Just seeing the way you were dressed…or rather not…" She grinned. "Well, I think she got the point."

He raised his brows and inclined his head.

"Oh, did I forget to mention she's divorced and looking for husband number two?"

Ignoring her comment, he swept Bella up and carried her to the bed, having every notion of showing her how alpha he could be.

"We have work to do, Devlyn. Catch a killer and—"

He laid her on the mattress, struggling to keep his desire in check. "We have some other business to take care of, Bella. And you're not talking me out of this."

She tucked her arms behind her head, her red curls spread out against the green sheets.

Reaching down, he unbuttoned her shirt; their gazes locked in shared appreciation.

"What do you have in mind? You know what Volan intends to do with me."

"He can't have you. I want you. Always have. I told you already. You just have to say you want me, too."

She furrowed her brows at him, her lips poked out in a sultry pout. "You know I can't."

"Because you're afraid I can't win against Volan." The notion that she felt this way about his abilities soured him. If he couldn't change her opinion of him, she could never love him fully. She'd proved herself an alpha female, being a loner and surviving so many years on her own, but he had to prove he could be an alpha male or lose the battle.

"I don't want you even trying. If we mate and he learns of it, he'll kill you."

Devlyn shook his head, his temper rising. "If I don't kill him first. Have you no faith in me?"

"He's a brute. I've seen what he's done to others—maimed or killed them outright. He'll destroy you."

"So, by looking for a human mate, you're doing what? If Volan finds you with one, he'll kill him like he did the boy. Would you find that any more acceptable?" he growled, unable to control his exasperation. He yanked off one of her shoes and then the other and tossed them to the floor with a clunk.

She bit her lower lip.

Leaning down, he kissed her lips tenderly, his tongue

stroking the full curves, the taste of wild blackberries flavoring them, feral and sweet like her. "Maybe you wouldn't care as much because you couldn't really love a human like you love me."

"You are *so* arrogant." Her voice teased, turning him on faster as his groin ached with need.

He yanked off his trousers and dropped them on the floor. "That's what you love about me…about our kind. You don't really want some human. Believe me, if you got hold of one, he'd never satisfy you."

She cast a raking glance over his nakedness. "The way you can?" A gleam in her eye and the smile on her lips was invitation enough, an unmistakable challenge.

He growled, "You better believe it." Every fiber of his body was ready to prove it.

He unfastened her belt and unzipped her pants. Smiling sinfully, she never twitched a muscle to stop him. Although mating as a human could occur any-time and with relish, the wolf's side demanded mating from January through April. And he intended to ensure that she was well satisfied for the rest of that time and beyond.

Suddenly, a deep male voice from the next room said, "You have mail, madam."

Devlyn spun around, but seeing no one, he stormed out of the room to kill the intruder in her office.

Bella laughed and chased after him. "He's my email butler, Devlyn."

Staring at the monitor, he read the message Bella had posted on a local board.

> Mystic Red seeks male interested in lifetime
> mate, who loves to hunt, free-spirited and wild
> in nature, Portland, Oregon.

"Damn it, Bella."

Bella ran her hand down Devlyn's bare back, trying to coax some of the tension out of his tight muscles.

"When did you post this message?" he growled.

"An hour after we fell asleep. I woke and couldn't get back to sleep. I couldn't quit worrying that the lives of other women could be at stake."

He turned to her, his face stern, teeth clenched, jaw set. "So you decided you'd be the bait? Without asking for my input? I thought we were doing this together. What if he decides it's a hoax? That you don't really want him for a mate? That you only want to turn him over to his pack to determine his punishment? What if he tries to kill you?"

She traced his ribs with her fingernails, beguiling him. "I've never done anything useful in my life. I'm a website graphics designer, but I've never truly done anything that makes a difference—well, except for caring for childless human couples during my teen years by mutual arrangement. Several provided a home for me when I needed one badly. I acted the loving adopted daughter and took care of them when they grew too old to care for themselves."

He caught her wrists to stop the sweet torture that her fingers did on his aroused body. "They never caught you slipping out of the house to take a run on the wild side?"

Shrugging, she admitted as much. "A couple of times, but they scolded me for sneaking out to see a fellow, even though, of course, I hadn't. In each case,

I took care of the couples in their advanced years until they died. When I finally reached the age of majority and could live on my own, I did so, using the money and properties they had bequeathed to me. I moved from time to time so as not to alert others that I aged so slowly and to keep Volan from finding me."

Rubbing her face against Devlyn's whiskery cheek, Bella loved the feel of his scratchy stubble against her skin, undomesticated and wolfish. "But I've never done anything for our own kind. You saved my life once. You're a hero in my eyes. I want to help stop a killer who could expose all of us for what we truly are before it's too late."

"It doesn't matter to you that I don't want you to do it?"

"Of course it matters to me. I want you to protect me."

His dark eyes sparkled with desire. "You want me to be your mate."

"I don't want you to die, Devlyn."

"Damn it, Bella. I don't want you to die either. You want me to allow you to jeopardize your life to save others, but you refuse to be my mate because you're worried I'll risk my neck? I've already gambled my life for you once. I wasn't that powerful a swimmer when I was young and carried you across the swollen river. I was determined at all costs to save you. Even now, trying to protect you against this killer, I'm risking my life. So why not take the chance against Volan?"

Devlyn shook his head when she didn't respond and searched through the thirty-two messages she'd received. "Lots of damned nutcases living here."

"Yeah, I didn't expect to get that much of a response."

"I think you've been too cryptic."

When she ran her hand over his toned bare butt, the muscle tightened. He flicked an interested glance her way, but she tried to keep his mind focused on the task at hand. "What would you have me say, Devlyn? 'Red *lupus garou* female seeks mate. Horny right now. Only a red *lupus garou* male need apply'?"

"You might have half of the *lupus garou* population in several states applying for the position. Lord knows how many are looking for a red." Sitting down at the keyboard, he typed, Little Red Wolf seeks mate. Preferably big gray wolf terminally in lust with her.

She hit his shoulder. "Be serious."

Grunting, he deleted the words. "I *am* serious." He typed, Rufus lupus female seeks mate in Portland, Oregon, area only.

"A red wolf seeks a mate? The humans will think she's a nut and—"

"The *lupus garou* will know she's one of them, a loner, looking for a red wolf pack to join."

"Okay, sign it as Rosa."

"But what if Thompson—"

She combed her fingers through Devlyn's shoulder-length brown hair, highlighted by the sun, satiny smooth to the touch, soft, where the rest of him was hard. "He probably wouldn't be looking at the personals for the local community. And if he did, he'd never figure it out."

Devlyn rubbed his chin.

"Do it, Devlyn."

He flashed her an annoyed look. "You sure are bossy."

"You love me for it," she teased.

He clicked on the send button and scanned the email responses to her first message.

> Hello, Mystic Red. I'm High-on-Poppy. Would you be my love forever? Just blows my mind what we could do together, wild thing. Set the world on fire. Looking for your loving response. HOP

Devlyn looked back at her as she read over his shoulder. "Sounds fun loving, huh?" she asked.

"Idiot, hopped-up human."

They looked at the next message.

> Hey, Mystic Red. Want to be my sweet thing? Don't you just hate zoos? If I could, I'd free all of the wild animals. And eat the grazers. I never did catch your name, so guess Rosa will have to do for now. Email me and we can arrange to get together. Sooner than later. Lovesick in Oregon. Al

She shuddered. "Alfred."

Devlyn looked back at her, all at once his posture dark and wolfishly protective. "What?"

"He's the one from the zoo. The one who wanted me."

"Red *lupus garou*," he muttered. "Damn it, Bella, what if he's the killer?"

"What if he is? We could catch him then."

The email butler, dressed in his tux, walked across the screen and then stopped and faced them. "You've got mail, madam."

Devlyn clicked on the next message.

> Hey, Rosa, I posted to your old message.
> Guess you were afraid I wouldn't catch it.
> So how about a date? A romp through the
> Cascades? Email me. Al

Devlyn rose from his chair and shoved it aside. "I don't like this guy."

"He's smaller than you. You can beat him if we get into a bind."

His expression turned stormy. "Damn it, Bella. You think I can only whip smaller guys?"

The darkness in his voice startled her. She hadn't meant to cut his masculinity in half. She touched his lightly haired chest. "I didn't mean it that way. I just meant you could protect me."

"Like hell you did. You think I can only whip a smaller red's ass but that I'd buckle under when the competition's a little more my size." With his long stride, he stormed off to the bedroom.

She fought chasing after him to console him. It wasn't their way, and he wouldn't appreciate it. It would emasculate him all the more. Her stomach clenched into knotted ribbon. Damn *lupus garou* male pride.

Turning to the computer, she typed in a reply.

> Hi, Al, hadn't seen your previous response.

> Meet me tonight at the Papagalli's Dance
> Club. See you there at seven. Rosa

The response was immediate.

> Hey, Rosa, what's your real name? Al

Had he been waiting for her response all of this time?
Desperate to get in touch with her? Or was he an internet
junkie too?

She stared at the question. What was her real name?
She typed: Rosa.

> All right, Rosa it is. I'll play the game for now.
> Don't you think a place a little less crowded
> would be better? Al

Having no intention of meeting loverboy in private,
she tapped her fingers on the desk, considering the
best response.

> I love Papagalli's. Besides, I believe in court-
> ship, don't you? Rosa

> Whatever you want, Rosa. But…I don't believe
> in long courtships. See ya, sweet thing. Al

Then a new message popped up.

> Male rufus lupus seeking female. Have cabin

in the Cascades for hunting and wild romps in
the woods. Where can we meet? Charlie

She reread the message. Was it just some nutty human?

Hey, Charlie! What do you prefer to hunt?
Rosa

Deer. What about you? Charlie

How about two-legged mammals? How about red-headed women? Are you the killer, Charlie? She tucked her hair behind her ear and then typed,

A male rufus lupus. Rosa

I like a lupus with a sense of humor. Can we
have lunch this afternoon? Charlie

Don't you work? Rosa

A significant pause followed. She chewed on the inside of her cheek. Come on, come on. Let me know what you do.

Independently wealthy. But if you're working...maybe tonight? Charlie

Liar.

Do you know Papagalli's? Rosa

The dance club? Charlie

Yep. Make it for seven? Rosa

The more the merrier.

See you there. Oh, what will you be wearing?
Charlie

Something black. And you? Rosa

Something to match. Charlie

Most everyone wore black to the club, and she had no plan to stick out. Another *lupus* would smell her scent. Humans wouldn't have a clue as to who she was, and best to leave it that way.

The kitchen door to the garage slammed shut, sending her heart skittering. Jumping up from the chair, she nearly knocked it over in her haste and headed for the garage. She didn't believe Devlyn would run off and expose himself to the world while the police were looking for them just because she'd angered him. She yanked the door open.

He'd taken the SUV.

Her heart sank. Damn him!

Still, she hated herself for having said he couldn't fight a gray, stomping his male wolf ego into the ground.

Trying not to worry about him, she toasted a slice of bread and coated it with wild blackberry jam, the smell reminding her of picking berries fresh over the summer. The tart sweet flavor touched her tongue, and instantly the image of Devlyn crowding her while she leaned over blackberry brambles filled her mind with wishful thinking. Attempting to clear her mind of the foolish notion, she finished her toast and headed out to the greenhouse.

The fragrant scent of Colorado wildflowers comforted her and she pruned, watered, and weeded for a couple of hours before she returned to the house. Because of the time she'd spent in the zoo, the website contracts she received were piling up, so she headed back to her office, trying to ignore the fact that all she really could think about was Devlyn and making up with him.

But the making up would come only after she got over being mad at him for leaving like he did and worrying her sick.

While she designed a redwood forest for a lumber company, her email butler walked across the screen.

She clicked on her email messages. Ten new messages. But the address of the sixth message caught her eye: *Argos*.

> Bella, I'm worried that we haven't heard from
> you. Can we meet somewhere? I have some
> news I'm sure you'll want to hear. Argos

She rubbed her temple. Was Volan dead? That's the only news she'd want to hear. Had another wolf infiltrated the pack and was now the leader?

> Argos, where are you? Bella

> I'm here, in town. I'm using the main library's

computer, but there aren't many patrons and I fear someone's following me. Can we meet somewhere later? Argos

She took a deep breath. Argos and Devlyn could both protect her if she were meeting the killer red wolf tonight. She considered telling him about the wolf they were trying to catch, but decided against it. He'd be just like Devlyn—his only concern would be returning her home. Argos wouldn't agree to her risking her life over a red *lupus garou* from another pack.

Papagalli's Dance Club. Seven. Bella

See you there. Argos

Email messages were an addiction. She had no ability to shut them off; instead, she began to read all of them. Most had the same kind of message. Red male *lupus* wishes to meet with female of his kind. Can we arrange to rendezvous and when? Like soonest? She responded to all of them:

Meet me at Papagalli's Dance Club.

The biggest crowd Papagalli's had ever seen on a Thursday night would show up. She sent the last of the responses zinging into cyberspace and then returned to working on clients' web pages.

A nagging at the back of her mind gnawed at her— that Devlyn was living a James Bond life of danger when he stormed out of the house. He had no right to worry her. But she knew he had to get away, stretch his legs, work his anger out on his own. Still, she had every intention of giving him a tongue lashing when he returned home for worrying her so.

She groaned as the thought of his tongue sliding down her skin popped into her mind. Maybe a little bit of wolf courtship would smooth out the rough edges of what she'd said to hurt his ego.

Bella worked for several hours on web pages, getting so wrapped up in her designs that she hadn't noticed the time slip away. When she realized the noon hour had arrived and Devlyn still hadn't returned, a slice of worry cut into her heart.

She walked into the living room and stared out the picture window. No sign of the SUV. Damn him for leaving.

A knock at her front door forced a shudder down her spine. She stalked toward the door but then hesitated.

What if the police had caught Devlyn? What if they came for her now, too?

# Chapter 7

PEERING OUT THE PEEPHOLE, BELLA FOUND CHRISSIE standing on her doorstep and figured the questioning would truly begin. Taking a deep breath, she yanked the door open, relieved it wasn't the police. "Hi, Chrissie."

Her next-door neighbor looked a bit startled, her blue eyes wide and her lips parted. She was wearing a short chiffon skirt and flowery blouse, a little too sheer for the weather and a lot too dressy for just dropping by. "Oh, I...I wondered if you might like an apple pie. To thank you for taking me to the grocery store this morning."

*An apple pie?* Chrissie had always been generous with Bella, relishing their friendship because she was estranged from her parents—they had told her the guy she married was no good and were still mad at her for not listening to them. Now she was raising her two kids on her own and Bella couldn't understand how Chrissie's parents could be so insensitive. But the kids were the ex's, too, and that made all the difference in the world to the parents.

Bella sighed.

Had Chrissie thought Bella had left the house and not Devlyn? Chrissie had never baked a pie before when Bella had helped her with errands. She was after the man hunk, only she wasn't taming that big gray.

Bella should have been annoyed, but she was more

amused than anything. "Thank you, Chrissie. I have to warn you, though, Devlyn's more of a red meat kind of guy. Not all that much into sweets."

The kitchen door slammed shut and Bella jumped slightly. She glanced back at Devlyn, furious he'd taken off, but glad to see him safely home. He strode across the living room, his expression still stormy, his back stiff, a light sheen of sweat above his brows shimmering in the living room's natural light.

"Who says I'm not into sweets?" he countered, his brows raised, challenging Bella. "I like my dessert, often, just as much as any other guy."

She knew damned well he didn't like sugary treats all that much. Was he trying to undermine her? Get in good with Chrissie for Bella cutting his masculinity down earlier?

"Well, that's good then." Chrissie beamed at Devlyn and handed the pie to Bella, pausing as if waiting for an invitation.

"I guess your kids are due home soon," Bella said, hoping they were.

"Not for another three and a half hours." Chrissie looked at Devlyn, a smile still curving her lips. Her dark curls framed her sweet face like a gray *lupus garou's* might when in human form. She stood taller than Bella, too, more like the females of his pack, and she definitely had the hots for Devlyn.

Placing his hands on his hips, Devlyn turned to Bella. "I took a run to work out some tension and then picked up a couple of things for us to eat. Didn't care for the slim pickings in your fridge. Maybe you can fix the steak for us. You know how I like it—on the bloody side. I'm going to hop in the shower." He wiped his cheek on his sleeve. "I smell kind of…ripe."

She couldn't help giving him a crooked smile. Yeah, she could smell the scent of him, all male, sweaty, and totally lovable. "Um, yeah, well…"

He waited for her response. She wanted to tell him she would join him, but she couldn't, not unless she told him she'd be his mate. Otherwise, she'd let things go too far.

He raised a brow, challenging her. "Coming?"

As a mature *lupus garou*, Devlyn proved hotter than the blue flicker of the flame—a *wicked* wolf, and all hers if she'd just give the go-ahead.

She turned to her neighbor. "Um, Chrissie, thanks for the pie. I'll talk to you later."

Chrissie's green eyes bulged like a Pekinese's.

Bella smiled. "Sorry, that's the problem with renewing old relationships. They can be awfully demanding."

Chrissie stammered, "Uh, yeah, well, okay. Talk to you later."

Bella closed the door and then turned to Devlyn. "Where the hell have you been?" she snapped, irritated to think she'd worried so about his safety.

"Running. I already said so," he retorted, his own voice still angry. He stormed off in the direction of the bedroom.

After setting the pie on the coffee table, she dashed after him. "You do not like sweets, liar."

He turned to her, his eyes dark. "I do too love sweets, Bella. Your kind of sweets." But he wasn't smiling.

A surge of lust coursed through her body. She wanted

him, really she did. But…"You've been gone for hours. You couldn't have been running all that time."

"I took a trip to the Cascades."

Her heart sped up. "Because?"

"The killer might have run there sometime or another." His hard gaze pierced her. "Were the reds aware you had a cabin there? That you took your jaunts there?"

She bit her lip. "I saw two in their wolf forms and smelled their scent on the breeze. I thought the murdering wolf might have been one of them. But I didn't know at the time what he smelled like. How did you know I had a cabin there?"

"Found paperwork in your office when I went to email Argos."

"You could have asked. So, did you find any clues?"

He shook his head. "But what bothers me is, if they knew you were there, why didn't any try to approach you?"

"They did, except they must have smelled the hunter nearby and took off right before I was shot. I'd only smelled their scent in the area the weekend before. Tons of forests exist in Oregon. The clan must normally go somewhere else, probably closer to Portland, maybe around Mount Hood."

"Then somehow one of them must have been in the area near your cabin, getting away from the rest of the clan. Maybe the one who murdered the human girl was with her there and he picked up your scent. If he let it slip to anyone else, any of the eligible males would have been searching for you after that." Devlyn snorted. "Good thing I came along when I did."

Despite agreeing with him silently, she hmpfed back.

He motioned to the bedroom. "Join me?" His offer was more than a proposal to shower with him. It was tantamount to joining him as his mate.

"I've already showered."

Turning his back to her, he stalked into the bedroom. "Fix lunch, then. I'll be out in a few."

His demand and dismissal should have bothered her, but they didn't. What annoyed her were her own actions, or rather inactions. She listened to the shower turn on and his shoes drop on the floor. If she joined him, he'd be one satisfied wolfmate, but she couldn't do it. It would be like sacrificing him to the devil wolf, Volan. She couldn't stomach the idea that the pack leader would kill him.

When Bella didn't join Devlyn in the bathroom, he knew he'd have a hell of a time convincing her that he was the only one for her, but he wasn't giving up. Then it occurred to him. What had she been doing the whole time he'd been gone?

He finished his shower, grabbed a towel, and wrapped it around his waist.

With a quick stride, he returned to her office and checked her email. He read through the messages she'd sent in response to her red wolf invitation, not believing she'd invited half of the world to a dance club that night. More worrisome was Argos's cryptic message to her.

The old pack leader wouldn't return for her unless something terrible had happened, but he would have said if Volan had been killed.

He turned as Bella entered the office.

"Your bloody steak is ready." She glanced down at his towel. "Going to dress, or eat like that?"

He rose from the chair and crossed the floor to her. Taking her shoulders in his hands, he massaged them lightly. "Which do you prefer?"

Her gaze took in his bare chest. "Men don't come to the dining table half-dressed."

"Just the answer I was waiting for." Yanking off the towel, he dropped it on the floor. "Ready?"

She glanced down at the towel and then back at his eyes, ignoring his full-blown erection. "I hope you intend to pick up after yourself." She turned and headed down the hallway.

Following her, he enjoyed the wiggle of her cute little butt covered in the tight black denims. "Is that what you're wearing tonight to meet all of your suitors?"

"Something a little sexier."

"Don't see anything unsexy about the jeans."

She glanced over her shoulder. "Did you practice your smooth words on human females for all of those years?"

"Did it have the right effect on you?"

She gave a half grunt. "No. So what do you think about my plan?"

"Sounds like it could be a circus." Sitting down at the head of the table, he smelled the rich blood of the fresh meat, warm and rare like he preferred.

She sat down opposite him. "Yeah, I thought maybe the more possible candidates we could draw out—"

"*You* could draw out." He still couldn't curb his anger with the notion of her acting as the killer's live bait.

"I thought if a red acted aggressively about my seeing others—"

He pointed his steak knife at her. "What if that's

the problem? What if he can't deal with other reds and because of that is having a difficult time finding a female to mate with him? What if the only ones he's able to interest are human, but when he changes into the wolf, they're terrified of him? As a wolf, he could bite her and still change her, but it's not the same as having a mate who is willing. Most males nowadays wouldn't want a female who has to be forced to accept him."

"You're right." She sliced off a piece of meat. "So then we find one who cowers or is angered when others are interested in me."

"Might work." He guzzled down a glass of water. When she raised her brows, he said, "Run took a lot out of me."

"From what I saw, it didn't take much out of you at all." She licked her lips. "Chrissie was drooling over you. I could have beamed her for thinking she could have…" She quit speaking.

"Could have me, when you already want me?" A healthy appetite for sex quickly displaced the anger and anxiety he felt.

"Why would anyone *not* want you? I mean, you're so…so…"

"Untameable?"

She bit her lower lip, her gaze drifting down to his naked chest.

"Say it, Bella. You want me. It's really easy. Just say it. I won't bite…too hard."

She shook her head and changed the subject. "You know, when I tried to decide whether to buy a wooden table or a more modernistic glass-topped one, I chose wood because it reminded me of the great outdoors. Only now, if I had glass, it would give me a better view."

He grinned. "Bad Bella."

She chuckled, never having enjoyed her home so much as she did now with the big gray wolf sharing the space. "I sure could get used to having you around."

"I'm all yours."

But would he agree to stay with her? Here? Away from Volan?

"What do you think is up with Argos?" she asked. "Do you think Volan could be dead?"

With the serrated edge of his knife, Devlyn sawed at his meat. "No. Argos would have said. I don't like it that someone's following him. He's not as agile as he used to be. Not as wary either."

"Maybe we shouldn't go tonight." Poking her fork into her meat, she considered Devlyn.

"What? And disappoint all of those panting suitors?" He couldn't help the sarcasm that laced his words. He didn't want her seeing red *lupus garou,* damn it, and he didn't want them catching sight of her or thinking that they had a chance with her either. He carved off another slice of meat. "We'll go. I'm not delaying our return home to the pack any longer than I have to."

"You shouldn't have left the house earlier like you did," she scolded, her brows knit in a cute little frown.

"Did you worry about me?"

"What do you think? Here I'd have these dates I couldn't break, and you'd be sitting in jail downtown. Who would protect me?"

"Are you sure you weren't worried you wouldn't have me to snuggle up to tonight?"

She gave a small growl.

He grinned. Yeah, she worried about him and wanted him, if she'd only allow herself to commit to him. He was wearing her down, bit by bit. Maybe, after the dance club, he could encourage her to say yes.

She took another bite of meat and then licked her lips.

Preferably before the dance club.

Bella turned from Devlyn, unable to stand his attentions any longer—the way he watched her lick the steak blood off her lips, the hungry look in his eyes, daring her to say she didn't love him or to say she did, the smile that stirred when she considered his bare chest.

He was so quiet that she glanced up from her meal to see if he was still there. Looking satiated, he leaned back in his chair. "So what do we do until tonight? Want to take a nap? We barely got any sleep. You must have been up before the sun rose."

"You won't want to sleep."

He winked, his lips curving up. "You're right. But we'll have a long night ahead of us, and you know how we are…lovers of the night. We won't do well without an afternoon nap. Game?"

"I've got to do the dishes."

He stood, and her eyes riveted to his erection. Heat pooled between her legs and her gaze returned to his. He grinned. "Really, just sleep. I can't help it if every time you lick the salt and blood off your lips, it gives me ideas." He grabbed his plate and walked to her end of the table. After planting a kiss on the top of her head, he seized her plate and carried the dishes into the kitchen. "I'll take care of these while you get into bed. Be there in a few minutes."

He was right. The *lupus* part of them required a long afternoon nap. Then they'd enjoy the night. Well, maybe not so much enjoy it tonight, but they'd be better prepared, more alert. *If they slept*.

"All right. But," she said, pointing down the hallway, "remember to pick up your bathroom towel."

"Gotcha. Don't you love domestic life?"

She snorted. "Right."

Life with Devlyn would be anything but domestic.

Before she retired to the bedroom, she entered her office, planning to check her email and then shut down her computer.

Twenty-two more messages. She blinked. Most had to be humans, looking for what they must have thought was a wild woman. Well, she was a little on the wild side.

She scanned through the messages, but one in particular caught her attention.

> Hey, Rosa! Why did you say you wanted to see me at the club but had already told Alfred you were meeting him? Even Nicol said you invited him. I don't want to make this some kind of a group mating scene. What's up? Ross

Ross must have been the other at the zoo. Bella's heart fluttered at high speed. Jeez, was he the killer? Oh hell, she never thought there'd truly be several from the same *lupus garou* pack that would contact her.

She turned when Devlyn walked into the room. He lifted his towel off the floor. "I thought you'd be in bed already."

"We have a problem."

He joined her at the monitor and read the message. "Damn."

"What do I do now?"

The look that flashed across his face startled her. It was as warm as a breath of sunshine and there was something more that she couldn't read. He touched her hair and then kissed her cheek. "We'll figure something out."

He reread the message. "Okay, how about, 'Sorry, Ross, but I don't know any reds in the area. This is as much a selection process for me as anything. It's a female's choice, too. If you don't want to come tonight, we can make another date. I won't make a choice until afterward.'"

She nodded, typed in the message, and sent it.

When no one responded, Devlyn nudged her arm. "Let's lie down. He's probably not at the computer. After we nap, we can see if he replied."

"Just sleep, Devlyn."

"Of course. I want you alert and ready tonight."

He slipped his hand around hers and pulled her from the chair, his touch gentle and warm, like a boyfriend on a first date. She looked up at him, wondering what had gotten into him. Did he think he had to act human to change her mind about him?

She glanced down at his erection, stirring a surge of interest. She couldn't help the deep chuckle that erupted from her lips.

He gave her a squeeze. "Yeah, you make it happen, Bella, all of the time. When you agree to be my mate, I'll have to wear a lot fewer clothes most of the time."

"You can't wear any fewer than what you have on now, stud."

"Your neighbor would approve. When I walked into the living room, I kind of imagined she wished she could see me the way she saw me earlier in the day."

He released Bella and took his towel into the bathroom. Unbuttoning her blouse, she watched him walk back into the room. "I have a feeling Chrissie thought I drove off this morning and not you. I believe," she said, pulling off her blouse, "she thought she might visit with you a bit and see what she's been missing since the divorce."

"She wouldn't have gotten it from me."

Although Bella was glad he made the remark, she wondered how many human females he'd been with over the years. It shouldn't have mattered, but a smidgeon of envy ran through her veins. Well, more than a smidgeon. Gallons. If Chrissie pushed it any further, she'd see a new side of Bella—a wolf's territorial side.

"Dollar for your thoughts." Devlyn unbuckled Bella's belt.

"A dollar?"

"Inflation."

"Just thinking how the wolf in me might respond if Chrissie makes any more advances toward you."

"Hmm, now that's sounding mighty possessive." Devlyn nuzzled her face, as if he were starting the wolf courting process.

"I'm a mite territorial, sometimes." She nipped his ear. "We're supposed to nap."

"We will." But the darkness of his eyes and the huskiness of his voice said otherwise.

After unfastening her bra, he slipped the straps off her shoulders. His warm fingers trailed down her arms to her fingertips in a sensual brush. Pulling her hands to his face, he kissed them, his gaze focused on her fingers.

"You sure know how to warm a girl up, but—"

He kissed her lips gently. But when she wrapped her arms around him and tried to kiss him back, he broke free, his actions confirming that he wanted to control how far they went.

When she tilted her chin up, he kissed her neck with gentle brushes of his lips against her sensitive skin. "You smell of wild rose, Bella." He ran his tongue down the hollow of her throat while she scarcely breathed. "Breathe. I don't want you passing out."

Running her fingers through his damp hair, she hmpfed. "Right." Yet she did feel light-headed with him touching her so tenderly.

He traced her nipple with his fingertips and she drew in her breath. Leaning down, he swept his tongue, wet and warm, over the tip of one breast and then sucked.

She groaned softly.

His fingers slipped down to her jeans and struggled to remove them. Her whole body thrilled with his touch; remembering to breathe was the least of her worries.

How she wished he'd give up the quest to fight Volan and stay with her forever. She'd do anything for Devlyn then.

He discarded her jeans on the carpeted floor and ran his fingers over the waistband of her panties. Again she tried to touch him, but he growled at her.

"I'm supposed to growl at *you*, Devlyn," she said, kissing the nape of his neck when he took the nipple of her other breast in his mouth, "if you go too far with me. You're supposed to whine for more."

Lifting his head, he gave her an evil grin. "We're not in our wolf states, Bella. For now, I'll growl when you go too far with me." He yanked her panties down and knelt and then buried his face in her crotch. "But you sure smell fine."

She tangled her fingers in his hair and was ready to give in to him when he stood and eased her onto the bed, growling a curse under his breath. "Sleep. You're going to make me an old wolf before my time."

Crawling into bed, she wished the erection he held out to her could be put to good use, as her body readied itself for his penetration, moist, hot, and aching deeply, longing for satisfaction.

"I'll join you in a moment."

"Can I…"

Shaking his head, he walked out of the room. She groaned and turned away, knowing he would relieve the tension she'd created in him, by himself this time. But she couldn't have him without putting his life in real danger. Volan was danger. And she knew if he learned she wasn't coming home soon, he'd be coming for her.

# Chapter 8

*HER HEART PUMPING AT TWICE ITS NORMAL SPEED, BELLA fled the fire. The searing heat singed her fur, the pads of her paws, and choked the breath from her. And then he appeared, the gray wolf, a large, fearless juvenile, intent on only one thing: grabbing her and carrying her across the swollen river.*

She whimpered and Devlyn tightened his hold on her. "Bella, you're safe."

*The nightmare…the damnable nightmare that she'd had for years.*

She ran her hand over Devlyn's arm, wrapped securely around her waist. Folded over her like a butterfly's protective cocoon before hatching, he made her feel safe and secure—until he turned her over to Volan.

"Did you sleep well?" he murmured against her hair.

"Yes. And you?" she whispered back, not entirely ready to shrug off the relaxed state she was in despite the vivid nightmare.

"I had an ache when you squirmed against me."

She smiled.

"You seemed restless and whimpered in your sleep. Are you still having nightmares about the wildfire?"

"Sometimes." She kissed the palm of his hand.

His chest swelled against her back. "You have other nightmares?"

"Sometimes." *Those* nightmares she didn't want to discuss with Devlyn. She worried he'd rashly take action against Volan for what he'd tried to do to her as a youngster.

"Nightmares about what?" he prompted.

She shrugged a shoulder. "You know how night-mares are. You often can't remember them when you wake." She glanced at the window. The lightness of the sky indicated they had another couple of hours before they went to the club.

"Devlyn, you said Argos had taken you in. What happened to the rest of your family?"

He ran his hand over her hair in a sensual caress that sent another wave of desire sliding through her. "They died."

"In a wildfire like mine?"

"No."

She waited for an explanation, but he didn't seem to wish to speak of it any more than she wanted to tell him about Volan. Yet curiosity caught hold. "Devlyn? What happened?"

"Men killed them. Set our house on fire. I'd gotten into trouble earlier in the day for playing in the creek without letting anyone know where I was. My father made me sleep in an outer building, where we stored leather goods, to punish me when we all lay down for our afternoon nap. My four younger cousins snuck out to stay with me. Their parents had died in a flash flood three years earlier."

He paused.

"Devlyn?"

"I heard the screams, but flames already engulfed the

house. I couldn't save anyone, not even my brothers."
He took a deep breath. "We were triplets, did everything together, along with my cousins, except for the
morning I'd played down by the creek."

Bella listened quietly, envisioning the heat of the
flames devouring everything in her path the day Devlyn
found her. She blinked away the tears.

"My cousins and I didn't leave the smoldering
remains of the house for days, somehow thinking that
if we stayed long enough, we'd wake and discover the
horror had been an ugly nightmare. Then hunger forced
us to change into our wolves and we ran.

"For weeks we survived on our own, living off the
land, not daring to turn into our human forms in the wilderness. We never would have survived, yet the phase of
the new moon was fast approaching. I knew inevitably
we'd have to face new perils soon."

Chill bumps covered her arms. She could imagine
how he must have felt—not much older than she when
she lost her family, all of them alone, having to protect
his younger cousins in the wilderness, terrified, and
worse, his heart aching for the only family he'd ever
known. She'd never have survived that long had she
been on her own at such a young age.

He took a ragged breath. "We kept moving west and
then we ran into Argos and some of his pack hunting
and he took us in."

"I'm sorry, Devlyn." Her heart ached for him. The
painful loss of her family had never faded entirely from
her memories. "I didn't know. You must really hate
humans for what they did to your family."

"The human males, although in truth it was probably my uncle's fault. He'd gotten into a drunken brawl in town and killed two men. At least I suspected it was because of his rash actions that men came out to the ranch and burned the house."

Now she could understand why Devlyn grew angry when she said she wanted a human male for a mate. "You've been right about me all along, Devlyn. I could never find a human that interested me."

He traced her breast with his fingers, triggering a lustful desire to have him make love to her. "I know," he said softly. "That's why you have photos of us all over your fridge. But *more* of me. And a bigger one beside your bed."

He was never going to let her live that down. "You're so arrogant. No female could ever put up with you." She pulled the comforter over her shoulder. "I bet if you could get away with it, you would say the original *lupus garou* was a gray."

"He was," Devlyn said with conviction.

She looked over her shoulder at him. "You can't be serious." But his expression was completely resolute.

"Sure. The first was a gray. I can't imagine you'd ever heard otherwise. Somewhere along the line, a smaller gray female turned a redheaded Scot and he started a pack far away from any of the gray clans. Their pups were smaller, some gray, some more red. The reds began to turn other redheads until they were able to find mates among the *lupus garou*."

"Bull. Ancient Scots were big men, not small."

"No, really."

"You know, just because you're bigger and stronger doesn't mean you were first. My grandfather said the first *lupus garou* was a red—that he was a berserker, a Norseman, who prayed to Odin, the Scandinavian god of war and death but also of poetry and wisdom. Odin could change into any form he liked, but a bear and a wolf were his best known forms. He was thought of as the ultimate alpha wolf when he turned into that beast. The berserker human was a redhead, and after losing his wife and children to a raiding party of Norsemen, he beseeched Odin to give him the power to right the wrong done to his family and his people.

"Odin took pity on the Norseman and gifted him with near immortality by extending his longevity, and the ability to change into a wolf—a red wolf—whenever the moon made its appearance."

Devlyn kissed Bella's ear. "All right, same story, except the Norseman had dark-brown hair and amber eyes, and he was a hulking brute of a man. Big, not small like a red."

Bella grunted. "He was a red."

Devlyn didn't say anything for several seconds, and she thought he'd fallen asleep. But then his hand slipped under the covers and caressed her shoulder. "Is that why Vernetta knocked out your baby teeth? Because you tried to convince her that the first *lupus garou* was a red?"

Bella growled, the memory still making her angry even after all these years.

"Was it? When Argos brought us male juveniles home from a hunt, you were pacing in Argos's cabin, your mouth bloodied, gaps where you should have had teeth, your eyes feral. Vernetta said you fought with her about the legend of the origin of the *lupus garou* kind, but she wouldn't say what you said, and you'd never speak of it to any of us, not even Argos."

"Well, she was wrong."

"She sure as hell was. If Argos hadn't stopped me, I would have knocked her teeth out in retaliation, except hers were all permanent. I don't think I've ever seen Argos so angry as when he found out what happened to you either."

"You should have seen how angry I was!"

Devlyn leaned over and licked Bella's shoulder. "I did. You couldn't eat anything solid for a couple of weeks. And until you could, Argos wouldn't allow Vernetta to eat anything solid either."

Bella smiled. "She was pissed." Then her smile faded. "The first *lupus garou was* a red."

Devlyn chuckled. "Whatever you say, Bella honey. Whatever you say."

Figuring she'd never change Devlyn's stubborn mind, she pulled back the covers. "I should check the computer to see if Ross responded."

"All right. I'll fix us something to eat."

"Hmm, a man who cooks. What else could a girl want?"

His hand drifted to her belly.

"A lot of loving…I know. But we've got to get going. Do you have a change of clothes?"

He burrowed his face in her hair as his fingers dropped lower. "Brought my bag in this morning."

His actions heated her, but she fought fulfilling the yearnings. "Have anything black?"

"As dark as the midnight sky when the moon is new."

"Okay." Turning, she kissed his lips.

He didn't kiss her back, only gave her a half smile. She assumed he didn't want to get too worked up if he couldn't relieve his ache for her. She was a little disappointed, loving the way he showed her the intense side of his feelings for her. But he was right…keep it cool.

After slipping out of bed, she yanked her panties on and fastened her bra. Then she had another notion. What if they lived in hiding, like she'd done for so many years? What if she could convince Devlyn to give up the pack and remain with her here, or wherever he wanted to go, but some place far away from the threat of Volan?

The idea seemed reasonable to her, but she figured Devlyn wouldn't go along with it. Not with being a male *lupus garou*. Hiding wasn't in his nature. Plus, he'd already told her how important his family was to him. But they could start their own family and find their own territory to establish.

He climbed out of bed and headed for the hall, turning to smile at her as she folded her arms and looked him over. "Chrissie would die if she knew you cooked in the raw."

"He'd do something else, but his selected mate's not agreeable enough yet."

Joining him, she raked her fingernails down his chest in a teasing caress. "Keep it up and maybe you'll change my mind."

"I intend to keep it up *and* change your mind." He snapped the elastic of her bra strap and then strode down the hall.

*One hot lupus garou,* but he couldn't be hers unless he met *her* demands.

Once he reached the kitchen, she entered her office, turned on the computer, scanned the messages, and found Ross's note.

> Meet me at Millie's Ice Cream and Sandwich Shop at six tomorrow evening on First Street.
> Ross
>
> See you there. Rosa

She tapped her fingers on the desk and then headed for the kitchen. "Ross wants to meet me at a sandwich shop tomorrow evening at six."

Devlyn pulled out a package of German sausage links. "How about these?"

"Looks good." She glanced down his naked torso and then up.

He shook his head. "You are one bad little red wolf."

"Yeah, I know. And I really do apologize for being so wicked. Forgive me?"

He chuckled under his breath. "*Nooo,* but I don't think you're going to give me what I want to make up for it either."

She cleared her throat, switching to a much tamer subject. "So what do you think about Ross?"

"He's afraid of the competition. He'd rather go for you without the others around, which makes me suspect that he could be the killer."

She ran her hand over Devlyn's well-muscled

buttocks. Instantly, the muscles tightened, and he growled.

Ignoring his protest, she kissed his shoulder. "But you think he'll be at the club still?"

"I'd bet on it, Bella." The sausages sizzled in the pan, and he poked them with a fork. The spicy aroma wafted through the air. Her stomach rumbled. "He'll want to see what kind of move the other guys make and how you react. Not to mention, he's probably dying to see what you look like in human form." Glancing back at her, he raised a brow. He continued to stir the sausages. "How do you think you're going to prove who it is?"

"I'll ask them what they think of what happened."

"Has the latest killing even been on the news yet?"

"Oh heck, I don't know." She hurried into the living room and turned on the television.

After flipping to the local nightly news, she held her breath as the newscaster pointed to a map of Portland where four locations were circled in red. "In the most bizarre case in the history of Portland, Oregon, the killings of four young women—all midtwenties, all natural redheads, every one of them no taller than five foot five, one every day for four days, ending three days ago— have baffled police. Preliminary reports in the ongoing investigation show a wolf did the killings.

"In other news—"

Bella shut off the TV and collapsed on the sofa.

"Are you all right?" Devlyn called from the kitchen.

"Four women have been murdered, Devlyn."

"I heard." He joined her in the living room and pulled her to her feet, his eyes dark, intense, worried, his hands rubbing her arms in a gentle sweep. "Are you going to be all right?"

"Yes." The word was nearly a whisper.

"I don't want you to do this if you're afraid."

"I'm not afraid. I just don't want to see anyone else get hurt." Her gaze met his. "If he doesn't kill tonight, it'll mean he's one of the ones who contacted me, don't you think? He'll wait to see if I agree to be his mate?"

"Maybe. Unless it bothers him that you're being choosey. He might still try for a human female then."

"Oh," Bella said, rubbing her temple. "He can't kill as a wolf tonight. Not until the quarter moon appears."

Devlyn took a deep breath and led her into the dining room. "Yeah, I don't know what I was thinking. He won't be able to for another four days."

"We have to find him before that can happen."

"He can still kill them as a human."

"But he probably seduces them first in his human form and then tries to convince them to experiment with something really wild, don't you think? Then he turns into the wolf and they go ballistic. But for now, he may have relations with them until the change is possible."

"You might be right, but I really don't want you mixed up with this maniac."

Bella didn't want to be, either, but she was sure that she already was.

<hr />

After eating, Devlyn and Bella returned to the bedroom to dress so she could face the crowd of female-hungry reds. She frowned at the meager selection in her closet—meager mostly because she worked out of her home or took a run on the wild side on the weekends in the woods *sans* clothes. "We should arrive early, don't you think, Devlyn?" Bella pulled a slinky emerald-green dress over her head. "I was going to wear black, but I'm not in the mood. What do you think?"

When he didn't answer, she glanced in his direction.

"You look good in that, Bella. *Too* good." His expression was brooding but mixed with a wolf's lust.

"Do you want me to wear something else?"

"Do you have anything ankle length with a high neck and long sleeves? Preferably black...and baggy?"

"No. How can I catch the killer if I hide?"

"I don't want you exposed to him in the first place." He buttoned his black shirt with jerky movements.

She figured he didn't want to expose her to the other reds either. "Devlyn, none of them is coming home with me tonight...only you."

She applied green shadow to her eyelids and blush to her cheeks and then grabbed fistfuls of red curls and held them against her head. "Up or down?"

He groaned. "Wear a black wig. Or a big floppy hat."

She released her hair. "Okay, down...less work."

"I really don't know how you talked me into this."

"You love me."

"If I had any sense, I wouldn't allow this," he grumbled, his brows knit in a hard frown.

She crossed the floor and grazed his mouth with hers. "You're an angel. My guardian angel. And you'll watch out for me. But, about my question, should we arrive early?"

For an instant, his smoldering gaze held her hostage, then glancing outside, he shook his head. "We're already too late for that. Ready?"

"As ready as I'll ever be, under the circumstances." She squashed the urge to shudder and pulled a shawl over her shoulders.

~∙∙∙~

When they arrived in the vicinity of the club, they parked a quarter of a mile away from the redbrick building in an attempt to avoid others seeing their vehicle or that they were together. She walked to the club ahead of him, the music already beating a gypsy rhythm to stir the dead. Cars filled the parking lot to capacity; others spilled into the road, silent against the curb.

She entered the club first, while Devlyn lagged a short distance behind.

A kaleidoscope of colored lights flashed overhead as the music pounded in her ears. She imagined she wouldn't be able to hear anything for hours afterward. The scent of perfume, cologne, and sweaty bodies wafted in the air, but it was a minute before she picked up the smell of a *lupus garou* nearby. *Too nearby*.

"Rosa," a deep voice said.

A chill prickled the nape of her neck and she turned. "Alfred."

"You're fashionably late." His chestnut eyes studied her too intensely, looking from her hair all the way to her strappy heels. He'd added some kind of greasy stuff to his hair, making it appear darker, less red. He seemed taller than he had at the zoo. She glanced down at his shoes. Elevated.

Alfred offered to take her shawl.

Once she removed it, his face brightened. "Certainly worth waiting for." Then a dark shadow crossed his face. "I saw Nicol here, though. He said he was meeting you also. I told him to try back some other time."

He seated her at a small round table for two near the highly polished dance floor.

"A gray *lupus garou* pack raised me, Alfred. I haven't been with my own kind since I was small. I don't want to select a mate from the first red wolf I meet."

He waved for a bartender and then turned back to her. "I see. The red alpha pack leader isn't good enough for you?"

So Alfred *was* the pack leader of the local red *lupus garou*. But she noticed at once that his smell wasn't the same as the smell of the one who'd been in the apartment where she and Devlyn had discovered the murdered girl. That was good. He'd want to find the rogue as much as they did, then.

"Actually," she said, "that's some of the problem. A pack leader is already after me—of the grays."

Alfred's eyes widened. "He's not from around here. Can't be. We have no grays in the area."

"No, from Colorado, where I lived originally."

He relaxed. "It's not his territory. Not to worry. A gray from another area won't have any success here with our females."

She wished his reds could do away with Volan. Then she'd offer herself to Devlyn as his mate.

Although she assumed he wouldn't like it if the only way he could have her was if reds from another pack killed Volan. Of course, if Alfred and his pack eliminated Volan, Alfred would be sure to think that *he* could claim her.

Wishing life were less complicated, she took a slow breath. "As pack leader, why haven't you already found a mate?"

"They're either much too young or much too old. You can't imagine what a stir you've created with your sudden appearance. We had no idea that a lone female was in the area. You must keep an awfully low profile. And we never fathomed you'd escape from the zoo. We had planned to storm the place to rescue you later that night." He turned to a bartender. "A beer and..."

"A Bloody Mary," Bella said.

He smiled and then grew serious. "So, who stole you away from the hospital? A gray?"

"Yes. He had orders to return me to the pack leader in Colorado. But something else came up."

Alfred fisted his hands on the table and snarled, "*No* pack leader from another territory has any say here."

Despite his outburst, Bella kept her words cool. "He's a gray. So far, Volan's been unbeatable."

The bartender returned with their drinks and Alfred paid for them. Bella sipped hers while Alfred raked his eyes over her in too leering a manner. "He won't be welcome. If he arrives here, I'll have a committee give him a grand send off."

Pack leaders—well-thought-of pack leaders—took the lead. He should be the one making plans to take

Volan down. Already her estimation of him had sunk to the depths of the Marianna Trench.

She made no comment concerning his threats about Volan, which seemed to make him uneasy. Did he assume he hadn't said the right thing to win the red's heart? He had that right. He'd have to look, act, and feel like Devlyn to get close to her.

Alfred cleared his throat. "I thought maybe tomorrow night we could—"

"I have other plans."

He tapped his fingers on the table, his eyes narrowed, and his lips formed a thin line. "I *don't* want a long courtship. I need a mate." He spoke abruptly, like a pack leader used to getting his way.

But with her, he had to tread lightly. She wasn't one of his pack, and she had no intention of ever being one. "And I told you I'm not going to choose a mate when I haven't seen some more eligible bachelors. Mating for life means something to me."

His eyes darkened and he frowned.

Despite his look of aggression, she wouldn't back down. She glanced around the club, hoping to catch sight of Devlyn. Leaning against a pillar near a set of tables, he observed her from the east side of the building. Her whole body thrilled to know he served as her protector, but it was the way his gaze locked with hers, mesmerizing her, claiming her, that stirred her to the core.

She gave him a knowing smile and then turned to Alfred. "So, where's Nicol?"

He pointed in Devlyn's direction. "The curly redhead

who's nursing a drink at the table over there, fuming and watching every move we make."

"Ah." She caught Devlyn's eye and then motioned to the red-haired man with her head.

Devlyn nodded and moved in to sit beside Nicol at the table.

She searched for Argos but, regretfully, saw no sign of him.

"Looking for someone?" Alfred asked, touching her hand as she held on to her glass.

She pulled away from his icy touch, concerned Devlyn might overreact to Alfred's attentions toward her. "An old friend. He wished to speak to me about some problem, but I don't see him."

"How old a friend?"

"Ancient. He's about seventy and retired as our pack leader before I became a teen."

"If you're referring to this gray wolf pack from Colorado, he's *not* one of your kind. *We* are."

She leaned back in her chair, not liking the comments he made about *her* pack. It didn't matter how different they were. They took her in and cared for her when she would have died without their help. Alfred hadn't even asked how her family perished and she ended up with a gray pack. He seemed more interested in getting her to agree to be his mate than anything else, but didn't he know that meant trying to convince her she was someone special?

He reached his hand out to her. "Let's dance."

Her heartbeat quickened. She'd have to dance to keep up the charade, but she didn't want to, not with him. She glanced back at Devlyn.

"Nicol won't ask you. I am." Alfred still held his hand out to her, and she took a deep breath, weighing her options.

—m—

Devlyn watched every move the slick red *lupus garou* made toward Bella. Twice, he'd had the urge to break up the party, claim her for his own, and take her away from the club—damn the reason they were here in the first place.

When Alfred reached his hand out to Bella, Devlyn knew he was asking her to dance. The thought sent a shard of ice straight into his heart. He wanted no one else near her feeling the heat of her curvy body and smelling her sweet scent.

Nicol spoke, distracting him. "She sure is hot." He looked over at Devlyn. "Got yourself a mate?"

"Yeah," Devlyn said, and it was no lie. Bella was his mate, if he could only convince her she wanted only him. But dealing with Volan was another matter.

"You didn't bring her?"

"She's preoccupied with work right now."

"Ah. So what do you do?"

Devlyn considered the man's calculating brown eyes and his unruly mop of red hair. "Leather goods. You?"

"Professional hunter. Take folks into the wilds—the rougher the terrain, the meaner the prey, the more they love it." Nicol's eyes darkened with a hint of malice.

Devlyn returned his attention to Bella. "You're not here much of the time, I take it."

"I'm here and then I'm gone. I still need a mate, if that's

what you're getting at." He pointed his beer at Bella and Alfred. "Now that's what *I* was supposed to be doing."

"He's your pack leader?"

"Yeah. But from the looks of it, she's taking it really slow."

"What's your leader like around women? Is he aggressive?"

"Don't really know. He's never had a *lupus garou* the right age to pursue." Nicol gave a smug smile. "But she sure is keeping him at arm's length. His face is even reddening a bit."

Devlyn knew his must have been too, as hot as he was getting. He downed his drink and then ordered a bottled water to chill his blood.

When Alfred tried to move his hand lower down Bella's back, Devlyn rose from his chair, ready to force one red male to cool it with his intended mate.

# Chapter 9

BEFORE DEVLYN COULD RUSH TO THE PARQUET FLOOR, the music changed to a fast-paced dance and Alfred released Bella. Curbing his temper, Devlyn sat back down at Nicol's table.

"Hell," Nicol said to Devlyn and motioned to another man—about the same shorter stature, around five foot ten, with reddish-brown hair. "Ross is headed this way. Guess he'll think I couldn't score again."

Devlyn took his eyes off Bella and stared at Nicol. "You said you hadn't courted any *lupus garou*."

"No, human females. They're all right, but nothing like one of our own kind. Too tame."

"Ever thought of changing one?"

Nicol's eyes grew big. "Why would I want to do that?"

"To have a mate. I considered it a time or two," Devlyn fabricated—anything to convince Nicol to talk about his relationships with human women. "I thought I might find the one I liked and then, if she were agreeable, change her. Like in your pack, we have a shortage of females who are the right mating age. So...yeah, I've considered it."

Nicol nodded. "Yeah, me, too. But it wouldn't work. A human would be afraid."

"Ever have a problem when you're getting it on hot and heavy and then you have the urge to change?"

Nicol stared at the table, grabbed his beer, and chugged it down. "No...no, and you?"

"A time or two," Devlyn lied. "You know, during the full moon."

Nicol slid his gaze away and nodded at Ross when he sauntered over to the table. Devlyn rose from his chair and offered his hand in greeting. Ross ignored him, and, amused, Devlyn overlooked the insult and sat back down.

"This is Devlyn," Nicol said, "and, Devlyn, this is Ross."

Ross sniffed the air and then frowned. "You're a gray. Not from around here."

"Yep." Devlyn wanted to add, 'Going to make something of it?' But this wasn't the time to act macho.

Ross's gaze shifted from Devlyn to Nicol and then to Alfred and Bella. He rested his hands on his hips. "Man, that's her, eh?"

"Yeah, as you can see, Alfred got to her first."

Devlyn finished his water when Bella sat at the table with Alfred again.

"Are you going to ask her to dance?" Ross asked Nicol.

Nicol rubbed the back of his neck. "And start a fight? You know Alfred won't let any of us near her when he's around."

Devlyn stood. "I'll ask her to dance." It was time to do something with that testosterone that made him testy where Bella was concerned.

"But you're a gray," Ross said, his voice astounded.

"And have a mate," Nicol reminded Devlyn.

Inwardly, Devlyn smiled. "Yeah, well, it's just a dance. Not a proposal."

"He's got to be crazy," Nicol said under his breath when Devlyn moved away from the table.

"He's a gray," Ross retorted.

Yeah, he was a gray and he would dance with that hot little red number. Nothing would stop him, certainly not one horny red pack leader.

———

*Now what the hell?* Bella stared at Devlyn stalking across the floor, forcing dancing couples to move out of his way or get run over. He was going to blow their case, yet from the way he acted, it didn't matter. She knew he'd have a fit when Alfred moved his hand lower on her backside. And she knew he would watch Alfred's every move and not have missed the red's action.

But this was not the way to handle it.

Her breathing accelerated as she tried to think of how to rectify the situation.

Before she could say anything, Alfred turned and saw the *lupus garou* targeting his date.

"He's a friend," she quickly said.

Alfred didn't look back at her but continued to stare down the impending threat. "The one who wants you?"

"No, the one who rescued me from the hospital."

He turned to her briefly. "The one who wants to take you back to the gray pack to hand you over to the leader?"

"He saved my life when I was little. He's changed his mind about turning me over to Volan."

Alfred shifted his attention back to the menace who stalked across the club, their eyes locked in combat, the wolf way.

When Devlyn reached him, he stretched his hand out to Alfred. "I'm Devlyn and I understand you're Alfred. I've been visiting with two members of your pack. They say you're a great leader."

Bella waited in breathless anticipation to see if Devlyn's words helped soften the confrontation.

Alfred took Devlyn's hand, but his lips tightened when Devlyn squeezed hard, his own hand much larger. Devlyn's arm muscle grew taut and Alfred's eyes watered.

She took a deep breath, hoping Devlyn's show of strength would make Alfred back down.

"Has Bella told you we're from the same pack?"

Alfred flashed her a satisfied look at having found out her real name. "She said grays raised her, yes, and that you'd planned to return her to your pack leader."

Devlyn looked over at Bella for an explanation.

"I also said you'd changed your mind."

Devlyn's lips turned up slightly. "I haven't had the pleasure of dancing with my wolfmate," he said to Alfred. "I hadn't seen her in years. Never had the chance to dance with her back then."

Devlyn showed all of the signs of wolf posturing.

Instead of waiting for Alfred's response, Devlyn pulled her from her seat, slipped his arm around her waist, and held her close as he moved her to the dance floor.

"Oh jeez, Devlyn." She frowned at him when he drew her deeper into the mob of dancers. "Could you make it any more obvious you have the hots for me?"

Grinning at her, his hands moved down her backside and cupped her buttocks. "If you must know, yes."

She encircled his neck with her arms. "Now listen, I wouldn't let him get away with such behavior toward me. You're ruining the whole thing. What will he think?"

Devlyn slipped his leg between hers and rocked against her heated core. "What he already knows. I've claimed you." He glanced back at the table where the other reds sat. "Maybe this will work even better."

She scowled at him. "What if they decide to gang up on you for trying to steal a red from their territory? They're not going to allow it. Not from a gray."

He grunted.

Sliding her hands down, she cupped his butt and tugged him closer. "Is this helping your plans?"

Chuckling, he kissed the top of her head. "Yeah, a few more moves like that and we'll have to return to the vehicle and finish them."

She breathed in his heady scent. "You sure smell good."

"Taste good, too, if you want a bite."

"Ah, Devlyn, what are we going to do? You know I want you, but…"

Raising her chin, he dropped his mouth open to speak, but the words wouldn't come.

"What's wrong?"

"That's all I've waited to hear, Bella. You said the magic words."

He captured her mouth with passionate aggression, his tongue plundering her, claiming her as he'd done so long ago. His hands roamed over her back and then down to her buttocks again, and he pulled her against him. Adrenaline running high, she trembled. She couldn't deny her feelings for him.

But she couldn't take the words back now. She'd committed to him, just as if she'd said 'I do.'

"I mean—"

"I know what you mean. Do we go home now and consummate our relationship or fake this charade a little longer?"

"I haven't seen Argos yet. What if we miss him?"

"He can get in touch with you the same way." Devlyn worked her toward the front exit.

"You can't mean to take me home this instant."

"Yeah, we have unfinished business, honey. And it's not waiting any longer."

She glanced at Alfred. Nicol and another wolf had joined him.

"Ross and Nicol," Devlyn said when he saw her look at them.

"They're planning on stopping you from taking me out of here, don't you think?"

"Damn it." Devlyn's brown eyes turned black as his jaw clenched in anger.

His intense posture sent a shiver down her spine. "What's wrong?"

"New plan. Zoo man Thompson's near the front exit looking for you. Let's find a back way out."

As soon as he guided her toward a rear exit, Alfred and his wolfmates blocked their escape.

"What if Alfred says he won't let us leave unless I'll agree to be his mate?" she asked, her heartbeat quickened.

"You're already spoken for." He hurried her toward the exit.

All three reds glared at Devlyn, stood their ground at the rear door, and wouldn't let them pass.

"We have some trouble," she said to Alfred, trying to diffuse the fight she feared was about to erupt any second. "Thompson, the man from the zoo who tranquilized me and put me there in the first place, is standing at the front door of the club. He probably has police officers standing by."

"Will you go with me?" Alfred asked.

"I promised myself to Devlyn."

Swallowing hard, Alfred's Adam's apple moved up and down. He crossed his arms. "No deal."

"We'll help you catch the red who's killing the women in the area."

He narrowed his eyes. "How do you know it's a red *lupus garou?*"

"I have evidence. We'll help you and your pack catch him."

"Why?"

"Because," she growled, frost surrounding each word, "he threatens to give *all* of us away."

He looked over at his mates, but they waited for him to give the word. Seconds hung like hours while Thompson's gaze shifted around the room. Her chest tightened.

"All right. Come on then," Alfred finally said, his words ominous. But, considering that the zoo man searched for her, guarded relief washed over Bella even though Alfred didn't seem to be buying the bit about her being Devlyn's choice.

"What evidence do you have that it's a red?" Alfred asked, shoving the metal door open at the back of the club.

"Some of his fur."

A dark shadow crossed Alfred's face. "If you give it to me, we can have a DNA match done to find out which one of my pack he is."

She glanced back at Nicol and Ross. Neither seemed worried about the notion. "I don't have it with me. But I can meet with Ross tomorrow night as I planned—"

Devlyn squeezed her hand hard.

She frowned at him. "Devlyn will come with me, of course. Then I can turn it over to Ross."

Alfred nodded. "Ross can let me know the details, and we'll meet you there."

The smell of garbage drifted to them through the doorway on the chilly breeze. One security light dimly illuminated a section of the parking area, while the rest remained dark. A cat scurried past employee vehicles parked next to a dumpster.

Dread trickled down Bella's spine. What if Alfred and his pack ganged up on Devlyn with no one to see— no one to stop them? They could force her to give up the fur afterward. One female red *lupus garou* was no match for three red males. Even one would be too difficult for her to handle.

"Coming?" Alfred prompted, walking outside, testing Devlyn's steel.

Still holding Bella's hand securely in his own, Devlyn followed. "Tomorrow night. And thanks."

"Thank you for assisting us in this matter." Despite

the words he spoke, Alfred's tone remained couched in hostility.

Devlyn nodded. "Tomorrow."

When Devlyn led Bella down the back alley, they caught Nicol's words. "You're not going to let her be his, are you? She's too much of a red for him."

They'd moved too far away from the three to hear the response when other voices in the dark caught their attention.

"I really think the chief's going to be ticked off about this. That guy and his girlfriend gotta be long gone from this area by now."

She recognized the men's voices. The police officers who were at the hospital—the ones Devlyn had knocked out. Her heart raced and her hands grew clammy. If they caught Devlyn...

Her big gray steered her away from them, slipping through the area without making a sound.

Thankfully, they'd parked far enough from the dance club that no others, not even the red pack, would see them leave unless they had followed them. The breeze blew in their favor, and no scent of the reds met them on the turbulent night air.

Devlyn opened the door for Bella and then hurried for his own. After climbing into the vehicle, he drove her home, his hands clenching the steering wheel.

Reaching over, she rubbed his back. "I don't think Alfred's ready to give me up, do you?"

"Nope."

"Did you get anything out of Ross or Nicol?"

Devlyn's back muscles relaxed with her massaging

them. "Just that Nicol is a professional hunter—the more dangerous the prey, the better."

"But women aren't dangerous."

"Maybe not to most, but if he's afraid of their reaction to the sight of him as a wolf, perhaps so. When I asked him if he ever thought about changing a woman, he said he had."

"He told you that? Without coercion? What with a killer on the loose, I would think he'd keep his mouth shut."

"I fabricated that I wanted to change a human female. You know how it goes. One tells of his darkest fantasies and the other doesn't want to be bested."

She stared at him, not sure whether to believe he'd fibbed or not.

When her hand stilled on his back, he glanced at her. "Humans killed my family, remember?"

"Men only, remember?" She couldn't curb the jealousy washing over her.

Reaching across the console, he squeezed her thigh. "It's good to know you care. I've never had a woman envious over me before." He winked at her. "Truly, Bella, I've wanted a mate for years. It's unnatural not to desire one when you live in a pack, but you're the only one I've ever wanted for keeps."

"Okay, so you fibbed to Nicol about wanting to change a human female." She began to rub his back again, relieved he had no interest in any other females but her.

"Yes. Then I asked if he ever started to turn wolf while he made love to a woman."

"You said this had happened to you to convince him to talk more?"

"Yes. A couple of times during the phase of the full moon."

She raised a brow. "And had it? For real, I mean."

"No." He chuckled. "You sure are suspicious of me. I'd never make love to a human woman during the full moon. I didn't trust anything like that could really happen, but I certainly didn't want to risk it."

"He said he had?"

"He didn't really say, but I got the impression he might have."

"Jeez. What happened?"

"Not sure. I must have gotten distracted."

She slapped his leg. "Typical man. When the story really gets good, you don't know the ending." She sighed. "What if Nicol had killed other women before the pattern emerged here in Portland? What if he'd done so in other countries where he'd led hunting parties? Out in the wild, where no one would suspect his actions? He could say it was a man-eating lion or something else that attacked the women."

Devlyn shook his head.

She wished he hadn't been so…distracted. "So… what about Ross?"

"I didn't get a chance to talk to him."

"Because?"

His lips turned up.

"What?" she asked, annoyed.

"I had to dance with you, Bella."

Frowning, she couldn't hide her irritation. "You were *supposed* to find out who the killer is."

"And you, with Alfred?"

Now that *she* was on the hot seat, she looked out the window and smoothed her dress. "I'm afraid I didn't get anywhere with him."

"Because?"

"I couldn't seem to broach the subject."

He snorted. "Except when you offered him the fur of the killer."

"Yeah, sorry. I couldn't think of any other way to solicit their help while avoiding the fight that seemed headed *your* way."

After a prolonged silence, he pulled into her garage and shut the door behind them. "I'm not sure it was a good idea. What if he switches it with someone else's fur to cover up the fact that he's the killer?"

"I'm not giving him the whole chunk. Just a couple of strands. That's all he'll need."

They climbed out of the vehicle, but before she could make it very far, he swooped her up in his arms and carried her into the kitchen. "I know it's a human tradition, but call me a sentimentalist. I always liked the idea."

"Carrying the lady across the threshold?"

"Yeah."

When he crossed the dining room, she chuckled. "We crossed the threshold a while ago."

"Yeah."

"You're taking me to the bedroom?"

"The wolf's version of carrying the lady across the threshold."

She laughed. "I like the wolf's version much better." She unbuttoned the top button to his shirt. "I can just guess what happens next."

# Chapter 10

AS SOON AS DEVLYN LAID BELLA ON HER BED, THE EMAIL butler on her computer said, "You've got mail, madam."

Devlyn growled, not wanting any distraction to keep him from fully claiming his mate. "You didn't shut your computer down."

"Sorry. By the time you return, I'll be ready for you."

He kissed her lips with feral possessiveness and then ran his tongue down her neck. "Better be."

Unbuttoning his shirt, he strode out of the bedroom, but when he reached the computer, his fingers poised to turn it off, a message from Argos caught his attention.

> Bella, I haven't returned to Portland. I found some-
> one had sent a message from my computer saying
> he'd meet you there, but it wasn't me. Argos

Devlyn cursed under his breath and typed in a reply.

> This is Devlyn. Who had access to your com-
> puter? We're safe for now, but I need to know
> who sent the message.

He added:

> Who knows her home address? Dev

The message came back quickly.

> Thank God, you're all right. I've been sitting
> at the computer all night waiting for your
> response in the hope all was well. Argos

> Who was it? Volan?

> Volan's the only one I can think of. I might
> have left my computer on when I ran some
> errands.

Poor old Argos. He wouldn't do anything on purpose to hurt Bella.

> I'm not turning Bella over to him. I want you
> to know that.

Devlyn rubbed his chin, waiting for an answer, respecting Argos above all others in the pack.

> Bella approves, I suspect?

> Yes.

Tapping his bare foot on the floor, Devlyn waited for his response.

> You'll have to fight Volan to the death.

> Yes.

I always knew it would happen, Devlyn. You're
following in my footsteps and, yes, I approve.

You and Myrta?

Devlyn couldn't believe the old codger had fought to
be pack leader over a female, too.

Yeah, can't see it, eh? The two of you watch
your backs. Volan's not one to play fairly if it
means losing Bella and his pack leadership all
at the same time. He'll be out for your blood.

Devlyn was glad to know Argos was on his side.

Does Volan know Bella's address?

No. She's always had a P.O. box address. I
don't know where her home is.

Is Volan there now?

Devlyn hoped it was a ruse, a veiled threat that he
was coming for them if Devlyn didn't bring her home
to Colorado.

No. According to others, he left sometime
this afternoon.

Devlyn breathed in the subtle fragrance of Bella
behind him.

> A red lupus garou has been killing here. We're
> trying to discover who he is. We'll be returning
> later than we planned. In the meantime, we'll
> keep an eye out for Volan.
>
> Devlyn...be careful.

"Is something wrong?" Bella asked, her sweet voice stirring him when she walked into the office. Her voice was threaded with worry, but seeing her wearing her red lace panties and bra forced the breath from his lungs. "Sinfully sexy" described his Bella. Just catching sight of her bra pushing up her already full-size breasts...just a bit more and the top of her dark nipples would be exposed.

He stood up from the desk chair quickly. "Yeah, something's wrong. Argos returned to Colorado and is still there. The message we thought he sent must have been from Volan."

Bella's face paled.

Wrapping his arm around her, he nuzzled his cheek against her neck. "Argos assures me he doesn't know where you live."

She shook her head.

Argos typed in a final message:

> Bring her home, Devlyn.
>
> You have my word, Argos. D

The next message made the hair on the nape of his neck stand on end.

Dear little Bella,

I sent trusted members of my pack to bring
you home, but it seems Devlyn has other
ideas. I should have killed him years ago. No
problem. Now is as good a time as any. Unless
you agree to be my mate. Think on it, angel. A
life for a life. Meet me at the club and agree to
be my mate and I'll let him live. Volan

Devlyn cursed under his breath, sure Volan's message would shake Bella's faith in his abilities. Shutting
off the computer, he tightened his hold on her, hoping
she wouldn't discourage what he craved to do with
her next. He kissed her cheek, but she seemed deep in
thought, not responding to his attentions.

He couldn't stomach the thought that she'd want to
cool it with him now. Not when he'd convinced her he
was the only one for her. "Bella honey, you haven't
changed your mind…"

Her dark gaze shifted from his chest to his face.
Tears pooled in her eyes, striking a chord in his heart.
He kissed her lips, trying to stir her compulsion to mate.
Once she was his, there was no going back. No acqui-
escing to the alpha leader.

He breathed in the peach smell of her hair, focusing
on everything about her that urged him to take his relationship with her all the way. "I'll kill him, Bella, before
he can have you. I swear it."

"We can't do it, Devlyn."

Unable to curb his anger, he growled, "Because?"

"Because of Volan!"

Grinding his teeth, Devlyn cast her a knife-edged look. "You still think I haven't got what it takes? That I can't best him?"

"I've seen what he's done to others who tried to take over the pack! I know how impossible he is to beat."

Devlyn took her hand and kissed it, attempting to get his rage under control, trying to persuade her to give him a chance.

She pushed him away.

Instantly, the bloodlust surged through his veins. "If all it takes for you to agree to be my mate..." He clamped his lips tight and stormed out of the office.

"Devlyn, wait! What are you going to do?"

He refused to give in to the panic in her voice. He'd come too far to back down now. "I'll kill him, Bella. That's what I'm going to do. I'll end this once and for all."

"No!" She grabbed his arm, but he yanked it free.

"Wait for me, Bella. I'll take care of him and be back shortly."

She didn't say another word, and when he climbed into the SUV, he glanced at the reason for his actions—Bella, his chosen, her eyes misted with tears, her lips pursed in anger.

Volan was as good as dead.

Bella watched Devlyn back out of the garage, her knight who'd get himself killed. She'd never share his love, have his children, be able to return to the pack.

The garage door shut, becoming an impenetrable wall between them.

"Damn it, Devlyn." He'd forced her hand.

She raced back to her bedroom, dressed, and yanked her gun out of the bedside table. *She* would end it once and for all.

After calling a taxi, she paced across the living room, waiting for the cab's arrival, her blood on fire. Could she kill Volan if she had the chance?

The image of him ripping her dress, trying to force himself on her, came to mind. She slung the leather purse over her shoulder. She could do it.

A yellow cab honked outside, and she hurried to meet it. "Papagalli's Dance Club," she said to the driver, her words rushed.

"Yes, ma'am. Hot date?" the driver asked, black dreadlocks jiggling when he talked, his voice sounding Jamaican. Steel band music thumped on his CD player while he tapped his thumbs on the steering wheel in perfect sync with the tune, his body rocking to the beat.

"Somebody's dying to meet me," she answered, jumping into the car.

"Lucky guy."

"Thanks. I need to get there fast to put him out of his misery."

The driver flashed a set of straight teeth, his dark skin making them appear ice-white.

On the way to the club, she pulled out her money but fought leaving her gun in her bag.

A few minutes later, he announced, "Here we are, ma'am. Fastest time I ever made."

She gave him a generous tip. "For your trouble."

"No trouble."

But she was already out the door. The heavy beat
of the dance club music filled the parking area, vibrating the ground. Except for the soft glow of streetlights,
the businesses on either side of the street were dark and
closed for the night, making the area the perfect place
for a *lupus garou* to stalk its prey. The temperature had
dropped several degrees, but it was the worry about
Devlyn fighting Volan that turned her blood to ice.
Before she reached the club entrance, movement to the
east caught her eye.

She whipped around.

*Volan.* His black eyes glittered with a mixture of
anger and unfulfilled lust. His grim look indicated that
he meant business.

So did she.

She fumbled to extract the gun from her purse.

He ran across the parking lot to intercept her.

*Damn it!* She knew she should've pulled the gun out
already.

Her skin grew wet with perspiration. The breeze
carried the smell of her fear to him. He'd like that. The
notion that she was afraid of him always empowered him.

She yanked the gun free.

His eyes wide, he froze a few yards from her. "Put the
gun down, Bella."

Dressed in all black, he was the picture of death. The
breeze tugged at his raven-colored hair hanging loose at
his massive shoulders. Everything about him was larger
than life. His thick neck, angular jaw, huge chest, and
large hands. *Unbeatable.*

She'd even considered that her memory of him

wasn't accurate. That because she'd been smaller, he'd seemed larger. But no, he was even bigger now that he stood so close again.

She swallowed, but the moisture in her throat had evaporated. "Leave us alone, Volan, and I'll let you live."

Smiling the most malevolent look she'd ever seen, he ran straight at her.

She staggered backward toward the safety of the club and bumped into the back of a van. She couldn't fire the gun like she thought she could. Heart hammering, she turned to run.

His heated body grew so close, it made the hairs on her arms stand on end. Stomping behind her, he stepped on one of her heels. Then he struck her in the back of the head.

The blow sent pain streaking through her skull. She fought the blackness that filled her vision. Fought giving into the bastard. Stumbling, she fell to her knees. He'd knock her unconscious and secret her away. He'd rape her like he'd intended so many times before.

Shoving her onto her back beside a bright-yellow sports car, he reached for her arms. She held them up to him, the gun shaking in her hands.

His face hard with anger, he stepped back. "Put the damned gun down."

She squeezed the trigger. Twice.

Silence.

A hideous chortle erupted. "You're coming home with me, Bella. Then you'll do what I say."

Again, he reached for her.

Only this time, she'd unfastened the safety catch. Two shots to the chest, the bullets slammed into his heart.

He grunted and clutched his chest, pain replacing his arrogant look. Like a giant redwood felled, he stumbled backward and collapsed on his back between the cars.

Her hands trembled. She eased herself up. For as long as she could remember, she'd feared the beast. She couldn't stop shaking, sure he would pummel her again. Her head still ached and she felt dizzy.

With her stomach crawling, she poked Volan's boot with the toe of her shoe. He didn't stir. He couldn't hurt Devlyn and he couldn't hurt her now, but she felt sick over what she'd done. Glancing around the lot in a panic, she saw Devlyn's rental SUV. She tore over to it and yanked on the passenger door. Locked. Her heart and head pounded as loud as the rock and roll beat blaring from the club. Racing around to the driver's side, she pulled at the door. It opened, and she nearly fell on her butt in surprise. Trying to get her nerves under control, she shoved her purse containing the gun into the backseat and then slammed the door.

Returning to Volan, she grabbed his arms and tugged. His massive body wouldn't budge. She dropped his arms and paced briskly next to his head, rubbing the back of hers where his iron fist had slugged her. Oh God, what was she going to do with him?

She seized his arms again and yanked, her back and arms straining. He was more the size of a grizzly than a wolf, and she couldn't move him even a fraction of an inch. She paced again. What in the hell was she to do? Get Devlyn to help her and undoubtedly have to face his anger, or pretend it didn't happen and get him to leave with her?

The headlights of an approaching car blinded her. She dashed into the din of the club.

Alfred and his buddies danced with human girls at the edge of the dance floor, too preoccupied to see her. Where the hell was Devlyn?

But then the song ended and Alfred and Ross headed for their table; the only sound now was the noisy conversation all around her. Her skin prickled for an instant, but she could barely glimpse them, so she figured she was pretty well shielded unless the ceiling fans in the place circulated her scent to them.

Nicol hurried to join Alfred and Ross. Alfred started speaking to them, his voice raised as he slammed an empty glass on the table. She moved closer to hear what the red leader was saying, but so many people congregated around her that she was still obscured from the reds' view.

"Which legend?" Ross asked, his eyes wide.

Nicol pressed closer to the table. "You mean the one about the gray?"

"Yeah, just what I mean. The gray ousted our leader, *what*, close to three hundred years ago?" Alfred said, his voice heated.

Ross tossed down the rest of his drink. "Oh yeah. Your great-grandfather."

"Hell, yeah. So what if this is a case of déjà vu? What if this bastard is going to try and take me down and 'cleanse' the pack?"

Nicol shook his head. "He probably doesn't even know about the legend."

"He doesn't need to know about the damned legend to do what happened before, *damn it*!" Alfred cast him an annoyed look and then leaned closer to his pack members. "Grays are not to be trusted, period. Particularly when one is after the pack leader's chosen bitch."

Nicol's lips turned up slightly.

"What?" Alfred bit out.

"She hasn't agreed to be your mate."

"She doesn't have to. Ancient pack law states that a lone *rufus* female in a red's territory is game if the pack leader doesn't have a mate." He tilted his chin up, waiting for anyone to challenge him.

Ross nodded. "Yeah, he's right about that. But if the rest of the pack begins to think of the legend...it could go bad for you. You know, they could worry that the scenario might have the same outcome. Gray wolf kills red pack leader and removes the bad seed from the pack because the reds couldn't do it." He gave a slight sneer.

Alfred moved so quickly that no one had time to react. He seized Ross's throat and growled, "Better hope not, because if he kills me, you'll still want the little red wolf, and the big gray will eat you alive."

Bella's skin chilled, and although she wanted to leave, she felt frozen to the floor. She hadn't heard of the legend they spoke of—probably because the tale was relevant to the ones who lived here and the story hadn't carried farther east. But it showed that the gray's arrival concerned them in a deeper way than she had suspected.

What else might she overhear between the reds? Who murdered the girl?

Alfred released Ross and sat back down. "Get us some more beers. I've got to figure out a way to eliminate this sorry gray before it comes to a real fight."

*He wouldn't fight fair*—that's what raced through Bella's mind. And she began to think that leaving the area might be the best thing after all. Then she smelled a trace of Devlyn's scent and turned. From the direction of the restrooms, Devlyn stalked, his eyes full of fury, his face hard.

Until he saw her.

Surprise registered and then anger again.

Legs shaking, she strode toward him, still fighting with her conscience which course of action to take. Get rid of Volan's body or just leave him dead in the parking area and sneak out the back way with Devlyn. She wasn't the sneaky type normally. But this was one of those times when she felt her life could depend on it.

Devlyn seized her wrist and pulled her toward the entrance. "What the hell are you doing here, Bella?"

"I came to…to tell you I'd be your mate, but…" She balked at going out the front way for an instant, still trying to decide what to do.

He stopped. "You agree to be my mate? Despite Volan?"

She nodded, tears threatening to spill.

"All right. You don't have to worry about Volan, Bella. He's a dead man. Just remember that." He pulled her tight against his chest, warm and loving, which made her feel even worse about what she'd done.

"I…we have to talk…outside," she managed to get out.

"What's wrong, Bella?" Devlyn grunted. "As if I didn't know. You're still worried Volan will beat me."

How could life be so damned complicated? She walked him outside but noticed a man and a woman standing where she'd left Volan's body between the two cars in the lot. From where she and Devlyn stood, they couldn't see Volan, but by the way the people were bending over, she figured they were checking him for vital signs.

She yanked Devlyn back inside the club. Too late to hide Volan now. "Too dark outside. Maybe too dangerous."

"I didn't see any sign of him, Bella. Volan, I mean. Listen," Devlyn said, pulling her toward a table, "after I had a chance to cool down, I thought about my actions. Killing him as a human is a foolhardy proposition. Wolf to wolf is the only way to resolve this. Since we're both here, why don't we stir the reds up a bit? See if we can make any more headway with them."

"I…I think we should leave."

He pulled her onto the dance floor and held her close. "I'll protect you, Bella. He can't hurt you here. Just play along with me on this and then we'll go home."

Volan would never return to hurt anyone again. Devlyn would take over the pack. End of worry. But she couldn't shake the fear of getting caught. Not by the police, but by the one she cared for more than anyone else in the world, her true love who would hate her for what she'd done. But he'd be alive, she reminded herself. He'd be alive even if he couldn't love her anymore.

The crowd shimmied to the heavy rock beat. Red, blue, yellow, and green lights swirled overhead and across the waxed dance floor. Women's flowery perfumes and men's spicy colognes couldn't disguise the perspiration covering the humans' skin while they worked their bodies to the music. But then the faint sound of a siren wailed in the distance. Bella's heartbeat kicked up a notch.

She caught sight of Alfred again, dancing with a

blond. Ross danced nearby with a brunette. Nicol, however, was nowhere in sight. The rear exit was clear. An easy escape.

With the music winding down to a slower paced dance, Devlyn pulled Bella close. "What's wrong, Bella?" He moved slowly, drawing her into the mating madness. "You're shivering."

"I…" She swallowed hard and moved Devlyn toward the rear exit.

He smiled and kissed her cheek. "I'm supposed to be the one leading, Bella."

Heart thundering out of control, she stared at the entrance, watching for the police. "I wish," she said against his ear over the sound of the loud music, "that you and I had no cares in the world."

"We won't, Bella, soon." He kissed her cheek and moved his hands casually up her back and then to her bottom. Wedging his leg between hers, he pressed her against his hard thigh.

She rubbed against him, shamelessly, wantonly. The silk of her dress slid over her thighs when his leg stroked her most erotic spot. "I said I'd be your mate. Let's go home."

He cupped her buttocks with his large hands and lifted her slightly against his firm arousal.

"We've garnered the reds' attention. We have to see how far we can take this."

With her head pressed against his chest, she couldn't see who watched them, but when she tried to separate from him to look, he held her tight. His hands roamed down to the small of her back. "We don't want anyone to know we're putting on this show for them, Bella. Just stay nice and close."

Annoyed, she bit his shoulder.

He laughed. "Of course it's not *really* a show. You know how I feel about you. I'd make these dance moves with you anywhere. In a subtle way, I'm trying to monitor the reactions of the reds."

"We should go, Devlyn."

"I've never seen a pack of *lupus garous* observe anyone so intensely. You sure have them worked up."

"You have me worked up, Devlyn, but I really want to…"

He leaned over and kissed her cheek. "You can feel what you've done to me."

"That's why I'm ready to go to the SUV. To…to relieve some of your tension and mine." She moved her hands from his waist to his backside. "Are the reds angry?"

"Rabidly entranced. As if you were doing a striptease in front of them. If any one of them is the killer, I imagine you're unraveling his resolve to keep his murderous intentions under control."

"Devlyn, I'm really ready to take this to a more private location." She rubbed against his steel-hard arousal, trying to induce him to agree.

"A little while longer." His voice sounded husky and strained. He shook his head. "Damn, one's coming in for the kill."

"Devlyn?" Bella said.

Nicol joined them and, in a ragged voice, said, "I know you've claimed her for your own, although you told me you already had a mate."

Devlyn moved his hands to Bella's hips and parted

slightly from her. "I had made my intentions toward Bella clear years ago. Except I had to convince her to agree with me first. But, she is my chosen mate…no other."

"You both have agreed to this?" Nicol asked.

"Yes," Bella said, and Devlyn leaned over and kissed her mouth. Responding with equal enthusiasm, she wanted there to be no doubt in the reds' minds that she wanted Devlyn and no other *lupus garou*.

"May I ask her to dance?"

Devlyn hesitated and then asked, "Bella?"

"I think we should leave, Devlyn."

For a second, he stared at her, as if he finally realized something big was bothering her. He whispered in her ear, "If we make any headway, we can end this here tonight."

She glanced back at the entrance. No police, no more sirens.

Before she could respond, Devlyn kissed her lips and then left her with Nicol.

Disheartened, she held Nicol apart from her while Devlyn made his way to the table where Ross and Alfred sat.

"You must know, Bella, you're about to give our pack leader a stroke the way you dance with the gray. I've never seen his face redder."

"We can't help it. We're in love."

"It's evident." He studied her for a moment, swallowed hard, and switched topics. "Another gray arrived here earlier. He spoke with us and then left. He appeared to be pretty angry he missed you."

Her heart pumped in overdrive.

"Something wrong? You look like you're getting

ready to faint. We'll eliminate the gray, Bella, if he's a problem. You don't have to worry about him. He said you arranged to meet him here, but we told him you left with another gray. He didn't seem pleased. After he left, Alfred said you had told him an older man planned to see you. Not someone who appeared to be in his thirties."

"Argos. The man you saw wasn't him. Volan serves as the gray pack leader and intended to have me as his mate."

Nicol stiffened. "*He's* the one."

"Yes. He sent a message to me pretending to be Argos. We didn't learn of the deception until we returned to my apartment." She noticed the flicker of interest in his brown eyes. If the red wolf pack searched for her themselves, they wouldn't be looking for a house, but an apartment complex instead. Still, she clenched her fists, irritated that Alfred hadn't used his men to eliminate Volan when they had the chance. Then she wouldn't be in the hellacious bind she was in now.

"Alfred still wants you." Nicol stated the words matter-of-factly.

It was as though she had no choice in the matter. She'd selected a mate, and it should have been a done deal, but the reds wouldn't allow her to choose the gray. "But I've chosen Devlyn for my mate."

"He's not from here and he's a gray. As far as Alfred's concerned, the gray has no legitimate claim to you. You know, ancient law of the pack."

When she didn't respond, he took it that she didn't know about it. "The ancient law, you know. Where an unmated pack leader can take a lone red wolf for his own if she enters the reds' territory. Of course, the same applies if he has a mate already and one of his pack members needs one."

She took a steadying breath. The sooner she and Devlyn left the red *lupus garou* territory and the sooner they got out of the club, the better. "What about you?"

Nicol smiled. "A pack leader can lose his position if a new alpha male emerges."

She raised her brows. He didn't seem to be the emergent leader type. A follower, like Ross—that's how she had both of them pegged. "Like you?"

He shrugged. "There's been no incentive…until now."

That definitely could capsize the boat.

"And Ross?"

"He's been brooding of late. No telling what's going on in that dark mind of his."

"He and Alfred were dancing with human females when we first arrived. They both looked happy enough."

"That was before you showed up with the gray. As soon as you reappeared, they quit dancing and joined me at the table to watch." Nicol tightened his grip on her hand. "I want you to dance close to me like you did with the gray."

"I'm Devlyn's mate, no other's."

He shook his head. "A red belongs with a red…not a gray. No one here will sanctify your choice. As far as Ross goes, he puts on a good show. But, frankly, I wouldn't trust him."

"If you're thinking of ousting Alfred as the leader of the pack and taking over, it seems to me you're the one who can't be trusted."

He gave her a sardonic smile. "No one is to be trusted,

Bella, with a rare red female in our midst, who looks good enough to eat. No one." Taking a deep breath, his eyes darkened.

She assumed he could smell how Devlyn had aroused her, and Nicol's own hormones would be thrown into turmoil. She glanced back at Devlyn, who sat speaking to Alfred and Ross but kept his gaze focused on her and Nicol. Devlyn's face looked red and hard. If Nicol got too fresh with her, Devlyn would be at her side in a flash.

Right before the dance ended, Ross made his move.

Fearing she would have to dance with every one of the reds, each trying to see if they could stir the same kind of interest in her that Devlyn did, she knew the police would stalk in any minute and arrest her, as guilty as she must look.

Nicol kept hold of her hand, reluctant to give her up.

"Will you dance with me?" Ross asked her, ignoring Nicol.

"Of course, but remember, I'm Devlyn's mate." Glancing over at Devlyn, she frowned.

Ross's nostrils flared slightly as his eyes burned with hatred at the mention of Devlyn's name. Nicol snorted at her comment and then joined the others at the table.

"I thought the brunette you danced with was quite attractive. Have you known her long?" she asked.

Ross's thin lips tightened and his brown eyes darkened to nearly black. "You have no business taking up with a gray."

Her stomach constricted. Instinct compelled her to shove him away and tell him where he could go. She had every right to select a mate, and if he were agreeable, she and Devlyn would consummate the relationship, thereby making it a mating for life. Squashing her more violent wolf nature, she attempted instead to learn whether Ross was the killer. "I'm sorry there aren't more reds around for—"

"You won't be a gray's bitch, Bella."

She didn't care for his tone, ominous and threatening, but she fought telling him off. She already had enough problems with zoo man Thompson, the police, and one dead gray pack leader. Plus the notion of finding and stopping the killer. No way did she need three horny reds compounding her troubles.

Devlyn sat on the edge of his stool, ready to pounce on any of the reds should they take their actions with Bella too far. Although neither Ross nor Nicol had treated Bella other than with great caution, he still didn't like them touching her. They desired her, just as he did. As any of their kind would. Touching that soft, warm body, even with the faintest of brushes, forced his loins to react. He knew the same thing happened to them when they drew close to her. Yet he had every intention of learning who the killer was as soon as he could so that he could take Bella home to the pack.

"I'm surprised you didn't make a move for her earlier. She's lived here for three years. Or didn't you know?"

Alfred's eyes rounded, and his face reddened. "Shit," he said under his breath. "I thought…" He shook his head.

"She's pretty good at keeping inconspicuous, mainly from dodging Volan all these years."

"She should have been mine all this time." Alfred rose from the seat. "My turn." He didn't ask if it was all right with Devlyn. He strode from the table like a pack leader does, knowing that everyone had better follow his lead.

Struggling to keep his seat, Devlyn clenched his fists.

"Man, is Alfred pissed now!" Nicol chugged his beer and then grinned. "To think she'd been in the area all that time and no one knew it. We thought she'd been here only a couple of weeks." He shook his head in disbelief. "She's sure fine."

"What do you think about Alfred wanting her so badly?" Devlyn asked, trying to take his mind off Alfred's hands on Bella's hips.

When she moved them back to her waist, Devlyn smiled at her tenacity.

Nicol faced Devlyn. "I'd say you've got a hell of a lot of competition and a big fight coming if you want to keep her."

The truth was out. "You'd fight for him so he could have Bella?"

Ross finally returned to the table, his face crimson.

Devlyn glanced back at Alfred, dancing super slowly to the music.

"I'd fight *any* to have a chance to have her," Nicol said.

Ross glared at Nicol but quickly shifted his attention back to Bella and Alfred.

Steeling his composure, Devlyn watched every move Alfred made toward Bella, intent on ripping him apart if he did one thing that she didn't like…or that he didn't care for.

"Hey, Ross, guess how long the little lady's been in the area."

Ross looked at Nicol, waiting for him to answer. Devlyn could sense the tension building.

"Three years. Can you believe it? Alfred's really steamed over it."

"Shit," Ross said.

Nicol finished his beer and set the bottle on the table with a clunk. "I told Bella that Volan looked for her here. We didn't know he was the gray leader who wanted her, though, or we would have done something about it."

Hell, Devlyn must have just missed Volan.

"We're not through with him yet," Devlyn said. "He won't want to give her up."

Ross faced Devlyn. "Did you bring the hair sample with you?"

Devlyn hadn't even considered doing so. He shook his head. "We'll rendezvous at the ice-cream shop tomorrow."

"We could follow you home tonight," Nicol offered, with a sideways glance at Ross.

"Thanks, but no. Zoo man Thompson's hot on our trail. The more of us there are, the more likely we'll all be caught."

"Maybe you ought to stay with one of our pack. We have several widowed females, if you'd prefer to reside with one of them," Nicol said.

"We're making other arrangements."

Ross growled.

Devlyn turned to see what Ross was watching. Two uniformed policemen. The same ones Devlyn had knocked out at the hospital. And both were showing sketches to club patrons.

# Chapter 11

TRYING NOT TO CATCH THE POLICEMEN'S ATTENTION, Devlyn eased his way across the dance floor and reached for Bella's wrist. He attempted not to make a scene and quickly said to Alfred and Bella, "The policemen from the hospital incident are here. Got to go."

Bella's peach skin blanched and her eyes turned nearly black.

Alfred motioned for Ross and Nicol to watch their backs.

"Tomorrow, the ice-cream shop," Devlyn said to Alfred. Then he pulled Bella toward the rear of the establishment, not waiting for him to respond.

When they reached the back door, Alfred followed on their heels. "Tomorrow night." He looked at Bella with such longing—his dark eyes clouded over as if he were totally moonstruck—that Devlyn could have slugged him.

Devlyn yanked Bella out of the building, ran down a street parallel to their vehicle, and then dashed in front of the shops lining the street. Once at the SUV, Bella finally took a breath.

He hurried her into the car, jumped into the driver's seat, and they were off. Driving down the main road, he headed in the opposite direction of her home, just in case anyone tried to follow them. "Are you all right, Bella?"

She nodded, her hands trembling to fasten her seat

belt. "Did…did you find out anything from the reds about the murderer?"

He snorted. The notion that they stirred up a hornet's nest came to mind. "Only that Volan had arrived, and the reds all want me dead."

She ran her hand over his thigh and immediately he became aroused. "We can't let that happen."

He chuckled. "I don't intend to." He could handle any red. Even the three at once, as long as Bella wasn't there to worry about.

The farther away they got from the club, the calmer she seemed.

"Both Ross and Nicol intend to become the pack leader so they could have me. Now that they know Volan is the gray leader who's after me, they might attempt to gang up on him." Her voice still sounded strained, and he figured she'd balk about becoming his mate while Volan still lived, but he had every intention of persuading her again.

"Better him than me." He glanced at Bella, whose lips rose in a small smile. It wasn't a pack leader kind of comment to make, but she seemed to sense that he was joking.

Doubling back, he headed for her place.

"I told them I lived in an apartment. Just sort of let it slip naturally so they wouldn't be on to us," she said; her voice seemed more even now. "Even so, they probably figure I live in Portland, not Tigard."

"Good. If they speak to Volan, maybe they'll let him know this, too." He was glad he hadn't said anything about her house to the reds and ruined her ploy.

"I was wondering," Bella said, sliding her hand up and down his thigh in a slow, sensual caress, forcing his blood to pump faster, "if you'd cooled down too much since the dance club. We might put some slow music on at home and warm things up. I was thinking about your comment concerning dancing...*au naturel*."

Reaching over, he slid his hand down her dress. With little effort, his fingers slipped down the lace cupping one of her breasts, exposing one already hardened nipple. Rubbing his thumb over the protruding nub, he smiled when she moaned in ecstasy. "I'd say we're heating up just fine." He grinned at her to see the devilishly wicked smile on her lips. "Bad Bella."

"Hmm, don't take any more detours on the way home, unless you want to park out here somewhere."

He raised his brows at her suggestion. When she'd torn into the club and said she'd wanted to mate with him, he considered she'd done so only to get him away from Volan. Hell, whatever her reasons, if she said yes, he was game. "I *would* park somewhere out here, only zoo man Thompson, Volan, or the reds might catch up to us."

She growled low with amusement. "Here I thought you were my wild wolf companion, afraid of nothing."

"I'm not afraid of anything. Well, except that I won't risk your safety, no matter how much I desire to have you."

She began to unbutton his shirt. "Speed it up, stud, while I'm still hot. You're going much too slow."

He'd show her slow, when he had her naked body pinned beneath his...slow and hard.

When they pulled into Bella's housing development, they kept a lookout for any cars parked in the street that appeared suspicious. Not seeing anything to concern them, he drove into her garage and shut the door.

Now that everything appeared safe, Bella wanted Devlyn—before anything else prevented them from finishing the moves they had started on the dance floor. Volan was dead, but she didn't want to think about that. The police had no idea where she lived, and even the pain in the back of her head had nearly subsided. No one would stop her from having her mate.

Immediately, she unfastened her seat belt and grabbed Devlyn's.

Chuckling, he pulled his seat belt free. "I thought we were going to play some slow music and work up the—"

Tugging at his shirt, she yanked it free from his trousers. She had no intention of wasting any more precious time to set the mood right. "The loud music from the club's still ringing in my ears. I don't need it to get me in the mood. Do you?"

His low sensual laugh pushed her to work faster. Their lips touched with heated passion when his fingers struggled with her buttons and she worked on his belt.

"Hmm, fewer clothes next time, stud."

"I'd have to say the same for you, Bella honey." Devlyn unfastened her bra and slid the straps down her arms, kissing her skin from her shoulder to her fingertips.

They moved to the middle bench seat, where there was no console to hamper their progress. The soft velour fabric against her bare back sent a tingling through her body while he knelt between her legs. For a moment, he looked her over, his eyes smoky with blinding desire. "The thought of the reds touching you…"

"But only your touch drives me wild." She ran her hands down his naked thighs, the well-developed quadriceps tightening with her stroke. Already he was fully aroused and her eyes shifted from his washboard stomach to the full erection readied for her.

He tangled his fingers in the short curls between her legs, and a smile curved his lips upward. "Been ready a while, eh, Bella?" His voice was husky, filled with wolf-size craving.

"I told you I wanted you some time ago." She moved her hand to touch him, but he shifted out of reach.

"You touch me, and I'll never make it."

She growled. "You'll have to learn better control, my mate."

"Not with the way you arouse me, Bella. Maybe not until we're both old and gray."

She chuckled. "No way am I waiting to touch you until we're old and gray."

Bella's skin was velvet against Devlyn's mouth and tasted sweet and wild. He nestled his lips against her abdomen. Almost with a purring catlike quality, she growled softly.

Threading her fingers through his hair, she arched her pelvis toward him. She was ready to mate and she'd chosen him over anyone else…over both the gray and red pack leaders, human males, everyone.

Leaning his naked body against hers, he enjoyed her soft curves, fitting nicely against his hard muscles. She mewed her satisfaction. He growled his.

He wanted to take it slow, to enjoy every inch of her and to prove to her she'd made the right choice. Still, her touch heated a fire in his belly that couldn't be quenched until he had his fill of her and she of him. Taking it unhurriedly would test his resolve more than anything else he had ever done.

He cupped the swell of her breast, the dark nipple taut. When he licked the tip, she closed her eyes, stopped breathing, and stilled her fingers that were buried in his hair. "Breathe, honey."

She chuckled. "Quit talking and get to business."

"*Pleasure,* woman."

"Hmm, you don't have to tell me." Her fingers massaged his back muscles, kneading and stroking.

Shifting his body higher, he moved his mouth over her heated skin, across the collarbone, higher, to the hollow of her throat.

"Oh, Devlyn," she said, her voice washing over him like a heated spring, filling the emptiness. She arched her body against his, parting her legs, urging him on. Offering herself to him like a siren of the sea.

Brushing his mouth up her neck with whisper-soft kisses, he tangled his fingers in her long hair, squeezing the soft locks in his hands, thankful the redheaded goddess was no longer his fantasy, but tangibly real. Again she pushed her pelvis against his erection, making it clear she ached to have him fill her. Her hands slid down his back and cupped his buttocks, prodding him to enter her.

Making love to her felt more than right. She was feral and willing and throbbing with life. And she was his.

He nipped her chin and then conquered her mouth. Instantly, she flicked her tongue at his lips, teasing him. Catching her tongue, he sucked fervently, making her smile. Again she lifted her hips off the seat, pressing hard against him.

A groan issued from deep within his throat. He continued his slow pace to pleasure his mate, but Bella wasn't cooperating. Sliding his hands up her velvet-soft belly, he cupped her breasts, weighing each bountiful marvel. She marked his neck with her teeth. Another surge of craving crashed over him, titillating him as he attempted to use a slow touch. "You're beautiful," he said—but inwardly, not just outwardly, the most beautiful creature of their kind; fun, loyal, and full of heart.

"Quit torturing me," she breathed heavily against his mouth.

It was his turn to smile. "I haven't even begun."

Bella frowned at Devlyn, her blood already so hot she felt her car's heater was on the fritz and they were now in a sauna. His arousal pulsing against her waist and the ache between her legs was driving her mad. "Devlyn, I swear…"

He covered her mouth with his and with long, hard strokes, thrust his tongue deep inside. *Hurry up!* she wanted to scream at him.

His fingers slid down her abdomen and then massaged her deeply, as if preparing her for his penetration, which she'd been damned ready for ever since she spied him at the zoo.

Again she arched against him, trying to force him to hurry. He throbbed against her and she fought biting him again to get him to oblige. "Devlyn," she whimpered, bringing a devilish smile to his lips.

She growled in response. Two could play at this game. She attempted to work her hand between their moist bodies to his thickened length, but as soon as her fingers reached his navel, he grabbed her wrist, kissed her hand, and shook his head.

"Devlyn," she groaned, the pleasurable ache of his actions killing her.

"If you touch me…" His words trailed off and he worked his hand lower, tangling his fingers in her short curly hairs for a moment, and then dipped even lower.

But she didn't want his fingers. She wanted his…

"Oh," she moaned against his mouth when he kissed her hard and stroked her sensitive nub.

"Breathe, Bella," he said, his tone of voice amused.

But she couldn't breathe and still concentrate on the sensual strokes that filled her with a longing to reach… a peak of ecstasy that waited at the top, willing her onward.

Never had she thought being with him could feel like this. From their early days of nuzzling and playing, of nipping and biting, of his pinning her down, of her tackling him back…none of that had prepared her for the earth-shattering feelings he now stoked deep inside of her.

"Oh, Devlyn," she whispered against his mouth, loving the way he touched her, cared for her, wanted to make the sexual experience last for her. He'd searched for her for years—not to return her to Volan, but to have her like this.

His accomplished strokes sent streaks of pleasure rippling through her like electricity zinging through hot wires, running to the source but not quite tapping into it.

She murmured his name, half pleading with him to finish her off, half wanting it never to end. His actions stimulated every sexual nerve pathway at once and she moaned with deep satisfaction. Scaling the peak, her body trembled with spent passion, contractions rippling through her in an unending stream.

His eyes clouded over as he slowly bore into her. She hadn't expected him to be so large, or that she'd be so small. But every bit of him felt so good. Entering her gradually, he stretched her to the limit, penetrating her inch by inch.

"Breathe, Bella," he whispered against her ear, sending a trickle of heat down her spine. "Relax, or I'll never make it to your special chambers."

She breathed deeply, unclenching her pelvic muscles. He kissed her lips. "Much, much better."

Before she could prepare herself, he thrust deep, breaking the membrane. She gasped, unable to contain her surprise at the sting that followed, like a hornet's hot poker thrust into the skin.

"Are you all…"

She covered his lips with hers and thrust her tongue deep inside his mouth. With her arms secure around his back, she pushed her pelvis higher. No words now. She wanted his seed, his babies, all of him. No going back.

Rocking the SUV back and forth simulated a boat on stormy seas, their heated breaths fogging the vehicle's windows.

His Bella. She was saccharine and tangy, the old Bella, playful and ornery, and the new Bella, just as fiery, just as fun, but filling a burning need now that Devlyn couldn't have fulfilled when they were young. How he loved her, from her long shiny red curls to her perfectly trimmed toenails. Every inch of her soft, curvy, warm, and needy body.

Although he still longed to make it last, her hands stroked his back to the base of his spine, drawing him to the peak. Her tongue tangled with his, teasing and sucking. The way her body moved against his, deepening his thrusts, pushed him to the top before he could control himself.

His seed exploded deep inside her, and she spoke his name in a sultry, exhaustive way against his mouth, her body trembling with renewed orgasmic pleasure.

"Oh, Devlyn," she moaned, her hands shifting from his hair to his shoulders, her nails digging into his skin, her body milking him of every last seed.

"I wanted you, Bella, always have," he said and then encircled her nipple with his lips and sucked.

She ran her fingers through his hair. "I guess you kind of figured I had—"

Lifting his head, he raised his brows. "Loved me?"

"Had the hots for you. Couldn't help myself. Once you kissed me—"

"I knew you'd never been kissed like that since."

"You made it pretty hard for the competition, stud."

Nestling his face against her cheek, he hoped beyond hope he'd not hurt her too much. He'd wanted the experience to be the most pleasurable one she'd ever had.

Then, he wished to repeat the encounter until they were old and gray. He settled on top of her, their bodies warm and wet and tired. But alive. He'd never been so loved, so cared for, so desired. He loved every bit of her, the wild side and the tame. The cautious and the adventurous. For choosing him, when she could have had so many others. "Are you all right—"

"Considering we're trying to catch a red *lupus garou* killer and Volan will want to murder us both for what we've just done…yeah, I'm all right."

He ran his fingers over her abdomen in a sensual caress, sparking a surge of renewed interest. "I didn't hurt you too much?"

Realizing his sole concern rested on how he'd made her feel, not about other world events, Bella smiled. How could she have not recognized how wonderful he'd make her feel? How sensitive he could be?

She quickly squashed that reasoning. The dread of losing him in a confrontation with Volan had been all that had weakened her resolve to have Devlyn. She gritted her teeth, unable to shake the concern that Devlyn might still learn how someone had shot Volan and he died, the only way he could, from silver bullets. Well, snapping his neck would work, too, or drowning, but no way could she have killed him in either manner.

Taking a deep breath, she assured herself Devlyn would think the reds took care of Volan, not her. Nothing could have stopped her from taking the relationship she had with Devlyn to the max. They'd been destined to be together from the moment he'd saved her from the wildfire.

She kissed his lips and then sucked on his lower one and released.

"I always dreamed I'd have you for my own. But the dreams could never be this real, or this satisfying," Devlyn said.

"Hmm, did you dream of making love to me when I was gone?"

"You wouldn't believe how many times I thought I had you within my grasp, only to find my sheets wet, and no Bella."

She laughed. "Well, the vehicle's seat is wet this time, but you've got me to blame for it now."

"I didn't hurt you too much?" Devlyn repeated, his fingers stroking the curve of her hip with a much too sensual touch.

Already she greedily yearned to have him fill her again. "Only pleasure." She wondered why she'd ever thought a human could ever be better than the *lupus garou* who loved her so tenderly.

He studied her face and gathered her in his arms. "Good. I was afraid when you wouldn't breathe, I'd hurt you too much."

"Are all grays so...big?"

He chuckled under his breath.

She licked his salty chest, ready to show him how bad she could really be. How would it be to ride *him* this time? With *her* handling the joystick? How would it be to set the pace, to be in charge? Could the big bad gray handle the red's test?

"You're not finished, are you?" She raised a brow in challenge.

He slid his hand down her thigh. "Does my mate want more?"

"All you can give me."

"Let's go inside. Turn on some music, dance *au naturel,* and take it from there."

They carried their clothes into the house. As soon as they reached the living room, a solid rapping on the front door nearly gave her a heart attack.

The dreaded image came to mind of police officers standing on her front porch with warrants for her and Devlyn's arrest...

# Chapter 12

BOTH DEVLYN AND BELLA SCRAMBLED FOR THEIR clothes, but he had no intention of allowing his mate to face whatever danger waited at the front door. Wearing only his jeans, he stalked across the living room.

Bella whispered wildly, "Wait, damn it, Devlyn. Together!"

The sound of knocking at the back door surprised him further. With a quick look out the peephole of the front door, he saw another of their nightmares…not Volan, as he'd first assumed. But zoo man Thompson. Bella was still buttoning her dress when she headed for the front door, barefooted.

Devlyn said in a hushed growl, "Thompson."

Her face lost all of its color.

A gentler knocking at the back door sounded again.

Devlyn motioned for her to stay put. In several long strides, he reached the back door. Peering out the side window, he frowned. "Your neighbor, Chrissie," he whispered. He opened the door partway. "Yes?"

"Hurry, let me in."

"Do it," Bella said, her voice hushed, motioning for her to come in.

Chrissie hurried into the house and headed for the front door.

"What the—" Devlyn said.

"Go." Chrissie waved at them to go down the hall. She considered his bare chest and smiled. "Continue what you were doing. I'll take care of the menace standing on your front doorstep."

Bella stared at her and then looked at Devlyn. He joined her and pulled her down the hall and into her bedroom.

With the door slightly ajar and their sensitive hearing attuned, they waited while Chrissie opened the front door. "Well, hello there," she said in such a sexy voice, Devlyn chuckled under his breath.

Frowning, Bella poked him in the rib. The color hadn't returned to her face and her eyes were still darker than normal.

"Are you Miss Bella Wilder?" Thompson asked.

"Yep. What's this all about? You a cop or something? Got a badge?" Chrissie sounded as sugary sweet as could be.

"I'm investigating the disappearance of a red wolf from the zoo."

"You think I'd keep a red wolf in my house? Ha! Aren't they dangerous?"

"Were you at Papagalli's Dance Club tonight, Miss Wilder?"

Devlyn rubbed Bella's arm and whispered into her ear, "Breathe, Bella."

"I don't go to dance clubs," Chrissie told Thompson, her voice firm but still saccharine sweet. "What makes you think I was there?"

"Can I come in?"

Bella stepped back. Devlyn leaned down and kissed her cheek. "It's okay, Bella."

Chrissie said to Thompson, "You haven't established your identity as a cop yet. I don't let just any man into my house, despite the fact that you're a pretty hot number."

Silence. Then Thompson said, "Messages were sent from an email address that belongs to a Bella Wilder, at this residence. If you didn't send those messages, who did?"

"Just exactly who are you?"

"Thompson. I have connections with the Oregon Zoo, and, as I said, I'm investigating the disappearance of a red wolf."

"Got a first name?"

"Look, the wolf may be in danger. I think you and your friends have some notion that Rosa's safer in the wild than in the zoo, but, as I explained to your friend, releasing a red wolf into the wild can have dire consequences for the animal."

Chrissie's voice elevated. "Listen, I don't like zoos. Let the animals live in their natural habitats. That's what I say."

Bella shook her head and then took a step forward, in rescue mode. Devlyn gathered her in his arms, keeping her still.

Thompson cleared his throat when Chrissie didn't incriminate herself anymore. "That's just what I figured. So where are your cohorts?"

"What were they supposed to look like? Do you have their names?"

"All right, I'll humor you. The girl's a petite redhead with amber-colored eyes. No name though. We found her in the zoo, freezing to death—"

"Naked?" Chrissie asked, the tone of her voice raised in disbelief.

That would take some explaining.

Thompson's voice showed marked enthusiasm. "Yeah, that's the one. She's only considered a witness at this point, though."

"And…and she disappeared from the hospital, right? I mean, even though cops were watching her, some guy stole her away right out from under their noses." Chrissie sounded intrigued.

"Yep. Now you remember."

"The news was all over the papers. Sure, I remember. With a story like that, who wouldn't have?"

"The guy's tall, about six foot—"

"Ah," Chrissie said, as if she were putting two and two together and coming up with Bella's old acquaintance.

"Six foot one," Devlyn said under his breath.

Bella pinched his arm. "Shh."

"Dark-brown hair and eyes. Muscular. He tried to free the wolf from the zoo on pretenses he was transferring her to another zoo. Then he arrives at the hospital, frees his partner, and vanishes."

"Wow." There was another lengthy pause. "But why would she have been naked at the zoo, of all things?"

"Little lady wasn't talking. She ran off before we could extract the truth from her."

"But what has this to do with the dance club?"

"You signed off as Rosa, but the email said you were a red wolf seeking a fun-loving red wolf male. Rosa was the name I gave to the wolf that was stolen from the zoo."

"Ah, well, I had about sixty people here at a party earlier. Someone must have played some kind of a prank."

"Is that so?" Thompson asked.

"Yep."

"I want a guest list."

Bella's whole body tensed. Devlyn massaged her shoulders.

"You're not a cop," Chrissie reminded the zoo man.

"You're right, I'm not. But I can ask my friend, the chief of police, to issue a search warrant and—"

Bella stiffened her back again.

"Well, maybe, Thompson, we could work up that list over dinner. You're not married, are you?"

Again a pregnant pause followed.

Thompson cleared his throat. "No. Well, divorced, but—"

"Well, me, too. See we have a lot in common. You like animals and I do also. Maybe you can tell me more about this red wolf of yours. I'll grab my coat, and we can go to that new Chinese restaurant on Main Street. Got paper and a pen? I'll make that list for you."

Another prolonged silence. Then Thompson gave a nervous little cough. "All right."

He sounded like he'd gotten bamboozled into the dinner date, but maybe he'd find out what he wanted from Chrissie when he wined and dined her. At least that's what Devlyn would have tried.

Footsteps headed in their direction. Bella backed away from the door, but Devlyn prepared to tackle Thompson if he tried to enter the room. But it was Chrissie. She pushed the door open wider and grinned.

"Got a coat?" she whispered.

"What about your children?" Bella asked, her voice hushed and concerned.

"At their dad's the rest of the week."

"What about this list—"

"Don't worry. Your name will be at the top. Bella Wilder." Chrissie grinned again. "After I have a lovely dinner with Thompson, and maybe take in a movie, I'll try to make him forget he was after the two of you."

"How did you know about Thompson coming here to see me and—"

"My neighbor called and said Thompson had come to her house to see if Bella Wilder had a wolf in the yard or a strange man visiting or living with her. She knew you and I are best of friends and thought I could warn you. He came to my door next, but I sneaked around the back way to your place. I figured you might need my help." She winked at Devlyn. "You know it's awfully important to renew old acquaintances without a lot of interruptions." Her gaze shifted down Devlyn's bare torso.

Interrupting Chrissie's gawking, Bella handed her a dressy raincoat. "Thanks, Chrissie, for being such a good friend."

"Like sisters," Chrissie said, her chin tilted down. "I owe you for lots of times. What a wonderful night this is going to be." She exited the room with a definite spring to her step and strode down the hall.

Bella whispered to Devlyn, "Thompson is never going to know what hit him."

"Husband candidate number two, don't you think?"

Bella nodded. "Poor man. Wait until he finds out she's got a couple of elementary school–age kids."

When Chrissie reached the front door, she said to Thompson, "Maybe you can explain to me why the animals are so much better off in a zoo. Never know. You might even convince me to change my mind."

"Yeah, well, Miss Wilder—"

"Call me Chrissie. That's what everyone calls me. Here, can you help me with my coat?"

"Sure."

"Hmm, such a big man with large capable hands, but with a tender touch. I bet you keep all those wild animals in line, don't you, but with finesse?"

The front door slammed shut.

If Bella hadn't been trembling so hard, Devlyn would have laughed out loud at Chrissie's actions. Instead, he held Bella close and hugged the breath from her chest. Kissing her head, he said, "What do you want to do now?"

"My heart tells me to run...to hide. I don't want to go to jail or back to a zoo cage. I don't want to expose our people for what they are."

"What about the red *lupus garou* killer?"

"We have to stop him no matter what." She ran her hands over Devlyn's arms. "I hope Chrissie won't be hurt."

"What do you imagine she thinks about us?"

Bella looked up at Devlyn. "That you're some kind of wild guy. She's always thought of me as very tame-natured. Quiet lifestyle—no dating, carousing, partying. Just nature retreats from time to time. But since you arrived—"

Devlyn chuckled.

"I'm sure she thinks you're a bad influence."

"What do you think?"

"I'd have to agree…happily."

Kissing her cheek, he slipped his hands inside her dress. She shook her head.

"Ah, Bella."

"We have work to do. Play later. You know as well as I do—"

"We have to find the killer."

"And we won't find him—"

Devlyn smiled. "In your bed."

"You always could finish my sentences when we were young." She changed out of her dress and into black denims and a turtleneck.

"I always knew what you were thinking, lovely Bella."

"Not always." She pulled her hiking boots out of the closet.

"Oh? Tell me a for instance." He pulled his shirt on.

"The time I caught you kissing Vernetta."

"You wished it was you and not her." He buttoned the last of his buttons.

Bella growled. "I did not! I wanted to…to…"

"You wanted me to kiss you. Admit it, Bella." The scene played back in his mind like it was only yesterday. She'd just turned sixteen, he nineteen. Vernetta was twenty, but meaner than a bull on steroids. If it hadn't been for Volan keeping an eye on Bella, the *rufus lupus* would have been the one Devlyn would have shared his kisses with.

Bella growled again and yanked one of her shoes on, tied the leather laces, and then the other.

He smiled to see her cheeks on fire, now as red as her hair. "I only kissed her on a dare."

"Right," she snapped.

"Really. Three of my older cousins had tried to kiss her. She'd bitten each in return. They bet me that she would bite me, too."

Bella rose and folded her arms. "But she didn't. She kissed you back."

He buckled his belt. "Yeah, I won that bet, but I hadn't expected it. She wasn't the one I wanted to kiss."

"Volan," Bella said with disgust.

Devlyn laughed. "No, I didn't want to kiss him, either."

"No, Devlyn, I meant, ohhhhh…" She stormed down the hall in the direction of the kitchen.

He stalked after her. "You're right. I wanted to kiss you, but Volan was always in my way."

She grabbed her fleece-lined jacket and headed for the kitchen door to the garage. "But that day after the lake—"

"I had to have you, Bella." He pulled her into his arms. "I had to taste you, savor you, force myself to realize you weren't the one for me, only some lustful desire that drove me insane. Some dream I had that you were all I had imagined you to be and more, but just a dream. I had to wake myself from the dream, prove once and for all that you were nothing more than forbidden fruit. Tantalizing, tasty, but really just like all of the others. But once I felt you against my body, soft and curvy, wet and…hell, Bella, you were real and my dreams of you were real. Once I'd kissed you, held you close, I knew no one could ever replace you in my heart."

"And Vernetta?"

"Becoming an old wolf maid."

"Good." Bella separated from Devlyn, yanked the door open, and crossed the floor to the vehicle.

"Where are we going?"

She sighed deeply. "I was thinking of taking a drive to my cabin."

"I thought we were trying to catch a red *lupus garou* killer." He could tell by the gentle upward curve of her mouth she was thinking of something sinful.

She ran her tongue over her lips. "All work and no play…but truthfully, near there is where I smelled the reds before. Maybe we could find some evidence that we missed before."

"Gotcha." He jumped into the driver's seat.

"I only wish we could be in our wolf forms for a while."

Knowing she wanted him to make love to her in both states—in civilization, in their silky human skin, and in the wild, covered in sleek pelts of fur—he totally agreed. "Four more days."

"The longest I've ever had to wait for the moon to appear."

---

The two-hour drive to Bella's cabin seemed like it grew longer with every mile they drove. Maybe because her thoughts were in such turmoil. What if they discovered the killer in the woods? Or Alfred and his gang?

She shook her head at herself, annoyed she could work herself up likely over nothing. Alfred and his pack members wouldn't be running around in the woods unless they could change into wolves. And surely the killer wouldn't hang around there either.

Devlyn reached over and rubbed her shoulder. "A deep trench is dug into your forehead. Want to tell me what's worrying you?"

"Chrissie and the zoo man. *For starters.* What if Chrissie let something slip by accident? I know she's smart, and after having raised her two kids as a single parent for the last three years, she has a lone wolf's wariness. But Thompson is clever, too. What if he hit on Chrissie's vulnerability? She desperately wants a man in her life again. Someone who cares for her children, and believe me—they mean the world to her. But she wants someone who loves her and she loves in return, too. It could happen if she thinks he might be the one."

"I think she's got a lot more moxie than you give her credit for. I'll bet she doesn't give an inch. I can just see her talking Thompson around in circles over the wolves and what might have happened to Rosa. And all he'll get out of it is another commitment for a dinner out or some other kind of date."

Bella gave Devlyn a sly smile. "Yeah. I'm sure you're right. You certainly are observant. Most males aren't half as perceptive."

He cast her a smug look. "It's in the genes. So what else is bothering you?"

"Well, I worried that maybe Alfred and his pack would be running around the woods, but I dismissed that because I'm sure they wouldn't unless they were wearing their wolf suits."

"Agreed."

"But then I wondered if maybe the killer might be there, hiding somewhere."

Devlyn squared his shoulders and sat taller. "Maybe. If so, I'll take care of him and that will be the end of that matter."

She took a deep breath and released it.

"Do you have a problem with that?" he asked, giving her a quizzical look.

"No. He couldn't kill any longer. Mission accomplished. Then we could return home."

"What about Alfred and the rest?"

Bella touched Devlyn's hair. "They'll have to get along without me." She pointed to a gravel road off to the right ahead. "Turn there."

He headed off the main road and drove down the gravel road for five miles until they finally arrived at her cabin. Her Escape was still parked out front. Everything appeared the same as before, when she'd gone on her wolf run and Thompson had found her.

"You don't mind going home anymore?" Devlyn asked.

Hating that she was living such a horrible lie, she swallowed hard. "If...when Volan returns home, I have every faith you'll handle him."

Devlyn leaned back against the driver's seat. "If?"

"I meant when. It'll probably take him a while before he realizes we've returned to Colorado, don't you think?"

He cast a wary look her way and then opened his door. "Right." But he sounded like he didn't believe her.

Damn it, she had to get her feelings under control.

Not only that, but she worried he might smell her nervousness. Oh hell, of course he had. Except he said he saw the furrow in her brow instead.

He lifted his chin up and observed the thunderheads building overhead; she pulled her jacket on and zipped it up. She smelled the rain in the air and knew it wouldn't hold off for long. "Storm on its way."

"Maybe we can find something before the rain starts." He buttoned up his jacket and joined her. Slipping his hands under her jacket, he rested them on her waist. Brushing her lips, he pressed further and gave her a searing kiss. She kissed him back but trembled, and he pulled her tight against his body. "Tell me, Bella, what's really bothering you?"

She fought the tears welling up.

"Bella honey?" His dark eyes willed her to speak the truth.

She took a hesitant breath. "I've always felt safe here until the day Thompson shot me. I didn't think it would bother me, but, well, it…does. A…a little."

Devlyn nuzzled her cheek, warming the cold skin. "I thought so. No hunting season right now. Most likely no one will be tromping around in the cold and wet. And it's a weekday, so most everyone is in school or at work. Thompson's busy with Chrissie, so no worry about him looking to find additions for the zoo. But if you'd like, you can wait for me at your cabin and—"

She straightened her back. "No. I'll show you where I smelled the reds' scents. I didn't know what the murderer's scent smelled like before, but now that we both do, maybe we can pick it up here."

He kissed her nose and smiled. "Your nose is icy. Let's get this over with quickly then."

She agreed. Her veins already felt like they were filled with ice and her fingers and toes were beginning to numb. She reached into her pockets and pulled out a pair of gloves. "Let's go."

<div align="center">~~~</div>

For an hour, Devlyn and Bella searched for clues, listening to every sound they could hear—the shivering of pine needles and leaves; the whoosh of the wet, chilly breeze; the rustling of a deer moving through the underbrush; Bella's rapid breathing.

He moved closer to her and rubbed her arms, her cheeks, and her nose red. Part of him wished she'd stayed back at her cabin, but another part was glad she was with him where he could keep an eye on her. Twice, he'd smelled the scent of Alfred and Ross on the breeze; he thought it was an old scent, yet he didn't trust her being alone.

"You're not too cold, are you?" he asked, his voice hushed.

Her eyes had darkened and grown wide. He'd sensed it, too—someone watching, and a hint of something else. He moved closer to the smell and caught sight of drops of dried blood spread over a cluster of brown leaves. Bella crouched beside him, barely breathing, yet he could hear her heart beating pell-mell. He lifted to his nose a leaf covered in drops of blood and took a deep breath.

"Is it hers?" Bella whispered.

He shook his head, relieved but dismayed, too. They needed to find evidence of the red's complicity. "Rabbit's," he clarified.

Letting out her breath, she surveyed the area. He shifted his attention and made a wide sweep but saw nothing out of the ordinary. The breeze picked up and a clap of thunder shook the ground.

He glanced at Bella and saw her tremble again. "Do you want to go back to the vehicle?"

"No. We'll keep looking. Let's search where I was shot."

Admiring her determination, he grasped her arm and helped her up. "You let me know when you want to go back."

They moved at a slow pace, searching the ground for canine prints or blood and the branches for broken twigs or any other sign of a struggle.

Lightning streaked across the sky and another clash of thunder sounded like it broke the sound barrier. Devlyn stuck close to Bella and they moved away from the spot of the rabbit kill, climbing over moss-covered logs and through dense ferns, lifting their noses to smell any scents that could give them a clue about the murderer or the murdered girl.

When he smelled the water, heard it rushing over the stony creek bed, Bella seized Devlyn's hand and pulled him to a stop. "Omigosh, look, a family of mink," she whispered, her voice excited as she pointed through the trees to the creek's bank.

Devlyn's attention was rooted to the ground. "Fresh bear tracks," he warned. Looking around, he spied movement in the trees about twenty yards away. "Over there." He pointed to the striking cinnamon-colored black bear lumbering in the woods.

"We're upwind of him. I can't smell him."

"You're right. He's gotten wind of us," Devlyn said, his voice raised. He knew from experience to always keep upwind of a bear and to make noise so that he wouldn't startle one. Although a wolf could take on a bear, bears were known to have killed wolves, too. Certainly as humans, they didn't stand a chance if the bear decided to attack and kill.

"He was foraging in the blackberry bushes," Bella added, her voice just as loud. "We need to give him a wide berth."

The bear rose to stand on his hind legs.

"He's checking us out," Devlyn said, moving Bella away from the beast.

The bear lifted his nose and smelled the air and then exhaled a series of several sharp, rasping huffs.

The wind shifted and now they could smell him.

"He's agitated." Bella took hold of Devlyn's hand.

The bear's long snout curled up and he snarled.

"He's really not happy." Bella took a few steps backward. "I think he's going to charge."

As unpredictable as bears could be, humans usually couldn't tell what they intended to do. But as *lupus garous,* they could smell the bear's fear and agitation.

"Keep moving backward," Devlyn said in a firm, controlled voice. "Keep talking and moving away from him."

Bella stumbled over a broken tree limb behind her, and the bear dropped to his feet and charged.

Devlyn yanked Bella to her feet and shoved her behind him, but the bear stopped a few yards short and roared.

"We're going!" Devlyn yelled back at the bear. "I sure as hell wish I had my wolf teeth about now."

The bear stood facing them, either getting ready to charge again or waiting for them to withdraw.

Another fork of wicked lightning smacked the ground a mile away and deafening thunder boomed a second later, unleashing the rains.

Unruffled, the bear stood his ground despite the rain pelting all of them.

Devlyn maneuvered Bella back toward the edge of the forest next to the creek. "Ready to ford it?"

"I don't think we have much of a choice, although I hadn't really planned on wading today."

"Come on, let's go." Devlyn hurried her across the stony bank and pulled her into the icy water.

They started to cross the creek, taking it easy over the moss-covered stones while the bear lumbered toward them. As soon as Devlyn felt his feet slipping out from under him, he released Bella so he wouldn't pull her down with him, but she lost her balance anyway and they both fell into the creek.

"Damn, sorry, Bella honey." Both soaking wet, Devlyn scrambled to his feet, helped Bella up, and then moved her as fast as he could to the other side.

Her lips were turning blue and her pace was sluggish.

"He's not following us across the creek," Bella said, casting a glance over her shoulder, her teeth chattering.

"No, but we'll have to make a wide sweep north of him, where the land's not as steep, and head back toward the…" Devlyn pulled Bella to a stop on the opposite bank, and his gaze searched the woods for signs of anyone. He thought he'd smelled the murdering red. He thought he'd caught a glimpse of a dark-green jacket, nearly blending with the Douglas fir, withdrawing deeper into the forest. But the rainfall was so heavy and the water ran down his face so hard that he could barely see.

"It's him," Bella whispered, her voice on edge.

"Did you see him, too?"

She cast Devlyn a fearful glance. "Did you see him?"

"Not sure. Come on. We need to head north."

"You smelled him, didn't you, Devlyn?"

"Might have been an old scent."

He thought he heard her snort, but the sound was muffled in the rain.

For a good half hour, Devlyn and Bella moved through the forest. Although the woods impeded their progress, he didn't want them exposed along the rocky bank of the creek. And the trees helped deflect some of the pounding rain. But he couldn't help feeling that the red was following them.

He thought he heard a branch snap behind them once, but the rain poured down in such a torrent that it was hard to hear anything else.

"I think we should cross here," Bella said, her teeth clattering. "The terrain isn't as steep on the other side of the creek."

Holding her hand with a titan grip, he helped her across the creek and up on the opposite bank. When they reached the shelter of the Douglas firs, he pulled her to a stop and watched for any signs of movement in the woods they'd left behind.

Silently, they observed the sheets of rain pounding the branches and the creek bank while he tucked Bella under his arm and held her shivering body close.

Finally, she shook her head. "He knows we're watching for him. He won't move out of the safety of the woods."

"Maybe. Or he might have hightailed it out of here already."

She looked up at Devlyn and her expression told him she knew differently—that the killer wanted her. That he would stop at nothing to have a *real* red *lupus garou*.

Devlyn squeezed her hand and then hurried her through the woods as fast as they both could manage, hoping the rush in their pace would warm her up some. They were a good mile north of where they'd been, and everything was gray, from the sky to the ground, as the rain continued to pour; the visibility was dismal.

Devlyn was so intent on returning Bella to the SUV and watching for signs of a trap the murdering red might have rigged that he wasn't thinking of anything else. But, suddenly, Bella yanked him to a stop. "The odor's faint, Devlyn, but do you smell it?"

No matter how frozen she had to be, she was still searching for clues of the killer's movements.

Feeling waterlogged as the rain penetrated every inch of the clothing he wore, soaking him clear to the skin, Devlyn took a deep breath. *The girl's blood*. He went into search mode. His gaze glanced at the pine needles and leaves matted on the ground beneath woodland ferns. He breathed in the wet, clean air but also smelled signs of the girl. She'd worn a flowery perfume, and he smelled blood—her blood.

Bella had separated from him, inching along, searching for clues, her eyes glued to the ground, barely breathing, then taking a deep breath, trying to find the source of the smell. "Here, Devlyn!" she shouted.

But something buried under a fern a few feet away caught his attention. Using a stick, he snagged a blood-soaked bra out from underneath the plant. He lifted the lacy garment to his nose and took a deep breath. Her blood, her fragrance—beyond a doubt.

Bella came up behind him and stared at the bra. "You knew he killed her out here, didn't you?"

"He probably took her 'camping,' wanting to sequester her away from civilization. But his plan to change her and make her his mate didn't go as expected. He cared enough for her that he took her back to her apartment, cleaned her up, and dressed her in a nightgown before he laid her to rest in the bed."

"Then stayed with her until we scared him off." Bella's voice sounded choked with tears and she couldn't look Devlyn in the eye.

"I thought he was there because he needed a place to hide. But now I think he didn't want to leave her until he was forced to."

"But you knew she died out here."

"He'd washed her body, but her hair smelled of the forest and wood smoke. They must have had a campfire and she was in the path of the smoke." Devlyn glanced at the gold necklace in Bella's gloved hands, finally taking notice of it.

"Hers," Bella confirmed, shoving it into her jeans pocket. "Same perfume, traces of wood smoke, too." She pointed at the bra. "You aren't going to take it with us, are you?"

"No." He buried it underneath the leaves beneath another fern. "The necklace will be proof enough as far as the red pack is concerned. I wouldn't want anyone catching us with her bloody garments."

He wrapped his arms around Bella and pulled her tightly into his embrace. She was shivering; not wanting to prolong their staying here, he whispered against her ear, "Let's go home, Bella. We've found what we came here for. It's time to go home."

---

Bella knew she was close to being hypothermic again and, even though Devlyn wanted to return to her cabin first, she wanted to go home instead. "I don't have any dry clothes for you, and I used the last of the wood for the fire. The rest of the firewood is too wet to use. And firewood is the only kind of heat I have at the cabin." She couldn't say a word without her teeth rattling together and she clenched them tight, but the shivers continued to shake her to the core.

But when she saw the SUV, her spirits lifted and her pace quickened. Devlyn opened her door in a flash, and cold, wet, and tired, she somehow managed to climb into the vehicle with his help. How he could not be shivering, she couldn't imagine.

He slammed her door shut and hurried to the driver's side. Then he turned the engine on and switched the heater on high, the first cold air chilling her further until they were halfway down the gravel road and the car began to warm up.

She peeled off her gloves, her hands shaking and numb, and held her icy fingers up to the vent. "If we show the necklace to Alfred and his buddies, one might react to the sight of it," she said, her whole body still trembling. She struggled with her jacket zipper, annoyed that her fingers still weren't working right. "I know none of them are the killers, but they might know who is."

Glancing over at her, Devlyn gave her a worried look. "Are you going to be all right, Bella?"

"Yeah, I just need to remove these wet things."

His lips curved up a smidgeon. "I can warm you up a bit."

"I hoped you'd say that. What about you? Aren't you freezing?" She jerked her drenched jacket off and tossed it into the backseat. Even her turtleneck was wet, and her jeans were soaked.

"I could use some warming up, too."

"Hot chocolate should do the trick."

He chuckled, dark and seductively.

She smiled and fumbled with the leather ties on her boots. Having a devil of a time untying the wet laces, she finally managed and sent the boots flying into the backseat. After peeling off her socks, she unfastened her seat belt, and Devlyn gave her a raised eyebrow look.

"I'll help you take off your coat," she said, unable to control the shivers still, even though the interior of the SUV was warm now and, because of all of the wet clothing inside, the windows began to fog.

Devlyn switched the heater to defrost while Bella unbuttoned his jacket. "That hot chocolate's sounding better by the second."

She helped him shrug out of his jacket and threw it over the seat to join hers. Then she started to work on the buttons on his shirt; his face was etched in a permanent wolfish grin.

"Something tells me you aren't going to wait for me to make some cocoa when we get home."

"Something tells me you're right." He leaned over and kissed her cheek, his lips cold.

She'd definitely have to warm them up.

By the time they arrived home, Bella had managed to remove his shirt and, in a comical maneuvering, his boots and socks. As soon as he pulled into the garage and shut the door, they both shed the rest of their wet clothes. Then together, they gathered them up and dumped them in her dryer where she put the load on high heat for an hour.

Shaking hard, she hurried with him toward the door leading to the kitchen, the ice-cold garage doing a number on her already chilled blood.

Devlyn yanked the door open, intent on getting Bella in a hot shower and taking the warming up process to new sexual levels, but the sight of zoo man Thompson sitting at the dining room table, sipping hot cocoa with Chrissie, nearly compelled Devlyn to have a stroke.

# Chapter 13

IN HER NAKEDNESS, BELLA GASPED, AND DEVLYN'S temper spiraled when he saw the enemy—zoo man Thompson—seated at her dining room table, cozy as could be. Devlyn shoved Bella behind him, hiding her nudity from the wolf lover, and slammed the kitchen door on their escape. He hit the button for the garage door opener and then met Bella at the SUV before she could open the door. He yanked it open and she scrambled into the car. As fast as he could, he raced around to the driver's side.

If it wasn't one damn thing, it was another. Why in the hell had Chrissie brought Thompson back to Bella's house?

*Damn.* Thompson thought Chrissie was Bella, and it *was* her house. She probably couldn't get rid of him without arousing suspicion. Or maybe she hadn't wanted to get rid of him so awfully bad. Devlyn growled deep inside.

He jammed the keys in the car's ignition and turned the engine on, but Chrissie hurried into the garage, waving at them. Devlyn rolled down the passenger's window and scowled. If Chrissie delayed their escape—

"I told Henry everything." Chrissie winked at Devlyn. "About how you and Bella were old friends who were in love with each other. How Volan Smith—you know, the guy you worked for, Devlyn—wanted the red wolf and how he had the goods on you so you had to release her from the zoo. Only you didn't. Volan set the red wolf free when you refused to go along with it. But he had taken Bella hostage and left her naked in the zoo's wolf exhibit in the wolf's place. He thought it was funnier than hell in his sick twisted mind, except that she could have died."

Devlyn clamped his gaping mouth shut and then finally said, "And?"

"Well, Henry's really a pretty great guy. He wants you to give a description of this Volan Smith so he can notify the police. Of course, he wants you to make a statement to the police about everything that happened also."

Bella glanced at Devlyn. "What about the knocked-out police officers and Thompson at the hospital? They'll blame and arrest you for that."

"Extenuating circumstances. Volan threatened to kill Bella. Left her for dead already, right, Devlyn?" Chrissie asked. "You knew no one would believe you and worried Volan would get to her at the hospital. Overcome by concern for her, you took any measure you could to protect her."

Bella shook her head. "I don't trust Thompson. What did he say about the wolf?"

"He wants her back. But I told him Volan's the one that got her out, and he's the one who'll know where she is."

Devlyn nodded. "He thinks she's his."

"Did he own her before?" Chrissie asked.

"Yeah. But she ran away."

"That's what I told Henry. He thought humans had owned her before."

Chrissie glanced at Devlyn's naked chest. From where she stood, she couldn't see anything more, but he imagined she wouldn't mind taking a peek to see what else she might get a glimpse of—if she hadn't already gotten enough of an eyeful earlier.

"When the two of you are more dressed, maybe you could come in and talk to him?"

"Our clothes are wet and in the dryer," Bella said.

Chrissie raised her brows. "Want me to grab them for you?"

"Sure," Bella said. "But I don't want Devlyn arrested. Maybe Thompson won't press charges, but the police most likely will. The worst of it is, Volan is after me, even now. Devlyn's my only protection."

Chrissie's eyes widened. "Oh, yes, of course, if Volan's still on the loose and after you." She pulled a ring of keys out of her pocket. "You can wait at my house while Bella talks to Henry," she said to Devlyn.

Devlyn shook his head and climbed out of the SUV, the door shielding him from Chrissie's view. "I stick with Bella."

Chrissie whipped around, dashed for the laundry room, and yanked the dryer open. In a jiffy, she headed back to Bella's side of the SUV and handed the warm damp clothes to her. Bella passed Devlyn's things to him, and while she tugged on her turtleneck, Chrissie hurried for the kitchen door with one backward glance before she closed the door behind her.

Devlyn yanked on his pants, growling under his

breath. "Of all the damned things to happen. I should have known."

Bella objected, "But you can't go with me. He'll—"

"I'm not leaving you for a second, Bella. At any time, that bastard could show up." Devlyn finished buckling his belt while she tugged on her denims.

Nodding, she acquiesced to his leadership, but he could tell she wasn't happy about it. This time it didn't matter. Any male who wouldn't protect his mate could never lead a pack; if Thompson had any ideas of having Devlyn arrested, he'd make sure he changed his mind. Even if it meant knocking him out again and running for the hills with Bella.

When Bella was more presentable, Devlyn grabbed her hand and then paused at the door to the kitchen, but everything was quiet in there. He glanced at Bella, but she was waiting for him to make a move. Steeling his back, Devlyn twisted the knob and pulled the door open.

Thompson stopped pacing and stood watching them, his blue eyes shifting from Devlyn, the one he most likely felt threatened by, to Bella.

Instantly, Devlyn felt possessive of his mate and wrapped an arm around her shoulders. Thompson, taking the cue, sat down at the table again, playing the part of a nonthreatening male adversary.

Devlyn walked Bella into the kitchen and shut the door.

"Chrissie told me the whole story," Thompson said, glancing in her direction.

Leaning against the bar countertop, Chrissie smiled

back at him, and Devlyn fought the urge to laugh. The woman would have made a great seductive gray female in their pack, but he was sure Chrissie wouldn't agree.

"*But,*" Thompson continued, "the police are going to need a description of this Volan Smith."

"He's still after me," Bella said, trying to move toward the fridge.

Devlyn finally released her, fearing the others would think he acted like a clinging vine. He couldn't help feeling possessive when it came to her, blaming it on his wolf nature. He was sure Bella wouldn't fault him too much for it.

She pulled a picture from the fridge, the rest half burying it.

He moved in closer and glanced over her shoulder. Sure enough, it was a recent photo of Volan. "Why did Argos send this to you?" He couldn't help the irritation that laced his words.

"So I'd know him if he ever came for me."

"Oh." He definitely had to get a grip on his emotions.

"He was an old boyfriend?" Thompson asked.

"No," both Devlyn and Bella said, and she looked up at him. He gave her a small smile.

Chrissie's version of the story didn't hold a thimble of truth. They'd have to concoct something that was more factual than not.

Bella squeezed Devlyn's hand as if to encourage him to let her explain the situation. "I was adopted after a wildfire killed my family. He was my adoptive brother, only he wanted me for more than a sister."

"He tried something with you?" Thompson asked, his

face stern, as if he would have protected her from the menace, too, if he'd been able.

Bella glanced at Devlyn, and the look on her face revealed a mixture of shame, regret, and anger. All at once, the idea that Volan had attempted to rape her when she was underage raced through Devlyn's mind. Was that the reason she kept trying to run away? Argos had grown too old and couldn't fight Volan, so he had wisely stepped down as leader of the pack. Although the pack would sentence a rogue wolf to death for such a crime, it couldn't do it if the wolf happened to be the leader and unbeatable.

Devlyn frowned at her, his heart thundering, both with concern that Volan had tried to do something so dastardly and with anger for her not telling him. He knew she'd been hiding some deep, dark secret, damn it. The nightmares she was having…"Bella, did he?"

Bella ran her hands over her jeans and stared at the floor. Her words were no more than a whispered croak. "Argos stopped him."

"Damn it, Bella, why didn't you tell me? I would have killed him! Why didn't Argos tell the rest of the—"

Her eyes shot up in warning.

"Family," he said, swallowing the word he'd almost used.

"You were adopted, too?" Chrissie asked, her eyes as big as melons. "A brother, too?"

He nodded. "Yeah." He knew what Chrissie was getting at. He and Bella shared an incestuous relationship, although they wouldn't have been blood relatives. "We weren't raised together for long before she ran away."

They had been, but humans wouldn't understand the *lupus garou* longevity, nor would they understand the workings of a pack. Besides, they were different kinds of wolves, sharing no close lineage—a red and a gray.

Befuddled, Thompson just stared at them.

Chrissie collapsed in her chair. "So, that explains why you don't go out with guys and you stay home most of the time. And have a post office box and all."

"But about Rosa," Thompson said, "why would he want her?"

"She's like a wild pet," Bella explained.

Devlyn linked his fingers with hers. He couldn't believe Argos hadn't at least told Devlyn to protect Bella. Then he realized Argos couldn't have. No one could have protected her back then.

She handed the photo of Volan to Thompson.

Frowning, he considered the picture. "I saw him at the dance club tonight."

Bella's face paled. "Yeah, he pretended to be Argos, my adoptive father, in an email to me."

"You were at the dance club?" Thompson said in surprise. "I—"

Bella gave an elusive smile. "What name did you use on your email to me?"

"Charlie. I thought maybe there was some kind of conspiracy to free all red wolves. I knew it had to be you, the unnamed girl from the hospital, or at least I'd hoped so."

"Charlie, the one who's independently wealthy." Bella noticed Chrissie's eyes grow big. "Volan doesn't know where I live, for now. But he's pretty cagey. He'll find out sooner or later."

Thompson glanced at Devlyn. "I won't press charges against you for knocking me out."

Devlyn raised a brow. "Who said I struck you?"

Bella's fingers tightened around his.

He gave her a reassuring squeeze back. "You didn't see who hit you, did you? Volan was there. That's why I had to rescue Bella from the hospital. I discovered he'd already knocked out the police officers. He must have gotten to you later."

Thompson rubbed the back of his head as if remembering the pain. "Yeah, you could be right. I only assumed it was you because I'd seen you at the zoo earlier and then again at the nurse's station. Downstairs, the receptionist said you'd left with a half-dressed, redheaded woman in a man's oversized clothes. I just assumed—"

"No one could have protected Bella if I hadn't slipped her away from the hospital."

Bella's fingers still squeezed his, cutting off the circulation, waiting for Thompson's final verdict.

"Yeah," Thompson said, nodding. "I'm sure I got a glimpse of this fellow right before he hit me. He's the one all right."

Devlyn wrapped his arm around her waist, glad that the zoo man could help corroborate their story, made up as it was. Now the problem was, if the police did arrest Volan, they'd have no proof. Plus imprisoning Volan wasn't the solution. Like any *lupus garou,* if he were exposed to the full moon when it shone in all its glory,

Volan's wolf coat could appear. No way could they risk Volan's imprisonment. To secure Bella's freedom, Devlyn had to kill Volan.

"You need to make a statement to the police about what he did to you, Miss Wilder," Thompson said.

She shook her head.

Thompson turned to Devlyn. "Can I talk to you for a moment, alone?"

Devlyn embraced Bella and then released her. "Yeah, we can talk out back."

Bella frowned at him. Devlyn had every intention of keeping the zoo man on their side. One less problem to have to deal with. Or at least he hoped.

He joined Thompson on the covered brick patio, and the two sat on a pair of cushioned, high-backed rockers. The rain had slowed to a pitter patter, but Devlyn felt damp through and through.

Thompson said, "I'm sorry about the little lady, but she needs to report this to the police. I can see she's terrified of this man." He shook his head. "I don't know why your family wants to keep this under wraps, unless it's to protect the family name. But Miss Wilder shouldn't have to fear for her life."

Thompson paused as if lending weight to his lecture, allowing Devlyn to soak in his words of wisdom. "I can tell she believes you'll protect her no matter what, but you can't kill him. Let the police handle this."

"I didn't mean I'd kill Volan for real." Of course Devlyn would kill him. It was the only way to save Bella. "It's just a saying. I'm not the killing type."

"Anyone's got it in them if there's enough at stake."

Thompson glanced back at the house. "I'd say that the little lady is pretty high stakes."

The highest. "There can't be any leak of her address to the media, Henry. She'd be a ready target if that happened."

Thompson folded his arms. "You think if I tell the police, they'll question her, need her address, and somehow this Volan will find her?"

"Yeah, that's exactly what I think." But more than that, the reds would locate her. And the killer of the female humans could, too, if he wasn't one of the pack. In any event, as soon as Thompson vacated the premises, Devlyn was taking steps to move Bella to another location to keep her safe.

Thompson reached underneath his jacket and Devlyn's back stiffened. "Got something I want to read to you," Thompson explained when he noticed Devlyn's reaction. He pulled out a newspaper clipping and shook out the folded paper. "This was in the *Mail Tribune* about Wolf Creek and some trouble they were having. Namely, a barbecue that was held in the neighborhood there. A nonprofit wolf sanctuary that takes care of abandoned and abused wolves once raised by humans was negotiating the purchase of the Golden Coyote Wetlands, one hundred acres of land near Wolf Creek. One of the men threatened to use the wolves for target practice."

Devlyn's neck muscles tightened.

Thompson took a deep breath and proceeded. "The thing is, people have painted over their signs, caused lots of other vandalism at the current facility, and even attacked the founder's home. These people who take in wolves to raise as pets have the best intentions. Or maybe not always, but they take in a wolf thinking that it's different and they can handle it. Then they find out they can't. The abused animals have no place else to go. My point is that, if people like the one who was threatening to kill wolves learn that a red wolf is running through the woods, releasing Rosa into the wild will get her killed."

Devlyn nodded. What else could he do? *Lupus garous* generally knew to stay out of the human's way when they took a run in the wild, except in Bella's case. He figured she had been distracted when she sensed other reds nearby. He didn't like it that people were mistreating real wolves, but he didn't want to sound too interested. "The founder's name?"

Thompson refolded the paper and shoved it under his jacket. "Probably best if you didn't know it."

Why? Because Devlyn might try to release those wolves into the wild? Seal their doom? But he *would* discover the name soon enough. And then? He'd make a private donation. Maybe, with additional funds, the founder could find a place far enough away from civilization where the wolves could live out their days in peace, like the insurance company did for a couple of pairs of red wolves in North Carolina at the Alligator River National Wildlife Refuge.

Thompson waved Volan's picture. "I'll run this photo by the police station on my way home. I can't promise anything about keeping Miss Wilder and you out of this forever, but for now, I'll say I received an anonymous tip about your circumstances. No addresses, no statement." Thompson shoved the photo inside his jacket. "In the meantime, I'll ask the chief, a good buddy of mine, to pull the warrants for your arrest and trash them, as a case of mistaken identity. The fact that I swear out a complaint against this Volan Smith striking me at the hospital should get the ball rolling as far as getting him into custody."

Somehow, Devlyn didn't figure Thompson's plans would fall into place so easily.

Thompson tapped his fingers on the arm of the chair. "Then Miss Wilder and you can come forward with further charges. But remember what I said." He rose from the chair. "Convince her to press charges. It's the only way to put the bastard behind bars."

Devlyn intended putting Volan six feet under, not behind bars.

He stretched his hand out and gave Thompson's a firm shake. "Thanks for helping us."

"Because of circumstantial evidence, I've pinned the blame on the two of you, and put you both at more risk. I'm the one who should be apologizing. If you need any further assistance, feel free to call me." Thompson pulled a business card from his pocket.

"Thanks." Devlyn hoped his movements didn't appear too rushed as he grabbed the patio door and yanked it open. And he hoped removing Chrissie from the house wouldn't take too much effort.

All he could think of was moving Bella. A cousin's condo in Sacramento might be a good bet.

But would Bella agree to leave? He'd grown used

to her unpredictable behavior. Thinking he'd have the situation well at hand, she'd surprise him. So, when he planned their next move, he had an inkling he'd have a fight on his hands.

Drawing himself taller, he entered the dining room as Bella sat at the table watching him, her face showing her concern. A paper napkin she'd been toying with lay in shreds on the tabletop. She quickly released the tortured paper and placed her hands in her lap.

Trying to reassure her that he'd take care of her, he smiled. He glanced at Chrissie, whose focus had returned to his bare chest where his shirt still hung open.

Thompson said, "Night, Chrissie. I'll call you tomorrow."

Grinning at him, she twisted a dark curl around her finger. "Sure thing. I'll be waiting."

Devlyn let Thompson out and then locked the door. Now, for Chrissie's removal.

He stalked back into the kitchen. For a second, it didn't register that Chrissie had already left. He looked inquisitively at Bella.

She rose from her seat. "She told me to say good night to you and slipped out the back door. She figured we had more getting acquainted to do, and she needed to get some beauty rest for her date tomorrow with Thompson."

"Bella, listen," Devlyn said, drawing close. He rested his hands on her shoulders and leaned down and kissed her cheek. "For your own protection, you have to leave here."

# Chapter 14

BELLA KNEW DEVLYN WELL ENOUGH TO RECOGNIZE HIS intense, anxious posturing meant that he wanted to move her somewhere safe before he even spoke the words. She scowled at him. "You're not going to hide me away while you search for the red killer and face Volan on your own. What kind of a mate would that make me?" In the worst way, she wanted to say that Volan was no longer a threat, that she knew Devlyn could handle the killer, but she squashed that notion right away.

She assumed Devlyn felt as hemmed in as she did. The closer it got to the moon's reappearance, the more the wildness inside them screamed to be released. Just a run in their wolf coats would do the trick. Just a stretch through the wilderness would curb the urge to remain in wolf form for very long. She craved the wind in her fur, the smell of the pines, the damp earth, the crisp fresh water, the woodland animals—that further spawned the desire to hunt.

She took a steadying breath. Being together as wolf-mates for the first time would be a truly special experience they'd never forget.

"Devlyn, listen. I want to be there when you make the murdering red pay. I want to be part of the solution, to make a difference in our world."

"Bella, we do it my way," he said again. "You'll stay

with my cousin in Sacramento. It's fairly close by and I'd feel a whole lot better if you were out of harm's way there."

Ignoring his words and hoping he wouldn't realize she was not about to go along with his new scheme, she slipped his damp shirt off his broad shoulders. "Let's dance to the music this time. Nice and slow."

Running her fingers over his chest, she traced the muscles that relaxed under her ministrations. Already his fingers yanked at her turtleneck.

His actions warmed her. "Chrissie really likes Thompson, but she wanted to know what you're taking that makes you such a sexy hunk."

A smile tugged at the corners of Devlyn's mouth.

"She said she's seen more of you out of clothes than in them. Although we kind of blew her mind when we both came into the kitchen from the garage naked."

"Did she ask why?"

"She gave us an out. Said that we were really smart to dump our wet clothes in the dryer like that and not track all that water into the house. Not to mention, it saved us the trip running back out there with the wet clothes after we changed into dry things. She talks a lot when she's nervous."

Devlyn chuckled.

Before Bella could touch his belt, Devlyn pulled away from her, and her heart sank. Instantly, she felt she'd failed in her mission. She had no intention of going along with Devlyn's plan to sequester her away with one of his cousins she didn't even know. Disappointed, she realized her charms weren't as powerful as she'd hoped.

He strode across the floor to her stereo and perused the selection of CDs stacked in a three-foot-high wooden shelf. *The music*.

Instantly tickled, she worked on removing her belt.

"What did Thompson think about our awkward state of undress?" he asked over his shoulder.

"He was interested in Chrissie's reaction, I'm sure. If she were agreeable, maybe he'd try some moves like that with her in her garage."

Shaking his head, Devlyn flipped through some of the CDs. "Hope she doesn't have a compact."

"She does, and with Thompson's big frame, they'd probably blow a couple of tires."

Devlyn glanced back at her, a grin plastered on his face.

"*What?*" She unbuttoned her jeans and slid the zipper down. Already the ache between her legs filled her with urgency. She glanced at the bulge in Devlyn's jeans. Although she meant for them to take it slow and easy, already she wanted to rip his clothes off and get on with the sensual dance moves that would drive her to the edge of the abyss.

"Thompson was so busy trying to get an eyeful of you, he didn't see the big bad wolf's temper rise."

"Nah, you shoved me through the doorway too quickly. Besides, he probably saw only one bare breast, if that."

"Even that would be more than I'd be willing to let him see."

She dropped her jeans on the carpet. "What did you boys talk about?"

"Thompson's going to leave us out of the picture for the time being."

Bella let out a sigh. "Thank God."

"Yeah, but he still wants you to report the attempted rape." Devlyn's eyes darkened in anger, yet compassion showed in their depths. "You should have told me, Bella. You shouldn't have had to face Volan alone. No wonder you ran away three times."

"Six, but who's counting?" She wasn't sure why she mentioned it. Maybe to show how determined she truly had been.

He growled and then stuck a CD in the player and turned the music up. The instrumental songs were perfect for slow dancing, with a beat in between for some jazzier steps.

"I would have protected you." He stalked toward her.

She shook her head. "You would have gotten yourself killed. Then where would I be today?"

Placing his hands on her cheeks, he tilted her face up to him. "I would have thought of something."

Silver bullets? No, Devlyn was too honor bound to have stooped so low. Not like she'd done. She closed her eyes, trying to erase the image of Volan's dead body out of her mind.

Devlyn kissed her lips.

She took a deep breath and opened her eyes.

"You were too young. So was I. Nobody had the strength to fight Volan. Argos somehow found the power that one time, but he couldn't have done it on repeated occasions."

"How many times did Volan try with you?" Devlyn

asked, his words dark and incredulous. "I thought there had been only the one time."

"Three. I knew he'd keep trying. The other times, pack members approached and he'd skulked off before they saw that he had attempted to rape me, afraid to show what a bastard he really was, I suspected. But I couldn't stay. I'd always hoped you would be strong enough someday and that we could be together again. I felt terrible leaving you after you kissed me that day, terrified he'd killed you because of your kissing me. But unable to save you, either."

She wanted to assure him that he couldn't have helped her, nor could any of the pack members. That everything had turned out as well as could be expected under the circumstances. That he should have no regrets. But she also wanted him to know how badly she'd felt in leaving him behind to face the beast alone.

"You couldn't have done anything for me, Bella."

She touched his cheek, lightly covered in brown stubble. He was right of course. And had she interfered any further, it would have been worse for them both. She knew it in her heart, but she still couldn't reconcile having left Devlyn behind to fight the monster.

"I ran, but I came back. I slipped into the village to learn that you were alive and our healers were taking care of you. Volan was searching for me, but I figured he'd never suspect I'd return to see if you'd made it all right."

"I wish I'd known. I wish… Well, I understand how terrified you must have been…of him and what he would have done to you."

She nodded, not wanting to relive the most horrible time of her young life. "Then I disappeared for good."

"And you wrote to Argos."

"As soon as I could. I wanted him to know I was all right. We agreed it was safer for you if you didn't know."

He growled again and then kissed her cheek. "He should have told me."

They rocked slowly to the music, but she barely heard the tempo. His hands swept down her sides, heating her nerve endings. His gentle touch, not pressuring, heightened her anticipation of what would follow, stirring her faster than if he'd started quickly with stroking her already aching nub.

The music faded further into the distance. She concentrated on the feel of him, his rough fingers against her skin in whisper-soft caresses. The smell of his musky body mixed with the fragrance of sandalwood soap. The sound of his heavier breathing, as his heart beat rapidly against her fingertips, matching hers. She licked the hollow of his throat, tasting his slightly salty skin, eliciting a deep-throated groan from him.

Moving her hands lower, she fingered his belt buckle. He leaned down and fondled her breast with his mouth, not pushing for satisfaction quickly, instead increasing the sensitivity of her skin to his touch.

Taking it slowly was tantamount to getting her way in the scheme of things, but she didn't believe she could handle his measured moves. Already she craved having him deep inside of her. Coupled together they were as one. No one could claim her then. She was his and he hers. Nothing else mattered.

She skimmed her fingernail down his zipper, stirring his rock-hard erection that was straining against the denim.

He growled when she ran her fingernail over his denim-covered arousal again. "Tease," he whispered against her cheek. Leaning over, he took her nipple in his mouth and sucked hard.

Who was the tease? Already she was thoroughly wet from his touch and yearning for much more. She pulled down his zipper and watched his erection spring free.

This time she wanted to touch him but fought the urge, fearing she'd send him over the edge too quickly and he'd send her away. Slow and easy. Slipping her hands around his waist, she pulled him against her body, sliding her leg between his. Again they rocked to the beat of the music.

She pressed her bare skin against his arousal, rubbing at a gentle pace, and his growl was more a moan this time. Still partially clad in his denims, he raised his leg and grazed her nub with the well-worn fabric covering his taut leg muscle. The soft material brushed against her supersensitive spot, exciting her further.

Her own muted growl erupted.

"Remind me," he said, licking her cheek, "to thank Thompson for capturing my little red wolf so I had the chance to free her and make her mine."

"I wasn't happy to see you at the zoo, you know."

He smiled. "The smell of you, ripe and ready for mating, nearly drove me insane. That poor wolf they tried to mate you with must have been truly agonized. I know I was."

"My heart nearly stopped to see you there. Then I realized you'd only come to take me back to Volan."

Devlyn moved his hands to her buttocks and lifted, pressing her harder against his arousal. She moaned as his leg massaged her more intensely.

"He'd ordered me to bring you back. But as soon as I saw you, I knew I couldn't. Not to him, not as his mate, but as mine."

She lifted a brow, amused. "You thought I'd agree? What if I hadn't?"

He kissed her mouth, pressuring her to part her lips. When she leaned her head back and opened herself to him, he thrust his tongue into her mouth and squeezed her buttocks. Her hands stilled on his hips, her senses overwhelmed with his bold erotic moves. Barely able to stand, she trembled with excitement.

Her reaction to him spurred him on. His hands shifted to the small of her back and pressed her against his leg, strategically rocking between her legs to the music.

The increased tempo of the melody matched his more aggressive actions, stimulating her further. The crescendo drew her higher, toward the sun, the moon, and the planets in the far distant galaxy, to the stars that clung to the black velvet night, well beyond the earth and the gravity that held them captive. Her hand shifted to capture his leg and increased the pace.

"Ah, Bella," he groaned.

She moaned his name.

A smile stirred on his lips, and he hugged her tightly.

The influx of the orgasm rippled through her like a never-ending tumultuous waterfall. She kissed his mouth with enthusiasm, loving him for bringing her to climax without concern for his own cravings. She desired to transport him to the top as well but hoped they could continue the action for much longer, ensuring that her plan to keep him from sending her to his cousin would succeed.

Yet, loving each other like this, whether they left her home or not, proved more important to her than anything now. He released her body and yanked off his jeans, his own mouth kissing her back, not wanting to part from her, she imagined, as she didn't want to separate from him, not even for a second.

Bella's moves against Devlyn's body couldn't have been any more erotic, and when she came with just the rubbing of his thigh against her nub, he nearly spilled his seed. Even now, he fumbled to ditch his jeans so that he could penetrate her slick, wet folds before he lost it.

She wasn't just any *lupus garou,* but the best part of his life growing up. Fond memories of the good times of their youth still lingered in his mind, even now as he maneuvered Bella to the velour couch.

He tried to take it gradually, moving to the slower pace of the music again. He danced her toward the couch, his leg still deeply entrenched between hers, keeping her warm for the follow-up play.

Their hips swayed to the music, their greedy fingers exploring each other's backs. The notion of moving her faded away. The only thing that concerned him now was filling her again.

"Bella, I want you like a wolf does."

She nodded.

Did she feel the pull of the moon? Did she want to mate with him in the wild like a male wolf committed himself to a female? He could barely wait to breathe in the pine scent blowing in the breeze, mixed with the musky smell of her, or feel the cool air against their fur-covered skin, their noses touched in greeting, or tackle her in playful fun and then mate with her among the pine needles that carpeted the forest floor.

Climbing onto the couch on hands and knees, she wiggled her tight little butt suggestively and then grinned over her shoulder at him. He nearly laughed. Yeah, she was ready all right.

He ran his fingers between her firm buttocks and dipped them between her honeyed folds. Her body still shuddered from her orgasm, sending a streak of urgency into his overheated system. He leaned his pelvis against her smooth round bottom and pressed his erection into her channel, driving deeply, and then slowly pulled out.

Her breath nearly ceased when he reached underneath her and pressed his fingers against her abdomen, moving down to her curly hairs, and then her swollen nub. Stroking with renewed focus, he urged her to come again as he sought to give her pleasure. He thrust into her tight sheath, clutching him like a warm, wet, velvet glove.

He'd never imagined how good life could be with Bella at the center of it. The pack was important, but Bella was everything.

When he penetrated her deepest chasm, the music heightened the rhythm. Her pelvic muscles tightened. He closed his eyes and concentrated on the way she squeezed him tight, grasping him, as he pulled back, regaining her hold, when he thrust forward. The sensation heated his sweaty body and, with a final plunge, he released his seed. But his fingers still fondled her nub until her inner muscles shuddered, convulsing around him in orgasmic delight.

Turning her over, he lay down on top of her to feel her warm, soft body beneath him. Her eyes had darkened, and her body was glossy and lightly flushed. She was the most beautiful creature in the whole world, and all his. She felt so right to him, fitting perfectly against his body, moving in sync, every part of her exciting him beyond belief. But it wasn't just the lovemaking that hooked him. It was everything about her…the way she acted so agreeable and yet so aggravating at the same time. The way she'd wanted him but denied her love for him, fearing for his safety. The way she'd lived in silent terror under Volan's threat but never once told Devlyn, in an effort to keep him safe.

He'd wished he'd been stronger then, more able to protect her, more of a hero to her, but he couldn't continue to regret the past. The future stretched out before them. Taking it one day at a time had to suffice for now. Although he wanted to take her away from here, safe from all the evils of the world, he couldn't ruin the special moments they shared. Sleeping with her was as much a pleasure as any other moment he spent with her. Wrapping his arms around her for a few hours in blissful rest was the only plan he had for now.

Later, after they were well rested, he'd insist that she go to his cousin's place.

She raked her fingers through his hair, no doubt tangled and a mess. Her lips turned up. Seductive minx.

"Let's go to bed for a while, Bella." His voice was

still husky, but tired, too. He climbed off her, but before she could rise, he slipped his arms under her and lifted her from the couch.

"I could have walked, Devlyn. You must be worn out."

He growled. "You're talking to a gray, Bella." She didn't mean any insult, but the idea still gnawed at him that he hadn't been able to best Volan yet. Any comment about his stamina remained a sore spot with him for now. He'd tried to remark with a lighthearted air, but Volan—damn him—angered him even more as the news of Bella's past was revealed. He kissed her cheek and carried her into the bedroom. Before long, he was folded around her under the covers.

Bella snuggled with Devlyn, her head on his chest, listening to his steady breathing and heartbeat that lulled her toward sleep. One hand lightly stroked her back and the other touched her hair. She couldn't have been any happier now that she rested with the *lupus garou* she'd always loved. Wild and single-minded when it came to pleasing her. On the other hand, she couldn't deal with the cold truth that she'd killed Volan, and Devlyn would probably never forgive her. Or maybe knowing that Volan had tried to rape her as a juvenile would change his mind. She kissed his chest and then cuddled her cheek against it.

Living among the humans, she'd become only a shell of what she was. She gripped Devlyn tighter, not wanting to lose him again, ever, but feeling the ugly truth would come out sometime or another. He was bound to hear that someone had shot Volan outside the dance club. Oh man, and Thompson would place Devlyn and her at the club. They had the biggest gripe against Volan.

The situation couldn't get any worse. The police would consider Devlyn the most likely suspect. Hell, he said he'd kill Volan himself, right in front of Thompson.

She could leave a note, explaining to the police and Devlyn that she was the one who killed Volan for his attempting to rape her. The best scenario would be if she left Devlyn, ran somewhere else, lived the miserable life of a loner—anything to keep the police from arresting her mate.

"What are you thinking about, Bella?" Devlyn whispered, dreamily, half asleep.

"About how much I miss the pack, of being with them, of running wild as the wolf with them. Being on my own hasn't been the same. Running as a loner is… lonely, to say the least."

"You felt you had no choice." His fingers stroked her shoulder.

She nodded against his chest. "But…"

"What, Bella?" Already his voice sounded darker, more awake, wary.

"I think we need to make a stand, don't you?"

She meant against the reds—then she would be history—but she realized at once she should have said it differently. She wasn't used to playing alpha male games—let the male think he's making up all of the important plays, agree sweetly like the good mate she should be, and then ensure somehow that she got her own way.

She closed her eyes, waiting for the explosion.

"After we've had a good rest, my cousin will come for you and take you to California for safekeeping."

She clenched her teeth against speaking her mind and saying something hurtful. She reminded herself they both were exhausted, and she kept her lips sealed.

One thing he'd learn about her, he might be the alpha male, or at least was attempting to take on that role, but she was a lone wolf…a rogue, and had been for years. She played by her own rules, and until now—well, until she got thrown in the zoo—she'd done well enough on her own.

"Bella?" He waited for her agreement, but she couldn't give it.

"Sleep, Devlyn. I'm exhausted."

He continued to stroke her hair and back. "I'm calling my cousin when it's light out. I want you to stay with him while I take care of the reds."

No way was he going to tell her what to do. Yet, from his definitive tone, he expected to do just that, and she'd obey.

She glanced at her alarm clock. Dawn would break in another three hours or so. He *thought* she'd go along with him, just like that.

Wait until she woke up later. Once she had some sleep…she'd…

She yawned. She'd do something about it.

When Devlyn began to snore, she lay awake for another half hour, aggravated that she couldn't quiet her mind and sleep. Finally, she slipped out of his arms and left the room.

In her office, she turned on the computer and checked

her email. Argos was asking for an update. She clicked on his message but hesitated to answer. She wanted to ask his advice, but she couldn't. Despite being like a father to her, he had been a pack leader. He was sure to think she'd done the wrong thing in killing Volan the way she had.

Not bothering to send a reply, she checked the rest of her email. Alfred, Nicol, and Ross had all sent her messages.

She ignored them and stared at the subject of the last one.

Wicked Bella.

Her heart raced. The reds knew her real name now. Was it the murdering red who had learned her name from the others? The sender used her own email address, so no clue there. The other reds always used their real names so she'd know it was them.

She poised her finger on the mouse, took a deep breath, and clicked. The message opened up and the breath caught in her throat.

I'm invincible, don't you know, sweet Bella?
Invincible. Volan

A photo finished loading, a picture of the devil wolf himself, his unkempt black hair straddling his shoulders, his eyes and lips smiling without humor, his skin pale, not ruddy like it had been when she first spied him at the club.

How…how could he have survived?

"Bella?" Devlyn called out from the bedroom.

She turned off the computer, her heart racing. When had Volan sent the email? Before or after she killed him? How could he be alive? No, no, he wasn't alive. He'd sent the email to her before she met him at the club, angered that Devlyn wasn't bringing her home to him right away. That's why he called her wicked Bella. But the invincible part threw her.

Invincible because he could survive silver bullets?

"Bella!"

"Coming." She strode back to the bedroom, her skin prickling with fear.

Volan couldn't be alive. According to the legend, silver bullets that penetrated the brain or heart or were left elsewhere in the body and not removed right away could cause death. But what if the legend were just that—a made-up legend and not really true? Think, think. Had she ever known of a case where a silver bullet killed a *lupus garou*?

No, death because of fire, a cousin broke his neck when he was in his human form and jumped into a shallow river bed, but no one she actually knew had ever been killed by a silver bullet.

Reluctantly, she climbed back into bed, and Devlyn wrapped his arms around her, tightening his grip. His touch should have warmed her, but she was chilled to the center of her being. She was so stiff, Devlyn whispered into her ear, "Sleep, Bella honey."

But she couldn't. She tried to relax, tried to let Devlyn think everything was all right. But her mind wouldn't shut down.

Volan had to be dead. Otherwise, she'd made love to Devlyn thinking Volan was dead. She'd given herself freely to the man she'd wanted forever, only to get him killed. She didn't have to worry about Devlyn being arrested for Volan's murder, but now she fretted over her original fear—Volan was indomitable, as she'd always known, and he would terminate Devlyn.

Unless, Volan was really dead. He had to be.

She thought back to the dance club and the events that led up to her killing him and afterward. He went down like a felled redwood. And he didn't move again. For several minutes, he didn't move. But she hadn't checked his pulse, either. Did he have a pulse? She groaned inwardly.

But…but what if he'd been wearing a bulletproof vest?

No. Why in the world would he have done that? He was an alpha male pack leader. He could control her, he'd think. And she was certain he'd never believe she'd shoot him with silver bullets.

So what in the hell had gone wrong?

Devlyn took a heavy breath, and she sensed he'd fallen asleep again.

Then another distressing thought hit her. What if silver bullets did work as the legend stated, but the old-time blacksmith who'd made them for her had taken her silver and kept it? What if he'd used some other compound and the bullets weren't really silver at all?

She considered what had happened that day so long ago when she'd thought Volan was close on her trail and she'd found a smithy working at his anvil, his large, sinewy hands pumping the bellows to heat the fire. The sign hanging above the blacksmith's shop in the Arizona town proudly advertised his skills: wrought iron work, horse shoeing, wagon fixing, wagon wheels, pulling teeth.

But all she'd cared about was whether or not he could make bullets. *Silver* bullets.

She could still envision the way the big man stared back at her, his muscular arms bulging under his linen shirt, his bushy black brows raised, his mouth embedded in black whiskers and partially opened.

"Silver bullets," he'd repeated, like a parrot.

Bella had offered her most winsome smile. "My brother collects old bullets from the American Revolution, Civil War period, various types. A collector. Anyway, he was saying how he had about every size, shape, and kind of bullet known to man except for one."

"Silver bullets."

"Yes, sir. He's turning twenty-five and I wanted to give him a real keepsake. Will these be enough silver spoons for the job?"

The smithy wiped his sweaty hands on his apron and considered the silverware. Looking back up at her with eyes as black as the coal in his fire, he asked, "Are you sure you want to do this?"

"Yes, I'm sure."

"Come back in three hours. I have several other jobs before yours, miss."

"Yes, yes, thank you."

And then she'd left to spend time in the mercantile, purchasing some dried meat and other items for the trip she'd have to make. The widow MacNeil that she'd lived with had died the month before. Bella had stayed there long enough and needed to move on, especially if Volan had learned she was there. After buying her stage-coach passage for Idaho, she returned to the smithy's shop. He had already gone, but a note was left on a table with six silver bullets: for Bella MacNeil.

Then she'd left with her treasure, her protection against Volan. For the first time ever, she wasn't afraid.

Which made her wonder again, did the smithy keep the silver for himself and give her regular bullets?

If so, she had one more chance to protect herself. The gun at her cabin. Different smithy, this one at Donley's Wild West Town a few years ago in Chicago, when Bella thought it might be prudent to have two guns, one at each residence, both filled with silver bullets. Or at least she hoped.

Devlyn's arm twitched, and she breathed in his mas-culine scent.

God, how she loved her big gray, and how she hated having to leave him. But if Volan was truly alive, the nightmare would never end. As soon as they found out who the red killer was, she would run again.

An hour into her slumber, Bella woke. What was the sound she'd heard? A grinding of metal against metal? A key slipping into the front door lock?

# Chapter 15

BELLA LISTENED BUT DIDN'T HEAR ANY FURTHER sounds. Slipping out of Devlyn's arms, she was surprised he didn't wake. Her heart beating hard sent the blood rushing into her ears.

Maybe she'd dreamed she heard something. Maybe a branch scratched at the window out back. So why had it sounded like a key in the front door?

She pulled on her jeans and a T-shirt and then seized the 9 mm from her bedside table drawer where she'd hidden it again, minus two bullets. Silver or regular? She growled low under her breath but reminded herself that Volan *could* be dead.

Taking a step out of the bedroom, she listened with her fine-tuned hearing and sniffed the air for any sign of an intruder. Nothing. She turned in the direction of the kitchen. The house remained dark, although she could see like a wolf in the middle of the blackest night.

Her heart thundering, she crept closer to the kitchen. She sensed something, a hushed word, a faint rustling, something out of the ordinary. Then the smell…

She tilted her chin up, readying her weapon. It wasn't Volan's smell. *His* remained imprinted on her memory forever. She sniffed again. A red? But the scent confused her. More than one? Damn, the three of them?

Alfred entered the living room from the kitchen. Ross

and Nicol came from the dining room. All three paused when they spied her gun.

"Silver bullets," she said, loudly, hoping to wake Devlyn. She didn't want him to know she had a gun loaded with silver bullets, or at least what she thought had been silver bullets. Wolf to wolf combat was the way they settled things. However, she had no choice at the moment. "They were meant for Volan if he ever found me. But I have enough to use on the three of you also."

But in truth, she didn't want to waste the bullets on these three—silver or otherwise. She knew Devlyn could make them leave.

She listened behind her for sounds of Devlyn stirring. Poor old gray. She'd worn him out. *Wake up, Devlyn!*

Alfred inched toward her.

"You don't believe me?" She continued to speak loudly. *Devlyn!*

"I believe you, Bella, because you're scared of the gray, Volan. But I don't believe you'd use the bullets on one of us. We're your kind, no matter how much you choose to deny it."

He could see through her better than she'd hoped, and she didn't feel he would listen to reason. She tried another tactic. "One of you might be the killer of all those women," she lied, knowing none of their scents had been in the murdered girl's apartment. Then again, any one of them, or all three, could be covering for the bastard who killed her, which was just as bad. "I'd be doing the rest of our kind a big service if I ended his life."

"But which one, Bella? Which one of us would you choose? Surely you wouldn't want to kill two innocent *lupus garou. Two of your own kind*." He repeated the last words, attempting to sway her. "Of course, that's saying that one of us *is* the killer. It could be any of my pack, or even a lone, rogue wolf. No doubt some are living here. Why, look at you, sweet thing." Alfred's lips curved up. "Who would have ever thought we had a female right under our noses, living as a rogue for all of this time?"

"But we found evidence of her in the woods when we…" Ross said, but Alfred waved his hand to silence him.

He continued to cross the floor at an easy pace, his step shortened, trying not to force her into a corner where she might use the weapon on him. The others waited. *He* was the alpha male. It was his business to take her, to make her obey him. To force her to tuck her tail, whimper, and bow her head.

Having no intention of giving in to the red's words or actions, she lifted her chin and drew herself up as tall as she could. Then, remembering the gold necklace she found in the woods, she pulled it out of her pocket. "Recognize this?"

Alfred stared at it but didn't say a word. Nicol looked a little green.

"Never saw it before in my life," Alfred said. "What of it?"

"The killer dropped it after murdering one of the women. Sure you don't recognize it? Nicol seems to."

"That's a lie," Nicol snarled.

Something wasn't right. Did he know the killer? The girl the red had murdered?

She shoved the necklace back in her pocket. "Well, it's evidence that will put the killer away. As for the three of you, I want you to leave my home this instant."

Alfred sneered. "We can't, Bella. You belong to our pack now. Most important—you belong to me. I thought I'd made that abundantly clear."

The thought that she'd be Alfred's soured her stomach. "I thought we had a date later today, to bring you the fur sample." She took a step back toward the hall, hoping to keep him talking until she could wake Sleeping Beauty.

Alfred cast her a sinister smile. "I'll have the sample now. And you along with it." His dark-brown eyes suddenly focused on the hall behind her.

She thought she heard it, too. The sound like the shifting of a body on a mattress from the direction of the bedroom.

For a second, Alfred hesitated. Then he directed a deadly glower at Ross. Under his breath, he growled, "I thought you said he wasn't here."

"Listen, Alfred, Nicol, and Ross," she said, hoping that, if Devlyn heard her conversation with the reds, he'd realize they had three to handle. "I've already told you. I'm Devlyn's mate."

Then, as if worried the big gray would soon be more of a threat than Bella with her silver bullets, Alfred lunged at her.

---

Slowly aware something wasn't right, Devlyn had sensed he no longer wrapped Bella securely in his arms.

His eyes shot open. As groggy as he was, her harsh words, spoken loudly in the living room, forced a surge of adrenaline to spike his blood, readying him instantly to face the threat.

All that raced through his mind was saving Bella. He heard her say the reds' names, warning Devlyn that the three had broken into the house.

Naked, he rushed out of the room and down the hall. Before he reached his mate, Alfred lunged at her, shoving her hand up.

Devlyn's gaze pivoted to the gun she held. What the hell?

Alfred forced her to drop the weapon, and in the ensuing struggle, kicked it underneath the sofa. Instantly, Devlyn dove into Alfred. Knocking him aside, Devlyn broke the red's grip on Bella's arm.

Alfred jumped back. In a flash, he yanked a knife out of a sheath attached to his belt. Taunting Devlyn, he waved the weapon in front of him. He struck and then retreated.

With agility, Devlyn withdrew from him, away from Bella's direction, allowing her to escape. Facing the others, he ensured that they couldn't strike at his back in case they had the cowardly notion to do so.

Neither advanced for the moment, waiting for their leader to take care of the gray, as any pack *should* do.

"You can't do this," Bella screamed at Alfred. "You have to fight each other in your wolf form. It's our way!"

"He's too much of a coward," Devlyn goaded the red on. "He can't get you any other way."

Alfred's face reddened and his eyes narrowed

to angry slits. His lips formed a thin, grim line as he growled. Without warning, he slashed at Devlyn.

Devlyn jumped out of the path of the ten-inch blade. Bella gasped. Even now, Devlyn could smell the red's putrid fear. The red hunched over, like a *lupus garou* who knew he couldn't win. Yet, Alfred couldn't show his pack that he was unable to triumph over the female he had chosen for his own.

In an attempt to rile Alfred, to rattle him so that he'd make a fatal mistake, Devlyn provoked him further. "What's the matter, Alfred? Can't convince a human girl to agree to be your wolfmate?"

"You can't pin those murders on me."

Nicol advanced on Bella in two bounds. She dashed toward the kitchen. Both Nicol and Ross tore after her, forcing a splinter of ice down Devlyn's spine. They wouldn't endanger her, just take her for their own. *That* thought sent another charge of adrenaline through his system, urging him on to eliminate the threat.

Alfred sliced the air with the knife, aimed at Devlyn's chest. Devlyn dove out of his reach, the blade whooshing past his ear.

A drawer drew open in the kitchen and then slammed shut.

Alfred stabbed at Devlyn's throat. He dodged the blade. But Bella's situation distracted Devlyn. Not liking that he couldn't see what was happening to her, he backed toward the kitchen.

She growled. Nicol yelped. After what sounded like a chair crashing, Bella reappeared in the living room, brandishing a bloodied carving knife. Nicol and Ross followed some distance behind her while she backed away from them, her weapon readied.

Blood dripped from Nicol's arm, but he and Ross approached her anyway, one on either side. Checking on Bella, Alfred turned for an instant.

Devlyn grappled for his knife. Alfred swung at him again. Leaping out of the way, Devlyn narrowly missed the blade cutting his torso.

Bella waved her knife between Nicol and Ross. "Give it up," she snarled. "I don't want to hurt either of you."

"Volan will never let you have her," Devlyn said, hoping to talk some sense into them. *He* would never let them have her, but he hoped maybe the threat of two grays wanting her would make the reds cease and desist.

When Alfred continued to attack at him, Devlyn realized he had only two choices. Either he took Bella home to his territory where he assumed the reds would leave well enough alone, not wanting to fight a pack of larger grays, or he had to kill the reds at the first glimpse of the moon, when they all could appear in wolf form, here in their own territory.

Ross grabbed for Bella's arm. Nicol hesitated on her other side, favoring his bloodied arm. As soon as Ross seized her wrist, she struck at him with the knife, slicing across his arm. He screamed in pain, released her, and jumped back.

Devlyn couldn't help the swell of pride that filled him. In the same instant, he pounced on Alfred, knocking the red to the floor.

Alfred's head hit hard against the carpeted concrete.

An "oof" from deep within his chest escaped his lips from the jolt. A string of curses followed.

Devlyn pinned him to the floor with his bigger frame. He grappled with Alfred's arm, trying to free the knife from his hand, but it slipped and cut the red across the abdomen. Alfred squawked.

"Don't make a move toward them," Bella warned Ross and Nicol.

Managing to bend the red's wrist back, Devlyn pressured so hard that Alfred's thumb could no longer grasp the handle. Devlyn yanked the knife out of Alfred's hand.

Bella waved her weapon at Nicol and Ross. "I didn't want to hurt you. Any of you. But if you don't leave now—"

"He can't have you," Nicol said, backing off. Ross followed him. "The gray can't have you."

Devlyn let Alfred up. He would have killed them all for trying to take his mate, but only if they'd been in wolf form. As humans, they were bound to obey human law. As wolves, the law of the jungle prevailed. The strongest and most cunning won. Survival of the fittest.

"You can't have her," Alfred said, standing, his face flushed and his eyes haunted. "She's a red and in our territory." His words were dark and menacing, but he bowed his head like a beta wolf in front of the alpha male, defeated and not willing to be whipped any further, submitting to the gray, no matter how much it hurt his male wolf pride.

"We fight like wolves the next time," Devlyn said, his gaze intense, forcing the reds to agree.

Even if Alfred and his followers didn't like the idea of dealing with him wolf to wolf, their failed attempt at taking Bella had wounded the red pack leader's pride too deeply to try again. Plus, their injuries would need time to heal. Then the moon's appearance would tell all.

They would make their stand in the wilderness, Devlyn against Alfred at first and then facing the others. Whoever desired the female red would make his move.

"By the next moon," Alfred said, clutching his stomach, the blood soaking his shirt, his eyes hostile but his face turning pale. He glanced at Bella, who was still holding the kitchen knife at the ready. "You'll be mine, sweet thing. Be ready." He staggered toward the front door with the others trailing behind, clutching their bloodied arms.

"They must have followed us here," Bella said when Devlyn locked the door behind the reds' hasty flight, returning the knife to the kitchen. "They must have had lock picks like you carry."

Nothing mattered to him for the moment except the gun she'd wielded and the secrets she'd withheld from him. "Where did you get the gun, Bella?"

She headed for the bedroom, her hips swaying suggestively with her walk, her buttocks covered in the tight jeans, tantalizing him. But she refused to answer him.

He hastened after her, wearied from sleepless exhaustion and fighting with the red. The hyped-up adrenaline that readied him for danger started to drain as the threat vanished. Yet a new energy stirred, a deeper, more primal urge.

He chastised himself. They needed sleep more than anything else.

His gut clenched with irritation. He would kill Volan,

proving to Bella and to the pack that he served as the alpha male, no other. In the ancient way they had to end this. Not with a man-made invention. Besides, only fictional tales stated that a silver bullet in the heart or brain could kill a *lupus garou*. Nothing in ancient *lupus garou* folklore made reference to such a thing, although many of his kind believed there might be a thread of truth in the fictional stories.

He combed his fingers through his unkempt hair as he entered the bedroom. Standing before the bed, Bella pulled up her T-shirt slightly, her eyes averted, her fingers unzipping her jeans.

Hell, she'd probably end up wounding herself and never get a shot off at the wolf.

"Bella," he said, drawing closer as she pulled off her pants, invading her space. "What kind of bullets are in the gun?"

She glared at him.

*Silver bullets.* He knew it. Just the way her eyes darkened and narrowed into daggerlike slits. Damn her. She couldn't take down Volan. He had to. What the hell was she thinking? "You can't use them on him, Bella. He's *mine*."

She took a deep breath. "If he comes around and you're not here to save me, he's *mine*." She yanked off her shirt.

She wouldn't win this argument. *He* would be the alpha male of their pack. The gun and its deadly bullets would have to go.

Instantly, the sight of her perky breasts, the nipples already hardened and darker from her exertion, the quickened pace of her breath, and the redness of her cheeks turned him on. She glanced down and frowned at his erection, beckoning to her to give it release.

At once, he throbbed with a deep-seated primal lust, inspiring him to take her again. He couldn't help that the sight of her sent his blood rushing south. She could feign being mad at him all she wanted. But the way she licked her lips and folded her arms under her creamy breasts…the way her heated eyes took in every inch of his body, she wanted him, too.

"What if they return?" she asked, her gaze shifting to his eyes.

Just the opening he was looking for.

"They won't, sweet Bella." God, how he loved her. "Alfred and his gang will wait for the next phase of the moon. As *lupus garous,* he and the others must honor this."

"But they're afraid of you. They're worried about some legend to do with a gray. Do you think all of them will be honorable enough to hold up the bargain?"

"Their wounds would put them at too great a disadvantage. They wouldn't risk it." Devlyn frowned. "What was the legend they were concerned about?"

She ran her finger around his nipple and he sucked in his breath.

"That some big gray got rid of a red leader who was bad for the pack."

"Ah." His lips curved up. "My great-grandfather."

"What? The gray couldn't have been your great-grandfather. He killed Alfred's great-grandfather, so he must have been from this area, not Colorado."

"Alfred's great-grandfather?" Devlyn shook his head. "Ever hear of the Gold Rush?"

She tilted her chin down, giving him a look as if she knew better. "In California, not Oregon."

"Over seventy million dollars in gold was panned out of the Rogue River. My great-grandfather had the gold fever bad, but after he had the run-in with the red pack leader living in the area and because none of our kind lived there, he returned to Colorado to be with our pack." Devlyn combed his fingers through Bella's hair, separating the silky strands over her shoulders. "Who would have ever thought my ancestor was the one to set things right with this same pack. But it appears the bad seed continued through Alfred, and he managed to take over like his great-grandfather."

Bella licked Devlyn's nipple and his groin tightened. "Alfred would have a heart attack if he knew you were a descendent of the same gray."

He chuckled. "Maybe we should send him an email and tell him so...end his misery sooner." Placing his hands on either side of her cheeks, he lifted her face to his. "I want you, Bella, more than I can say."

Her hands swept down his sides, stirring him all over again. He moaned. How could a small red *lupus garou* female bring him so quickly to his knees?

Devlyn climbed into bed first and reached his hand out to Bella. When her fingers touched his, he wrapped his hand around hers and pulled her on top of him. His brown eyes, as dark as midnight, gazed into hers with the familiar longing of a wolf desiring the satisfaction only his mate could fulfill.

She leaned over and kissed the corner of his mouth, loving him for everything he stood for. Brushing her lips over the rest of his mouth, she ended with a kiss on the other corner. He tangled his fingers in her hair.

"I promise I won't use the bullets on Volan, unless—"

His face darkened. He rested his hands lightly on her hips, adjusting her squarely on top of his rigid erection, and impaled her.

"Unless," she continued, sucking in her breath as he penetrated her, stealing her thoughts briefly, "I have no other choice."

"By no other choice, you mean that he has killed me. I won't have you using the gun on him for any other reason."

*Damned male wolf pride.*

She slid up his erection and down again, holding him tight within her, stroking his needs as he reached his fingers between her legs and began to stroke her.

She licked his nipple. "Yes, that's what I meant."

"That if I were dead—"

She clamped her mouth over his, not wanting him to say another word about the fact that he might die in this fated confrontation with the alpha gray.

"Make love to me, Devlyn, as if we haven't another care in the world."

She didn't think either of them could manage to climax with as little sleep as they'd had, but his spine-tingling strokes over her swollen nub sent her hormones spiraling toward a cataclysmic end. She nearly sank down, so close to reaching the climax, unable to think of anything else, and then the white-hot heat washed over her. The heart-stirring waves of completion clouded her mind with awe and deep satisfaction.

She would have curled up against Devlyn's chest and drifted off to a dream-filled, wondrous sleep if it hadn't been for his rolling her over and finishing her off. He felt so good, every inch of him diving into her, her own body still pulsing around him, clutching him and releasing, a vague awareness drifting to her that he had finished.

He released his warm, wet seed deep inside of her and collapsed on top of her with a tired groan. "You…" he said, his words a heavy whisper, "are unbelievably wonderful."

She wrapped her arms around him. He turned over onto his back so she could sleep with her head against his chest, one leg propped over his.

A wolf that exposed his belly gave the other wolf complete power over him. He was all hers, every inch of the hunky, muscular, very slick gray *lupus garou*.

His hand swept down her backside and then touched her wet folds from behind. He could have his way with her all morning long if that's what he desired. She raised her leg up to expose herself to him further. He hummed his pleasure against the top of her head. He pulled her leg even higher against his belly. He groggily whispered, "Hmm, Bella, one hot little red wolf."

"Ready anytime, Devlyn."

He chuckled. "Making up for lost years, honey."

She wiggled against him. "Fill me up whenever you have the urge."

His sexually hungry growl meant she wouldn't have

to wait very long, which suited her fine. She brushed her
face against his cheek, smelling the spicy, male scent of
him, hoping that nothing else—like red *lupus garous* or
Volan—would disturb their sleep or other, stimulating
activities they might wish to explore later that morning.

Yet she wondered what happened to Devlyn's plan
for her to stay with his cousin? Had he given up on that
notion? Or would she have to fight him all over again
when they woke?

Worse, the threat of Volan still hung heavy in her
thoughts. Was he dead or not?

---

Early the next afternoon, Devlyn found Bella gone,
*again*. Searching through the house, he found no sign of
her. But the fresh, sweet fragrance of cut flowers sitting
on the dining room table in a glass vase caught his eye.
He glanced outside and saw the greenhouse door open.
Then he noticed Bella's silhouette against the green
glass building, and the prickle in his gut dissipated.
Stalking across the yard, he reached the greenhouse and,
with a squeak, shut the door behind him as he entered
the building.

He stared at the plants in wonder. Colorado wildflowers from alpine columbine and aspen daisies to scarlet
paintbrush and fireweed.

"Do you like it?" Bella asked, watering a trough of
violets, barely looking Devlyn's way.

He considered Bella in the ankle-length robe she
wore, the forest-green velvet clinging to her curves, her
hair dangling in a fiery display in contrast against the

fabric, her feet bare. "What's not to like?" His voice was already several shades huskier than normal.

He placed his hands on her shoulders and nuzzled his face in her hair. "You smell like a garden of flowers."

"That's because we're standing in a greenhouse full of them," she teased, leaning against his chest, pressing against his heavy groin.

He took her hand and ran his nose over the silky skin. "Your hand smells like roses, and your hair like Persian lilac. *You* smell like a floral garden." He nudged his cheek against her throat and she moved her head so he had better access. His hands dipped lower, to the tassel tie belted at her waist.

"I have work to do," Bella said, but she didn't stop him, either.

"The work will get done, but this can't wait." He pressed his arousal against her backside and she smiled.

"If we keep doing it, I won't be able to walk normally for a week."

"Hey, just think if we were in our wolf coats."

Bella laughed. "Well, I've seen a wolf and his mate go at it, but…"

"Half an hour at a time? Multiple times? Just know what you're getting yourself into when the moon appears." He pulled her robe open and slid his hands over her breasts.

She turned and smiled when she saw he was wearing jeans but was barefoot and shirtless. "You're dressed. Kind of."

"Easily remedied." He tackled his zipper. "Afraid Chrissie's kids might peek through a knothole in the redwood fence and see something they shouldn't?"

"Good thinking. But I believe Chrissie's the only one who might do something like that, particularly now that you're around." Bella kissed Devlyn's chest, her hair dangling against his nipples, raising them into tight knots. She licked one and hummed.

Devlyn broke free and locked the door. Thankfully, the greenhouse windows were fogged up enough that only Bella and Devlyn's silhouettes could be seen from the outside.

He yanked off his jeans and slipped the robe down Bella's shoulders, exposing every inch of creamy skin. She was every guy's wet dream and more.

After spreading the fabric over the mossy floor, he motioned to the makeshift bed. "My lady?"

She laughed. "So gallant."

"Only for a minute." Without further ado, he swept her off her feet, and she squealed. "I hope Chrissie doesn't think she needs to come to your rescue."

He pressed a steamy kiss to Bella's ear and then set her on the robe. Grasping her knees, he moved them apart, opening her to his touch. "My garden princess. I see you missed more than just me in our home in Colorado." He kissed one shoulder and then licked the other.

She cupped his face and looked into his eyes, hers dark-amber gems. "I never ever thought my garden could bring me *this* much pleasure."

He gave her a wolfish grin. "You always know the right words to say, Bella honey."

"But you always know the right moves to…ah, Devlyn," Bella mouthed against his lips, his tongue probing hers, his fingers separating her womanly folds.

The fragrance of sweet flowers scented the greenhouse, but Bella was the most irresistible flower of them all. Her hands shifted downward, pressing his buttocks, pressuring him to enter her.

With a single hard thrust, he impaled her, entering her secret garden, deeper with every movement, rubbing her mound, pushing her toward the top.

She matched his enthusiasm, rocking against him, striving for deeper penetration, until he found sweet release, planting his seed inside her, his body on fire.

Nipping his shoulder, she stifled a cry, her internal muscles clamping down on him, milking him for everything he had.

Totally spent, he rolled off her and pulled her on top of him. "I like this garden room of yours very much," he said, his voice drenched in passion. He winked at her.

"I just bet you do. But I had lots of work to get caught up on and now I'm...well, awfully relaxed."

He wrapped his arms around her and held her tight. "The work will get done."

*But it didn't.*

---

For an hour, they slept in peaceful bliss in the garden of flowers while a storm raged around them. A bolt of lightning crashed close by, shaking Bella from her state of slumber. She frowned at Devlyn, who opened one sleepy eye and gazed at her.

"I had work to do," she groused.

His lips curved up in a wicked smile. "You sure did."

After helping her up, he grabbed his jeans and pulled them on.

When she slipped her robe over her shoulders, he pulled her into his arms and nuzzled her cheek with his. "What can I do to help?"

She groaned. What she wanted him to do was take her back to bed and ravish her all over again.

His eyes lighted with fire and he grinned. "Does my little red wolf need some more—"

She pulled out of his embrace before he talked her into returning to the house. "Here," she said, handing him some gardening clippers. "Cut off the dead flowers. I'll finish watering."

After finishing the chores in the greenhouse, Bella and Devlyn made a wild dash through the rain to the house. Intending to wash their bed linens, she declined taking a shower with him for now or she'd never get the cleaning done.

"I'll fix us something to eat as soon as I'm through here," he hollered from the bathroom, the steamy spray muffling his words.

She finished stripping the bed. "All right by me." But what she really wanted was a good four more hours of sleep. She dumped the dirty sheets on the floor and remade the bed with fresh linens. By the time she had finished showering and dressing, Devlyn was in the kitchen cooking—in the raw again.

She dumped the linens in the washing machine, started it, and then wandered into the kitchen, feeling as though she could move at only half speed. Sitting down, she leaned against the dining room table.

Devlyn glanced over from his cooking, the long German sausages sizzling in the frying pan for their brunch, filling the kitchen with the scent of spicy pork. Bella leaned her elbows against the table and rested her head against the palm of her hand. She cast a tired smile in his direction. He smiled back.

Soft, pale-blue sweats covered her curvy body. Already he was prepared to slip her sweats off and make love to her again. Only he'd done so three more times that morning, and the final time, when she rose from the greenhouse floor, she'd been a little stiff, like a cowgirl who'd been riding a bull too long.

Her eyes appeared blurry. She hadn't had enough sleep, nor, truthfully, had he. Once they ate, he planned on taking a nap with her, although he feared to get any sleep he'd have to move to her couch. The memory of making love on the couch filled his thoughts, her tight bottom wiggling suggestively at him, the smile playing on her lips, the feel of her soft buttocks pressing against him when he entered her. He chuckled. Well, he couldn't think of one place she'd be safe from his advances.

He poked at the sausages and then flipped them over. "Blueberries all right this morning?"

"Mmm-hmm."

"Some sourdough muffins?"

This time she didn't respond. He turned to look at her. She cradled her head on the crook of her arm. Her cinnamon curls cascaded over the table, like a silken red waterfall. She'd closed her eyes, and her face appeared totally at rest. He chuckled.

But then a knocking at the back door just about unhinged him.

He stalked to the back door and peeked out the curtained window. Chrissie smiled back at him, her brows raised.

Growling under his breath, he opened the door. Her gaze instantly focused lower, on his nakedness. He motioned for her to come in. "Be right back. I'll throw some jeans on." Even though Bella was going to wash them.

"No need to on my account," Chrissie said dreamily while he strode down the hall.

It didn't matter to him that she saw him in the raw, but if he'd stayed that way with Chrissie in the house and Bella had known, that was another story.

After he yanked on a pair of jeans, he stalked back to the kitchen. Chrissie had served up the sausages and muffins, preventing them from scorching, thankfully.

"Did you want to eat with us?" he asked, assuming there was no polite way of getting rid of the woman. On the other hand, since she'd saved their butts the previous night, they kind of owed her.

Chrissie glanced at Bella. "Looks like you might have a time waking her to eat. What did you do to tucker her out so?" A smile appeared. "Forget it. I already know the answer."

He ignored her, wishing Bella didn't have such an intrusive neighbor. Leaning over Bella, he kissed her ear. "Bella honey, do you want to eat?"

She murmured something inaudible.

"Okay." He lifted her from the chair and carried her down the hall to the bedroom. After laying her on the mattress, he hesitated. He didn't want to disturb her slumber, but since they didn't wear anything to sleep in, and he intended to join her after he ate breakfast…

The decision was already made for him. He slid her sweats off, first the pants and then her shirt. He groaned to see her sweet body. Never would he get his fill of her. Hurriedly, he pulled the comforter over her. Then he strode out of the room, shutting the door behind him before he changed his mind and joined her.

When he reached the dining room, Chrissie had already poured glasses of milk for them.

"I would have gotten you some orange juice, but you don't seem to have any."

He downed the milk. "Milk's good for growing bones."

Chrissie sighed. "And muscles. Don't forget the muscles."

"Do you often visit Bella in the morning, or did you have some news?"

"I didn't mean to barge in on the two of you, but since it was later in the morning, I figured—" Chrissie's cheeks reddened. "Well, I assumed you'd both be up and ready to face the day." She buttered her muffin and lifted it from the plate. "In truth, I wanted to tell you that Henry called me earlier and said he'd talked to the police chief. The warrants for your arrest and Bella's have been rescinded."

Somewhat relieved, Devlyn nodded. "Thanks so much for all of your help last night, Chrissie. I don't think we had the chance to express our gratitude."

Fingering her muffin, she grinned. "Do you eat Wheaties?"

He stabbed a sausage. "Meat, and lots of it."

"Ah. I'm sorry for making up a story so different from the truth. I worried that when Henry heard the real version, he would have been madder."

"Well," Devlyn said, lifting his forkful of sausage, "I'm glad it all worked out fine."

He got the distinct impression something was bothering Chrissie, but he wasn't used to having human friends or the way in which they were afraid to speak frankly. With *lupus garous,* if they wanted something, they normally came out and said it.

Dipping the butter knife into the blackberry jam, he coated his muffin, the smell of the wild berries tantalizing him. He envisioned Bella bending over to pick the strong, flavorful fruit in the wilderness, her denims hugging her buttocks. Licking the sweet, tangy jam off his muffin brought an image of the wild to him, creating the urge again to run through the brambles, to chase Bella through the woods on a carefree romp. The idea of finishing breakfast and joining her in bed quickly filled his thoughts.

He looked up from his muffin to see Chrissie watching him with adoration in her eyes. Or maybe a bit of lust. Inwardly, he smiled. She couldn't handle a *lupus garou,* no matter how badly she thought she wanted him. "Is something bothering you?"

She looked back at her plate and then up at Devlyn. "I'm worried about this Volan. Henry showed me the picture of him and said that if the man came around my place asking about Bella, he wanted me to know what he looked like. He feared the man might get violent, considering how he left Bella naked at the zoo in subfreezing temperatures. He must have wanted her dead." She watched him for his reaction.

"He's dangerous all right."

"There's something else. I thought I heard car doors slamming in the middle of the night. As sleepy as I was, it took me a few minutes for the noise to register. Then I wondered who it would be that late at night. So I threw on some clothes and looked out the living room window, but I didn't see a soul, only a jeep parked in front of my house. I watched for quite a while and then, figuring whoever it was wouldn't be returning any time soon, I walked into the kitchen to get a drink of water. But I thought it odd that the vehicle was parked in front of my house. When I returned to the living room window and peeked out, the jeep had disappeared."

Devlyn took a deep breath. "Maybe it was someone at the wrong house."

"I instantly thought of Volan and called Henry, but I couldn't get hold of him. I was going to come over here to check on you, but the house remained dark and, well, then the jeep vanished."

"We must have been sleeping like tired, old dogs." Chrissie grinned.

He got the impression she didn't think they were all that tired, or old, or that they had been sleeping. Although about now he sure could use a nap. He grabbed his plate and pointed to her half-eaten breakfast. "Done?"

"Sure." She jumped up from her chair.

He carried the plates into the kitchen. "We watched movies until way too late last night. I hope you don't mind, but I'm going to join Bella for a nap."

"Oh…oh, sure." Chrissie headed for the back door. "If you two need anything from me, be sure and holler."

The door shut on her hasty exodus, and he returned to the bedroom only to find Bella gone. For an instant, the image of the reds ferreting Bella away flashed through his mind. He tore into the bathroom, hoping she was taking a shower, although he didn't hear the sound of the shower spray or smell any dampness in the air.

As he suspected, she wasn't there.

He stormed out of her bedroom, down the hall, and into her office.

Sitting in her chair with her chin propped in her hands and wearing her sweats once again, she stared at the monitor. Bright colors zigzagged across the screen, darting hither and thither against the stark blackness.

"Bella?"

She gave a start. "Oh, Devlyn."

He crossed the floor and knelt at her side. "Bella, what's wrong, honey?"

"I woke and didn't find you with me. Then I heard Chrissie talking to you in the kitchen, but I was too tired to speak to her. I couldn't sleep, and I wondered if I had any new messages to clue us in about the killer."

He touched her cheek and then looked at the screen saver.

Sighing deeply, she nestled her cheek against his hand. "I guess I forgot what I was doing."

"What you are doing is taking a well-deserved nap, now, with me. We'll look at the messages later. We're both too exhausted to make any sense of anything."

She raised her arms to him. "Help me up."

"I'll do even better than that." He lifted her in his arms, and she nestled her head against his chest.

"I see you put on some jeans."

"I didn't think you'd approve of Chrissie seeing me without."

She gave a low growl. "You're right. I can be awfully possessive."

"All right by me." He carried her down the hall to the bedroom and deposited her in the bed. "You shouldn't have gotten dressed."

She touched his zipper and instantly his arousal strained against the denim. No wolf could ever get him worked up as fast as Bella.

Knocking at the back door interrupted them and sent a ripple of anger shooting down his spine. "Now what?" Devlyn growled.

"If it's Chrissie, I'll take care of it." Bella sounded grumpy and climbed off the bed.

Knocking sounded again, louder this time.

"Maybe we should ignore her. I told her I was taking a nap with you."

Bella's lips turned up. "What did she say to that?"

"I think she didn't believe we were going to nap."

"Not with her pounding on the door every few minutes." Bella swept her hair out of her face, and he wanted to kiss her pursed lips.

"I'll take care of it." Devlyn stormed out of the bedroom, figuring an annoyed male might persuade the woman to vamoose more easily than his mate would. Before he could make it to the back door, Bella's feet tromped on the carpet behind him at a hurried pace to keep up.

When he turned to look at her, she smiled. "Didn't want you to be too brusque."

"Not me." But he had the feeling that, if Bella weren't so tired, her neighbor might see the darker side of Bella's persona. Yanking open the door, he tried to quell the ire building in his own blood.

Chrissie gave a nervous smile. "Uh, I'm sorry, folks, to disturb you again." Twisting a piece of her dark hair between her fingers, she looked quickly from him to Bella—who stood slightly to the left of his shoulder— and back to him again.

Wary that something was seriously the matter, he motioned to the living room instead of sending the woman packing. She glanced at Bella, as if asking if she approved. Smiling wearily, Bella nodded.

Devlyn linked his fingers with Bella's and followed Chrissie into the sitting area.

"I'm sorry, Bella, Devlyn, but something's been bothering me." Chrissie took her seat on the couch.

Devlyn and Bella sat on the love seat opposite her. Immediately, Bella rested her head against Devlyn's shoulder. He wrapped his arm around her and squeezed.

"Henry told me not to say anything to you, but I think he mentioned it to me, hoping I would tell you. He really admires the way the two of you seem so much in love. He knows that Devlyn is only trying to protect you, Bella. But, well, something about your story didn't add up."

Bella kept her head on Devlyn's shoulder, but her whole body tensed.

"What did he say, Chrissie?" Devlyn prompted, wondering if he would have to take Bella back to Colorado earlier than planned and forgo solving the red *lupus garou* killer mystery. Bella's safety was tantamount, above all else.

"Can I have a glass of water?" Before anyone could respond, Chrissie hopped up from the couch and headed into the kitchen. "Sorry," she hollered. "I'm a little nervous."

Bella shook her head.

Devlyn kissed her forehead and gave her another squeeze of reassurance.

"Yeah, like that," Chrissie said, pointing with her index finger wrapped around a glass of water. "He saw how caring you are toward one another. Refreshing to see."

"What didn't add up, Chrissie?" Devlyn asked, trying to curb his irritation.

She sat back down on the couch. "It was the zoo scene. Volan has never been sighted anywhere. At the hospital, the zoo, nowhere."

"At the dance club," Devlyn reminded her.

"Yes, yes, of course. But that's the first time."

Devlyn attempted to look unruffled by the revelation. "Henry said he remembered Volan struck him."

"That's the problem. You and Volan are similar in build and have similar coloration."

"No," Bella said. "Devlyn's hair is brown and Volan's hair is black."

"Devlyn's hair is dark brown, and inside it looks nearly black." Chrissie sipped some of her water. Her gaze shifted from Devlyn back to Bella. "The thing is, Devlyn is the one who's always in the picture, not

Volan. Then there's you, Bella. But he's trying to protect you. Henry understands that. He said he's sure you
told the truth about Volan as far as being afraid of him
and what he'd do to you. But it's the other part of the
story that doesn't fit."

"What doesn't add up?" Devlyn asked again.

"Why didn't Volan grab Bella at the hospital? If he'd
already knocked out Henry and the cops, how come he
didn't get Bella? Where was he? The receptionist said she
never saw the man. The police said they'd been knocked
out from behind and had never seen who hit them.

"Henry believes it was you, Devlyn, fearing for
Bella's safety; you couldn't explain the situation to the
police adequately, so you knocked them out and stole
her away."

She paused, waiting for confirmation of what she
said, but when they remained silent, she continued.
"The real problem is the zoo. If Volan didn't release the
wolf and leave Bella in the pen naked, who did? Henry
knows you wouldn't have, Devlyn. You would never
risk Bella's life like that. The only conclusion he can
come up with is that you're protecting someone else.
Maybe this Argos, your adoptive father? Maybe he's a
bit crazy and he—"

"No," Bella said.

Devlyn rubbed her hand. "Why is Henry so sure Volan
wasn't at the zoo earlier? What proof does he have?"

Chrissie swallowed hard. "The police arrested Volan
early this morning."

Bella sat upright, her heartbeat racing.

Chrissie studied her. "He had airline tickets."

Devlyn took a steadying breath.

"The airline verified that Volan's flight was delayed in Denver, so he couldn't have made it to Portland in time to free Rosa, the red wolf, or to leave Bella there. He was still stuck in Denver when someone rescued Bella from the hospital. Henry wondered if perhaps Volan had an accomplice. He figures if Volan flew to Portland and then showed up at the dance club, he really had come after Bella."

"Is Volan still in jail?" Bella asked, her voice hollow. Already her cheeks had grown as pale as the fresh fallen snow of the Great Rockies.

Chrissie shook her head. "Once he could prove he had nothing to do with the zoo or hospital incident, the police couldn't hold him any longer." She sat forward on the couch. "Listen, I've known you for a long time, and I've never seen you so scared. I know what you say about this Volan guy is true. Henry believes it, too. But nobody can help you if you don't go to the police and make a statement about what he's done to you."

Devlyn grunted. What had happened to Bella had occurred way before Chrissie's grandfather was even born.

"Oh, and Henry knows Volan's connected to the zoo somehow, because he'd tried to get Rosa transferred to the Denver zoo. That's why Henry mentioned that maybe you knew of an accomplice Volan might have had working for him."

Devlyn couldn't think of what to say. Bella's hand turned ice cold, and he rubbed it, trying to warm it.

"No one gave Volan any indication where Bella lived, did they?" he fairly growled.

"Henry wouldn't tell the police her address. He feared someone might leak it to the press, to Volan, or to his accomplice, because he must have one. Unless…" Again she swallowed hard. "Unless, the two of you freed Rosa and…" She shook her head. "But you wouldn't have left Bella to freeze to death in the pen. So what really happened?"

# Chapter 16

BELLA GRIPPED DEVLYN'S HAND AS IF AN OCEAN current tugged her out to sea and she would drown if she let go. Her mother had always warned her to stay away from humans. They'd never accept the *lupus garou*'s ways. Now, so many years after her mother's untimely death, those words haunted her.

Bella could never explain the truth to Chrissie. Yet she'd cherished her friendship with her...until now. But protecting her mate and the *lupus garous* took priority.

Immediately, she wanted to return home, to the grays that had taken her in, to a life where she could run with the pack and share the bonds that made them alike as well as the differences that made them unique. She wearied of hiding who she was, wanting nothing more than to be Bella, *lupus garou,* free to run on the wild side on moon-filled nights and enjoy the gifts being human meant, too.

On the other hand, the notion that Volan was confirmed to be perfectly alive, searching for her, and that he would kill Devlyn filled her with dread. Hell, after she shot him, he probably wanted to kill her, too.

Chrissie wrung her hands while the silence stretched between them. Devlyn waited for Bella to answer Chrissie's question as to what had really happened at the zoo that night when Rosa escaped and Bella was left to freeze to death in the pen.

Weaving a new story, like a black widow spider ties the silken strands together into a web full of holes and deceit…how could she spin another lie like that?

"I don't know what to say." Sometimes the truth was better off said.

"Henry told me you're hiding the truth. That you're afraid of more than just Volan. I've been your friend for a long time and I want to help. So does Henry." Chrissie looked at Devlyn and then faced Bella again. She rose from the couch. "But Henry and I can't help if you're not totally honest with us."

Henry and Chrissie couldn't help even if they *were* totally honest with them. Despite liking the two of them so much, Henry and Chrissie couldn't refrain from being terrified if they knew of the real existence of *lupus garou*. No, Bella and her Rosa, one and the same, would have to remain a mystery to Henry, Chrissie, and any other curious human. Although Bella contemplated telling Chrissie that she feared the killer of redheaded women was after her, to give Henry and his police friends another reason why she was so concerned, she worried their interference could delay Bella and Devlyn's locating the murderer and ending his terror.

Chrissie sighed. "All right, if you change your mind, I'll be next door as usual. Um, do you think I could borrow some flowers from your greenhouse to make an arrangement? Henry really loved the way your house is filled with plants—like an extension of nature's beauty. He's genuinely into that sort of thing."

"Take whatever you'd like. And thanks for all of your help, Chrissie. We're just really tired, and neither of us can think straight," Bella said.

"Yeah, all those late-night movies," Chrissie said, winking.

Bella looked at Devlyn. He smiled back at her.

"See ya." Chrissie headed out the back door.

Devlyn pulled Bella from the couch. "Now, we get some sleep. But now I'm worried things are getting too hot around here for us."

"We have to catch the killer." Bella had no intention of leaving the Portland area until they did. Yet Devlyn had made no mention of her going to California with his cousin again, and she wondered—although she wasn't about to bring it up—why he had let the matter drop.

Devlyn walked with Bella to the hall and then made a detour to the front window. He peeked out and then turned and faced her.

Her heartbeat quickened when she saw the concerned look on his face. "Company?" she asked.

"Yeah. Seems we have some guard dogs on our tail."

"The police?"

"Plainclothes stakeout. Maybe Henry's worried that Volan's accomplice will show up unexpectedly. Or Volan himself."

She swallowed hard at the thought that Volan truly lived and could arrive any time on her front doorstep and that the final scene would play out between Devlyn and him...

Devlyn crossed the floor to join her. Taking his hand, she enjoyed the strength, warmth, and size of it, knowing he'd always be there to protect her if he could. They walked toward the bedroom, their steps betraying the tiredness they both felt.

Bella yawned. "Henry must have assumed that the jeep pulled up in front of Chrissie's house in the middle of the night meant trouble."

"Yeah. He probably wishes he'd had someone watching us before this."

They stripped out of their clothes, intent on getting sleep. Both considered the other's body with interest. The knowing look they shared turned into grins.

Devlyn drew her into his arms. "Sleep. Then I'll have something ready for you." He rubbed his cheek against hers.

His touch triggered interest, yet she yawned again. Both chuckled. "Can't wait to see what gifts you want to bestow on me."

She wished, as they climbed into bed and snuggled together, that nothing else mattered. That the red who killed the women had already been caught and put out of his misery, and Volan, too. That they were again home with the pack and Devlyn now served as the leader. But none of those wishes would come true without a fight, and the fear that the one left standing might not be the right one sent a shiver down her spine.

---

Later that evening, Bella woke to find Devlyn gone. Lightning flashed across the dark sky and distant thunder grumbled. A steady rain beat against the bedroom window at a slant, a perfect setting for snuggling longer under her down comforter. Listening for sounds of Devlyn in the shower, she touched her wet hair and remembered showering with him already. The memory of his large hands massaging her breasts, slippery with peach soap, heated her body. She tilted her nose up and smelled for any signs he was cooking dinner, although she vaguely remembered licking whipped cream and blueberries off his chest sometime earlier. Worried she might grow weak from lack of food, he'd enticed her to eat a bite. Heaven knows how her snack had ended up on his chest.

Domestic life with Devlyn was anything but domestic.

The email butler announced a new message. *The office*.

Slipping out of bed, she peered into the oval mirror hanging above her dresser. Her hair rested about her shoulders in a tangled, fiery-red mess. Well loved... that's the way she appeared. The image sparked a secret little thrill. Her left cheek wore a faint redness...the result of his nuzzling her with his scratchy stubble of a beard at sometime or another in their bedtime romps.

A telltale hickey graced her right breast. She quirked a brow, trying to recall when he'd done that.

Without dressing, she wandered into her office. Devlyn sat at the desk, staring at her computer, intensely reading the messages.

Running her hand over his naked back, she felt his muscles instantly tighten. He turned and pulled her into his lap. "Bella honey."

"Find anything?"

He slipped his fingers between her legs. "Mmm-hmm, nice and wet, too."

She chuckled. "I mean about the reds, or the killer or something. You sure have a one-track mind." She was damned thankful she'd deleted Volan's message to her earlier.

"You distract me something fierce. But no. And I don't think we will either until—"

"The moon appears." She'd hoped everything would be resolved in the next few days before that happened.

But the way of the wolf would dictate the final draw. Everyone waited for the day to arrive, or the night, rather, when the moon began its sliver of an appearance. The waxing crescent that would grow until the moon swelled into a full sphere…the phase that would send *lupus garous* running through the wild in their wolf pelts, anxious to feel the wind at their backs and the feral freedom their wolf forms presented them. The reds would make their final move.

Then…Volan would seek Devlyn out to make his kill. She shivered and ran her hand over Devlyn's. He stroked her nub, and she arched her back when he worked her hormones into a delicious frenzy.

Yet the notion still plagued her: three more days and their fate would be sealed.

---

The next afternoon, Bella heard kids' laughter and looked out the front window. Like a lumbering grizzly, Thompson chased after Chrissie's kids on the front lawn as her son, Jimmy, tossed a beach ball to her daughter. Mary missed the ball and Thompson feigned running for it. All squeals, Mary dashed after the rolling ball and grabbed it just before Thompson reached it.

Chrissie stood watching them, her face beaming.

Bella took a deep breath, and Devlyn moved silently in behind her and then wrapped his arms around her. "What's all the racket about?"

"Looks like Thompson's as good with kids as he is with animals."

Devlyn shook his head.

Bella turned and nipped Devlyn's chin. "I've been thinking."

"I can tell this is going to get us into some tight places."

"Yeah, well, you know me."

He ran his hand up her sweatshirt and cupped a breast, quickly moving to the nipple and sending a spine-tingling jolt straight through her.

"Yeah, I know you. What's brewing in that one-track mind of *yours?*"

She gave him a small smile and pressed her mouth against his in a lingering kiss. He responded, wrapping his arms around her in a tight squeeze, and she felt his arousal beckoning to her. He nudged her back toward the bedroom.

"I've been thinking," she began again. "If the murdering red was so fond of the girl he killed, why would he have found others and killed them, too? Then Nicol's reaction to seeing the necklace bothers me also. He really looked sick when he saw it."

"And?"

"I want to search his place. Find out if there's any sign of a girl murdered there. Maybe we're dealing with

two killers, not one. Or maybe he knew the girl inti-
mately before the killer murdered her. Maybe she was
at his place before she was killed. I just want to discover
how connected he is to what's happened."

"You want the truth before I take Nicol down."

She took a deep breath and raked her fingers through
Devlyn's hair. "Yeah. I want to know that, if there was
more than one killer wolf, we'll find them both and get rid
of the threat. What if we left the area after we eliminated
one murderer, only to discover the killings continue?"

"Against my better judgment, I agree. Would you
stay home on this one?"

She gave him a get-real look.

He shook his head and pulled her back to the bedroom. "Didn't think so. Why did I even ask?"

"Because you always want the best for me. But what
if you left me alone and someone came for me, despite
your thinking that they'll honor the agreement?"

"That's the *only* reason why I'm allowing you to
come with me."

She hit him in the shoulder. "You are sooo controlling."

"Yeah, and you love me for it." He swept her off her
feet and carried her into the bedroom.

Pleasure before business.

~~~

An hour later, Devlyn watched over Bella's shoulder
while she hacked her way into the police headquarters
files.

"Do this often?" he asked, not believing how devious
his little red wolf could be.

"When I need to."

She printed out a page and pointed to the printer where five more pages rested in the tray. "Okay, we've got all three of the reds' addresses, the time of the killings, and the locations where the police found the bodies. Can you think of anything else we might need?"

"We already have a police escort."

She groaned. "They've been parked across the street for so long I almost forgot they were there." But then she smiled, the look pure evil. "I've never attempted anything like this, but it's worth a try." She accessed the police station's computers again and sent a message to the sergeant in charge of the surveillance teams watching her house.

> Pull the surveillance watch on Bella Wilder's house. We'll reinstate it if we have further evidence that it's needed.

She sent the message off and looked up at Devlyn, her brows raised.

"But will it work?"

"Maybe. For a while possibly. Won't know for sometime, probably. Want to get something to eat before we go investigating the reds?"

"Why couldn't you have gotten rid of the search warrants on us in the same way earlier?"

"Ha! This might not even work. We'll just have to wait and see."

In the meantime, Bella hastily made tuna fish sandwiches while Devlyn kept an eye on the SUV parked across the street.

The vehicle wasn't moving.

Bella joined him at the window, plates of sandwiches in hand. "Didn't work yet?"

"Nope."

"We have another problem, too."

He took his plate and nodded. "Thompson."

"But, maybe, Chrissie and the kids will keep him preoccupied." She motioned to the window. "They've all gone inside the house."

"Let's hope so." Devlyn began working on his second sandwich when the police SUV's engine started and the vehicle began rolling down the street away from Bella's house.

"Let's go," he said, already halfway to the kitchen.

Bella hastily ate her sandwich and raced after him. "Wait! Got to get the papers with all the addresses on them."

Devlyn shoved the empty plate onto the kitchen counter and hurried out to the car. He punched the garage door opener, jumped into the SUV, and started the engine. Bella dashed into the garage, her expression harried.

Wishing he could have sent her home to his cousin, he took a deep breath. The situation could get really hairy if they ran into any of the reds while they searched their homes.

---

Bella considered the Oregon map as Devlyn drove out of her residential area. "Head for Beaverton, west of Portland. That's where Ross lives. Nicol's place is farther out, and Alfred's ranch home is south of Portland." She rifled through the papers and pulled out the one that listed their occupations. "According to a website that Nicol advertises on, he's a professional game hunter and takes people on tours, but you found that out already when you spoke with him earlier."

"Yeah, but not where he actually hunts."

"Well, here's the listing. He's a fourth-generation big hunter game guide—"

Devlyn snorted. "As in he's all four generations."

"Bet you're right. He charges fifteen hundred to thirty-five hundred dollars for hunts in northern Idaho for mountain lions, black bear, antlered deer, and elk."

"Not too far away then."

"Nope. But then he also schedules two trips a year to South Africa for antelope, buffalo, and kudu, for a price ranging from five thousand to ten thousand. And here's his schedule. He's on a hunt in Idaho for three days." She looked over at Devlyn. "He'll be home when the first of the moon appears."

"In time for the fight."

Suppressing a shiver, she ran her finger down the page to a listing for Alfred. "Okay, so Alfred owns a cattle ranch. Probably eats the cows on occasion when the moon's out."

"Wouldn't be surprised. So what does Ross do for a living?"

"Owns a meat packing plant. Probably where Alfred sends his cows after fattening them up. He's located in Woodburn, a few miles south of Portland."

"Woodburn."

"Yeah. According to the history of the place, men were burning the brush, clearing the area to lay railroad tracks when the fire got out of hand. They have a big tulip festival, and I've collected bulbs for my garden from there."

He offered a sexy smile. "Never took much notice of flowers before, but I sure do like that greenhouse of yours. In fact, I wouldn't mind working out with you there on a regular basis."

Bella rolled her eyes. "My plants would all die from lack of care."

He laughed. "So where does Alfred live?"

She held up two fingers. "Two places. One's in Portland, probably to keep closer ties to his pack in the surrounding area, and a place south of that… Well, he had a place at Cottage Grove near the Row River where he initially had his cattle ranch. The river was named Row for the quarrel two men had over sheep- and cattle-grazing rights. Knowing the way Alfred is and his great-grandfather's legend, I wouldn't be surprised to learn he was the man who killed the other rancher. But he's moved his ranch closer to Portland, near the Willamette River by Salem. That's an hour south."

Devlyn shook his head. "So, Ross is probably at the meat packing plant, running things. And who knows where Alfred is."

"Turn down that street there," Bella advised, pointing right. "Cross four more street intersections; the second house on the left is Nicol's."

When they reached the red brick home, Bella said, "Problem is, after we've checked out Nicol's place and taken the drive to Ross's, it might be close to closing time at the meat packing plant. If he's even at work at all today because of his injured arm. Heck, Nicol might not have even gone on his hunting expedition."

Devlyn parked the SUV in Nicol's driveway and considered the house. "No lights on, unless he's sleeping. Wonder if any of the rest of the pack live in the vicinity. Next-door neighbors, even."

He climbed out of the SUV and Bella joined him. "Gray-haired lady peeking through her blinds across the street is watching every move we make," she said.

At a leisurely pace, Devlyn checked the mailbox and pulled out a flyer. Then he headed straight for the front door as if he were a regular visitor. "No sounds inside the house. Won't take long for us to check out the place, sense any signs of blood, see if either the murdering red or the girl were here before. We'll be gone long before anyone can get here."

"Unless someone calls the police."

Devlyn picked up the newspaper lying on the front step, shoved it under his arm, and brought out his lock picks. Within seconds, he had the door open and they were in.

Both listened for any sounds that would indicate that Nicol or anyone else was in the house, but they heard nothing. The place was silent, vacant, unless Nicol was cowering somewhere or sleeping.

"The neighbors will see us drop off his paper and mail for him, stay a few minutes, and then leave without taking anything, and figure we have to be friends of his."

"Is that how you and your cousins got away with snooping through people's homes when you were younger?"

"Works like a charm. It's the sneaky ones that get caught. And, thankfully, it's cold enough here that no one will be suspicious of us for wearing gloves either. Although it won't matter at the reds' places. They'll smell that we've been there, and catching a trace of your scent will drive them crazy to know you were there and all they can enjoy of you is the delicious fragrance you left behind." He lifted his chin and took a deep breath. "Smells like Nicol and the strong odor of dead animals."

Bella pointed at the stag heads mounted over the mantel as she made her way across the jungle of a living room. The couch covered in zebra and the chairs in leopard skins caught her eye, and she wondered if Nicol killed one of the women and took a trophy from her, too. When she walked into the cluttered kitchen, she found dirty dishes stacked in the sink, and the kitchen counter was buried in papers and half-eaten sandwiches, dried out and spotted with spreading black mold.

"A woman's been here," Devlyn called out from down the hall. "Well, make that a few."

But was one of them the murdered woman?

Bella peeked into the fridge. Half-soured milk and green, fuzzy cheese. She wrinkled her nose and shut the door. Ransacking the drawers, she found nothing.

"Computer back here. You want to hack into his email?" Devlyn shouted.

Bella bolted for the sound of his voice and found him hunched over the keyboard, Windows starting up on the screen. He moved out of the chair to let her sit down.

"AOL. He's got it set up where he can just log in automatically." She clicked enter and the page took forever to upload. "Direct dial-up." She studied the email message subjects and chose one that said, "Looking forward to Sunday!" dated three weeks earlier.

> Here's a newer picture of me, and, yes, Nicol,
> my hair is really red! Not a Clairol-bottle red!
> I've told all my friends how we've met on the
> dating service. They're going to try it next, too.
> Got any brothers?

"Omigod, Devlyn, he was looking for redheads on an online dating service. Look." As if Devlyn already wasn't. His heated breath caressed her neck while he looked over her shoulder.

Bella's breathing slowed as she clicked on the attachment. After several excruciatingly slow seconds, the picture appeared. "It's her," Bella said. "I recognize it from the police photos in the papers—the murdered girl, Linn McGowan."

She hurriedly looked through several more emails, finding pictures of four more redheads from the online dating service.

"Where's Linn's residence?" Devlyn asked, his voice hard.

Bella pulled the papers out of her jacket pocket and fumbled through them. "South side of Portland."

"What about the other redheads he'd contacted?"

"The other girls listed in this dating service live in other parts of Oregon. They're not among those found dead here in Portland. He may never have met them once he found Linn."

"Or if he did and they met bad ends, he might have killed them in other locations of the state, and the police may not have connected them with the killings here."

Bella's stomach clenched while she sifted through the emails and then she shut the computer down. "What about his bedroom? Find anything there?"

"He's been with a few women in there. I thought he might not have brought the woman who was murdered here. But maybe so. We'll have to check out her place to pick up her scent and compare."

Bella headed into the bedroom and took a deep breath. "Lusty little red wolf. Ready to go to Linn's place?"

Devlyn pulled out a date book from his pocket and flipped it open.

"Nicol's?"

"Yep. Found it on his desk. When was the girl murdered?"

"A week before the mystery red's murder."

"This just about confirms it then. 'Date with Linn, noon.'"

"What if he met her somewhere else?" Bella asked, as Devlyn guided her out of the house, pretending to lock the door, and then escorted her to the car.

"In his little black book, he had listed several dates with her beforehand. The last one is the day she was found murdered. I'd bet either he brought her here at least once, or he went to her place sometime during their courtship before her death."

"The neighbor's still watching us. She undoubtedly took down our license plate number."

"No problem. We've acted above suspicion. Why

would anyone break into a house and then not haul off computer equipment and a bunch of other valuable items?"

"You're right." Bella snapped her seat belt in place. "Do you want to chance going to Woodburn to search Ross's place? We should make it before his business closes for the evening."

"Yeah. Then we can check out the murdered girls' places."

"And Alfred?"

"We'll have to leave him until tomorrow, unless we want to try investigating his place while he's there."

"We might have a police surveillance car back at our place before we return home," Bella cautioned.

"Okay, Bella honey. We'll make it an all-night sleuthing venture. The hunt is on."

———

The sky was dark, with massive clouds threatening to rain, and the air was heavy with cold moisture. Devlyn hoped the impending storm would hold off until they were through. He sure preferred his drier Colorado weather to this.

The search for Ross's place took longer than expected because, even though his address was Woodburn, he lived a couple of miles out on a gravel road. Because of the thick trees and winding road, they couldn't see the houses hidden back off the lane until they were right on top of the drives leading to them.

When Devlyn finally spied the redwood house tucked back in the forest, he pulled off the main road and parked a few hundred yards from the place. Lights were on inside, and two vehicles were parked out front.

"Still want to check it out?" Devlyn asked, glancing at Bella.

She rubbed her arms. "No. Let's go to where the women were murdered. Maybe we'll pick up Ross's scent at one of their places. Then we can check out Alfred's house in town."

Devlyn pulled back onto the main road and returned to Portland, where Bella directed him to Linn's apartment. The rain was spitting by the time they reached the apartment's door, and Devlyn mused that folks in Oregon couldn't ever tan—they just rusted.

Devlyn picked the lock, but before they opened the door, a woman wearing pink foam curlers in her white hair, a pin-striped housecoat, and purple sneakers peeked out her door. She gave Bella a sad kind of smile. "Hi. You must be Linn's sister. The poor thing. When I was laid up with a broken leg several months ago, she brought me canned chicken soup—she didn't cook, you know. I told the police there were half a dozen guys or more seeing her. She told me it was some online dating service."

The woman shook her head, making the curlers jiggle. "Darn foolishness and dangerous, I thought. Meet them at church, I told her. But she wouldn't go to church. Do you go to services? See, if she'd been in Bible studies and listened to a sermon about the Lord and not seeing whoever murdered her that Sunday, she'd have been fine, I figure. I was away at a social gathering after services so didn't get home until that evening. But by then it was too late. She sure wasn't lonely. Do you need anything?"

"No, thank you," Bella said in a small voice.

Devlyn rubbed her arm and the neighbor smiled. "You two must be newlyweds. Congratulations."

"Thank you," Bella said.

Devlyn pushed the door open. "It was nice meeting you." He didn't have time for niceties. Then he closed the door after them.

Taking a deep breath, Devlyn pulled Bella into his embrace. "Are you okay?"

"I...I didn't expect a nosey neighbor."

But he knew Bella's upset was due to more than that. The more they learned about the dead girls and the reds, the more personal the situation got.

"The old woman's lonely. Probably doesn't have anything much to keep her occupied. But I bet you anything that, if it was Ross's doing, he planned the Sunday killing because the next-door neighbor wasn't going to be home."

Bella agreed and turned on Linn's computer. Before long, Bella was hacking into her email. "The only emails linking her to the dating service were sent to nine other men. Nothing that she emailed to Ross."

"He deleted them to cover his trail," Devlyn concluded. He took a deep breath. "His scent is in here, and the smell of antiseptic and blood. He cleaned the place thoroughly, but he didn't expect *lupus garous* to be checking for his scent."

They combed through the rest of the place and found nothing but the smell of Linn's blood and perfume in the bedroom.

"He never took her to his place," Bella said.

"Too wily. He left the other guys' emails to her so the

police would consider them all suspects. I imagine that, when he learned she was seeing other guys and not just him, he was pretty pissed off."

A knock on the front door nearly gave Bella a heart attack and she let out a squeak. Devlyn gave her hand a reassuring squeeze and then answered the door while Bella turned off the computer.

The old woman next door gave Bella a kindly smile. "Linn felt so badly that my favorite gold necklace had broken, she gave me hers to keep. Said she didn't really ever wear it. But, since you're her sister, I'd like for you to have it."

Bella began to object, but Devlyn took the necklace. "Thank you. She'll treasure it."

As soon as Devlyn and Bella climbed back into the SUV, she let out her breath. "Why did you take it?"

The old lady waved at them as Devlyn backed out of the driveway and Bella waved back at her.

"Do you see how similar it is to the other one we found in the woods? I have a hunch that's why Nicol was concerned when you showed him the other. Maybe he even gave it to Linn, but when he went to remove it, he couldn't find it because she'd given it to her next-door neighbor."

"Hmm, sounds like Linn didn't have any sentimental attachment to it, maybe not to Nicol either. Wish we could have found a diary of hers or something."

"If she'd had one and it had any reference to him, he would have destroyed it."

Devlyn smelled the necklace and nodded. "His scent is on it."

"So he was the last one to see Linn alive."

"I'd say that was a safe bet. What about the location of the other two murdered women?"

Bella searched through the papers. "Omigod, I didn't see this before, but one lived only a couple of doors down from Alfred's townhome." She looked over at Devlyn. "He couldn't have killed a woman, too."

"Let's find out."

Bella was sure Nicol had murdered one of the girls because of the way he seemed so upset over the necklace. But Alfred had wanted the patch of red wolf fur she'd found in the murdered girls' apartment when she and Devlyn were on the run. Did he think Bella had found it in the apartment of a girl he might have been seeing?

"No houses," Devlyn said, driving through the development. "Condos, duplexes, townhouses. I can't imagine he'd want a place so compact, no yard, front or back."

"He has a big ranch. He probably doesn't stay here that often. Maybe just for pack business."

"Or picking up women."

Bella glanced at him. "Yeah, way out on the ranch, all he'd have was a bunch of cows."

They drove slowly past Alfred's place, where six vehicles were parked.

"The girl's place is two houses down. There—in that duplex. Looks like no one's home next door."

Seeing a police lockbox securing the front door, Devlyn pulled around the back under the metal carport. A lockbox secured the back door, too, but at least Bella and Devlyn were hidden from prying eyes.

For several seconds, Devlyn tried to unlock the box

using his tool kit. Bella's skin prickled with uneasiness. Eyeing a side window, she moved closer to check it out. When she pushed against the windowpane, trying to move it up, it didn't budge. Glancing over at Devlyn, she saw him watching her, waiting to see if she was successful. She gave him a lopsided half smile and pointed to the lockbox. "Can't get it open?"

"Take me a few seconds more." He went back to work.

Looking up, she found another window directly above the locked one. Devlyn was struggling away with the lock, getting a little more aggressive, but not making any headway. Bella surveyed the area but couldn't find anything that would help her reach the upper-floor window except for a plastic trash can on wheels.

"Devlyn, do you want to see if you can hoist me up and I'll check the window—see if it's unlocked?"

He grunted. "It'll only take me a few more seconds to unlock this."

"Fine, have it your way." She grabbed the garbage can and rolled it underneath the window.

He stopped what he was doing and gave her a disgruntled look. "Here, you'll end up breaking your neck," Devlyn warned, shoving his lock pick set into his jacket pocket.

He lifted Bella onto his shoulders, and, as if she'd been on an exhibition cheerleading squad for years, she nimbly balanced herself on his shoulder blades. When she shoved at the window, it didn't budge.

Devlyn snorted.

"Just hold still and I'll try again. It might just be a little stuck."

Bella pushed again and thought she felt a tiny give. "It's unlocked. I see the latch is turned. But it's a bit cemented in place."

"Maybe we should switch places, and I'll open the window."

"Very funn—oh, oh, here it goes."

The window suddenly gave, sliding up, and Bella lost her balance, her feet slipping off Devlyn's shoulders. In a desperate attempt to avoid falling, she grabbed the windowsill and hung on, her gloved hands smarting where the metal window grooves dug into them.

Devlyn grabbed her feet and then lifted her until she could pull herself through the opening. As soon as she clambered into the bedroom, she knocked over a bunch of makeup jars and a mess of other items on the dresser, sending them crashing to the wooden floor.

"Are you all right?" Devlyn called out.

Bella got to her feet and peered out the window at a worried-looking Devlyn. "A cat burglar I am not. I'll open the window down below. Be just a second."

She glanced at the sheets and floral comforter torn in shreds, half dragging on the floor. Not good. And she could smell the blood in the room, too. But not just what must have been the girl's blood. She smelled a hint of Ross's blood, remembering the scent after she had sliced him with her knife in the living room. She shivered to think she'd danced with two murdering reds and hadn't had a clue.

Stumbling through the living room where the couch and overstuffed chairs were ripped to pieces, stuffing scattered everywhere, she finally managed to make it to the kitchen. The room looked as if an earthquake had hit here, too. Or a wild animal had torn up the place.

Her boots crunched through broken dishes and shattered spice jars, the smell of cinnamon and paprika mixing in a nauseating medley. Reaching the kitchen window, she unlocked it and yanked up the glass. "I smelled Ross's blood upstairs. She must have drawn blood when he tried to murder her. The smell of her blood is scattered throughout the duplex, too."

Devlyn stood inside the kitchen, surveying the damage. "He tried to make it appear like a burglary."

"How can you tell?"

"Computer hard drive's missing, but keyboard's still at the desk. Monitor's gone. No printer, but there's the cord." Devlyn pulled open several kitchen drawers. "Silverware's gone, but the spatulas, serving forks, and knives are all here."

She followed Devlyn into the living room.

"No television, no stereo. And I bet upstairs you won't find any jewelry," he said and sniffed the air.

Bella's gaze shifted to the Disney prints on the living room walls, all knocked askew. The brightly colored pictures complemented her floral seating arrangement, bright and cheerful—at one time. A collection of family photos hung on another wall, featuring the redheaded girl herself surrounded by what looked like her mother and father and a younger brother and sister, all with gleeful blue eyes and wide smiles. The Cinderella Castle spires rose in a lighted backdrop behind them.

Bella clenched her hands into fists. The reds who had

murdered these girls were no more than savage killers. Now, she had no regrets if any of them should die at Devlyn's hand. But her concern that he'd be overwhelmed by the three of them worried her more than anything.

When they reached the stairs, Devlyn motioned to the carpet. "Blood trails all of the way up. Scratches on the handrail indicate that she was still struggling to get away from him."

"Was he enjoying the torture?" Bella asked, sickened at the way Ross's twisted mind worked.

"More like a rabid wolf, no control."

"But the police must have been baffled. She was killed in the same manner as the others. The police reports said canine saliva was found in her bite wounds. Why would Ross have tried to cover his tracks with a faked burglary?"

"Maybe he didn't fake it. Maybe he really did burglarize the place."

Bella considered the possibility and agreed. "That could be. I wonder if he was looking for something that connected him with her, too. Did he date her first, like Nicol had Linn? Or had he just stalked her and then attempted the change?"

"Not sure. Either could be a viable possibility."

Devlyn shut the bedroom window and then led Bella back downstairs.

"Where to now, Bella? The last murdered girl's place, or do we check out Ross's house again?"

"What about his meat packing plant? It should be closed for the night." She climbed out the kitchen window; Devlyn followed and then shut it.

A clap of thunder let loose another bout of rain, but thankfully the carport kept them from getting wet.

"Let's find the other woman's apartment first and check it out."

"Boy, I really thought that, since this one lived so close to Alfred, he targeted her, not Ross," Bella said.

"He probably saw her outside of her duplex sometime when he was visiting Alfred."

"Do you think Alfred killed the other girl then?" Bella climbed into the SUV.

"If so, the red pack's doomed unless we can take care of the bad seeds."

They drove around the front of the townhouse and pulled to a stop at the street. A police cruiser drove on by slowly, the officer glancing in their direction. Bella's heart nearly gave out.

"We could be the resident next door," Devlyn said, trying to reassure her.

"Right." But she didn't feel at all reassured. That's all they needed right now—some cop asking them why they were in the parking area of the unoccupied duplex when they didn't live there. "The last girl on our list is Lisa Campbell, the first girl reported murdered. Her place is located on the other side of town."

Devlyn drove them past Alfred's place, but it was even more crowded with cars now. The time was nearly eight when they reached the victim's house. But already they could see a dilemma. Lights were on in several of the rooms, and three vehicles were parked out front.

"Looks like it's a little busy for a visit, Bella."

She ground her teeth. "We have to know if Alfred

killed her. Since he appears to be preoccupied in town, let's take a country drive and check out his cows." But she couldn't shake the eerie feeling that someone was watching them.

# Chapter 17

DEVLYN NOTICED BELLA CHECKING OUT THE SIDE VIEW mirror again and saw the tension in her stiffened spine. "See anything?"

"I thought I saw a black Humvee. Twice now. But when I look back, it's gone, vanished in the rain."

"I've seen it before."

Bella looked at Devlyn. "When?"

"When we were at the dance club. I saw it parked there and then again when I took a look in the Cascades for any evidence of the murdering red's complicity; it followed me for a while and then disappeared."

"A red? Or Volan?"

"Volan would have confronted me. The windows were too dark; I couldn't see the driver, but I gathered he was a red—wary, questioning, but something more. I can't pinpoint the gut feeling I have about it, except that, even though he's hostile—a red not liking a gray in the red's territory and has his sights set on the only female red wolf who's young enough to be pursued—he doesn't seem to have any evil purpose."

"Like reporting our actions to Alfred."

"Right." Devlyn was more curious than worried about the red's business.

The downpour worsened along the highway, and Devlyn hoped that the rain would help hide their clandestine activities when they reached Alfred's ranch.

Bella tapped her fingers on her door's armrest. "This means he might be one of the older males who wants you to eradicate the killers from the pack."

"Possibly."

"You don't think so?" she asked, her voice elevated in surprise.

"When I was alone, he followed much closer, more aggressively, letting me know he was there and watching. But when you're with me, he hangs back, almost as though he knows he has no chance with you when I'm around."

"The mystery murdering red?"

"Maybe. But I don't really think so. The one who followed us into the woods, the one we recognized as the murderer, behaves differently. Skulks more in the background. I wished I'd paid more attention to who else was at the club that night. The Humvee was there, which meant this red was watching you…us. But I sure didn't get a whiff of either the murderer or this guy."

"Hmph," Bella said, folding her arms. "As hot and sweaty as the humans were getting, covered in their cloying perfumes and colognes, I had enough of a time trying to smell the reds we met up with."

"I was concentrating on a female red in the midst of a bunch of lusty red males. I should have known there would have been more of them there." Devlyn peered into the fog, trying to locate the turnoff for Alfred's ranch.

"I hacked into the files at the county courthouse; he owns the deed on a seven-hundred-acre spread. Tax records show he has 760 steers on the ranch and gets paid on the gain at a rate of thirty cents per pound per day with a gain of three hundred pounds. Not too shabby. He pays a tax assessment on the irrigation water from a canal, but, according to this, he doesn't need the irrigation water and has fought with city hall about reducing or doing away with the tax."

Devlyn snorted. "Why would anyone need irrigation water in a place as wet as this?"

Bella chuckled. "Ready to go home to Colorado and dry out?"

"You bet."

"Okay, there's a river on his property and his main house sits on a hill high above the ranch."

"Main house?"

"Yeah, he has a second home, mobile home, and a bunk house, machine shop, three large granaries, two loafing shed barns with feeders, an additional barn, and two sets of corrals with portable scales."

"Holy crap, Bella honey! Can you imagine how many reds work for him and probably live on the property?"

Bella frowned at him. "But Alfred's not there."

Devlyn shook his head. "No, but most of the rest of his pack might be."

He turned off onto the ranch road along the river in a pretty valley surrounded by timbered mountains. They spotted several elk, cows, yearlings, and horses on higher ground; some of the lower-lying pasture lands were under water.

All of the buildings rested on the hilltop above the valley, and Devlyn shut off his headlights and crawled along the road, trying to get as close to the main house as he could without garnering anyone's attention.

"The Humvee's behind us again," Bella whispered, as if the guy could hear them. "But he turned off his headlights, too."

"Maybe he hopes to box us in, if he backs Alfred. On the other hand, I wouldn't have expected him to turn off his headlights. He's got to know we realize he's following us."

Devlyn parked some distance from the house in the dark, and then he and Bella headed through the pelting rain for the backside of the place, where windows enjoyed a view of the valley. He glanced up at the eaves and roofline. "No security cameras."

Bella motioned to the bunkhouse a couple of football fields away, where several pickup trucks were parked. "No need," she whispered, "when he's got such a huge security force nearby."

Devlyn grabbed the doorknob on the back patio doors and smiled when the door opened without resistance. "He must feel really secure out here with all his hired muscle."

Inside, the place was super elegant—leather couches, Persian rugs, crystal chandeliers, oil paintings of the Oregon coastline. And brass wolf sculptures. Devlyn didn't bother turning on the lights, not needing them anyway, and made his way through the three spacious living areas, searched the kitchen, which was big enough to serve large parties, and then headed to the bedrooms, both he and Bella dripping water everywhere.

Every one of the bedrooms was outfitted for guests,

with bathrooms for each, dressers and sitting rooms, and balconies. In the last one, the room was larger than the rest and even more highly appointed, with a brown velvet comforter on a raised bed, massive oak furniture that filled the room, and oil paintings of men and women hanging on the walls, maybe his family over several generations.

Bella grabbed an old leather-bound book off a shelf in a sitting area.

"His journal?"

"Werewolf legend."

Devlyn made a face as she stuffed it into her jacket. "Humans don't have a clue about the real *lupus garou* legend. And *lupus garous* aren't permitted to set down the oral history in writing, which is why *some* clans became confused as to what the real story is," Devlyn said while Bella sat down at Alfred's computer.

Her fingers flying at the keyboard, she retorted, "Right, gray clans got it mixed up, you mean." She let out her breath in exasperation. "Nothing on his computer, email, files, correspondence." Bella scanned the rest of his computer. "Not a darned thing." She looked up at Devlyn as he paused while searching through dresser drawers. "I smell lots of reds who have been here, which would be typical. Pack probably meets here regularly. And the murdering red? I smell him here, too."

"I got a whiff of him in one of the guest bedrooms. But no humans. Alfred probably figures it's too dangerous to bring them to his lair."

Then he thought he heard a faint sound of something, but before he could listen further, a woman suddenly called out from the foyer, "Hello?"

"Damn," Devlyn said under his breath, wondering why he hadn't heard the front door opening.

He locked the bedroom door and hurried to open a back door onto the patio. Bella turned off the computer and joined him. But as soon as they sneaked around the side of the property, trying to reach their car, the heavy rain instantly dousing them, a woman ran outside, yelling into a phone, "Someone's broken into the master's house! Yes, yes…I don't know. It smelled like a gray. And a female red. What? What do you mean keep them here? They're not here! Oh, oh, I think I see a vehicle down the road in the dark. Yes, it's a black SUV."

The woman was shrieking so loud Devlyn was sure whoever was listening had to hold the phone away from his ear or lose his hearing. Devlyn rushed Bella down to the SUV, and both jumped in just as a couple of truck engines rumbled to life.

"Oh hell, Devlyn. The cavalry's coming." Bella wrung out her hair and wiped the rain water off her face.

"We'll make it, honey." But he wasn't sure they would. With nowhere to turn easily and the shoulders along the gravel road pure mud because of the hammering, constant rain, he headed straight for the pickup trucks in a dare-to-hit-me mode, chasing one off the hill. The pickup got stuck in the water-drenched mud. But the other truck was still game.

Bella gripped the seat and looked out the side view mirror. "The Humvee's behind us."

Again, Devlyn wondered if the Humvee driver intended to box him in. But instead, the vehicle slipped on past him and headed straight for the pickup.

"Jeez, Devlyn, he appears to be on our side. Or plain nuts."

At the last second, the pickup veered, clipping the Humvee's front fender, causing the pickup to spin out of control and plow into the side of one of the barns. The Humvee flipped around, too, and ended up facing Devlyn's vehicle.

Devlyn paused, making sure the Humvee driver's vehicle wasn't incapacitated.

For a second, the two vehicles faced each other in a gunfight standoff, and then Devlyn turned his SUV around in the gravel and drove slowly, watching to see if the Humvee followed them. When it did, he nodded, assured the guy's vehicle was fine.

"Wonder who the guy is. Could use him for backup when the going gets rough," he said.

"I'd sure like to know his story." She sighed deeply. "We didn't find one lick of evidence on Alfred yet."

"I think he's too wily to keep anything around that could incriminate him. The only other thing would be if we could get in the house of the last girl who was murdered. If we smelled him there, that would cinch it."

When they reached the main road, Devlyn turned his headlights back on for the benefit of other vehicles.

"The Humvee went in the opposite direction."

"Too bad. I was beginning to like the guy."

"He could be bad news."

"That he could." But Devlyn's gut instinct told him the mystery red wasn't.

For several miles, Bella watched her side view mirror. Because of the bad road conditions—the water puddled up in ponds in places on the highway and the rain ran down the windshield like a continuous rampant waterfall—Devlyn concentrated on what was in front of them.

"Maybe we can check out the girl's place now."

Bella stared at the headlight shining on her side view mirror and studied the forest-green SUV skulking behind them. "I think someone else is following us."

Devlyn looked up at his rearview mirror. "Saw one like it parked at the mobile home on Alfred's property."

Bella made a face. "Great, then they know we're on to them. Well, not that they wouldn't know already. I imagine the woman who ratted on us probably called Alfred at his home in Portland and warned him that we were snooping around his country estate."

"Well, tit for tat. He broke into your place. Payback can be hell."

"Yeah, we dripped water all over his expensive carpets."

"And you stole his favorite bedtime book. So what did you learn from the human-concocted 'werewolf legend'?"

She flipped through the book, scanning several pages, and then gave a ladylike snort. "A human wrote it."

Devlyn raised a brow. "What did it say?"

"Why should you care? You already said humans don't have a clue."

"You're right. So what did it say?"

She cast him an annoyed look. "A Scandinavian white wolf was the first *lupus garou*."

Devlyn laughed out loud.

Bella threw the book into the backseat. "I told you it was a bunch of nonsense." She glanced back at the vehicle following them. "Can you lose the SUV?"

"I could do better than that." He jerked the rental SUV over to the shoulder of the road, and the green one jammed on its brakes and stopped several feet behind them.

Her heart skipping beats, Bella grabbed Devlyn's arm. "What if the SUV's packed with reds? You can't fight them all."

The other vehicle idled behind them. Devlyn's neck muscle tightened and his knuckles turned white from the grip he had on the steering wheel.

"Devlyn, we might as well return home if they know what we're up to. Even if we managed to lose them, the word's probably out that we're investigating the murders."

"I imagine by now the whole pack knows and every one of them will be watching for us, either at Ross's place, his packing plant, or the murdered girls' houses, if they don't know we've been at any of them. Unless they've checked them out and found our scent there." He gave a satisfied smile.

"Right." Bella let out her breath. "Hell, that means Alfred's involved. Otherwise, he'd terminate Ross and Nicol himself for creating all of this mess. And the other red, too."

Devlyn glanced in the rearview mirror. "Unless he's a loner—not part of the pack." He pulled back onto the road and headed for Bella's house.

The rain would let up intermittently and then pour hard again in places, but she could still see the green SUV following them. Twice, the rental SUV Devlyn was driving slid like a skater out of control on the water-logged road.

"Nearly worse than the ice in Colorado," he groused under his breath.

When they finally neared Bella's house, the green SUV suddenly headed down a side road and took off. But Bella and Devlyn had a new surprise waiting for them.

Two police cars and a fire engine, their lights flashing, were parked in front of Bella's place; her stomach took an instant dive. Smoke was billowing into the night sky in the backyard behind her house. Her greenhouse and shed were on fire!

Devlyn pulled into the garage, barely parking before Bella jerked open the door and leapt from the car and dashed out the garage door to the backyard.

"Bella!"

She heard Devlyn's heavy footfall behind her as a policeman tried to block her path to the greenhouse. Despite the intermittent heavy rainfall, the roof protected the fire blazing inside and the firemen had to use hoses to bring the blaze under control.

"My plants," Bella cried, trying to get to her shed, but Devlyn gathered her against his body and held her tight.

"You can't go near it, Bella," he said, half commanding, half trying to console her.

Another vehicle screeched to a halt in front of the house and Thompson, Chrissie, and her kids piled out of the car.

"Omigosh, Bella," Chrissie said, running to join her. "What happened?"

"Vandals," one of the policemen said. "Whoever did

it broke most of the windows in the greenhouse, trashed the inside, and then poured gallons of gasoline everywhere. Luckily, the wind died down before the blaze really took hold or the house might have caught fire."

Thompson rubbed Chrissie's arm. "Why don't you take the kids in the house and I'll be over in a little bit."

But Chrissie looked devastated and didn't seem to want to leave Bella alone. Shivering, her kids stood out of the rain on the back patio, their eyes and mouths wide as they gaped at the fire. Chrissie gave Bella's hand a squeeze and said, "Call me." Then she hurried the kids to her house.

Thompson shoved his hands in his pockets and stared at the dwindling inferno. "Police called me to say that whoever set fire to your greenhouse must have been the one who hacked into the police headquarters and sent a bogus message to Sergeant Reddy, who pulled the police detail watching your place." Thompson shook his head. "This Volan character is sure vindictive."

*Volan?*

Bella was sure the reds had burned the greenhouse, probably in retaliation for snooping around Alfred's house. She tried to get closer to the building to see if she could pick up the reds' scent, or Volan's. But Devlyn wasn't letting her get any nearer, and she growled at him.

Without warning, an explosion rocked the greenhouse. Splintered glass and wood flew across the backyard, and Devlyn yanked Bella behind the garage while everyone else took cover.

"Hell!" one of the firemen said. "What did you have in there?"

"Fertilizers, garden chemicals, gas for my mower, not sure what else," Bella said, making her way back to where she'd been standing, her eyes filled with tears and her heart in her throat. In the next instant, the greenhouse roof collapsed, and everyone dashed for safety again.

Once it appeared the greenhouse was settled in ruins, the fireman returned to put out the rest of the flames, now smoldering in the twisted metal, glass, and wood debris.

"Thankfully, your next-door neighbor Mr. Sherman called in the vandalism," one of the policeman said. "Mr. Sherman said he thought the guy was going to torch the house, so he began yelling on the phone to 911 all the details about the guy—big, dark-haired, sounded a lot like Volan."

Thompson looked back at Bella and Devlyn. She hoped she didn't look as guilty as she felt. "You didn't hear or see anything?" he asked.

The policeman offered, "They weren't here. They just arrived shortly before you did."

Thompson looked from Bella to Devlyn, and she knew he was waiting for a report, but neither of them said anything.

"Guess it was good you weren't home then," Thompson said, "or Volan might have tried to do more." He turned this attention to the police officer. "Is the watch back on the house?"

"You bet. Police Chief Whittaker himself directed it. He said there's to be no more foul-ups, or heads will roll. Now, only *he* can change the order."

Bella exchanged a glance with Devlyn. Their sleuthing

days appeared to be over unless they wanted a police escort tailing them or they could think up some other creative way to get rid of a tail.

—◦◦◦—

Early the next morning, even though it was dark, with threatening storm clouds hovering overhead like a permanent menace, Devlyn reached out for Bella in bed, but he found her gone. He listened, hoping to hear her butler announcing new email or the sound of her cooking in the kitchen. *Nothing*. And then the rain, *pitter-pattering* at first, followed by a roar as it drowned the area, filled his ears. He was sure if he didn't leave here soon, his skin would start wearing a coat of green moss or mold.

Shoving the covers aside, he headed out of the bedroom. She wasn't in her office. She couldn't be in the greenhouse now. The thought of the ruined greenhouse sickened him. When he returned her to Colorado, he'd build her one twice as big.

He strode through the living room, but then he saw her standing in the green velvet robe on the back porch, staring at the burned wreckage. Growling at the insidiousness of whoever torched her building, he pulled the door open and stalked outside.

She took a deep breath and rubbed her arms. Devlyn pulled her into his embrace and kissed the top of her head. "Come on back inside, Bella honey. I'll make you something to eat."

"Was it Volan or the reds? That's what I can't quit worrying about."

"The reds. Volan doesn't know where you live."

She looked up at him. He gave her a small smile. "I sniffed around the wreckage when you were sound asleep last night. I didn't want you to worry, but I knew you'd be more concerned if it was Volan."

"I couldn't make myself check it out." She let out her breath and, for the first time since they'd found her greenhouse on fire, she relaxed.

"Come on inside, Bella. I know Chrissie's kids are back at their dad's, but I don't want Thompson to see me dressed like this, if he's still at Chrissie's house, in case anyone peeks over your fence."

Bella glanced down at Devlyn's nudity and her lips rose a hair. "You are one big, very bad wolf, you know?"

"And all yours." He coaxed her back inside the house, ready to prove it.

"What about investigating the reds further?"

"We're done with that for now, honey. Time for the big showdown as soon as the moon makes its appearance. I'm sure at that time we'll resolve the issue of the murdered girls once and for all."

⁓

Later that morning, Chrissie pounded on the back door, her face solemn. Bella let her in and glanced at the blueberry pie Chrissie was holding.

Chrissie handed her the pie. "I'm so sorry about your greenhouse. I wanted to come over last night and say something more, but Henry stayed late and helped me take the kids over to their dad's place. Then, well…" She shrugged.

Saddened about her greenhouse, Bella managed a

small smile, glad that Chrissie had found someone she enjoyed being with after her husband had dumped her for a much younger woman. "I'm thrilled the two of you hit it off so well. Come in."

"I'm sorry I've been kind of distant, too. Henry and I have been dating up a storm, and, well, you know how it is when you've getting involved with someone. I have to make time for the kids, too, so it's been a juggle."

"No problem." Bella headed for the kitchen and Chrissie followed, glancing around the living room. Bella was sure she looked for signs of the naked hunk and was glad Chrissie hadn't come any earlier in the day.

"Devlyn still sleeping?" Chrissie took a seat at the dining room table.

"Devlyn's looking over some emails. Want a slice of pie?" Bella carved up a piece.

"Sure. Things have been awfully quiet over here. Well, except for the insurance people and the arson investigators tromping all over the place." Chrissie took the plate Bella handed her. "I wondered if you needed me to run out and get you anything. I imagine you don't want to leave the house after what has happened, and Devlyn shouldn't leave you alone."

No one needed a neighborhood watch program with Chrissie acting as the eyes and the ears of the whole community. "We've been rather preoccupied, but we have plenty to eat and are just fine."

Chrissie sat at the table and considered Bella's neck.

This morning, at least, Bella's appearance was neater, although she imagined Chrissie was looking at the hickey gracing her throat. Bella's hair rolled in shiny waves over her shoulders and down her back. No one would suspect Devlyn's hands had tangled her curls in the throes of passion only half an hour earlier.

Chrissie scooped up a bite of crust, stained blue and dripping with berries. "Are the two of you getting married?"

"We've already done so." *In the lupus garou way.*

Chrissie's eyes widened. "When?"

"About the time we first had our reunion." How could Bella explain that, for *lupus garous,* selecting a mate meant for a lifetime and the traditional human-contrived marriage vows meant nothing? Hell, half the human population ended up divorcing the same mate they promised to share their lives with together forever. Hmph. Look at Chrissie, even!

Chrissie seemed saddened not to have been told earlier. But then she looked at Bella's unadorned fingers. Explaining the lack of a wedding ring would be even harder.

"Allergic to metal." Bella flipped her hair back and pointed to her ears. "No earrings, no bracelets, no necklaces. Can't wear any kind of metal." In truth, most jewelry hindered their turning into the wolf. If it didn't, it would be lost with the change. Or, in the case of pierced-ear jewelry, what would someone think if they found a wolf with pearls or gold secured to the leather of their ears?

Chrissie glanced at Bella's wrist. "Jeez, I never realized." Her gaze met Bella's. "I never noticed you don't even wear a watch."

"Nope. Can't."

"How do you tell time?"

"Clocks. When I'm in the Escape, it has a clock.

The computer has the time. The oven, microwave, my alarm clock in the bedroom…clocks surround me. If I'm somewhere that I don't know the time, I just ask." She couldn't let Chrissie know she had an innate ability to know the time, from the elevation of the sun in the sky.

"I would have liked to have been present when you got married," Chrissie said softly. "I would have gotten you something."

Bella's heart wrenched. She hadn't wanted to hurt her feelings. Bella gave her a hug, and Chrissie reciprocated with a heartfelt embrace. "Chrissie, you have been the best of friends, and I don't want to ever lose that. But I imagine you know I left my heart in Colorado, and, now that Devlyn has found me, we'll be returning there soon."

"Oh." Chrissie sniffled. "Oh, sure, I knew it would happen someday because of all of the pictures of your family you keep on the fridge. I can't tell if it'll ever come to that, but, if you're back there and Henry and I, well, if he, you know…"

"Asks you to marry him?"

"Yeah, I realize it's way too early, but, if it did happen, would you be my matron of honor?"

Bella smiled. "You bet." She might even entice Devlyn to come with her to the wedding. Actually, she was certain he wouldn't let her return alone.

"Devlyn, too. I'd want him to come. You could use my extra guest room."

"He'd love to."

Devlyn walked into the dining room, but despite the smile that lifted his lips, his countenance was dark. "What would I love to do?"

Chrissie groaned and the two ladies separated. "Tell him later. I'd hate for him to think I was scheming where Henry was concerned."

Bella smiled. "We'll keep in touch. What with the internet, you can keep me posted. We can email each other daily. I'll check your blog every day, and you can upload your kids' drawings. It'll almost be like I haven't left." She waved at the pie sitting on the counter. "Chrissie baked us one of her famous blueberry pies. Want a piece?"

"Yeah, I could use some quick energy." He winked at Bella. "You know how much I like blueberries, and…" He reached into the fridge. "Whipped cream."

Chrissie quickly finished the last bite of her pie. "I've got to go. Enjoy. I'll talk to the two of you later." Her cheeks colored crimson as she hurried out the back door.

Bella touched Devlyn's arm. "You embarrassed Chrissie."

"She loves it." He dabbed whipped cream on top of his pie.

"So what's the bad news, Devlyn?"

As he met her gaze, his brown eyes darkened. "Alfred wants us to meet him, and he wants to fight me for you. His whole pack will be there. He's laid down the challenge and—"

"You'll win, Devlyn. I have no doubt about that. But we need to find the unknown killer, not establish your right to have me to the satisfaction of a bunch of reds."

"It's a challenge I can't refuse. If we weren't in their territory and you weren't one of their kind, I'd have to agree with you. But under the circumstances…"

She growled at him and stabbed her fork into her pie. "We have more important concerns. We don't know for sure that Alfred killed anyone."

"This is important to me, Bella. At least while we're here, I have to prove to the reds that you're mine. That no one can make a claim to you."

She attempted to curb the annoyance she felt. She hated this part of being a *lupus garou*. The part that could mean her losing Devlyn. She was certain he could win against the red, but the problem was that two more reds wanted her. They wouldn't allow him time to recuperate. And she couldn't help feeling that the reds should be handling this matter with Ross and Nicol. Neither one of them was the leader and both of them had murdered girls. So why didn't the pack take them down?

Because Alfred approved it.

Fine. Despite the objections Devlyn would raise, she'd take her gun, to even out the odds a bit if he needed her help. Even if the bullets weren't silver, they'd do enough temporary damage to save Devlyn's hide until he could heal. No red would have her who hadn't earned her justly. Hell, no one but Devlyn would have her.

Then the image came to mind of Volan, standing before her one second, lying on the ground dead the next, and alive after that. She quashed a shudder that threatened to undo her resolve. Still, the bullets had knocked him out for a time. Thinking it might work better, she'd aim for the head this time.

"When and where are we to meet?" she asked, not at all happy about the circumstances.

"Wolf Rock, as soon as the moon makes its appearance. I still say you should have stayed with my cousin."

"Well, I think you already decided I was a better asset here with you than off with some distant cousin of yours." She raised a brow, hoping that was his reasoning.

He grunted. "The notion had occurred to me that he might make a play for you himself."

She laughed. "So that's the real reason you agreed to let me stay by your side, mate of mine."

She pointed to a map of the Cascades. "Wolf Rock is close to my cabin." She twisted her hair between her fingers, trying to ease the concern that chilled her skin. "But what about the escort service we have out front?"

"One of the reds' older couples is coming to see us. They'll drive our Suburban out of the garage and, hopefully, the police will tail them. They'll be heading east, toward Colorado. If that doesn't work, Alfred said he'd work up another plan."

Then all would be decided. At least with the reds. With Volan, that was another matter.

———— ∿ ————

Two days later, still several hours before the waxing crescent of the moon appeared and the first clear day since storms had pelted the area, a knocking at the front door made Bella's heart nearly leap out of her chest while she worked on a pressed flower picture of a variety of Colorado wildflowers, a parting gift for Chrissie.

Devlyn pulled Bella from the kitchen stool where she'd been working at the counter and held her close, kissing her cheek. "Let's get this over with and return to Colorado."

"But the killer—"

"I think we'll find out at Wolf Rock which one is the mystery murderer."

Yeah, despite her considering otherwise, she assumed the murderer would be the right age to want to run the pack if Alfred and the others fell.

Together, she and Devlyn went to the front door to let the reds in.

The man and woman appeared to be in their seventies, both gray-haired. They must have assumed the police wouldn't guess their ploy. And being that the couple was older, the police wouldn't see them as a threat to Bella or Devlyn either as they approached the house.

To her surprise, the woman hugged Bella, and the man slapped Devlyn on the back in greeting. Then he reached over to hug Bella, and Devlyn growled low.

She frowned at him to cool it, but the red male tensed and backed off.

After showing the police that these people were friends, not foes, Devlyn closed the door.

The woman quickly donned a long, red wig, while the man covered his gray hair with a dark-brown one. The woman eyed her for a moment and then gave an evasive smile. "I see now what's got our boys stirred up. Haven't seen a marriageable one like you in a while."

"Who's the rogue who's killing the human females?" Bella asked, figuring if the woman knew she wouldn't tell her but that her response itself might give a clue.

The woman snorted. "He's a lone wolf. Got to be. Not one of the pack."

"If he's looking for a mate and a loner, why doesn't he come for me, then? Only the three from your pack have approached me."

The woman glanced at the man. Her reaction clued Bella into the truth. Nicol and Ross were definitely in on the killings. Alfred's role was still not confirmed, but she highly suspected he was in on them, too. All three were sure to fight Devlyn. And maybe even the mystery fourth.

Devlyn handed the man the Suburban's keys. "Be sure to turn it in at the rental company when you're through with it."

The old man grunted.

Ditching the SUV somewhere in the wilderness and then running like a wolf were more what the old man had in mind. At least that's what Bella would do if the roles were reversed.

The man motioned to the woman. "Let's go."

The two disappeared into the garage, and Bella and Devlyn posted themselves at the front door. A bead of perspiration trickled between her breasts as they watched out the window to see if the police would take the bait.

# Chapter 18

THE RENTAL SUBURBAN PULLED OUT OF BELLA'S driveway and headed through the development, an older couple from the red *lupus garou* pack driving it. After a moment's hesitation, the unmarked police car followed.

"Now what, Devlyn?" Bella asked. Her voice was tight and worried. Her cheeks flushed faintly.

He hated to see her so concerned, and he wrapped his arm around her shoulders. "Now we wait for—"

A different Suburban, this one black, pulled in front of the house.

"Is it a red escort? The police wouldn't send someone else, would they?"

"I don't think so." Devlyn started to walk outside.

Bella tugged at his arm. "Wait for me. I've got to do something."

He couldn't help looking at her in disbelief.

"My mother always said to use the bathroom before I went anywhere," she hastily explained. "Just don't leave without me."

He tilted his chin down. "I won't be leaving without you, honey, that's for certain."

Her eyes held a wealth of worry. She nodded and whipped around, disappearing down the hall.

Folding his arms, he watched out the window while a man climbed out of the vehicle. Again, this one appeared older, only his hair was nearly white. They must have thought Devlyn and Bella wouldn't feel threatened by pack members who were way past the age of scrapping well.

Bella soon joined Devlyn and placed her hand in his. "Sorry, I really had to go to the bathroom."

Her hand was ice cold, and he hated that she seemed so scared. Gripping her hand tightly, he tried to warm it up on the way to the SUV.

Once inside the vehicle, the man glanced at them through the rearview mirror, his gaze shifting from Bella to Devlyn. He snorted and then drove the vehicle past Chrissie's house. Plain as day, Chrissie was watching out the window with a phone pressed against her ear, her brow wrinkled with concern, her hand waving in distress as she spoke. Devlyn looked back and observed her as she bolted outside and recorded the license plate of the vehicle on a slip of paper.

"Great neighborhood watch, eh? A force of one," Bella whispered to Devlyn.

"Yeah, hope Henry doesn't have the police chief put an all-points out on us before we make it to our destination and take care of business."

She sighed deeply. "They'll think we're in on some kind of bad-guy caper, what with leading the police astray."

"They might think we've been coerced into leaving with them. Hopefully, we'll be long gone before they question us further. The killings of the women will stop—"

She shook her head. "But Rosa will never be found."

"She'll be with me in Colorado, if anyone knows where to look."

She nestled her head against his chest. "Do you think Henry will suspect you're going to fight Volan?"

"Yeah, I do."

"He'll try to stop you."

With a light caress, he rubbed her arm. "Yeah. Only wouldn't he be surprised to find Volan's not there, and instead three other men are waiting to have a piece of me?"

She ran her hand over his thigh, instantly stirring his libido. He cast her an interested smile and glanced at the driver, whose eyes remained glued to the road as they drove out of Portland.

"Bella," Devlyn whispered in her ear and then slipped his hand down her shirt and worked his fingers under her lace bra. "Why don't we move to the seat that's way in back?"

She gave him a soulful smile. "All right, stud."

They had a long drive out to Wolf Rock. No sense in wasting precious minutes.

"Need some tension relieved?" she whispered to him as she climbed over the back of the middle seat, her bottom suspended at the top of the seatback for a moment. Immediately, he ran his hands over her butt and squeezed.

"Yeah, you always bring it out in me."

—✦—

Two hours later, they arrived at their destination at the base of Wolf Rock, an ancient volcanic plug, a barren rock face in summer, now sporting a topping of fresh snow like a whipped cream–topped sundae. Devlyn stared up at the daunting monolithic rock: rising over forty-five hundred feet, the nine-hundred-foot pinnacle towered above them, surrounded by the Willamette National Forest.

The fragrance of ponderosa pine and Douglas fir scented the cool, crisp air. Birds chirped in the cover of the forest. A hawk screeched high above, soaring, searching for his next meal, all of it belying the deadly confrontation that would soon take place. Other than the black SUV, there was no sign of anyone else yet.

"No climbers," Devlyn stated, wondering if they were on the other side of the rock face.

"Not allowed," Bella explained. "From January 1 through July 31, raptors nest up there and no one wants to piss off a mother eagle. And, really, hikers only climb between August and October unless the roads are blocked with snow."

"Good time for a rumble, then."

Bella ran her hand over Devlyn's arm. "Yeah."

But she didn't sound like she thought the time was good for the coming fight.

The driver turned to look at them. "Seems I drove a little faster than usual. If you want to get out and stretch before the others arrive, you can."

"Who killed the human women?" Bella asked, combing her fingers through her hair.

Devlyn couldn't believe she'd ask another red that question. Then again, he could. She wasn't really the shy type. Still, he didn't believe any one of the red pack would tell them if he or she knew who had done it.

"Sad state of affairs when *lupus garous* can't find a

mate. Unnatural. In the beginning, there was only one. Of course, you probably know the story. Some say he was from some other world, or a genetic abomination; others say a virus mutated him. Anyway, he had to change a human woman to satisfy the wolf's urge to have a mate. Then more were changed, until all we had to do was mate with our own kind, no longer needing to change humans in the ancient way. Somewhere along the line, the males outnumbered the females and that led to the imbalance that has caused all of the trouble."

Bella frowned. "The first *lupus garou* was a berserker gifted with the change by Odin's will."

The old man nodded. "That's another version."

She growled. "It's the true one. And the first was a red."

The old man's lips rose in a sly smile.

"Well, he was," Bella insisted.

"Never gave it much thought what kind of wolf the original *lupus garou* was. I suspect it could've been a red."

"But," Devlyn interjected with authority, "it was a gray."

The old man's eyes caught Devlyn's gaze, but he wouldn't respond to the bait. Then he took a deep breath and stared out the windshield, glancing up to look at them through the rearview mirror.

Devlyn nodded for him to continue. He squeezed Bella's hand when her breathing grew shallow.

The old man sighed. "It's not right for a *lupus garou* to do what's been done." He shook his head, sorrow filling his voice. "Not right at all. If the woman couldn't accept him…well, in the old days it was different. She had no choice, and, once she was changed, she acknowledged it, learning to love her new life. Today, it's not the same. We can't just kill a human because she won't accept us."

Bella said softly, "All of us are at risk with their actions. They'll expose all *lupus garous* to manhunts and extermination if they learn the truth about us."

"That's what I've said all along. They'll be the death of us."

"How can we help put a stop to this?"

"By that mate of yours fighting tonight."

Bella's eyes widened. "It's all three of them then—Alfred, Nicol, and Ross—and a fourth?"

The man studied her in the rearview mirror. "You would have made an exceptional alpha female for our pack, but it won't ever happen. Not the way you're attached to the gray." He gazed out the window again. "When it's all said and done, we'll be leaderless, but one of the older males can guide the pack in the interim. Maybe we need someone with more sense than strength for a while. Although…" He shook his head.

"So there's another who might be fit to take over?" Bella glanced at Devlyn. "Does he drive a Humvee?"

"He's a loner, for the most part. Been gone for most of the year, some say searching for a mate somewhere else in the States. But he's not been successful as far as I hear. By the way, he only just learned about you, missy."

"Would he take over?"

"If your mate gets rid of some of the bad seeds, I suspect he might come down from the mountains."

"But what about the other murdering red? The one that's sneakier than the rest?"

The old man remained silent.

Bella tightened her grip on Devlyn's hand. "They all took part in the killings—one for each girl, four of them."

This time, the old man glanced up at the mirror, and the look in his eyes revealed the truth. Four younger males had taken part in the killings. All seeking a mate. All failing. They were bound together in the killing spree, and, with so many involved, the rest of the pack feared speaking out against them.

Devlyn knew then it was his destiny to fight them when their own could not. To right a wrong that could hurt all *lupus garous* in the end.

"Who's the other red?" Bella asked again.

"Simon."

"Simon? We haven't met this Simon."

"He's the least aggressive of the pack in their age range. I'm sure he was there when the others went to meet you at the dance club."

Bella swallowed hard.

Devlyn wrapped his arm around her shoulders and pulled her close. He tried to think of another red he might have missed, who'd watched them, quietly surveying the female he wished to make his own at the dance club. But Devlyn had been so intent on Ross, Nicol, and Alfred that he never thought there'd be anyone else. Kissing her cheek, Devlyn whispered, "I'll be all right, Bella."

"There'll be four of them, Devlyn."

"They won't attack all at once, not in front of their pack."

"If anyone can do it, it'll be your mate," the old man said. "In truth, and I'd be burned at the stake for saying so—your gray is the only one who has a chance at saving this red pack from extermination. And it's rattling Alfred a bit to think the gray devil wolf from his great-grandfather's day did away with that bad hombre, too."

"But if you have no others to lead the pack and this other one won't leave his mountain home..." Devlyn said, concerned about the pack dying out without younger leadership.

The man's wizened face lifted, and his eyes turned brighter for an instant. "Leidolf returns to the city on occasion—checking out the pack, we figure. Mainly after he learned your mate was here, too. We believe he plans to take over once the gray culls out some of the bad wood. Leidolf's name means 'wolf descendant.' Some say his line ties in directly to the original *lupus garou,* one of the rarest of our kind, with only a human or two thrown into the mix."

"A red royal," Bella said under her breath.

Devlyn grunted. *A royal, my ass.* That kind of lineage didn't make him a better wolf.

"Yeah, he'd be a royal all right. Give our clan a good name. We could certainly use the likes of him to give new life to the pack. Alfred hates him because he fears the elusive *lupus garou.* An animal magnetism surrounds him, and whenever he appears, we're drawn to him. If Alfred and his gang are banished, we hope the rogue will agree to be our leader."

"But what if he's not strong enough?" Bella asked.

The man chuckled. "Alfred tried to take him several months ago, but the red took care of *him* instead—sent

Alfred to the healers. Even though Alfred denied that
the loner had torn him up good. He insisted he'd tangled
with a cougar. But we all know better."

"So why hasn't he taken on Alfred and his gang?"

The old man shook his head. "Too many of them, missy.
No red could hope to fight four fit males and survive."

Bella leaned her head against Devlyn's chest. "We
should have gone home to Colorado when you said."

"No, Bella. You were right all along. We needed to
be here, to set things right. Just have faith in me."

He wished she trusted his abilities more. Already the
adrenaline flooded his system, preparing him for battle.
Both mentally and physically, he readied himself.

Still, the sound of tires rolling on gravel startled him,
and they both turned to look behind them.

"Here they are. Time to give it all you've got, young
man."

Devlyn would. He wouldn't give Bella up to a pack
of reds, if he had to fight every last one of them. Proving
to any wolf that he'd claimed her, particularly to her
own kind, gave him great satisfaction.

Four SUVs barreled up, scattering the gravel on the
shoulder. Two parked in front of them, two behind, as
if wedging them in, allowing them no chance of escape.

The sun had nearly faded from the sky, and already
the reds were ditching their clothes in the vehicles. Bella
and Devlyn waited. Despite the old man's words, the
gray was not likely a welcome sight among the reds,
and the notion that Devlyn—instead of a red—would
kill their leader most likely didn't bode well with many
of them. As the old man said, there were many who

probably felt that Bella could solve their problems by mating with one of the reds and thereby end the killings. What was done was done, and it wouldn't be repeated, but the problem was that, if Alfred won the prize, Ross, Nicol, and Simon would still be without mates. And they would continue their killing spree.

The urge to mate ran in their blood. Desiring a mate who would race in the wild with them proved tantamount. Sexual relations with a woman in human form only wouldn't be enough to satisfy them.

Bella would have had more of a chance at changing a human male—with their more warlike, hunter attitudes—than a male *lupus garou* would at changing a female human. Devlyn was well pleased when she'd said she'd given up that notion.

When night fell and the sliver of the moon sat suspended against the navy velvet backdrop, Devlyn and Bella exited the vehicle. The reds had already turned into their wolf forms, but Bella seemed reluctant to remove her clothes. Surprised to see her shyness, Devlyn realized she hadn't been with her own kind for eons, and living with humans had changed her. Then he reconsidered. She didn't want to become a wolf because it meant that then he would, too, and the battle would begin.

Because he didn't want the reds to see her nakedness, he stood in front of her, with the SUV at her back, the door wide open to provide her some privacy.

Her eyes filled with tears, striking a chord of sympathy deep inside of him. She had to be strong, his alpha female, forever by his side.

"Be strong for me, Bella honey. I need your strength to win."

She swallowed hard and nodded.

"I love you." He kissed her lips; it was the last time he could touch her in their human form until he finished with the reds. He wanted to do so much more, to assure her in some way that he'd come out on top. Until he fought the others and won, he figured that no amount of convincing would work.

They deepened the kiss, and growls erupted behind them.

Bella wrapped her arms around him in a warm embrace, ignoring the reds' dislike of Devlyn and his mate showing such affection. "I love you, too, you big gray. You'll win. I know it."

But she didn't sound sure.

"You'd give me hell if I didn't. Are you ready?"

She nodded.

"All right, let's do it, Bella darling."

Bella took a deep breath and began to change as Devlyn kept her shielded. Once she had dropped to all four paws, he shape-shifted, glad to be in his wolf form and ready to finish this.

He rubbed her face with his muzzle and then moved away from her. His heart thundered with determination.

Bella watched her big gray with sadness in her heart. She couldn't help but worry about how he would fare. But worse, she knew she had to leave him once it was over. Had to run so that he wouldn't fight Volan.

Here, if he began to lose the battle, she'd change into her human form and get the gun. After all, four against one wasn't fair by either kind's standards, *lupus garous* or humans. And regular bullets were better than nothing.

Even though her wolf coat kept her warm, she shivered. She couldn't shake the fear that one of the reds might seriously injure Devlyn.

The wolves formed a jagged circle while Devlyn and Alfred faced off in the center. Although Alfred was decidedly smaller, he was wiry and moved quickly, pacing back and forth, highly agitated and aggressive. Devlyn's larger build had the power of the pounce and the pinning that had always beat her when they played as youngsters and preteens. But this was entirely different. This was a battle to the death.

She assumed that, if Devlyn had not learned that Alfred was one of the killers, he would have let him live, barely, just to make the point that Bella was his and no other's. Then Alfred could heal and come back to run the pack, if another hadn't taken it over. But Alfred and his companions in crime warranted the death sentence, and Devlyn would mete it out if he could.

Devlyn stood stiff legged and tall—a show of dominance. His ears were erect and held forward, his hackles bristling. He held his tail vertical and slightly curled toward his back, alpha posturing at its best and not to be trifled with. His lips curled up, and he bared his incisors. Alfred promptly growled, showing off his canines. If Devlyn dove in and got Alfred just right, his powerful jaws—twice as strong as those of a German shepherd's—could crush the large bones of his prey.

Alfred continued to pace, which was not normal for two wolves fighting for the alpha male role. She wondered if her kissing Devlyn with such affection had unmanned the killer red.

Appearing not to want to attack the red unprovoked, because of his size and the fact that he wasn't in the red's territory, Devlyn waited.

Alfred finally whipped around, as if he got the courage to take a nip at the gray, and leapt nearly six feet into the air.

Devlyn sidestepped where Alfred would land. As soon as the red's paws were planted firmly on the ground, Devlyn attacked.

Devlyn's teeth sank into the red's flank. Yelping, Alfred scurried away, his side bleeding, his ears flattened, his tail straight down. The rest of the wolves waited, tongues panting, as if they stood at a sporting exhibition, watching to see which fighter won.

Bella fought the urge to rush into the fray and bite the red who could have exposed their kind for what they were, to give back a little of what they'd done to the girls they'd murdered.

Devlyn watched Alfred, never taking his eyes off him, calculating his next move, conserving his energy for the next three in line. He was a crafty wolf, and she loved him dearly for his size, strength, and cunning.

Limping slightly to the side of the circle, Alfred paced again, only slower this time, not as steadily or as sure of himself. He never looked at her once, just at the ground, already exhibiting signs of defeat. The way he acted, he appeared to think he'd lost the fight before he'd even begun. He was probably right. The last two wolves might have a chance to take a bite out of Devlyn when he was tired and worn down. But not the first.

Bella hoped with all her heart that Devlyn wouldn't be hurt, even a scratch, despite the fact that they healed quickly.

Attempting the same maneuver, Alfred whipped around and leapt through the air. Maybe it worked for him when he became the alpha leader for the reds, but with Devlyn, it didn't.

Devlyn lunged this time and grabbed Alfred's throat, instantly crushing his neck. He had to end the game quickly if he were to conserve enough strength to fight the other three.

For a minute, no more, the reds watched him when he released the dead body of their alpha leader. The deed was done. No one had time to reflect on the sudden shift in power.

Instantly, Ross attacked. His teeth snapped at Devlyn's neck, but Bella's gray mate lithely avoided Ross's wicked canines.

Her heart pounded ferociously.

Grabbing Ross's ear, Devlyn tore the leather. Ross whined in protest and dodged out of the way.

So much for the bad red wolf who'd killed his victim so brutally.

Sitting on her haunches, every nerve on edge, Bella tried to stretch her muscles to release the tension.

Devlyn faced Ross, but he got a glimpse of her. His tongue hung over his teeth as he panted, but his lips curved up slightly as if in a smile. He'd beaten Alfred, and he'd done it for her. He was one proud big gray wolf.

Bowing her head slightly to him, her eyes gazed into his, showing him how much she loved him and how proud she was of him.

Ross attacked again.

Bella stiffened her back, but Devlyn was prepared. He immediately responded with a bite at the red's right shoulder. Bleeding profusely, Ross yelped and bolted away.

Bella glanced at Nicol; his eyes darkened, his body tensed. As soon as Devlyn finished Ross, Nicol wouldn't wait either, but which one was the sneaky Simon?

Fear niggled at her that he was an emergent leader. The kind that waited until the battle ended before he rushed in to take over. Was it as Ross and Nicol had said? There wasn't any reason to take over the pack until she came along?

She stood. Then realizing her anxiety might bother Devlyn, she lay down and rested her head on her paws as if the whole matter served simply as a pleasing walk in the woods.

Ross stood still at the edge of the circle, panting hard, his chest filling and emptying with intense breaths. No longer just a spectator, he battled for his life. Fresh blood matted his fur. The rest stood on end as he raised his tail behind him. His posture indicated that he wasn't ready to give up the fight, not yet.

Neither was Devlyn. He stood ready, his body somewhat relaxed between sparring, to allow him time to rest.

A wolf howled in the distance. As unique to wolves as fingerprints were to humans, Bella immediately recognized the warning sound...Volan.

# Chapter 19

THE SOUND OF VOLAN'S HOWL NEARLY MADE BELLA'S heart stop. Devlyn's ears pulled back and he narrowed his eyes. His tail pointed straight out, parallel to the ground. Undoubtedly, he sensed the added danger when he caught the sound, too.

It just couldn't be Volan. Not when Devlyn had so many reds to fight. Bella continued to recline on the ground, pretending not to be bothered, to show Devlyn that she believed in him with all of her heart. But she couldn't smooth down the hair standing erect on the nape of her neck or tail. She couldn't relax her tail, fixed straight as a spear, her body on full alert, ready to react if Volan made a sudden appearance.

Then she reminded herself that she had her gun and it could give him a lot of heartburn for a while.

Ross ran toward Devlyn with his teeth bared. Fire burned in the depths of his brown eyes. Devlyn responded, his leg and back muscles moving like a waterfall, fluid and powerful. Grabbing Ross by the throat, he snapped his neck in two.

Ross fell limply to the ground; Bella stopped panting. For now, Devlyn had proved himself once again the winner. Taking a deep breath of pride, she admired her mate for his skill and ingeniousness. She thought of how Ross and the other wolves had killed those helpless

women and how, if they'd had a chance, they would
have killed Devlyn. For those reasons, she had no regret.
It was the way of the wolf, the only reason they had
survived as long as they had.

Still, her anxiety heightened, worrying that Devlyn's
energy would dwindle.

Nicol lunged at him. No rest in between, calculated
to wear the gray down.

Most of the wolves still stood. A couple of the older
ones, their red fur now graying, lay down, but all kept
their eyes fixed on the fighters.

Nicol got a lucky strike—because she couldn't concede
it was anything else—and grazed Devlyn's neck with his
wicked canines. Devlyn snapped and growled with his
teeth bared, the sound deep and basslike, extremely menacing. Nicol quickly retreated from Devlyn's killer canines.

Bella suppressed the urge to dash into the battle and
bite the red back. She sat up instantly, unable to pretend
any further to be so relaxed about the fight.

Nicol pounced on him again, but Devlyn snapped his
jaw at him, nearly catching the red's leg. Hearing the
sound of Devlyn's powerful jaws clamping together so
close to his body, Nicol yelped.

Bella searched the crowd again, looking for a male
wolf about the right age that might be Simon. Her eye
caught that of a red who was watching her, not the fight.
He stood taller than Alfred had, but certainly not as big
as a gray. But he looked as if he could have put Alfred
down. Her stomach tightened.

She faced Devlyn, who sprung at Nicol and pinned
him down by the throat.

Nicol whined and squirmed. Devlyn had the best of him. Why didn't he finish him off? Not to do so was cowardly, and it was not the wolf way...not the *lupus garou* way. Not when the red had murdered a human woman and risked exposing all of the *lupus garous*.

Devlyn's chest heaved with exhaustion. Worn out, he rested before the kill, knowing that Simon would attack as soon as he let go of Nicol. Bella settled back down, glad she'd figured out his reluctance to finish Nicol off.

The wolves grew restless as he continued to wait. Several wolves held their tails straight out behind them, indicating their apprehension. Then, with resolve, Devlyn clamped his jaws down on Nicol's throat, crushing the neck bone with a powerful snap, ending the fourth-generation big-game hunter's life instantly.

The one who'd been watching Bella immediately leapt for Devlyn, nearly sixteen feet through the air, the longest distance a wolf could leap. This time, Devlyn didn't react quickly enough. Simon knocked him on his hip.

Bella lunged forward, but two of the other males blocked her from interceding. Females fought females, never males—the unwritten rule passed down from generation to generation.

She growled at them. They bowed their heads to her, showing that they had no intention of fighting her but wouldn't move out of her path.

Again she growled, baring her teeth at one and then the other, preparing herself to attack. She couldn't watch Simon hurt her mate. The strain of the fighting and the tension that had built up in her system keyed her higher than an active volcano built up steam, ready to explode.

When neither of the reds would move, she snarled and snapped at the one to her right, intent on having her way. Immediately, the one to her left pounced, pinning her to her side against the pine needle floor. She wriggled with frustration but couldn't free herself because of his heavier weight and bigger size.

Devlyn caught her eye and snarled, angered that another male would force her down. If he hadn't had to fight Simon, she knew he would have taken care of the male that now dominated her. Devlyn whipped around, his teeth connecting with Simon's right front leg.

Simon yelped and dodged backward.

The two tore into each other again, snarling and biting with wicked intent.

Bella squirmed to get free again and then growled low. More enraged than she'd ever been, if she could have freed herself, she would have torn to shreds the red who pinned her down.

To her horror, Devlyn tucked his tail, bowed his head, flattened his ears, and lay down on his belly. Her heart nearly quit when she saw his defeated posture. His neck and mouth bled, but he didn't seem to have any serious injuries. If he didn't fight and kill the red, a known murderer...

A male, maybe in his late fifties, moved forward cautiously, baring his canines at Simon. The younger wolf turned to face the new threat.

Devlyn remained in his subservient position, watching the reds fight, avoiding looking at Bella.

It finally dawned on Bella. Devlyn couldn't kill the last renegade red. He had to force one of the reds of the pack to do it. The one who did would become the new leader. They couldn't have a gray best the last red and take over the pack.

Just like the gray devil wolf that had infiltrated Alfred's red pack so long ago. The leadership had become stagnant and corrupt just as Alfred's was. She'd never considered that Devlyn's great-grand-father had forced change—not by taking over as he could have easily done, but by helping them rid them-selves of the cancer in their pack—and then left. That another red wolf had taken over. But she bet his great-grandfather hadn't had to fight four reds, one after another, either.

The older male charged and tackled Simon. They bit each other, snarled, and snapped their mighty jaws. They dodged and charged and bloodied each other's pelts. Then Simon made the fatal move. He turned the wrong way, exposing his throat at the inappropriate instant, leaving himself open to the kill.

The older wolf took him by surprise. Without hesita-tion, he ripped out Simon's throat, and the younger wolf was instantly killed.

Then something drew their attention toward the woods, and everyone turned to look. Standing in the mist of the forest, a red male wolf considered Bella with unspoken longing, but his neck and leg were bleeding, his tongue hanging from his bloodied mouth, as though he'd tangled with a much bigger beast and lost. Had he come to fight for the leadership but been thwarted? And now was he too torn up to fight well?

He glanced at Devlyn and bared his bloodied teeth.

The new leader bowed his head to the loner. The two stared at each for a moment and then the wolf turned and dove back into the forest, disappearing in a heartbeat.

"It's him, Leidolf," one of the older women said, already having turned back into her human form. "He'll be back." She smiled with admiration. "He has the look of leadership in his eyes, his stance. And he would've taken on the others if he hadn't been injured and that delayed him. He'll be back."

There was no time for jubilation, or for the wolves to show their allegiance to their new pack leader. Sirens sounded from a distance, creating a panic. The wolf that pinned Bella down jumped off her. She snapped at him, missing biting his leg by inches.

Devlyn rushed to join her as the other wolves scattered, quickly changing into their human forms. Some dove into the vehicles and donned their clothes. Some grabbed the lifeless, bloodied bodies of the reds, once again turned into human form, and deposited them in the trunks of their vehicles.

Only the new red alpha male leader remained for a moment, staring at Devlyn, not challenging him, but instead giving him thanks.

Devlyn bowed his head and then raised it in acknowledgement.

The wolf dashed for one of the vehicles, but before Bella and Devlyn could return to the SUV that had brought them there, the driver tore off. She realized then they'd never have taken the gray and her back with them to the city. Only if the gray had died would they have taken her into the pack.

She touched her nose to Devlyn's, and he licked her face. They pressed their muzzles against each other. They had only one option available to them now—run like the wind and seek shelter in her cabin.

At short spurts, they could run as fast as twenty-eight miles per hour, but because of Devlyn's fight, they ran at a trot. Her cabin was located only a couple of miles away. They'd make it. As long as zoo man Thompson didn't find Rosa running with the injured gray male, or they didn't cross paths with Volan. Involuntarily, a shiver ran through her.

With the cool breeze in her face and the two of them trotting nearly shoulder to shoulder, she suddenly realized that the gun she'd so carefully hidden in her clothes still rested under the seat in the black SUV. Her security blanket was ripped away from her. Now they had nothing but to fight Volan the way the wolf would. Even wounding Volan temporarily would have been to her advantage—until she could find another old-time smithy who could fashion silver bullets.

Then she recalled the gun in her cabin. Different smithy, and maybe real silver bullets. If they could just reach it in time.

Analyzing the rustle of the wind through the trees, birds' sweet whistling tunes, and the sound of Devlyn's and her pads tromping on the needled floor, she listened for Volan. Tilting her nose up, she breathed in the air, smelling a deer nearby, the scent of a raccoon, the fragrance of pine...no Volan.

Devlyn acted as wary, his ears twitching back and forth, channeling in on the sounds, sniffing the air.

When the cabin came into view, she filled her lungs with air and wanted to shout for joy. Instead, she whimpered in her most happy wolf way. Devlyn rubbed her face with his, sharing her tentative liberation.

As soon as they reached the front steps, they changed into their human form. Standing on the porch, Devlyn pulled Bella into his arms and kissed her thoroughly.

The tension drained from her body. Devlyn had won. He'd shown his cleverness, superiority, and prowess as a born leader by allowing the older male to take down the final rogue wolf. She wondered if the mystery red wolf would give up his loner ways and take over the pack. But then she speculated again about whether she could convince Devlyn to start a new pack.

A lone wolf could do so, with his mate, and then he wouldn't have to fight Volan. How she wished he'd agree with her, but his heart was set on returning to the family that had taken him in. She had to admit that the notion of being with the pack again filled her with longing.

Taking an exasperated breath, she asked, "Did you hear Volan's howl?"

"Yeah." Devlyn rubbed her arms. "Telling us he knows where we are and that we have no choice but to return home to the pack."

"We don't have to, you know. We could start our own."

Devlyn's eyes hardened, and she knew then that she'd never be able to convince him to stay away from Volan. "I told you years ago, Bella. He would come after you and our children. I can't risk it." He glanced down at her clothes still lying on the chair on the porch.

"I took a run and ended up in the zoo."

"I remember it well, although it seems like eons ago."

Grabbing her clothes, she headed inside the two-room cabin.

Devlyn dashed around her. "Let me take a look around first."

She smelled it then. The slight odor that was Volan. Her skin chilled, but it had nothing to do with the cold cabin.

Devlyn quickly inspected the bedroom and bath and rejoined Bella in the living area. "He's not here."

"But he's been here."

"Yeah."

"Do you think he'll come back?"

"No. He'll want to prove to the pack you're his. Trying to kill me here and then returning you to the pack wouldn't be enough."

She dumped her clothes on a tweed-covered couch and took Devlyn's hand. "Let's get you washed up then. I'll take care of those bites and…"

He leaned over and licked her neck. "I need something else. I'm a bit…tense."

Glancing down at his full-blown erection, she lifted a brow. "After all you've been through?"

He wiggled his brows.

She laughed. "I know just how to handle it."

He growled softly. "How well I know."

They made it halfway across the living area when the front door slammed open, banging against the wall.

Volan stood in the entryway, his mouth red with blood, and she wondered if Leidolf, the loner red, had tangled with the demon. He was dressed in denims and a sweatshirt that were as black as his mood. His black hair hung loosely at his shoulders, and he looked as if he'd fallen out of bed in a hurry and hadn't had his first cup of coffee yet. But the demonic look in Volan's black eyes had nothing to do with missing a mug of caffeine. His unfulfilled lust for Bella showed in every angry line creasing his stern face.

Volan took in Bella's nakedness, inhaled a deep breath, smelling the air—or, rather, her, trying to tell if Devlyn had mated with her already. His look couldn't get any harder. He shifted his attention to Devlyn. "I gather you were straightening out a matter with a pack of red wolves in the area, which delayed your bringing Bella home to me."

"She's mine, Volan," Devlyn said, moving Bella behind him. "You can't have her."

Volan tsked. "*You* can't have her. Pack laws. She's my choice."

"Those aren't wolf laws. She chose me. You're out of luck."

"My rules then. Come on, Bella." Volan stretched his meaty hand out to her. "I'll let him live if you come with me now."

Devlyn gripped her arm tighter, worried she might agree to be Volan's mate.

"However, Bella sweet, I'll have to teach you a thing or two about wolf law. Seems you've forgotten some of them while living among the humans." Volan touched his chest lightly. She noticed his skin still seemed paler than usual.

Had she injured him after all? Why hadn't the silver killed him?

Drops of blood trickled down his sneakers onto the wood floor. She looked up at him.

Volan turned his attention to Devlyn. "Lover boy's too spent to fight me. Wouldn't be a fair battle. Besides, we fight in front of the pack, end this once and for all. I challenge you to bring her home and battle me for her, Devlyn."

"I'll be there," Devlyn growled.

Volan turned and stalked out of the cabin, a slight limp to his gait.

Releasing her, Devlyn stormed to the door and watched Volan disappear into the woods. Bella joined him and bent over to inspect the blood.

"He's been wounded," Devlyn said. "That's why he wouldn't fight me yet."

"In the leg?" she guessed, wondering how her bullets managed to hit him in the leg when she was damn sure both bullets had hit his chest.

"Yeah, probably when he was in wolf form someone got a shot off."

"It's not hunting season."

"Right, but some wouldn't care if he was wearing his wolf pelt and got near their livestock."

—◦◦◦—

Before long, warm water filled the tub, and Devlyn reclined on his back as she climbed on top of him.

He kissed her lips and ran his hands over her breasts, heating her deep inside. "I have to say, Bella, you made me proud."

"I was afraid you'd be angry with me because I tried to help you."

He leisurely licked the bathwater off her cheek. "You love me and wanted to protect me. You didn't do it because you felt I couldn't handle him. It was just instinctive. An alpha female quality."

She washed his bloodied neck with care. Referring to her as having alpha qualities was the greatest compliment he could ever give. "I was so proud of you to submit to another red, to allow him to fight Simon for the right to be the leader of the pack." Knowing how difficult it was not only to pretend to cower before a red, but in front of his mate—it had to have been the hardest thing he'd ever done. Her chest swelled with pride to think such a great gray wanted her for his very own.

"I only did what my great-grandfather had done before me."

"Don't be so modest. I doubt *he* had to fight four reds, one after another. You created a new legend for this clan in your own right."

"And you, Bella. The red wolf that the gray fought for."

She leaned over and kissed his bristly cheek.

His fingers touched her nipples, making her whole body tingle. He sighed deeply. "With only one to battle instead of four, I hoped one of the older wolves would have the courage to tackle him."

"My clever wolf." She ran her hand over his length in loving strokes. Finally, he'd allowed her to touch him, without stopping her. She would have rested with him instead, anything, to feel his heart beating against her breast, to have his skin touching hers, warm and alive, to feel his breath against her cheek, to taste his salty skin, and to smell him, feral and all male. Her gray, for the most part uninjured and safe with her again.

His eyes clouded with passion as he studied her with admiration, his hands massaging the small of her back. When it appeared he couldn't handle another of her strokes, he slipped his hands down to her thighs, his fingertips drawing closer to her folds.

"You're still awfully tense," she said, her gaze taking in every inch of his glistening body, hard, muscled, and every bit hers.

He chuckled, the throaty sound triggering an ache between her legs. He lifted her and worked his way inside her folds. "This will definitely help."

Her nipples brushed against the hair on his chest, sending delicious chills of desire coursing through every nerve. He cupped her face and lifted it, claiming her mouth with a deep, sizzling kiss. Their bodies slid against each other while his erection penetrated her deeply. Up and down she rose on top of him, creating tidal waves in the bathtub. Water splashed over the edge of the tub and spilled onto the tile floor. They kissed and touched each other's skin with greed, giving not a care to anything else in the world.

Just as she envisioned climbing to the top of the snow-covered Wolf Rock, she rose higher with every plunge he made deep inside her. When she felt she couldn't take any more, he groaned out her name, filling her with his warm seed, and as she reached the peak of pleasure, her insides pulsated with orgasmic delight.

"You're too right for me," he whispered against her

mouth, tenderly, lovingly, the sound of a lusty, satiated mate.

Their tongues tangled, and she combed her fingers
through his damp hair. "For each other," she said, still
seated on top of him, never wanting to let go.

But something in his eyes told her he was concerned
about some matter. It didn't take her long to learn what
still troubled him.

He cleared his throat. "I always wondered, Bella, in
the old days when your friend drowned—"

"Elizabeth?"

"Yes. Why didn't you let me console you?"

"Volan saw you with me. I bit you to get you to leave
me alone. He hated when you got near me, especially
after I became a teen."

"But you let him comfort you! I thought you wanted
him."

"Right. That's why I ran away so many times."

"Then why?"

She glowered at him. "He threatened to kill you! He
told me if I let you touch me, he'd end your life. Damn
it, Devlyn, you weren't full grown then. He'd killed men
more his size. I couldn't let him hurt you."

Then tension left his body, but only for a second.

She cocked her head, thinking she heard a sound outside the cabin. Devlyn's whole body grew rigid. He'd
heard it, too.

Before they could disengage themselves from each
other, humans stormed into the house, their heavy
cologne preceding them. Zoo man Thompson forged
ahead at the lead and began to enter the bathroom first

but stopped when he saw Bella sitting on Devlyn, naked in the tub.

He wheeled around, shoving uniformed cops out of the doorway, and then hollered back to Devlyn and Bella, "Sorry, folks. We had word the two of you had been kidnapped."

Devlyn smiled at Bella and shook his head.

Henry cleared his throat. "Chrissie will be glad to hear that you're both...uh, well."

Bella chuckled under her breath and handed Devlyn a bath towel. "I only have the one." She pointed to a hand towel. "That wouldn't work I don't think."

He wrapped the towel around his waist. "I'll bring your clothes to you. I don't have any," he whispered in her ear. "The towel will have to suffice for now."

He walked out of the bathroom and returned with her clothes. He said for her ear only, "I'll give them the story."

"I'll listen to make sure our versions are the same," she said, her voice hushed.

Devlyn left the bathroom and shut the door. "Henry." He pointed to the couch. "Have a seat."

Henry sat down while the police milled around on the front porch. "When Chrissie called to say you were kidnapped, I had to take measures into my own hands. We hadn't reacted fast enough to follow the SUV that took you, so I broke into your home..."

Devlyn raised his brows.

Henry shook his head. "I'm sorry. I only wanted to get to you quickly before Volan killed you."

"And?"

"I found the email stating that someone wanted to

meet you at Wolf Rock. You wouldn't take Bella with you to meet him for fear she'd get hurt. I figured he thought you wouldn't come, so he ensured that you would by kidnapping you. Luckily, I was able to get the police's help, and we hurried to Wolf Rock as fast as we could."

His gaze fastened on the bite marks on Devlyn's neck. Although they'd been severe, the wound had already started to fade, the intensity of the pain lessening by the hour. Of course, some of the healing had to do with Bella's distracting him. Still, he was sure the wound looked pretty angry.

"We found a lot of blood, but no bodies. I'd come across Bella's cabin a few days ago, checked the license tags of the Escape parked out back, and verified that she owned the place. Anyway, I'd hoped, if you were still alive and able, that you'd made it here safely, as close as it is to Wolf Rock. We found traces of blood along a trail leading directly here, too."

Devlyn nodded. Either Henry assumed that more had happened and he was keeping it a secret, or he'd given them the best out they could have. "Yes, well, luckily her place was close enough."

Henry pointed to his wound. "A doctor needs to take a look at that."

Bella entered the room wearing her turtleneck and jeans. Her wet curls still dangled over her shoulders, and the dripping water darkened the blue turtleneck in spots. She joined Devlyn, and he pulled her onto his toweled lap. She smelled like lavender and female, and he had to fight burying his nose in her wet hair. What the heck?

He closed his eyes and pressed his cheek against her hair, took a deep breath, and opened his eyes.

A hint of amusement flashed across Henry's face.

"With Bella's care, I'll be better in no time."

"Yeah, with care like that…" Henry cleared his throat. "I guess I'd better let you give the police a statement about what happened then. We'll give you an escort home?"

Devlyn deferred the decision to Bella. She nodded. "We'd like that. We're going back to Colorado for a while. Let Devlyn heal up there."

Henry stared at her for a moment. "But that's where this Volan character is from."

"We'll inform the police when we get there about the situation," Devlyn said. "And listen, Henry, we sure do thank you for trying to rescue us."

Henry glanced back at the bathroom. "I didn't expect…well, I'm just damned glad we found the two of you alive and in pretty good shape."

"We'll need one more thing, however," Bella said, with a twinkle in her eye and a dimple in her cheek.

Henry rose from the couch. "Anything."

"He stole Devlyn's clothes. Well, mine, too, but luckily I had some clothes here already."

"You ran in this cold, stark…" Henry shook his head. "That sick bastard."

"I have an oversized pink sweatshirt Devlyn can wear, but the extra pair of denims I have won't fit him." She ran her hand over his thigh.

His muscle flexed with her stirring touch. Just a little higher, more centered, and she could touch something else she'd stirred.

"Let me talk with the officers. Maybe we can come up with something."

Henry walked outside and conversed with the officers.

Devlyn kissed Bella on the mouth. "Hmm, a pink sweatshirt, eh?"

"Yeah, I dare you to wear it."

"I'll take you up on it. Nothing I'd like better than to wear the smell of you, up close and personal."

She chuckled. "I'm glad you don't have a problem with it. Because I imagine that's all we're going to be able to come up with."

Although one of the officers offered his jacket to Devlyn, he couldn't be dissuaded from wearing Bella's sweatshirt back to her house. With a blanket wrapped around his waist, he walked outside to talk to the police officers. She overheard Devlyn say, "Volan brought a killer wolf with him and ordered it to attack me. When we heard the police sirens, he fled with his wolf in a black SUV, but we didn't get a look at his license plate. Concerned about Bella and my condition in the frigid weather without clothes, we headed for the warmth and safety of her cabin."

"Hell, I wonder if that's the same wolf that rancher Evans shot?" one of the men said.

"Someone shot a wolf?" Devlyn asked.

"Yeah," Thompson said. "At first we thought it was Rosa, but he described the wolf as a bigger gray."

Bella barely breathed. *Volan.*

"Did the rancher kill him?" Devlyn asked.

"Nope, that was the thing. He yelped, so Evans knew he hit him, but the wolf ran off. We've got men trying to track him down. A wounded wolf won't get far, but he will be dangerous," Thompson said.

So a rancher had wounded Volan after all. But it didn't explain his bloody mouth, and she wondered again if he'd torn into Leidolf. Then he could watch from a distance and see if Devlyn could handle four reds on his own? She wouldn't put it past the bastard. Then what? Fight Devlyn when he was worn out? Only he got shot. She smiled. Good one on him—the snake.

Hoping the police believed Devlyn's story, Bella returned to the bedroom to retrieve her gun. Her heart did a flip when she saw the braided rug that normally kept her secret cache hidden had been overturned, and she quickly lifted a loose floor plank.

Nothing but a scribbled message.

> *Naughty, Bella. Another gun? Threats work better if you back them up with real menace—silver bullets. I see you got it right this time. But you won't be needing this gun. Not anymore. Your soon-to-be mate, Volan*

Sniffing the air, she smelled Volan's faint odor. She glanced at the window; the cotton curtains rippled in the breeze. She dropped the crumpled note into her hiding hole and wanted to scream. Crossing the floor, she parted the curtains. He'd broken the window. Sniffing her shirt, she realized he must have touched her clothes on the porch and recognized that the place was hers. Had Devlyn seen the note?

She checked the bed. Volan's odor clung to the sheets. She wanted to throw up.

"Bella?" Devlyn called to her from the living room.

"Coming!" She hurried out of the bedroom.

---

On the way home, Bella tapped her thumbs on the steering wheel and then finally glanced at Devlyn, his eyes drowsy, as he leaned his head against the passenger's window. He must have seen the upturned rug. "Volan slept in my bed," she growled low.

"Yeah." He stared out the window.

Did he find Volan's note or not? Oh hell, no sense in keeping the situation secret. She squeezed the steering wheel and then loosened her hold. "He left a note."

Devlyn looked at her.

"Underneath the floorboard."

He didn't say a word, just watched her with a stern look.

"I...I had another gun; the bullets were meant for him."

"I know, Bella honey."

"You did?" Tears pricked her eyes.

"Yeah."

"But you didn't say anything."

"I didn't want to worry you that he'd found the gun."

"Would you have let me keep it?"

He ground his teeth and looked away. "Yeah. Even though I didn't ever intend for you to have to use it."

She took a steadying breath. "Thanks, Devlyn."

"What I have to know is why he knew about the

other gun—the one you threatened the reds with at your home—and why did you intimate that the bullets were silver when they weren't?" His eyes were hard, compelling her to tell the truth.

"I…" Oh hell, she couldn't keep the secret from her mate even if he hated her for it. "I shot him."

Devlyn's eyes widened.

"Twice," she added. "In the chest. Both times. And he fell. And he looked dead. But he wasn't. Only knocked out. But I didn't know that. You know, real bullets cause damage, too, except it's not permanent. But then he contacted me. And I didn't know if he'd sent the email before or after he died."

Devlyn raised a brow, his mouth almost curving up.

"So, I didn't know if the bullets weren't really silver or if Volan was really dead. Then we got the news that Volan was taken into custody, and that confirmed that he was alive." She glanced at Devlyn. "I don't blame you if you hate me for it."

"It's not our way, but, for your protection…I understand." He leaned over and kissed her cheek and then it seemed like the fight, the sex, and the adrenaline seeping out of every cell of his body finally hit him. He closed his eyes, and his head leaned against the cold window, where he slept for the two-hour drive home while the police escorted them the whole way.

When Bella finally parked in front of her house, Chrissie dashed out of her place to greet them. As soon as Bella and Devlyn climbed out of her Escape, Chrissie's gaze shifted from Devlyn's injury to the pink sweatshirt stretched taut across his chest and the green blanket wrapped around his waist. Her eyes grew wide.

Bella gave her a hug. "Thanks, Chrissie, for sending Henry to our rescue."

Chrissie looked at Henry, whose ears turned slightly red. He rubbed his chin. "Yeah, we'll talk about it later." He disappeared into Chrissie's house with her, but she cast a backward glance at Devlyn's blanket one more time, her eyes still huge.

Thank heavens the police took off.

Devlyn stalked into the bedroom, intent on changing and then returning to Colorado, while Bella paced in the living room.

She listened to him zipping his bag. Grinding her teeth, she glanced out the window at her compact SUV.

For now, Colorado and the pack beckoned for their return.

After giving Chrissie the picture of pressed Colorado flowers as a keepsake and assuring her she would keep in touch, Bella and Chrissie said their goodbyes. Devlyn helped Bella load everything she could fit into her Escape. Within the hour, and with Bella's heart in her throat, they were on their way, with Chrissie and her kids and Henry waving goodbye in the misting rain.

<center>~~~</center>

It took nearly the whole trip back to Colorado for Bella to realize that, although she wanted to show her independence and to run her life her own way, she wanted Devlyn more. She knew in her heart that he was meant to be an alpha male. Now that Devlyn was part of her life, her mate, and bound by wolf law to protect her, she had to give him the chance to prove himself worthy, or else she would forever damage his pride. She loved and admired him for being a male *lupus garou*. The good and the bad.

For humans, male pride only went so far, but for wolves, it was the whole basis of their familial existence. A part of Devlyn would never be satisfied unless he took over the pack in the wolf way, through brute force and resourcefulness, ousting Volan forever.

No matter how hard that was for her to concede, she had to give him the chance to show he could do it. To her, it didn't matter if he was the alpha male. It only mattered that they loved one another, but he needed more. The reassurance that he had the legitimate claim to her, that she was his and no one else's. He had to prove he could do this—to protect her from Volan, ultimately, to kill him, and to lead their pack.

And she prayed he'd survive.

Devlyn and Bella finally arrived in the Southern Rockies, midday. The pinyon junipers and pines scented the air, calling to them to take their fill and romp through the woods as they had done as youngsters.

Bella's eyes moistened to be home finally. She stared at the log cabin home, with its steep roof and wraparound porch. "This is your place, Devlyn?"

"Plenty of room for a bunch of kiddos," he said, reaching over to pat her belly. "Five bedrooms and 350 acres of prime wolf land. A stream runs right through the middle of it."

"The stream where we fished when we were little?"

"Yep. About a mile from here, my leather goods factory sits on two acres. Tanner and some of my other cousins are running things while I'm away."

"Oh, I should have asked before if you could support me in the fashion I've been accustomed to."

"Yeah, Bella, and all the little ones, too."

"Good." She climbed out of the Escape, weary of all of the traveling, glad to stretch her legs and to be home. "That means I don't have to spend *my* money."

He joined her on the porch and wrapped his arms around her. "You're independently wealthy?"

"Are you sure you didn't already know?"

He chuckled and kissed her cheek. "Here I thought I knew all about you."

"Not everything. Some secrets should be left that way, don't you think?"

"Absolutely not."

She smiled, then noticed a note fluttering on the door. "Someone left you a message." Already dread filled the pit of her stomach.

> *Didn't think you'd have the nerve to bring her to me after all. Argos said you were coming home. See you soon. Volan*

She touched Devlyn's neck where the red's canines had wounded him. Thank heavens, the area was completely healed, with not even a trace of a scar.

"Come on. We've tried your bed, the couch, the rental SUV, motel rooms, bathtubs, and showers. It's time to christen my place now. Plus rest up for tonight's big adventure," Devlyn said, crumpling Volan's note in his fist.

"Fighting Volan."

"Yep. The time has come. Well, in a few hours, but the notion is making me a little tense. Got something to relieve the tension?" The glint of devil flashed in his eyes.

"Now who's got a one-track mind?"

"*Only*...when you're around."

They'd barely walked into the house when Devlyn's phone rang. Answering it, he glanced at Bella.

She knew from the look on his face, Volan had called the pack to meet in the glade. The time had come to decide the leadership of the pack once again.

# Chapter 20

DESPITE LOVING HER WOLF FORM, BELLA THOUGHT SHE could live without it forever if it meant she and Devlyn would not have to face Volan's wrath; after all, keeping her wolf form meant that she could possibly lose the gray she dearly loved.

As before, she would be the dutiful mate and sit on the sidelines, relaxed and quiet, giving the illusion that she didn't worry about Devlyn's strength.

But as soon as the grays gathered for the evening spectacle, her heart sank. Crickets sounded their raucous tunes, frogs riveted from near the stream, and a breeze stirred pine needles with a whooshing sound. Cold and crisp, the smell of an expected snow touched the air. She wished the whisper of frost would harden Volan's joints and make him unable to dodge Devlyn's lunges. That Volan's teeth would fall out from disrepair. That his eyes and hearing were not so keen and he would make fatal mistakes, giving Devlyn the advantage. But he was not an old wolf, only in his midthirties, and he was a threatening figure.

Vernetta inched toward her in her wolf form, her dark-brown hair standing on end, warning her the move wasn't a social call. Suddenly, the idea dawned on Bella. If Devlyn succeeded in beating Volan, Vernetta would want to be the alpha female and his mate. Bella had been so worried that Devlyn would win, she never considered *she* might have to battle a bitch for the female alpha role. Especially since she had already mated with Devlyn, and she figured it was a done deal.

Devlyn cast a wary glance at Vernetta while he waited in the center of the circle alone, the grassy clearing surrounded by thick pines and a smattering of oaks shivering in the chilly breeze, a peaceful meadow any other time. Volan was the only wolf of the pack not in attendance. Now it was she, Bella, who had her mate worried. Not the other way around. He feared for her safety. Then alarm filled her soul. Would he give in to Volan, concerned that, if he did not, Vernetta might rip her to shreds?

Vernetta stood two inches taller than her and was heavier besides. Bella had never tangled with her, or any female before. Well, except for the time Vernetta had knocked Bella's baby teeth out, but Bella had been so much younger and smaller it really hadn't been a fight. For the first time that a wolf had tackled her in years, the red male had sufficiently pinned her down, but Vernetta wouldn't just wrestle her to the ground. She'd want blood to ensure Bella got the point. No *lupus garou* but her would be Devlyn's mate.

The smell of Volan pelted Bella before she caught sight of him. Turning, she found he'd sneaked up behind her, sniffing. She was sure he tried to see if Devlyn was still keeping her well satisfied. She snarled at Volan. He shoved his way between her and Vernetta, his black fur standing on end, his neck just as thick as she'd remembered it, his body hefty and deadly.

He glanced at the gray and then gave Bella a look of menace, the same kind of evil look that he gave Devlyn the day he'd kissed Bella so long ago. Vernetta wouldn't fight Bella to have Volan as her mate. This was clear in her posture when she slinked away, her tail tucked between her legs, but what disheartened Bella most was the way Devlyn's ears flattened slightly.

She wanted to scream at him not to give in. She'd fight the bitch with tooth and claw, but damn him if he gave up the fight before it even began.

His ears rose, and she bowed her head to him, trying to show she would fight for him as well as he fought for her. That she wouldn't give the matter a care when it was her turn to wage war, just as she'd struggle to keep her own emotions in check while he fought his battle.

Volan swung his head around and licked her face. Instantly she bit him, nipping his cheek. A love bite, that's the way he treated it. If a wolf could smile, he grinned at her. She snarled at him.

With a heavy lope, he ran into the center and confronted Devlyn.

Now was the moment of the face-off she'd dreaded all her life. Larger than most wolves, Volan was heavier-set than Devlyn, although Devlyn stood taller.

The hair on the backs of both wolves stood erect, as did their tails. They held their heads high and sniffed the air, attempting to sense signs of fear. They twitched their ears back and forth, listening, each anticipating the move of the other.

The standoff continued, and although most of the wolves remained tensed, waiting for the clash to begin, everyone kept deadly silent. Bella sat down, her back aching from holding it so laboriously taut, worrying that, if she didn't relax, she would cause her body to stiffen so much that she'd be unable to take on Vernetta.

Volan waited for Devlyn to make the first strike. Was that the reason Devlyn had waited for the reds to attack him? Because he'd learned it from Volan?

Never having witnessed fighting for the alpha male position between grays, she wasn't sure of the best way to win. She'd only seen the aftermath of the kill, when Volan had finished with the rogue wolves years earlier. Bella panted hard, trying to contain her nervousness, hoping that Volan would collapse and die right on the spot before either of them did anything.

Once she sat down, several others did, too, as if she'd clued them in. To her surprise, the old pack leader was watching her. When Argos caught her eye, he bowed his head slightly and then lifted it.

Taking a deep breath, Bella faced Devlyn and Volan, more confused than ever about pack politics. She'd been away much too long. Living with humans had caused her to forget some of the pack ways, and now she regretted it. She would raise her children in the pack and never again forget where she came from.

Devlyn flattened his ears again slightly. She wanted to bite him in the butt and make him quit it, but before she could think any further about it, Volan lunged for him, his canines extended viciously.

Devlyn dodged his action, swung around, and bit him in the shoulder. Volan yelped. She wanted to cheer Devlyn on, to jump up and down, but the battle had only begun.

The two parted and ran away from each other for a moment, gathering their wits and readying themselves for the next confrontation. Devlyn glanced at her, and she bowed her head to him again. He turned quickly when Volan flew across the center at him.

Had it irritated Volan that Bella showed her favoritism for Devlyn? It did. She'd rattled him. Yes!

What else could she do?

Volan hit Devlyn so hard with a frontal assault that each raised up on his hind legs and snapped and snarled at the other's muzzle. Bella jumped to her feet. Then, not wanting Devlyn to see her worry, she lay back down. Neither of the males won. Both dropped to their paws and separated.

This time, Volan paced along the edge of the wolf circle, his black fur glistening with sweat except for the patch of blood at his shoulder. He paced like the reds who couldn't beat her mate.

Devlyn stood still, watching him, wary of the next move, but seemingly in complete control. His chest heaved with exertion, but she sensed he wasn't tired yet. Not with the adrenaline coursing through his body. Not with the knowledge that he wanted her more than he wanted anything else in the world.

She glanced over at Vernetta, who was watching not the fight, but her, as if to say it was Bella's turn next. Bella lifted her head higher and turned to face Devlyn.

Volan conserved his energy this time. He didn't jump into the fray but instead trotted across the circle and again attempted a frontal assault.

This time he managed to bite Devlyn's cheek. The

blood dripped from his face and Bella bolted into the circle. Instantly, Vernetta charged her. Before they could clash, several males forced them back out of the circle. The position of alpha male had to be determined first. The females' fight would follow.

Now Bella wanted to pace, but she couldn't unless she did so outside of the circle. Then she couldn't see the fight. She forced herself to sit.

Devlyn and Volan had separated again, like boxers returning to their own corners of the ring.

Volan charged Devlyn again, not waiting such a long while in between this time. His action disheartened her. Worse, when he struck at Devlyn, her mate fell. She nearly died. Intent on protecting her mate, she dove into the battle, risking the grays' wrath.

Devlyn's cousin, Tanner, slammed into her from the sidelines, knocking her off her pads. The brief distraction allowed Devlyn time to get to his feet, and at once he lunged at Volan. Tanner snapped and snarled at Bella to get her to move to the outskirts of the circle. She growled back at him, the lowest, angriest growl she could manage, and then trotted back to her place.

The grays were too big for her to handle. How could she even think she could deal with Vernetta successfully?

Devlyn had managed to catch Volan's cheek with his canines and ripped a chunk from his face, the fur-covered skin hanging loose, covered in blood.

Devlyn lunged again. He grabbed the gray's thick neck and held on for dear life. Volan snapped his jaws in an attempt to get loose. He finally shook Devlyn off. The two parted company.

But this time...Devlyn paced.

By jumping into the ring, she'd shaken him. Seeing his cousin tackle her and the powerlessness she had against the grays...undoubtedly, Devlyn worried about her ability to fight for the place of the alpha female.

Her heart sank. She couldn't help it. When he was hurt, she had to protect him. She had to.

Okay, she wouldn't do it again. Just quit pacing, Devlyn, damn it!

Volan leapt through the air and knocked Devlyn down. She could almost hear the breath in his lungs whoosh out. She waited, breathless, while Tanner watched her. She gave him the evil eye. Apparently, he thought it his place to keep her in line, but she wasn't having any part of it.

When Volan dove for Devlyn's throat, Bella went for Tanner's. She couldn't hurt him, and he wouldn't risk harming her or face whoever was the victor as the alpha male, but for the moment, she would be the distraction.

As soon as she sank her teeth in Tanner's neck, he yelped. Volan snarled at them. He wanted the show centered on him, but she wouldn't release Tanner's neck despite his attempts to break free from her. Another of Devlyn's cousins bit at her backside. That did it.

She swung around so fast, he didn't have time to retreat. With her teeth snarling, she quickly bit his leg. He yipped and scurried off.

Devlyn made it to his feet and attacked Volan again, but instead of trying for his throat, he jumped against his back. With a powerful snap, he bit into the back of Volan's neck, crushing the bone instantly. Volan didn't make a sound, and his body fell to the pine needle–carpeted floor. Volan was the alpha leader no more.

Vernetta didn't waste any time in attacking Bella, but Bella's blood still boiled from Devlyn's cousins having attacked her. She wasn't in the mood for giving in to threats from anyone. Least of all from a female who lusted after Bella's mate.

Bella grabbed Vernetta's leg, biting only enough to make the female bolt away and limp off. Bella didn't want to kill her, just show her she wouldn't take guff from any gray female, not now or ever.

She hadn't even time to see how Devlyn fared.

Vernetta turned and bolted for her. Bella jumped out of her path and bit her broader backside. Vernetta yelped, but she turned around and charged again. There was no waiting it out, no resting between bouts.

The image came to mind of the black bear that Bella had faced years ago when she'd run away from the pack. She didn't back down then, and she wouldn't now. Vicious perseverance was the key.

Vernetta hit Bella this time with her canines, slicing her neck. *The throat.* If Vernetta got hold of her throat…

Bella swung her head around and grabbed Vernetta's neck and bit hard, not enough to kill her, but enough to show her that she was someone to respect. Vernetta tore free and then whipped around and lunged again.

Damn, the bitch wouldn't yield.

And Bella was quickly wearing out. The size of the gray overwhelmed her, and fighting with Devlyn's cousins hadn't helped.

Still, she wouldn't give up. Devlyn was hers…her

heart soared with the realization. He was the alpha leader now!

Vernetta slammed into Bella again, and both rose on their hind legs with the impact, only Vernetta's bigger size forced Bella down first. This time, Bella aimed low. Get the lower parts, like a wolf pup would do when tackling his mother.

Bella grabbed for Vernetta's foreleg, but she wouldn't nip it this time. With a powerful snap, she broke her leg in two. It would heal, but for now, it was the end of the game for the gray. Vernetta yelped, rolled over on her side, and then whined.

Bella turned to face Devlyn. He just stared back at her. Was he ashamed she could be so mean? That's the way she felt for an instant. Mean and crotchety.

Devlyn stalked toward her and nuzzled her face with his. Their noses touched, and they licked each other's wet cheeks. The wolves around the circle lay down and bowed their heads.

Devlyn had proved himself the new alpha male leader, and Bella had won her place as his alpha mate.

# Epilogue

FIVE MONTHS LATER, DEVLYN CRADLED BELLA IN HIS arms while they nestled on a new redwood porch swing he had crafted for her. She gazed at the beautiful greenhouse situated nearby—twice as big as her old one and already filled with rhododendrons and azaleas from Oregon, now her second home. "Chrissie wants us to come to her wedding in two months. She and Henry moved the date up, afraid I couldn't travel if they waited too long or, if they delayed it until after the babies are born, it would be harder for me to take them with us." She smiled up at Devlyn.

He grunted. "I knock Thompson out during my rescuing you at the hospital, and he wants me to be his best man at his wedding? Humans. No figuring them."

"Hmm, maybe it's the wolf in you he really likes."

Devlyn shook his head, his hand caressing her belly, swelling with triplets. She sighed heavily against his chest.

A wolf's howl in the distance brought a smile to her lips. "The Sinapu sure have made strides to reintroduce the gray wolf in the area."

"Yeah. No worry about hunters shooting *lupus garous* anymore or trying to put a wolf into the zoo."

"And even a few reds have been successfully reintroduced in the Smokies."

Devlyn ran his fingers through her hair. "Right. Once the humans realized that the reds they set free weren't wild enough and so were killing turkeys at local farms."

"Good thing the government's willing to reimburse farmers if wolves eat the farmer's livestock."

"Makes it easier for us to roam the area in our wolf states without arousing suspicion. But it sure was funnier than hell when Tanner got tagged as a successful reintroduction of one of the gray wolves. Nobody will let him live it down."

Bella smiled. "I couldn't be happier to be here with you like this, Devlyn, and with the pack again."

He held her tighter. "To think Argos's own mate had done the very same thing as you...distracted the pack leader so that Argos had a chance to win."

She chuckled under her breath and slipped her fingers over his bare chest. "I wish he'd told us sooner."

"Yeah, I would've had you help me out long before this. We're a team, sweet Bella."

"I agree. I'm glad Vernetta's leg healed properly, too."

"Did she tell you she had first dibs on taking care of the triplets?"

"Yeah." Bella smiled. All of the females of a wolf pack helped raise the alpha female's offspring. She couldn't have been happier to be home again. She'd lost her own red *lupus garou* pack but found the gray pack and the mate who'd forever be hers. "I guess your cousins aren't still sore at me for fighting them that day, although they've made themselves scarce whenever I'm around."

"On the sly, they told me that, once they'd seen your reaction, they knew you were the alpha female, even before Vernetta tried to take you down. Tanner said he was glad he didn't have to deal with that quick temper of yours."

"And you?"

"Spices life up just right."

She gave him a serious look. "When the triplets are old enough, they'll learn the true legend of how were-wolves came into existence."

He kissed her cheek and squeezed her good-naturedly. "Sure, Bella honey. The first was a Scandinavian white wolf. We still have Alfred's book to prove it."

She shook her head.

Another howl sounded from the wilds.

"He's looking for a mate, don't you think?"

Devlyn stood and lifted Bella from the swing. "Yeah, at least I've got mine."

"I love you, Devlyn," she murmured against his throat.

"No more than I do you. But for now, you have to earn your keep."

She nipped at his chest.

He laughed. "Or maybe I should say, I have to earn mine."

"Hmm." She snuggled against his chest. "You better believe it. I want to take a run on the wild side. Think you're up to it, stud?"

He growled. "I'm just the one to take you up on any-thing your heart desires, my little red wolf." He buried his face in her curls. "Anything."

Devlyn served as the alpha male, but Bella ruled his heart and soul...just as it was meant to be. She smiled. "Promises, promises."

He chuckled, deeply rapturous. "Yeah, and you know how intent I can be on keeping my promises."

"Yeah, makes me remember again why I selected you for my mate."

He laughed and kissed her ear. "Demanding wench, but I aim to please you for the rest of our days."

She ran her finger down his chest. "Good, because we still have a lot of catching up to do."

"I'm sure we'll never get caught up." He shoved the door open with his hip. "But we have all of the time in the world to try."

"Trying is all of the fun." She grinned at him, as he laid her on the faux polar bear rug resting before the fireplace. Then she pulled the leather strap free from his hair. "My sinfully seductive big gray wolf."

He pulled off his jeans and knelt beside her. She reached out to touch him. Shaking his head, he grinned back at her. "Bad Bella."

"Mmm-hmm."

*The End*

# NIGHT
## OF THE
# WOLF

**A Heart of the Wolf Novella**

# Prologue

*1840*
*Colorado Rockies*

THE WEATHER WAS SO DRY—TOO DRY. THOUGH THE RED wolf pack lived in stone or log cabin homes near the river, Serena Wilder's father had warned that any-thing—a campfire, an electrical storm—could set off a wildfire and destroy their lives.

Today was that day, the fire catching hold so fast that no one had time to locate each other. She'd been gathering thimbleberries for a pie, but tossed her basket aside, the berries spilling out onto the dry pine needles as the winds carried the flames through the dry brush. The pine needles and leaves discarded at the base of the trees added fuel to the already out-of-control fire.

Serena was alone. Her twin sister, Bella, was gather-ing kindling somewhere else; her cousins, uncle and aunt, and her parents, were all doing chores. The men had been hunting for food. Her mother and cousins? She didn't know. As a six-year-old girl, she couldn't run as fast as a wolf to escape the fury behind her, so she stripped and shifted into her wolf pup form and ran toward the river. The smoke was so thick, she could barely breathe, and the flames danced from tree to tree high above her, the wind carrying the crackling sound like a warning: *Run little wolf, or you'll get burned*.

But the smoke could kill her first.

The last few feet to the river, she leapt as far as her small legs could, landing in the wet reeds. Finding a beaver's den, she buried herself in the sodden wood. She howled for her family, but didn't hear any sign of them, just the river splashing over her hiding place. She prayed the flames wouldn't catch hold on the wet wood, but as hot as it was, she feared it could. The wind blew and fire snapped and popped as it burned everything in its path.

Crying wolf's tears, she felt a lump the size of her home lodged in her throat. She prayed her family had found refuge somewhere safe.

The fires raged, the ground too hot to cross, small fires still eating away at larger trees. Her clothes and her basket she'd woven were gone, burned up along with everything else. Rains came after that, putting out the fires, and once they'd stopped, she left the river and made her way to her stone house as a wolf. The roof and everything that had been inside, the furniture her father and uncle had made, was nothing but soggy, charred remains.

She discovered her mother, still fully dressed, lying beneath a rock ledge, protected from the fire a short distance from the house. But Serena couldn't wake her. She sat and howled for the loss of her mother, for her family. Slept there beside her, until Serena knew she had to eat and drink and find a way to survive. She never found anyone else—Bella, her father, or the rest of her family—but one day she heard a wagon coming, and, hating to do it, she shifted into her human form. Covered in soot, teary-eyed, and naked, she stood on the wagon trail, hoping someone would take care of her until she could fend for herself.

# Chapter 1

*Present Day*
*Omaha, Nebraska*

SERENA WILDER PACKED UP HER BELONGINGS AT THE library where she had worked for four years. This was her last day because she and two other women were no longer needed on staff. Between funding cuts and the newly-installed automations—automatic book check-ins and self-checkouts—she knew she had to find another job, but she hadn't had any success. She packed away her remaining wolf postcards—not of any wolves she knew, but just the generic kind her friends had given her, because they knew how much she loved wolves, though not the reason why—that she had tacked to the board above her desk.

Her other two laid-off coworkers—strictly human—had already left. Serena had always worked around books, from being a teacher in the early days, to working in the first libraries. She loved books. But she'd had to move so many times over the years, and she was always starting over. How could she not? Once she hit her late teens, she had aged so slowly. People would wonder.

Now she'd applied for unemployment compensation, but she had a "waiting week" before she could be paid for subsequent weeks. After that, the amount of her

highest quarterly earnings would be divided by thirteen
and then again by two. So her compensation would be
half of what she was already earning and wouldn't be
enough to support her.

Serena was worried about paying her share of the
house she was renting with a male gray wolf, Harold
Gaston, but he'd assured her she'd get back on her feet
and could pay him later. As a telephone line repairman,
he made more money than she did. They'd met at a
local diner, the first shifter she'd met in all her years
of moving about. They didn't feel anything for each
other in the way wolves who wanted to mate would.
Her momma had often shared the story of how she had
met Serena's dad. How they'd fallen in love from the
beginning. And how she and her sister would have the
same wolfish interest in another wolf when they were
older—just like that. When she met Harold, she didn't
feel any of the romantic feelings she thought she should
have; nothing about him made her heartbeat quicken.

Serena was an avid romance reader, but she'd never
been madly in love or even intrigued by a human, either,
though her mother and father would have frowned at
her even considering such a thing, if they'd still lived.
Wolves mated with wolves for life. Not with humans,
though she'd had a few human lovers over the years.

With their sensitive shifter hearing, she found sharing
a house with another wolf sure beat living in a noisy
apartment complex. And she liked being able to talk to
Harold about wolf shifter things that she couldn't with
anyone else.

She had the rest of her day planned—go home, run,

shower, and hit the road to apply for yet another round of jobs. Anything would do for now.

When she got home, she was surprised to find Harold standing inside, his sandy hair tousled, his small, black eyes studying her. She thought he'd had to work. He smiled at her, but he shoved his hands in his pockets. He seemed tense, troubled. "I had some business to attend to, so I took the day off. How are you doing?"

"I've left the library for good." She set her bag of wolf cards on the dining room table. "I'm going for a run. Wanna go with me?" It would make her feel better to run off some of the frustration she was feeling.

"No, I've really got to take care of some business."

He didn't say what his business was, but then again, they were just roommates; he had a right to privacy.

Then she realized why she had been so surprised to see him home, besides the fact that he was supposed to be working. No brand-new red pickup truck was parked out front.

"Having trouble again with your truck?"

"Yeah, pain in the ass. Total lemon."

"Is that the business you have to take care of?"

"It is."

"Did you want me to drive you then? I need to apply for some more jobs, but I'd be happy to help you out."

"No, I've got a friend coming by to take me to the dealership shortly."

But it was all a lie. *He* was all a lie. Maybe not the truck being a lemon part, but everything else...

When Serena returned home from running, she saw her car was gone. She panicked. Had someone stolen it? She raced through the house, looking for Harold, calling out to him. He was gone. So was her wallet and her car keys from where she'd left them on the dresser.

It didn't mean Harold had taken the car, but then she smelled the scent of a female gray wolf. He wasn't supposed to know any other wolves. Warning bells began going off. She told herself that he could have just met her. But why had her wallet, keys and car vanished?

She hurried to his room—everything was gone. She tried calling him, the call going to voicemail.

She pulled out her laptop and logged into his email—thanking providence that he'd given her his password six months ago to look up something for him when his phone went out on him at work and he desperately had needed the information.

She barely breathed when she saw he had a plane trip scheduled for him and a woman named Velvet Jamison this afternoon for Grand Cayman Island. Then she received an email on her phone from her bank thanking her for having an account with them and hoping she would consider opening another with them in the future. *What the hell?*

She immediately called the bank and was told that her account was closed.

"Tell me again how Harold Gaston could have cleaned out my bank account *without* my authorization."

"Whoever closed your account had two forms of valid ID. We'll notify the proper authorities, Miss Wilder."

A lot of good that would do Serena. The bastard

would be on Grand Cayman Island with *her* money, sipping a fruity cocktail with one of those flipping colorful umbrellas and enjoying the sun, while she was stuck here on this cold spring day in Omaha, Nebraska. He'd be beyond anyone's legal jurisdiction. And all her hard-earned money would be sitting safely in *his* Cayman account. Or he'd spend it all. At least she'd learned where he'd gone. She was glad he hadn't thought to change his password.

"What do I do now? He took everything I own!" Serena said to the bank clerk. *Well, not everything, but close to it*. "I have $150 in cash and that's it. He stole my car even!" Without enough money to pay $1,050 for this month's rent, Serena would lose the rental home too. At least it had come furnished, so she didn't have too much to leave behind when she packed up and vacated the place.

She again thought of *home*. She'd been thinking of returning to the old homestead, wondering if there were any shifter wolf packs out there. She kept feeling like there might be, like there had been in the past. There also might not be, but she hadn't had any luck in finding wolves in the places she'd been living—Tennessee, Georgia, Oklahoma, Arkansas, here. She hadn't returned to Colorado since the human family had taken her from there and raised her. She yearned to find a wolf to love, who would love her in return like her mother and father had loved each other. Like her aunt and uncle had loved one another too.

A distant memory stirred faintly. The walls of her family's stone house had still been standing. What if her family's home was still there? A dilapidated building, maybe? What if she could claim the land for her own? She remembered catching her father putting something beneath the basement's stone floor one Christmas Eve. He'd explained to her the importance of the documents there—money for a rainy day, although for most things they bartered; a will; a deed to the house. Even if the house wasn't salvageable, maybe the land was worth something.

She shuddered. She had never returned there. Not after the wildfire killed her family. All she remembered was the smell of smoke hanging thick in the air, gray ash covering everything. And she had never gotten the sight of her dead mother out of her mind, assuming, years later, that her mother had succumbed to smoke inhalation.

"Miss Wilder, we could give you a bank loan," the clerk said.

"A bank loan." Giving a bitter laugh, Serena wanted to kill Harold. "That would be the day." She wouldn't even be able to get that once they learned she'd lost her job. Thank God, she had a credit card phone case, and had her phone with her when she went running, but she didn't want to get herself in debt in the event going after Harold and her money didn't pan out.

She ended the call. *Harold, the snake*. She wanted every penny he'd stolen from her.

Except she needed money to get to him. And since they were both wolves, she really couldn't go to the police. Though the bank was sure to call them.

The only money she figured she could get her hands on quickly was her family's savings—if any of it was buried beneath the stone floor. It would be old money though; then again, may be worth a mint—if her home was still there and hadn't been torn down. If it was, after all this time, surely someone else would have taken her property for their own. Not one of her red wolf kind. A human usurper.

She ground her teeth.

She didn't want to see the woods where she had romped as a child. Or relive the horror she'd experienced when she had found shelter in the beavers' lodgings. She didn't want to set eyes on the home she had loved—not after her family had died so horribly there.

But she couldn't think of any other option for now. She had to have money, and then she'd go after the bigger prize. *Harold*. Teach him to mess with one of her kind. He'd never do it again.

First, she had to find her car. Taking a taxi to the airport in hopes her car was there, she discovered his scent in the long-term parking area closest to the entrance he would have used to reach his gate and backtracked to where he must have parked her car. Between that and using her spare keys, she finally located it, her driver's license and other set of keys sitting on the console.

Now, it was time to take the next step—return home after all these years.

—⁂—

Two days later in the Colorado Rockies, someone or something stalked Serena as she left her car behind on the gravel road. She headed in what she thought was the right direction of her family's home, after going through the small town near where they'd lived, though it had grown some in size. The livery was now a museum; the old hotel, renovated; the feed store was still a feed store; the post office, a shop. And myriads of other buildings that were once homes along Main Street were now shops, bed and breakfasts, or art galleries. But the town was still quaint, no large department store chains. A couple of gas stations, a grocery store, a bank, and a few other shops had been added. A few more homes spread out from the town. But it was still a sleepy Colorado country town.

Beyond the town, she'd located the rock formations she and her sister used to climb that reminded her of giant stepping stones, a monument to an earlier time. In her day, the road that traveled past the stones had been dirt. Now it was gravel, not even paved yet.

Serena slipped between pine trees, barely making a sound as her hiking boots padded along the pine needle–covered floor. Whatever followed her proved clever, always keeping downwind of her, no matter how many times she circled, trying to locate it.

*Keep cool, Serena. Don't let it rattle you.*

Yet, she couldn't help the way her skin crawled. Every fine hair on her arms stood at attention. Her heart beat wildly and the sound of her blood pumping hammered in her ears.

She'd lived among humans way too long and had forgotten how to use her wolf instincts. *Listen to the sounds of nature*, she warned herself. *What do you hear? Ignore your panic. Listen.*

The rustle of the new green oak leaves shivered in the

cool spring breeze. A distant creek gurgled over rounded stones as it had for thousands of years. A woodpecker pecked at rotting wood and a gray squirrel scampered up a nearby birch.

Something, whatever *it* was, watched and waited for her to make a move, as silent and cold as falling snow, as dangerously sneaky as a forest fire.

Damn *it*. Nothing would intimidate her in her woods. She hadn't thought they would be so green, as if the forest fire had never happened. She wasn't sure how she felt about that—as life went on without them.

She breathed in the wildness, enjoying the fragrance of spring. It stirred happy memories—sad ones, too. She'd only planned to find her home, the hidden money, a will, and the deed, but already she was feeling a pang of regret for not having returned sooner, for not taking back her family's heritage, if she could. She shook her head at the sentimental human part of the equation. All she came for was her money, the will, and the deed, so she could put the property up for sale after she took care of Harold and got what was left of the money he'd stolen from her. Afterward, she could live here until she sold off the property. But she'd been so upset over him, she realized she wasn't thinking clearly. How would she prove she was the descendent of the family who had owned the property in the first place?

A distant howl caught her attention. A wild gray wolf returned to the Rockies? She'd heard the Sinapu had reintroduced some into the area. *Sinapu* was the Ute word for wolves, and they were dedicated to the protection of the wild wolves and their habitat.

She stared in the direction, listening until she heard his mate call to him. Taking a deep breath, she wondered what it would be like to coexist with wild gray wolves in this day and age.

Would men ever be able to live with wolves in peace?

She hadn't lived in the wild for so long, she couldn't get the feel of it.

The fickle breeze switched directions. She turned her head to smell the scents. Nothing but the heavenly aroma of earth, pine needles, and oak leaves.

The sun withdrew from the tree-shaded sky, and her skin grew chilled. She rolled down the sleeves of her green sweater, annoyed she hadn't made any headway in locating her family's home.

The house had to be close by, she assumed.

She skipped over a fallen tree, then spied a clearing as the sky grew darker. Her heart sped up, and she dashed for the clearing.

A few more steps and she entered a landscaped yard. Not wild like it had been when her family had lived here. The natural earth-toned stone blocks still protected the home's exterior, though she assumed someone had scrubbed away the black soot that had covered it after the fire. She stood in awe, overwhelmed for a moment, tears filling her eyes. Memories of playing in the woods, her mother calling to her sister and her to return home, the aroma of apple cobbler and fresh fish coming to her all at once.

The roof…

She stared at it. Green metal? She wrinkled her nose. And…and the place had been extended out the sides and back. She growled under her breath and moved in closer to get a peek inside the windows. Aluminum-framed windows replaced the wood ones and were now adorned with forest green shutters, which were pleasing to the eye. What was that on the roof? A skylight?

A light flickered on in the living room. She stopped dead in her tracks. The warm yellow glow filled the big picture window, but she couldn't make out any sign of a person moving about inside.

Forever, it seemed she stood in the clearing, staring at her home, frozen with indecision. She wanted to check out the cellar. The moneybox, if still hidden, was down there, and the only way to get to it was by going inside the house.

On the other hand, the house belonged to her, and not just the hidden money, making her feel whoever lived here now had to go. They had no right to her home.

Mostly, she needed the deed and will to prove it was hers.

Her fists clenched and her jaw tightened. She wanted to scream, "Come out at once, or I'll huff and I'll puff and I'll…"

The faint snap of a twig coming from the woods behind her garnered her full and immediate attention.

She whipped around. In the dark woods, the iridescent eyes of a wolf shown.

Nothing else…just the eyes. A gray? Had to be.

She glared at it, showing she wouldn't be intimidated, or frightened or…

The front door of her house squeaked open, and she jerked her head around.

"Whoa," a man said, stepping onto her front porch, his hand still on the doorknob. "What have we here?"

One very pissed-off homeowner whose home had been stolen by this person. Not to mention all the changes that had been made to the property when it didn't belong to him.

A black SUV drove up on the gravel driveway and skidded to a stop. Two males got out, who looked eerily like the man on the front porch. If she had to fathom a guess, the three were more than just brothers—they were triplets. Both looked her over as if she was prime meat, taking in every inch of her, from her hiking boots to the top of her head with her red hair pulled on top in a chignon with copper clips.

"Jeez, Shawn, you didn't tell us you'd invited Devlyn's mate to the pizza party. What would he say?"

"Hey, Fisher, she was feeling well enough to go with Devlyn to attend that woman's wedding in Portland, Oregon," Shawn said, smiling broadly. "*This* little lady is someone else."

The men all stared at her, then the other shook his head. "Hot damn, we got another one of them in our midst."

"I'll say, Heath," Shawn said.

"Sure is going to cause some troubles," Fisher said. "Got any more sisters?" He directed the question to Serena.

She took a step away from them and away from the wolf. Fisher turned his attention to the wolf, but no one said a word. She wasn't afraid of the beast, but instead kept her focus on the men in front of her. *They* were her enemy.

"Are you lost?" Shawn asked, his voice deeply sensual,

but a tad concerned. He tilted his head to the side slightly. "She sure looks like her, doesn't she?"

Did he have a clue she'd come for her house? That he didn't have long to live here? The crap about looking familiar was a guy line for sure.

She studied him back, trying to determine if she had met him somewhere before. Dark-brown hair curled behind his ears and hung just below the bottom edge of his denim shirt collar. Her eyes drifted to his jeans — well-worn, stonewashed, faded, soft and hugging his muscled thighs, and...

"Miss?" Shawn said. "Are you lost?"

"Hell, come on in, miss, and share a beer and pizza with us. We've got plenty for all of us. I'm Heath. If you couldn't tell, we're all brothers." He lifted three pizza boxes, then motioned with his head to the other man. "That's Fisher, our youngest brother by five minutes." Heath was darker haired, amber eyed, and wore a plaid shirt, jeans, and hiking boots — the lumberjack look.

Blue-eyed Fisher grinned and raised three six packs of beer. He looked more like a cowboy, with a Stetson, well-worn cowboy boots, jeans, and chambray shirt with the western trimmings. His hair was a much lighter brown with golden highlights.

"And our oldest brother, Tanner, is..." Heath gave a small smile. "Well, he's roaming the woods right now."

Quadruplets? It took every ounce of effort for her to break free from her dilemma.

The hair at the nape of her neck stood on end. She knew the wolf was still behind her. Not close. Still hidden in the woods, still watching her.

The brothers' half-wild, half-pet wolf maybe?

"Would you like to come inside and use a phone?" Shawn asked.

She swallowed hard, the tears stinging her eyes. For now, she'd leave her beloved home behind. *For now*.

She turned and glanced in the direction of the woods. Her vehicle was off the road two miles through the woods. She'd have to search her house when Shawn and his brothers weren't around. She was certain they wouldn't agree to her looking for the deed while they were in the house. Unless...unless she came back later when they were sleeping off the beer.

The wolf, gray and blond pelted, his eyes a beautiful dark amber, had drawn several yards closer, watching every move she made. He was a large gray. His ears perked up, twisted back and forth, listening to the sound of her breathing, judging how panicked she might be.

He sniffed the air, but she was downwind of *him*. Her lips lifted at the corners slightly. Then she bolted in the direction of the creek, hoping to return when they were asleep. She didn't want them seeing her car and license plate, possibly learning who she was, yet.

"Miss!" Shawn yelled. "Miss! Shit!"

The men ran after her, but humans were so unattuned to the wild. She'd soon lose them in her territory. The wind kept shifting and she couldn't detect their scents.

The land seemed so familiar, coming back to her as she made her way through it—the terrain, the trees, maybe taller than before, closer to the house than before.

For now, she dreaded meeting up with the wolf that bounded after her in hot pursuit. Not because she couldn't hold her own against him, but because she feared being tracked. She'd do this her own way. She had no intention of being forced to tell them why she'd been studying the house...or who she was. If she could get her deed, a lawyer, and file her claim, she'd get rid of the squatters without much trouble. Except, she'd have to prove she was her family's descendent too. She was afraid if she didn't find the deed and will first, they could destroy them, and she wouldn't have any recourse. Then she'd have to use her credit card and go after Harold.

"Damn it, where'd she go?" Shawn yelled.

"Hell, Shawn, we've got to let Devlyn know about her right away," Heath said. "He'll want a report at once."

She scrambled into the creek, then made her way downstream several hundred yards. Around a bend in the river, she climbed into an oak tree, certain the wolf would lose her scent.

For some time, the men and the wolf searched for her, splashing through the creek. Their boots knocked rocks on the shoreline together occasionally, then their noisy search faded away. The wolf circled beneath her tree, then headed after the men.

She would have smiled when they passed right beneath her leafy perch twenty minutes later, unaware she sat right above them. She would have gloated at her cleverness. But tonight, Shawn and his brothers would return to her home, eat pizza, drink beer, and sleep in comfort in her home while she had no place to call her own.

"Come on. Let's call it a night." Shawn trudged back to the opposite side of the creek's bank.

Fisher chuckled. "I know she's somewhere close by. But Red's not about to let us catch her tonight."

Her blood warmed. They thought themselves hunters and she was their prey?

No. This was her land. *Hers*. And she'd have it back one way or...

"All right, stay out here," Fisher said to the wolf. He shook his head. "You always did have a thing for a red-headed, long-legged beauty. See you in the morning."

"Ah, hell," Heath said. "We all do. And there'll be trouble. You know it. Then Devlyn's going to be pissed."

"Wouldn't you know she'd show up when our cousin's gone," Shawn said.

Shawn and his brothers tromped off. Serena fumed. If the wolf had gone into the house with its master, she would have waited until everyone went to sleep.

Now she was stuck in a tree like a raccoon cornered by a hound.

For a while, the wolf sat. When she didn't move, he laid down, watching, listening, his ears twitching back and forth. She took in a deep breath and smelled the fishy stream, a hint of snow in the air, and realized how foolish she'd been to leave her jacket in the car. But if she left the tree, the wolf would hear her. Ah, hell. She rubbed her arms, her pants and boots wet from trudging through the creek. If she didn't get out of the cold, she'd freeze to death.

She began the climb down, and the wolf sat up and watched her. She swore the dumb beast smiled at her.

Before she could race off for her car, he leapt at her, and her heart nearly died a frantic death. He knocked her down, his paws on her back, his heavy weight effectively pinning her to the pine needle–covered ground.

She growled. "Get off me."

For several seconds, he held her there, not moving, though she tried to squirm out from underneath him. And then he leaned down, and she thought he was going to bite, but instead he licked her cheek.

"Get off me!" she screamed. She instinctively knew he hadn't meant to hurt her, but was playing with her like a big, friendly dog. Only he was all wolf.

To her surprise, he moved off. For a second, she sat up and stared at him. Then she jumped to her feet and bolted. He ran after her, but didn't tackle her again, though she expected it. When she reached her car, he paused.

"Afraid of cars and roads. Good. They can kill wolves." She jammed her hand in her jeans pocket. Then in the other. Panic coursed through her icy veins. Ohmigod, what happened to the car keys? If she'd lost them when she was running, she'd never find them now. Not unless she shifted into her wolf and, with her nose to the ground, could find her scent on them.

The wolf watched her, his eyes fixed on her, waiting for her to do something. She snorted. Her only other option was walking twenty miles to town. Fat chance. Or joining Shawn and his brothers for pizza and beer. *Great. Just great.* She wanted to take her property back in an impersonal way. The less she associated with these men, the less she'd care about having them evicted.

The snow began to fall. She was out of options.

Cold, wet, and hungry, her hands jammed in her jeans pockets, she headed back toward the house, the wolf trailing her like a puppy would its mother. "You know, you're supposed to go home with your master," she said, glancing over her shoulder at the beast.

He woofed at her. If she hadn't avoided making trips to the wilderness with a wolf for so long, she would have recognized the warning in his bark. But it was too late.

The land gave way and she tumbled down a steep incline, branches slapping at her, tugging at her hair and shirt, her hands reaching out to grab something that would stop her fall down the rocky terrain. She swore she'd kill Harold for all the trouble he'd put her through. She felt the impact with the immovable tree before she saw it, felt the pain in her ribs. She smacked her head before the night turned into a hazy gray, then faded to black.

# Chapter 2

FORMER ARMY RANGER TANNER GREYSTOKE MADE HIS way down the steep incline easily in his wolf coat.

When he reached the base of the hill, he shifted, shivered, and prayed the woman wasn't injured too severely. She was lying on her back, passed out, her red hair splayed across the brush. She was beautiful, ivory skin, red cheeks from the cold and the walk. When she was glowering at him, she had beautiful blue-green eyes, bluer than Bella's.

After seeing she was breathing normally and her heart rate was steady, he crouched down to lift her off the cold ground. She opened her eyes and studied him, every bit of him—from his muscles to his package. She was definitely a wolf, and he smiled.

He cradled Red in his arms and hoped he wouldn't injure her further, but he had to get her out of the cold. It didn't help that her pants and boots were wet.

"What's your name?"

"Serena," she said.

"I'm Tanner."

He struggled to make his way up the narrow wolf trails he and his brothers had made, and when he reached the top of the hill where it leveled off, he headed straight for the house. Changing out of his wolf form and running around as a naked human in the freezing cold wasn't the smartest way to travel, but he couldn't carry her any other way. He could have howled for his brothers, but damn if he wanted them to come to her rescue. When she opened her eyes again, he wanted her to see him, not one of his brothers.

He took in a deep breath, inhaling her sweet scent. Earlier, he kept tracking her smell and knew she had to be one of Bella's kind: a red wolf, maybe even a relative, who looked a hell of a lot like her. He'd say they were sisters, but Bella had said her sister had died in the fire many years ago.

Now every one of his brothers would want her. Could they even convince her to stay here? They had to get hold of Bella. Maybe she could encourage her to stay with their pack. That still left the problem with his brothers. And Devlyn, their pack leader. If the brothers fought over her, Devlyn would decide what to do.

Which meant Tanner had to make sure Red wanted him, not his brothers. He smiled and quickened his pace. As long as she didn't have as quick a temper as Bella, no problem. He was glad Heath was here; as the pack's doctor, he'd check her out.

Her eyes fluttered open and she stared at Tanner's bare chest for a minute, took a shallow breath, groaned, and closed them again. She'd heal. Their kind always did. But it might take a while. He listened to her steady breathing and heart rate. He shook his head, not believing how fortunate they were to have her here with them tonight. He was still concerned about her injuries.

Like what had happened between Devlyn and Bella,

Tanner had rescued his own little red wolf now. He smiled broadly, perfectly pleased with himself. Until he approached the front door of the house. He knew as soon as Shawn opened the front door, Tanner would have a fight over keeping her for himself. Not that she wouldn't have a say in it. Which meant he had to prove just how perfect a match they could be. At least he hoped so.

"What the hell happened?" Shawn asked, his brow furrowing, and Tanner knew his brother thought *he* had caused her injuries.

"She was returning to the house—at least she was headed this way—but lost her footing and fell down a steep incline. I tried to warn her. She hit a tree on the way down, smacked her head, and passed out."

Fisher and Heath came out of the den, then both crowded around while Tanner carried her to his bedroom.

"Hey, not in there," Shawn said.

Tanner gave him a look like he'd better cool it.

Shawn folded his arms. "Devlyn won't like it if you make a claim to her without his say."

"I'm in charge of his leather goods factory whenever he's gone. I'm the eldest of the four of us, and next in line to be the alpha leader if anything happens to our cousin."

Heath whistled. "Already tempers are flaring and we don't even know who she is or why she's here. Just because she's here doesn't mean she wants to stay. Let me take a look at her."

"She's come home," Tanner said, laying her on his bed. "I think she might be Bella's twin sister."

—∿∿—

The Greystoke brothers drove to the pack clinic with the mystery red she-wolf lying in the middle bench seat, her head on Tanner's lap. Fisher was sitting in the third seat in back, Shawn was driving, and Heath was sitting in the passenger seat up front.

"She's got to be Bella's sister," Shawn said, driving through the woods on the winding road to the clinic.

"Or a distant cousin," Tanner warned, her head sitting squarely on his crotch, heating him up. "We don't want Bella to rush home thinking we've found her twin sister when we haven't."

"You don't want her rushing home so she can say no to you having the red," Shawn said.

As if Bella would have any say in it, or would even be inclined to say no. The choice was strictly the she-wolf's.

"We called Devlyn," Heath said, "as soon as we saw the lady here. Either they have no reception or they're doing their usual thing and they have their phones turned off."

Shawn shook his head. "Knowing them, they're at it again."

The she-wolf finally roused enough to speak. "Where are you taking me?"

"To my clinic," Heath said. "I'm the doctor for the Greystoke wolf pack. Are you related to Bella Wilder? You're the spitting image of her, except your hair is a little lighter red, and your eyes are bluer. If you're not her twin sister, I'd venture to say you're a first cousin."

She tried to sit up and groaned.

"Where are you hurt?" Tanner asked, half holding her up, half wanting her to lie back down.

"My ribs. I think I bruised them."

"And your head? You passed out," Heath said.

"I don't remember."

Tanner wanted her to rest, but she struggled to sit up. He helped her, and then was going to buckle her seat belt, but as soon as he tried to lock the shoulder strap over her chest, she cried out. "Hell, sorry," he said, hating that he'd hurt her.

"Kill her before we get to the clinic, will you?" Shawn asked, sounding annoyed.

"I'm just bruised," she said, as if defending Tanner.

"What's your name?" Tanner held her hand to protect her if Shawn had to suddenly stop the car. Deer ran through the woods and sometimes they had to make sudden stops.

"Serena Wilder. You say my sister is alive?" Tears had filled her eyes and she looked as though she was fighting to hold them back.

"Hot damn!" Fisher said. "Bella's going to be ecstatic to hear the news."

"Yeah, our gray pack raised her. Devlyn rescued her when they were both pups, and she mated him when they grew up," Tanner said.

Serena sobbed. "A gray wolf?" She sounded like she couldn't believe her sister would do something so crazy.

Maybe getting to know the she-wolf would be harder than Tanner suspected. She hadn't grown up with them. She didn't know them. Had she even been raised by wolves after she left the area?

"Yeah, gray wolf. Why didn't you return before this?"

Tanner figured she probably believed everyone in her family had died, just like Bella had believed, and had never wanted to return and relive the horrific memories. He rubbed her shoulder gently, trying to calm her.

"I made it to the river and managed to survive while buried under wet branches of a dam. My dad had said beavers had built part of it. A rainstorm put the rest of the fire out, and when I couldn't find any of my family, I finally made it to the dirt trail. A couple of days later, a human family passing through in a covered wagon picked me up. They took me back east and cared for me until I was old enough to be on my own."

"So you felt nostalgic and came back to the old home-stead," Tanner said. "We're eager to have you in the pack. Bella will be thrilled to learn you are alive and well."

"I..." She frowned and wiped tears away. Heath handed her a tissue box from the console. "How come you're living in our home?" she asked, still sniffling.

"Bella inherited the..." Shawn paused. "Uhm, well, she thought she was the only one who had survived. She gave the home to us."

"She found the deed?" Her eyes widened, still filled with tears.

"Yes, in the basement. And the will, too." Tanner realized then that Serena must have been shocked to learn gray wolves had taken over her home. "We can move out. It's yours, Serena." Tanner wasn't going to get a consensus from his brothers on the issue. The house had belonged to both Bella and her sister. Serena had every right to live there now.

Trying to get her emotions under control, Serena couldn't believe how nice the gray wolves were—at least Tanner. She wasn't sure if his brothers would agree to give the house to her, making them all have to move. She was so shocked her sister had been alive all these years, and furious with herself that she had never come to learn that until now, missing all the time they could have been together.

One by one, the other gray wolf brothers agreed. "Hell yeah," Fisher said. "It's yours. We can stay with others in the pack until we build a place of our own."

"Agreed," the doctor said. "I've been meaning to build a place next to the clinic so I'll be right there if we have any injuries or sickness I need to take care of."

Shawn cleared his throat. "But if you need anyone to stay around and protect you—"

"I'm volunteering," Tanner said.

She smiled through her tears. "Thanks. I have to admit I thought I'd have to get growly with all of you to chase you out of the house."

They laughed, but Tanner suspected she wasn't joking.

Shawn pulled into the parking lot of the clinic, built all of stone, the roof metal like her home's. Tanner hurried out of the car to help lift Serena out, but Heath was right there for her. His light-amber eyes looked worried.

"It's nothing major, Doctor," she said, taking his hand, but holding her ribs lightly with the other and groaning when she got out of the car. "Where is Bella?"

"She and Devlyn went to a friend's wedding. It's

in Oregon and out in the country. They might not have reception," Tanner said. "We'll keep trying to reach them."

"I…need money."

Tanner frowned, looking like he was afraid that meant she intended to leave again soon. "I'd be happy to give you however much money you need."

"All of us would," Fisher hastily said.

She couldn't have appreciated them more for their offer. "Someone stole mine."

Tanner was now dressed in jeans, hiking boots, and a black T-shirt that molded to his sculpted muscles—the perfect balance, not the overdone kind. She recalled in vivid detail all those muscles she had gotten an eyeful of when he'd been naked, before he carried her to the house. His package was just as noteworthy, though she'd never admit she'd been peeking. He reminded her of hot baked buns, his wolfish scent woodsy, wet, and wild. And totally appealing.

Heath helped her to the front door of the clinic, while Shawn hurried to unlock it and turn on the lights inside.

"Who stole your money?" Tanner was immediately a growly wolf, and she thought he would tear into the man who did this if he could.

*Hmm*, that gave her an idea. She had thought she'd be dealing with this all on her own. But what if she had a male wolf to back her? She could pretend he was her new roommate and he could be there to lend some male muscle. Even better was that he seemed so eager to please.

Heath helped her to an exam room, but the brothers all crowded in at the door.

"Do you mind?" Heath asked.

"Tanner can stay," she said, wanting to talk further to him about Harold. If he was willing to pay for her trip and even come with her, she would go along with it.

Fisher and Shawn slapped him good-naturedly on the back. "Hell, he has her hoodwinked already," Shawn said, and he and his brother walked off toward the waiting area.

Tanner folded his arms. "Okay, tell me what this is all about."

Heath examined her ribs. "They feel okay, nothing broken. Let's take some X-rays."

He moved her into the X-ray room, set her on a table, and took the photos. While he developed them, Tanner came in and held her hand, his amber eyes concerned. "What's going on? Why did you return here?"

"I needed money to go after my roommate who was sharing a rental house with me. He took all my savings. Over one hundred and sixty thousand dollars' worth. He had grabbed my wallet that had my driver's license and debit card in it when I went running. He must have used a girlfriend to take out the money and even took off in my car. I'd just lost my job due to layoffs at the library where I'd worked. Luckily, I had some cash stuffed in a sock for emergencies, and kept my passport in there too. I used some of the cash on taxi fare to get to the airport, and then finally found my car. Between gas, meals, and lodging on the way out here, I used most of the money I had left." She sighed. "I didn't know if the house would still be standing, or if the basement was still there. I thought my dad hid some cash in a strongbox in the basement."

"You were headed to the car parked in the woods like you were planning to leave, but didn't. Why?" Tanner asked.

She ground her teeth. "I dropped the damn keys somewhere in the woods."

He smiled.

She growled.

He laughed. "We'll find them. We'll take care of you so you don't have to worry about anything."

"I want to get my money back. I worked hard for all that money over the years."

"I understand. Do you have a photo of him?"

"I do. I kept one so I could show it to people while I try to find him." She pulled out her phone and located one. They'd taken a road trip a month after they began rooming together a few months ago and he was standing close to the edge of a cliff. She should have had him step back a little bit when she took that picture of him.

They'd met at a diner, realized they were both wolves, and began to talk. What a mistake that was.

"Okay, so square jaw, small black eyes, sandy-colored hair, cleft chin, and looks like a wily wolf." Tanner gave her phone back to her. "We have cousins, Vaughn and his brother, Brock, who are Navy SEALs turned PIs. My brothers and I are Army Rangers, now working at our pack's leather good factory. As PIs, our cousins can help us locate Harold, if we can't."

"Oh, I know where he is. He's on Grand Cayman Island. I want to fly out there and get my money. *Now*. I don't want him spending it all before I can catch up to him and make him give it back."

Heath returned and showed her the X-rays. "Good news. No breaks. No hairline fractures even. It appears you have a couple of bruised ribs. With our faster healing abilities, you should be good in a couple of days."

"Thanks, Doctor."

"Heath. If you don't mind."

"Thanks, Heath."

"What do you plan to do when you catch up to this guy?" Tanner asked.

She snorted. "I'd love to end his miserable life. But he just took all my money, didn't injure me or anything. If I can get all he took from me, plus enough money to pay for the trip out there, then I'd be satisfied."

"You're sure he's on Grand Cayman Island?"

"I am." She reached down to pull out the confirmation paper from her jeans pocket, but her ribs hurt every time she moved.

"Here. Let me." Tanner helped her down off the table.

He reached in her pocket—she tried not to squirm at the way his heated touch was doing amazing things to her body—and pulled out the folded piece of paper showing the resort Harold was staying at and the flight he was taking. "Looks like we don't need to use Vaughn and Brock's services. If you want, when we return to the house, we can book a flight out first thing."

Things were definitely looking up! She couldn't wait to see Bella, but she didn't want to ruin her sister's chance to celebrate her friend's wedding. In the meantime, Serena had to get her money back before this scumbag ex-roommate spent all of it.

More than that, she wondered just what it would be

like to kiss the hot wolf who was signing on for this mission. An Army Ranger? *Beat that Harold, the telephone line repairman.*

# Chapter 3

Tanner was ready to rip Serena's ex-roommate to shreds for stealing her money, though he was thankful Harold's actions had caused her to leave wherever she'd been living and return home. "Do you want to show Harold's picture to my brothers and cousins?"

"Uh, yeah, sure." She handed her phone to Tanner and he leaned forward and handed it to Heath. "Everyone can stay at the house until we resolve this money situation with my ex-roommate," she told the brothers as they drove her home.

"Are you sure you don't need more muscle?" Fisher asked. "Four of us should be able to convince the bastard what a mistake he'd made."

"Who would be left to run the factory?" Shawn asked. "Tanner's in charge there."

"I'll leave you in charge," Tanner said.

The brothers smiled. Never in a millennium would he think to give up his position as the manager of the facility to one of his brothers for anything other than being near death.

"I've got to stay in case we have any medical emergencies," Heath said, handing the phone back to Tanner.

He passed it back to Fisher.

Fisher gave an exaggerated sigh. "The plant needs

me. Unless Devlyn declared a holiday for the staff and we could shut down for a few days."

"We have too many outstanding orders to do that," Tanner warned.

"Okay, so you're it. But if you need any help, we'll be out there in a heartbeat," Fisher said.

"Deal." Tanner got the phone back from Fisher. "Do you mind if I share the photo in a text to some members of the pack?"

"Sure. And thanks," Serena said, and for the first time, she seemed to relax.

"Are you sure you don't mind us staying at the house longer?" Fisher asked.

"We'll be gone and when we get back, we'll see what happens then."

"You can't mean to leave the pack after you return," Shawn said. "Bella would be devastated."

"I don't want to leave my sister. We need to catch up on everything that's happened over the years. Has she had any kids yet?"

Heath said, "I wasn't sure if she wanted to be the one to give you the news first. But since you asked, she's due to have triplets in a few months."

"Ohmigod, that's wonderful. Well, that decides it. I'm not leaving."

Everyone whooped and hollered, and she laughed.

The whole pack would be damned glad she was sticking around. They'd all make her feel welcome.

"Are you sure you're all right with us staying at the house tonight?" Shawn asked.

"I'd like the company."

"And you need to be watched in case you're in further pain or have any complications from your fall," Heath said.

Tanner and his brothers agreed.

As soon as they arrived back at the house, all the brothers coddled her—setting her up on one of the brown velvet couches with pillows and blankets and providing a steak dinner for two that Tanner prepared himself, since they'd both missed out on the beer and pizza. She seemed to appreciate that he'd fixed it for her, though she'd said she didn't want him to go to all the trouble.

He wanted to. What better way to prove he could be the right wolf for her? "Tell us all about this ex-roommate. Is he a wolf?"

"He is. And so is the woman he took off with. I smelled her scent in the house when I returned from the library, my last day after they gave me my layoff notice. I suspect he waited until the last minute to leave because he was always that way. He knew he didn't have any time left. Once I was home, I could have caught him at whatever he was up to. I'd asked him if he wanted to go for a run, but he hadn't. When I returned, I saw he'd taken my car without my permission. And I smelled the unfamiliar she-wolf who had been in the house. I tried calling him, then texting him, but he didn't answer. I assumed he took my car because his truck was in the shop and I was without a job. But I felt something was off. He would have told me he needed to borrow the car and asked me for permission to use it. That's when I checked the closet and realized he'd taken his clothes and a couple of suitcases. I started checking his email and learned where he'd gone. Grand Cayman Island. The bastard."

"And the woman?"

She hmpfed. "A gray wolf like him."

The brothers exchanged looks.

She sighed. "Okay, yeah, after the experience I had with him, gray wolves were on my blacklist. But you all have been great and I can't thank you enough for everything you've done for me already."

Tanner showed her his phone. "The earliest flight out for us here tomorrow is at 8:30 a.m., arriving there at 3:27 p.m. It'll take us an hour and a half to get to the airport from here."

"Okay, I'm game."

"Do you want us to drive you?" Fisher asked.

"No. That's a three-hour round trip for you. We'll just leave the car in long-term parking in case it takes a while," Tanner said.

His brothers smiled at him, sure that he wanted her all to himself. Which he did.

---

Early the next morning, Shawn handed Serena her car keys while she and Tanner had breakfast before they left for the airport. "We all looked for the keys last night so we could move the car and carry your bags into the house," Shawn said.

"Oh, thanks so much for all your help."

"How are you feeling?" Heath asked.

"Much, much better, thanks."

"We'll have to look the part when we get there. Do you have anything that you can wear there?" Tanner asked.

"Sure. I had to vacate my rental house. I brought everything I owned."

"You can leave what you don't need here and just pack up what you need for a summer vacation. Do you have a bathing suit?"

She smiled at him.

"If you don't have one, I'll have to buy you one."

"I have a bathing suit, though this is *not* a vacation," she reminded him. "What about you?" Swimming in the surf total appealed, if they could swing it.

"Absolutely. Sunscreen. Flip flops. Board shorts. Sunglasses. We'll need to look the part of tourists. ACP—an automatic Colt pistol, just for backup. I'll get in close to where they're staying to do surveillance. We'll rent a car. You can wait for me at the bungalow since Harold knows you. I can scope out the situation and then we can make plans."

"All right. Sounds like that will work." As soon as she finished eating breakfast, she hurried to repack her suitcases, so she had her laptop and camera in a carry-on, and her clothes and other essentials in a midsize bag.

Tanner had already packed and the guys were waiting for her to finish, then Shawn carried out her bags to Shawn's SUV.

The three brothers gave Serena hugs and wished her luck, slapped Tanner on the back, and then she and Tanner headed out. "I wish we could have reached my sister before we left," she said.

"I agree. She'll be glad to hear from you as soon as she's able."

Serena was feeling much better, both physically and mentally, about everything. Their faster healing abilities really were a godsend. And with the support of a pack, she felt she could manage anything. Even letting this go, if she had to. Family and friends were more important than anything, but she still had to give this her best shot or she'd forever regret that she'd let Harold get away with it.

She was certain Tanner could convince Harold to give up her money if she couldn't access his accounts covertly. And she felt good about getting to know the brothers better, even though she hadn't met the rest of the pack yet. Would she have trouble with any of them? No sense in borrowing trouble.

With her sister having triplets, she was excited about being part of that. Wolves naturally helped take care of other wolves' pups, and she was thrilled to be there for her sister. She couldn't wait to see her.

"I made reservations at a resort down the beach from Harold. Their place was full, but I thought it was better for us to have a little distance between us anyway; this way we can do some surveillance before we confront them."

"Sounds good. You won't be in trouble for taking off like this when your pack leader left you in charge at the leather goods factory, will you?"

"I don't believe Devlyn will fault me too much. Your sister is a different story. I can just imagine her being irritated with me for taking you with me in the event this guy fights back. What kind of a wolf is he? Alpha? Beta? Omega? A lone wolf?"

"He's a lone wolf, no pack. He's alpha, except when he did his cowardly, beta act of stealing my money and slipping away like a thief in the night."

"What about the woman?"

"I never met her. I have no idea where he picked her up. It makes me wonder if he'd planned this all along."

"Wolves don't have sexual relations unless they agree to mate because we make a lifetime commitment to one another. Had he led you to believe that he wanted that with you?"

"No. Neither of us had. For the time being, we just needed each other to share the cost of a furnished rental house. I couldn't afford a place of my own in Omaha, not on a library clerk's hourly wage. Renting an apartment would have cost more than splitting the cost of a rental house. I couldn't live in an apartment anyway. You know how it is with our enhanced hearing. Since he was a wolf, he was more compatible as a roommate than a human. I couldn't find any female wolves to room with. And Harold and I became friends. With us, there was more of a friendly vibe rather than anything physical." She shrugged. "I hadn't been around wolves for eons, and when I met him, it was the first time since the fire. I didn't know what it was like to feel anything like..." She hesitated.

"Carnal pleasure between wolves?"

She smiled at him. "Yeah."

"How long were you together?"

"Three months. Which makes me wonder if he

planned this or if it was something that just happened. He met another she-wolf, decided to mate with her, and help himself to my savings before they left? Or maybe she's a relation."

"So, the plane reservations were for two."

"They were. The woman's name is Velvet Jamison. Different last names, but that could be for any number of reasons."

"Velvet?"

"That was the name on the reservation. One male, one female."

---

After arriving at the airport, Serena and Tanner checked their bags and hauled their carry-ons onto the plane. She and Tanner had both taken laptops. Thankfully, Harold hadn't stolen that.

They finally settled in their seats on the plane, but they'd have two stops and would have to change planes both times before reaching their destination.

"What if he says he didn't take any of my money?" she asked Tanner.

"Why would you travel all the way to Colorado to look for a buried treasure in your parents' basement if you hadn't been robbed of all your savings?"

"I can show the account was closed, but he could just say I did that. I don't have any hard evidence it was him."

"Bastard."

Serena glanced out the window. "Makes me feel like doing what I initially wanted to do."

"Take 'em out permanently."

She squeezed his hand. "I know I shouldn't feel that way, but—"

"Not only did he take all your money, he hooked up with another she-wolf to pull it off."

"Right." She let out her breath on a heavy sigh. "I was angry. Then you and your brothers treated me so nicely, and it helped me to feel a little better."

"To know you weren't the only wolf left in the world with no one to watch your back?"

"I admit, I was feeling that way. You think you know somebody, and then you learn just how much that isn't so."

"Well, one thing about the pack, if anyone did that to another pack member, there would be hell to pay."

"I never thought there'd be a pack in the area where we'd lived. Not a shifter pack. And that gray wolves would be living in my home, or that my own sister would be alive and mated to the pack leader. It's all still a shock."

"All good, right?" He leaned over and pulled her against his shoulder so she could rest.

She smiled, then frowned. "Until we get to the island." Yet, this was nice, she thought. Resting her head on the hot wolf's shoulder, she breathed in his spicy, male wolf scent, listening to his steady heartbeat, feeling his warm touch. *Really nice.*

# Chapter 4

FROM THE FLIGHT SCHEDULE SERENA HAD FOUND FOR Harold and Velvet in the email, they had only arrived the night before, and their return flight was scheduled ten days from then, but they were traveling to Raleigh, North Carolina, instead of returning to Omaha. Tanner was surprised Harold hadn't changed his identity, probably figuring Serena wouldn't catch him because she wouldn't have any money to do anything about it. He couldn't go to jail as a wolf, because it was too dangerous for their kind if he needed to shift during the phase of the full moon. Not to mention that taking on two gray wolves when she was a smaller red wouldn't have been a good idea.

Harold would never suspect an Army Ranger wolf shifter would be hot on his tail.

Tanner and Serena had lunch between flights. When they arrived at the island, they picked up their luggage, got their rental car, and, before they went to their lodging, Serena directed him to go to a bank. There, she opened an account. If Harold could do it, Tanner figured, she could do it too. Then they headed for their lodging. In retrospect, he probably should have asked her if she wanted a separate place. He'd reserved a two-bedroom bungalow on the beach so that they'd be together, share meals, and he could watch over her. Not only was it something he'd do for any she-wolf who was part of the pack, but he also wanted to get to know her better. Plus, Harold might just want to try and scare her off, or worse.

He might have been sneaky about running off with her money, but no telling what might happen if she began stalking him to get it back.

When they walked into the bungalow, she took a deep breath and looked around. There was a cute little kitchen with sunshiny decor, and stairs leading to the bedrooms and one bathroom.

She set her bags down on the tile floor.

Tanner set his bags by the stairs.

"What if Harold had done this before to women he's hooked up with?" Serena asked.

"I was thinking the same thing. There's a good bet that he has."

"And that he'll do it again. Easy money."

"I agree."

She walked over to the living room window that looked out on the beach. "That makes me want to wring his neck again."

"Wait until we get your money back from him first. It would be different if he had some charitable reason why he took the money. Coming to the island to have fun with some new she-wolf? I don't think so. I need to run out and pick up some groceries and some dinner for us. Unless you want to have something delivered?"

"Go ahead and order something for us, then you can get some groceries and the takeout. Anything's fine with me."

He pulled out his phone and searched for a restaurant

close by that served takeout. "Chinese?" He joined her and showed her the menu.

"Sure. The spicy broccoli and beef for me."

"All right. I'd take you with me, but…"

"We might run into them. I feel like I'm on house arrest."

"Because of me?" He didn't want her to feel as though he was calling all the shots. He just wanted to make sure they didn't tip off Harold unless she had to.

"No. Because of them. I suspect she knows what I look like if she had to disguise herself as me when she went to the bank. Though it was a big bank, and I didn't know anyone personally. I didn't go in very much, just used the drive-through or made automatic deposits."

"Why don't we take a run tonight when it gets nice and dark?"

"As wolves?"

"Yeah. What do you think?"

"I'd like that. I'm glad you're with me. I was so mad, I was ready to tear into the two of them all by myself. I wasn't concerned about my own well-being. I didn't figure I had anything to lose at that point."

"I don't blame you. And I'm glad to help you in any way that I can. All right. I'll call in the order and pick it up when it's ready."

"I hope trying to get the money doesn't take more than a couple of days."

He hoped it did. Then he'd be able to spend more time alone with her on a tropical island without his brothers or anyone else's interference. He carried her bags up the stairs, then he called in the order to the

Chinese restaurant. Afterward, he carried his bags up and put them in his room.

He heard her setting the table for dinner. "View of the beach up there?"

"Yep. Both bedrooms. Food's ordered." He headed back down the stairs. "What are you going to do?"

She opened her laptop on the kitchen table and turned it on. "I'm looking for the layout of their cabana. I'm checking his email also. Okay, he received a confirmation for dinner for two at a Chinese restaurant for tonight—like now."

"Not the same one we're getting takeout from though, correct?"

"It's the same one. It's the closest one to both our places. If they see you, they won't know you anyway."

"But if they smell me, they might be able to smell you on me."

"Oh. Sorry. No more hugs for you."

"Hell, I'll kill the SOB for all he's done to you myself. I'll have them deliver the food here and I'll run to the grocery store while they're at the restaurant."

"Thanks for doing this and for everything you've already done for me."

He thought she was going to give him a hug for stepping in to be her hero. He must have looked hopeful, or eager, or something.

She smiled broadly, closed the distance between them, and gave him a warm hug. Warmer than she'd given his brothers when they'd said goodbye. And that told him she just might be interested in something more between them. He meant to give her a simple, sweet kiss; as much as he was craving something wilder, more passionate, wolfish even.

She began to kiss him back, as if searching for the truth. Was she just as passionate a wolf as he hoped she would be? *Hell yeah.*

He gave into the moment, holding her tight, kissing her soft lips, enjoying the heat of her body, the softness of her curves, and the sweet scent of the human and she-wolf combined. Her kisses became more insistent, needier, more passionate.

When they broke free of the kiss, they were breathing harder and their heartbeats were drumming. Her eyes darkened and she appeared dazed. Her arms were still wrapped around his back, and he was holding her close, the two of them gazing into each other's eyes. He knew by the way their pheromones were singing to each other that she had been affected by the intimacy just as much as he had. Not to mention he was fully aroused.

There was something between them, a connection between wolves they could build on.

"I'd tell you I shouldn't have done that with you because I don't really know you, but…I have to admit I've never felt that way with anyone I've ever kissed," Serena said.

"The heat? The desire?" He smiled. "Ditto for me."

Then she sighed and released him. "I'm going to unpack and change into something a little cooler."

"Save a swim date. We can go swimming and running after that long flight. I'll get the groceries and be right back."

"I would love to go swimming and unwind a bit

before we take care of business." She gave him a short list of what she'd like to eat—oatmeal for breakfast, dark-brown sugar, tea, and sandwich fixings.

When Tanner left, Serena unpacked her bags, and then changed into shorts, sandals, and a halter top. Returning to the kitchen, she opened up her laptop to try to learn anything more about Harold from his emails.

She still couldn't believe the way she'd felt when she had kissed Tanner. She'd had a few flings with humans over the years, which were fine as long as she wasn't mated to a wolf. But the craving to make a human hers? Or to take this all the way with a wolf like Harold?

Never.

Back in Omaha, she'd observed a male blue jay courting a female in spring, fluffing out his chest, his wings spread, trying to impress her. The female had been watching him, interested. Appreciative of all his hard work. In Tanner's case, he'd stayed near her when he was a wolf, had tried to warn her of danger, and had taken care of her after she'd hurt herself.

He didn't have wings to spread, but he was definitely in courtship mode, showing how protective he could be, and helping in any way to take case of this business too.

Drawn to him, she tried to tell herself she only kissed him to see if all wolves were the same as humans. Nothing to write home about. She had quickly learned that wasn't the case with Tanner. If she'd had someone to write home to, she would have told her she had found one hot wolf.

She checked more of Harold's emails. She kept thinking he'd remember she had used it once, and he would have changed his password. Maybe he didn't think she was that bright. He would never suspect she was just down the road from him, a beach's run from his cabana.

Then she saw another couple of email confirmations.

Harold and Velvet had paid for a stingray snorkeling excursion tomorrow afternoon and were going on a sunset catamaran cruise tomorrow night. They would be gone for five hours for the snorkeling trip. The catamaran cruise would take about three hours. She and Tanner should be able to... Shoot. She was thinking they could sneak into their place, find his laptop to see if she could hack into it and learn about his bank accounts, but Harold would smell their scent. Even if only Tanner went, Harold would wonder why a male wolf had been there.

The food arrived and she tipped the delivery man, then carried the food into the kitchen to serve it. She received a text from Tanner:

Did the food arrive?

She texted back: It did.

She told him about Harold and his girlfriend going out on the two trips.

Tanner texted back: Why don't we eat out for lunch and dinner tomorrow since they'll be gone for so many hours?

She texted back: We could.

She really didn't plan to stay on the island long. They could have a quick lunch, then break into the cabana. Or Tanner could. He could find the laptop and bring it out to the rental car where she could learn what she could on it. They'd still have the problem with leaving Tanner's scent behind. She suspected they might have to just threaten Harold to force him to give up her money.

I'll be right there. The grocery store is nearby.

See you.

She fixed them glasses of ice water, then looked out at the beach. She was a take-charge person, and sitting here doing nothing was driving her nuts. While Harold and Velvet were at the Chinese restaurant, she wanted to check them out and learn what the woman looked like. Was she similar in coloring and build, or just the opposite? Serena wanted to see how the two of them reacted to each other—intimate or just getting to know each other? Hotly craving each other?

She should have been angry that he'd used another she-wolf to help steal from her, but his actions had forced her into new circumstances—learning about her sister and finding a whole pack of eligible male wolves to choose from—which thrilled her. Harold had done her a favor.

Even though the Greystoke brothers said they'd take care of her and she didn't have to worry about money, she couldn't allow Harold and the she-wolf to get away with stealing her savings. Only an omega or beta wolf would let another wolf abuse her trust and do nothing about it.

She heard Tanner park the rental car out front, and

she hurried to help him with the groceries. He only had a couple sacks of groceries and took the opportunity to wrap his arms around her, bags still in hand, and kiss her as if she'd come outside to welcome him back home after he'd been away for eons.

She laughed and kissed him back, and did something so uncharacteristic for her when it came to a man—*but he was all wolf*. She rubbed her body against him in a way that said she was interested in being *more* than just one of his pack mates. That got him smiling in a hot, sexy way. After the official greeting, they entered the bungalow and shut and locked the door.

"Okay, I didn't want to text about all this stuff, but I was thinking we could search his place for any clues about where he might be keeping my money and how to access it. But then he'd smell that we'd been in his place."

"I have hunter's spray I brought with me."

Her jaw dropped, then she frowned at him as he put the groceries away. "Do you often use it to conceal your scent?"

"Only when necessary."

"Okay, then good. They're going to be gone for about eight hours on excursions tomorrow, so I figure we'll be able to slip into his place one of those times." She began to serve the Chinese food.

"I've got lock picks we can use. Standard *lupus garou* issue."

"What if we run into them when we're running or swimming?"

"I'll tear into him and make him wish he hadn't taken your money and your car."

That made her worry. She didn't want Tanner injured. And for what? Money? His life was too important. But she didn't want to emasculate Tanner by mentioning it, reminding herself that he was an Army Ranger. She'd jump in and fight the bastard though, if Harold got a lucky strike and Tanner needed her help.

After eating and washing up, they stripped out of their clothes, opened the door to the patio on the beach, and shifted, intending to enjoy the beach and ocean that night, the sun already having set. The dark was perfect for their night vision, but humans wouldn't be able to make them out.

They ran as wolves, then shifted and ran into the water as humans. She never imagined skinny dipping as a human with a wolf. She and Tanner swam, the full moon shining on the waves. She'd never been in the Caribbean or even to a beach before—lakes, ponds, rivers, yes—but this was beyond beautiful, and she loved it here. Too bad she wasn't on a vacation with the handsome wolf, not worrying about getting her money back from a crook.

Tanner took hold of her arm, pulled her close, and kissed her. Now this she'd never tried before—kissing a naked man in the ocean, the warm swell of water lapping at their waists, the sultry breeze ruffling their hair, the silky sand under their feet. It made her nearly forget her purpose here.

He nuzzled her cheek. "Are you ready to run past the cabana and check it out?"

"Yeah, let's go. I wish we could check out their place early, but they might—"

They saw movement on the beach, two gray wolves

racing down the white sandy beach, and Tanner quickly turned Serena away from their view. Since he was half a foot taller than her at six feet tall, he sufficiently blocked their view of her. He wrapped his arms around her and kissed her then, as if that was part of the charade. Though she had to admit Harold would never suspect she would be here with one hot wolf.

She kissed him back, her arms wrapping around his waist, her wet body pressed against his, and felt his cock stirring to life. For the moment, she didn't give a damn about Harold and the she-wolf.

But then Tanner pulled his hot lips away from hers and said, "Can you access his computer if he has it at their cabana?"

"I can."

"The Grand Cayman account would be new, wouldn't it?"

"He might have had it for a while. He uses the same three passwords for everything. He had them written down on a slip of paper in a drawer. I came across it one day while looking for a pen in his desk drawer."

"What if he's changed the passwords?"

"I can try to hack into the account."

"You're a hacker?" Tanner looked amused.

"Just a hobby. It came in handy when my coworkers at the library forgot their passwords on their computers. It was hush-hush, and we never breathed a word of it to management. If that doesn't work, we'll go to plan B: force him to tell us to give up the money."

He glanced over his shoulder. "We'll have time to search for his laptop when they go on the snorkeling trip. They're gone now and way down the beach. We should return to the bungalow. I don't want to run into them as wolves on the beach."

"Agreed. Let's go." She glanced down the beach and didn't see any sign of them. "Should we make a run for it as naked humans or furry wolves?"

"Wolves. We'll reach the bungalow faster. If we can't see them, they can't see us from this distance either."

They moved through the waves to get closer to shore, then shifted and ran for the bungalow's porch. Tanner shifted again, opened the door, and then Serena shifted and walked inside with him. He shut and locked the door.

"Now what?" he asked.

Her phone rang then, and she wondered who would be calling her. "Gotta get that." She grabbed her phone and saw that it was Bella; she was glad Tanner had added her name and number into her list of contacts for her. "It's my sister." She felt overjoyed at once. Not wanting to try and dress while talking to her sister on the phone, she climbed the stairs to the bedroom. "Omigod, Bella!" Tears filled Serena's eyes. "I can't believe you're alive! Or mated to a gray wolf." She slipped under the covers. "Or that you're having triplets!"

"I can't believe you're alive either, and now you're risking your neck, trying to get your money back from your ex-roommate?" Bella sounded annoyed with her, but she was sniffling too.

"In my place, you would have done the same thing." Serena knew her sister would have. She was too stubborn not to.

"I don't want you to risk your life over the money. We have plenty in the pack, and you don't have any concerns in that respect."

"At first, I felt I didn't have a choice. But it didn't change my feelings about him stealing my savings. It's mine. I worked hard for it. And I don't want him to feel he got away with what he did."

"Okay, I understand. I'm glad Tanner's with you. Devlyn is ready to send more than half the pack there to take the wolf down."

"We're fine. For now. If we have trouble, we'll be sure to call you." Serena heard Tanner talking on his phone downstairs and wondered if he was still naked like she was.

"I can't believe I'm really talking to you. Everyone's been trying to reach us. We finally arrived at a location where we had cell phone reception. You don't know how thrilled I am." Bella began to cry.

So did Serena. "I can't wait to see you, Sis. We'll"— Serena sniffled—"be home soon. I can't wait to hear all about your life."

"Same here. Don't do anything that will get you killed over there. I will never forgive you."

Serena smiled. "We'll be there soon. And I promise I'll be careful." But she'd also promised herself she was getting her money back, and she always kept her promises.

Still, they talked for two hours straight, and when they finally hung up, Serena felt as though they had barely been apart all those years. She wanted to know more, but it was time to call it a night. Though she was certain Tanner understood her need to reconnect with her sister, she didn't want him to feel neglected either. Not when he was willing to help her like this.

She threw on some shorts and a T-shirt and headed downstairs. He was dressed in shorts, watching out the window. "See anything?" she asked.

"I saw them return as wolves headed in the direction of their cabana. Did you have a nice talk with your sister?"

"I did. But we need to talk about so much more."

"I'm not surprised. Devlyn called me."

She'd wondered who Tanner had been speaking with. "Checking to see if we're all right?"

"Giving me hell."

Her lips parted. She was surprised Devlyn was angry with his cousin. "Because you didn't ask his permission first?"

Tanner closed the distance between them and pulled her into his arms. "Because I brought you here, risking your life without a solid plan and no backup."

"We're going to get the money by accessing his account."

"He wants us to wait. He's sending two of my brothers and our cousins Vaughn and Brock."

She didn't want to delay what she and Tanner intended to do while Harold and his girlfriend were on the stingray feeding excursion, especially when Serena only knew about that trip and the night cruise for certain. This was their best opportunity to grab the money surreptitiously.

She let out her breath. "When are they arriving?"

"Two days from now. The flight in was booked. They're going to try flying standby in the meantime."

"Okay, this is what we're going to do. We have Harold's itinerary for most of tomorrow. Beyond that, we have no idea when they're going to leave the cabana, or when they're going to return. To do this as covertly as possible, this is the best shot we have. If we get the money, the guys don't have to fly out here, unless they want to. And we can return to Colorado."

He smiled down at her. "You and Bella will really keep Devlyn on his toes."

She smiled up at Tanner. "Are you going to call him and tell him the plan?"

"Nope. If we're successful tomorrow, we'll tell him then. If we're not, we'll go with a new plan B. Wolf pack muscle."

"Okay, it's a deal. Thanks, Tanner. I hope you won't get into too much trouble."

"I'll just tell him you made me do it."

She laughed. "I doubt he'll believe that."

"He will. He'll know I'm trying to persuade a wolf to court me, and I'll do whatever it takes, within reason. As long as your life isn't on the line."

# Chapter 5

THE NEXT MORNING, TANNER AND SERENA PREPARED breakfast at the bungalow. Tanner made the works—omelets, bacon, hash browns, toast, and coffee. She had her oatmeal. But all he could think of as he prepared breakfast was that he hoped Harold and the she-wolf wouldn't cancel their plans so he and Serena had time to do what they needed to do.

"You said his laptop was in the shop." Tanner took his seat at the kitchen table with Serena to eat.

"It was. He picked it up two days before he left."

Tanner had a nightmare last night that he and Serena would arrive at the cabana and the wolves would be there. If it did happen, it just meant they'd have to force the truth out of them.

Movement outside the kitchen window caught his eye, and he noticed the palm tree fronds were flapping wildly in the wind and the waves were covered in white caps, larger than they were last night. He checked the weather app on his phone. "Hell." A tropical storm was approaching the islands.

"What's wrong?" Serena asked.

"Storm's coming in with gale-force winds of up to sixty miles per hour. It might veer off, but it might not."

"Oh great." She checked Harold's emails. "Damn it. The tour group has cancelled the excursions for both this afternoon and their catamaran dinner cruise. It's understandable, just not something I wanted to hear."

"Have they rescheduled for a later date?"

"No. They'll have to wait out the storm. If the docks are torn up, it might be canceled for the duration of their stay here." Serena sounded disappointed.

Tanner hoped they didn't have more trouble than that. "Says here, no flights in or out of the islands until further notice. So the guys will be delayed coming here to back us up also."

"What will we do?" She looked so disappointed that she couldn't just take care of this and be done with it. He reached across the table and took her hand, giving it a reassuring squeeze.

"We'll get it done." Though Tanner couldn't be sure how. If the storm destroyed their lodging, and Harold's laptop with it, then what? Not to mention a real risk to themselves if the storm was bad enough. "The tropical storm has developed about thirty miles offshore. We've got some food, but I need to return to the grocery store and pick up some more items just in case we lose electricity."

"I'll go with you."

"What if Harold and the she-wolf have the same idea?" Tanner really didn't want Harold to see Serena. Harold couldn't leave the island right away, but he might leave as soon as he could if he saw Serena was here, before she could get her hands on the money.

"All right. Get plenty of water, some spare gallons for cooking and washing up, and canned goods."

"Got it."

"I'll clean up our breakfast dishes. You go before everyone cleans out the grocery store."

"All right." He carried his dishes and coffee mug into the kitchen, then pulled her in for a warm hug and kissed her, already feeling possessive and needing her to know he was there for her.

She kissed him back in a way that said she appreciated it, their mouths open to each other, their tongues sliding against each other's. He groaned when she pulled away. "More later," she assured him.

"Then I'd better hurry."

It took him only ten minutes to get to the grocery store, and Serena was right; the place was packed. People, mostly locals, were stocking up. He smelled the panic, everyone in a rush to grab what they could.

Wheeling a cart in front of him, he picked up a couple of camp lanterns, flashlights, candles, several packs of bottled spring water, several extra gallons of water, canned goods, other nonperishable food items, a radio, and a propane stove. Tanner smelled a male wolf had just been down the aisle where he was picking up some chips, and he didn't believe there would be a lot of wolves vacationing on the island. He rolled his cart around the corner and saw a man and a woman clinging to him. Covertly, Tanner snapped a quick photo of them to show to Serena, wanting to know if she had ever seen the woman before, and he sent it to his brothers and cousins.

The guy had sandy, dishwater-colored hair; the woman, mousy brown hair. She pulled free from him and began wringing her hands, looking worried. He was laid back, smirking, his hand rubbing her back underneath her shirt. From the picture Serena had shown Tanner, that was Harold.

"I think we should leave," the woman said, most likely Velvet. She was about the same petite build as Serena.

"All flights have been cancelled because of the storm. We'll be fine. I've been through two of these here already. No big deal." Harold pulled her in for a kiss.

Tanner thought they'd known each other for a while. Or maybe the two of them felt something for each other that Harold hadn't felt for Serena and vice versa. Something that went deeper than just a physical attraction between wolves. Still, Harold hadn't needed to steal Serena's money or leave without telling her he'd found a she-wolf who meant everything to him. Which made Tanner suspect Harold was a scam artist and had planned this out in advance. And that the woman meant something more to him than someone he just used to grab Serena's money.

Tanner was glad Serena wasn't here to witness their display of affection.

He stayed out of the wolves' way, grabbing what he needed, hoping they wouldn't notice his wolf scent.

As wary as wolves were, he hoped they didn't catch sight of him halfway watching them. Though if they did, they'd probably believe he was just curious about them because he was a wolf too.

They finally checked out and left, not noticing Tanner, thankfully. Then he waited until their headlights turned on and they backed out of their parking space. Already the blue morning skies filled with white fluffy clouds had turned ominously dark gray, and spatters of raindrops began to fall as Tanner hurried to load the groceries in the car, then returned the cart to the store.

He received a call from Serena. "Headed back, just getting into the car," he said.

"Okay, I was worried. It's fixing to let loose at any moment. I looked into the emergency shelters. We'd have to bring our passports, ID, money, nonperishable food for three days, and three gallons of water per person. They take children, the sick, and the elderly as priority. They don't have room for a lot of people, so I figure we'll just stick it out here. I already closed all the outdoor shutters."

The winds were blowing him all over the road, and the rain was coming down in a torrent, so he was glad when he finally pulled into their parking space and cut the engine. "Okay, why don't you fill the bathtub with water? We can boil it if we need it. I picked up a small battery-operated radio and extra batteries in case the electricity goes out."

"I've been filling the tub. I've got the TV on and am watching the weather channel. Good idea on the radio."

"I'm here. I'll grab our stuff and be inside in a minute."

She headed outside to help him. "I never expected this." Neither of them had brought rain gear, so they were getting soaked as they hurried to carry the bags into the bungalow. "But I should have. We're in Hurricane Alley. The program I was just watching said this island has been hit or brushed by a tropical storm or hurricane every year and a half or so."

"I checked the weather report before we came, just to see if we had any bad weather coming. It showed nothing."

"I guess they pop up without warning sometimes. Suddenly there's a tropical depression that worsens, and then if you're in its path, watch out. We won't have to take a shower." She set the wet plastic bags on the counter and hurried after him to get the rest of the stuff.

He glanced back at her, considered her T-shirt plastered to her breasts, and smiled.

She chuckled and helped him get the gallons of water into the bungalow. Once they were done, he locked the door and pulled her in for a hug. "I like the wet look on you."

She smiled and rubbed her hand on his wet shirt covering hard abs. "I like the look on you too. What are we going to do while we wait out the storm?"

"I found some board games in the cabinet underneath the TV. We can keep tuned into the weather report while we're playing some of the games." He set the flashlights on the table while she made them some tea and coffee.

"Oh, the big set of dominoes. Ever play chicken foot dominoes?"

"Nope. I'm game." Tanner showed her the photo of Harold and Velvet. "I took this of them in the store. Recognize them?"

"That's definitely Harold. I've never seen the woman before."

He was glad she didn't seem perturbed about the woman.

They set up the dominoes, then sat down to play, the wind howling outside their shuttered windows. The news was updated periodically on the TV, the lights flickering.

"Hmm," she said, placing her double domino next to his single domino, making a "T." She glanced at the shuttered windows. "If we lose electricity, we may have to play a different game." Though they had enhanced night vision as wolves.

"We can. Tired of this one already?"

"No. I'm winning."

He laughed. "We just began."

The strength of the wind whipped everything into a frenzy. The roof started vibrating violently.

Tanner reached over, pulled Serena close, and kissed her cheek. "If it gets too bad, we can move under the stairwell. It has no windows and a narrow space that would offer the best protection."

"We should move blankets and pillows in there now."

"Let's do it, to be on the safe side."

They headed up the stairs to get the bedding, and she entered her room, while he gathered the pillows and blankets from his.

After they set up their makeshift shelter underneath the stairs, complete with bottles of water and a flashlight, they looked at it for a moment. Tanner wrapped his arms around her. "Are you ready for me to beat you at dominoes?"

She rubbed his arms, thinking of running to Harold's cabana to see if they had gone somewhere else to ride out the storm. "What if Harold and Velvet went to a shelter?"

"Children, the sick, and the elderly have priority. Remember?"

"Right. And he's an alpha wolf."

"And we're supposed to stay put during the storm."

She sighed. "All right. Back to dominoes."

The shutters rattled and so did the walls and roof. It was eerie sounding and gave her a chill. They settled on the couch and half watched the news as the weatherman reported the tropical storm was growing closer and picking up steam.

And then they were kissing. She wasn't sure how it happened. But she'd blocked his next move, taking the spot where he wanted to go next with his domino, and he tackled her. She squealed, then laughed as he pinned her to the couch and began to kiss her.

She gave into the kiss, forgetting about the howling wind and rattling bungalow. About Harold and her money. This is what she'd needed in her life, and no money could buy what she was feeling for the wolf—the hot yearning, the wolfish need.

"I think I could fall for you." She smiled up at him.

"I want to make that happen." Tanner sounded so sure of himself, she thought he might just be right.

Then the TV and overhead light flickered and went out, plunging them into darkness.

"Time to go to our shelter," she said.

"Agreed." He got off her, grabbed the flashlight and the radio off the coffee table, and she slipped her arm through his.

She and Tanner couldn't have sex or they'd be mated wolves, but that didn't mean they couldn't fool around. And she'd only do that with a wolf she really, really liked.

"So what do we do now?" she asked as they moved into the narrow hall.

"This small space isn't very accommodating for games or much else."

"We just got up, so taking a nap seems kind of silly." She joined him on their blanket bed on the floor.

"There's only one thing I can think of." He smiled at her and cupped her face.

"When the lights go out…"

Tanner began to kiss her again, and the way the bungalow was rattling, she really did wonder if they were going to make it through this okay.

But then he was on top of her, whispering, "I'll protect you." And she knew he would do anything to make that happen.

Serena never expected to be having afternoon delight with a hot wolf, hunkered down in a makeshift shelter with a tropical storm bearing down on their location. God, how she wanted this, the hot passion erupting between them, their bodies naked and rubbing against each other.

Their kisses became more insistent as the winds became more violent. What if this was the last chance she'd ever have at making love to a wolf? And the first. But consummating the relationship would mean a mating.

Still, they stripped off their clothes, and then she concentrated on every aspect of what they were doing: his hand massaging her breast; the sexy, sea-salt smell of his skin; the way his heart beat as rapidly as hers.

He was hard—from his arousal to his toned muscles— but his mouth was soft against hers, nipping and kissing, then pressuring until his tongue came into play with hers. Their tongues teased and stroked each other's.

Then his hand moved between her legs, and he began

to stroke her clit. Her hands grasped his shoulders as she clung to sanity, her breath short. She was barely breathing as he rocked her world.

But then he rubbed his engorged cock against her mons, the aching need compelling her to grab his hips and pull him harder against her. She shouldn't want him thrusting between her legs, but she sure as hell did. Her belly tightened, her blood on fire. He slid a finger inside her. The climax was so close, she could taste it, and then she let go and cried out with wild pleasure, right before he closed his mouth over hers again.

He rubbed his cock against her belly, her hands gliding up his arms. "Do you want me to—"

"Shhh."

So she moved against him, her hips rising, pushing against him, until he groaned, and she felt him spill his seed on her belly.

"Sorry," he whispered, kissing her forehead.

"Don't be. That was amazing." And she knew it wouldn't end there.

※

The storm raged on for hours, and finally sounded like it was beginning to die down a little. Serena and Tanner cleaned up, then dressed and went into the kitchen to make tuna sandwiches, adding chips and pickles and bottled water for lunch. They listened to the radio reporting that the storm was moving onward, but the winds and rain continued to pelt the bungalow until later that night. And then it was calm, everything quieting. The storm had moved out to sea.

The electricity suddenly came back on, and they went outside to see the damage. The waves were still huge, perfect for surfing. A few palm fronds were scattered about and red tiles missing on some roofs, but no major damage that they could see.

"Looks like we made it safely through that one."

"If we can weather a storm like that, we should be able to manage anything." Tanner pulled her in close, resting his head on the top of hers, his arms wrapped around her waist as they looked out to sea.

"Do you want to see how their cabana fared?"

"Yeah, sure. Let's go."

They headed down the beach toward the cabanas and everything there looked fine too. "I wonder if the docks and boats are all right," she whispered.

"We'll have to check the news and see what was damaged on the island. They might not report it until daylight tomorrow."

They returned to the bungalow, and she was glad the storm was over and that at least where they were, it hadn't been too bad. She didn't know what they would do if the excursions Harold and Velvet were going to take were canceled for the duration of their stay here.

"At this point, I don't see any reason for us to have separate bedrooms, do you?" Tanner asked.

She snagged his hand and hauled him up the stairs. "Wait, our pillows and blankets are still under the stairs."

They retrieved the bedding, then he chased her up the stairs. At the top, she hesitated. "Let's use your room."

He looked like one satisfied wolf. She figured she looked like one too.

———∿∿———

Early the next morning, Tanner checked Harold's email,
wanting to know if the excursions were rescheduled or
not, while Serena was taking a shower.

Wearing shorts and a T-shirt, her hair still wet, she
joined him, and he kissed her as if they were already a
couple. "You are the perfect wolf to wake up next to in
the morning, and ride out a storm with too."

"I only screamed once."

He laughed. "I jumped too, when I heard that big
bang."

She saw he had his laptop out and was checking
emails. "What's the verdict?"

"A few trees were down, some vehicles flipped in the
high winds, some roofs were badly damaged. But the
docks and boats on that side of the island are fine, and
the trips were rescheduled. Harold received confirmation emails for this afternoon and tonight."

"Yes!"

He was hoping they'd get this done and maybe skip
over to one of the Sister Islands, as long as they hadn't
sustained a lot of damage. "Flights have commenced
also, but the guys were delayed because of the flights
getting backed up yesterday."

"We'll be okay."

Tanner sure the hell hoped so. He made it through a
tropical storm on a small island with the she-wolf, and
he sure as hell didn't want to lose her now.

# Chapter 6

As the looming hour approached, Serena fought the nervousness she was experiencing, trying not to show it outwardly, but Tanner could smell it on her.

After hastily eating lunch, her stomach in knots, she spread her legs and arms so Tanner could spray the hunter concealer all over her, then she did the same to Tanner.

"Ready?" he asked.

"Yeah, let's do this." She thought he looked like he'd hoped she might have changed her mind. She wasn't giving this up for anything.

They drove over in the rental car and parked nearby. "I'll knock on the door to ensure they really have gone on the stringray snorkeling trip. If no one answers, I'll use the lock pick and you can join me."

"When he's on trips, he always hides his laptop under the sofa."

"All right. See you in a minute." Tanner gave her a hug and kiss, and then he walked to the door with purpose. The cabanas were separated by vegetation, and he didn't hear anyone about. He knocked on the door, and when no one answered, he texted Serena.

He pulled out his lock pick. As soon as he opened the door, Serena hurried to join him. "So far, so good," he said.

But anything could go wrong.

She quickly checked underneath the floral couch, but it sat so high, it probably didn't look like a safe place for Harold to hide his laptop. "Not here," she whispered.

"Checking the bedroom."

"He wouldn't have taken it with him. Not snorkeling. So it's got to be here somewhere." She looked in the kitchen. "Not in here."

He looked in the two bedrooms, smelled that both Harold and Velvet were staying together, which was no surprise there, but smelled they'd had sex here, or sexual activity. "The safe in one of the closets is too small for a laptop, unless it's really small."

She joined him. "I can't imagine he would have locked it in the rental car." She eyed the safe. "You're right. The safe is too small for his laptop. Unless he bought a new one for traveling. I can't figure him out. He always had plenty of money. Why would he have stolen mine?"

"Some people never have enough."

Harold's clothes were neatly hung up in the closet, Velvet's piled on a chair, but Tanner noticed the suitcase behind his shoes. "In there maybe?"

Serena grabbed the mostly empty black bag and set it on the bed. An airline security–approved lock protected it. She used her own key that would work on it and the lock clicked open. After she unzipped the bag, she found a leather case, his laptop. She pulled his laptop out and set it on the desk in the bedroom.

Tanner appeared as relieved as she was that it was there. Now if she could only get into his computer. "I'll watch for any sign of them returning," Tanner said.

"Okay, good. I'm into his computer."

"Anything yet?"

"He's so predictable. He has all his bank account links set up on his toolbar for one-click access. I'm trying the variations of his passwords to see if I can—holy cow."

"You got into one?"

"Yeah, and boy, has he got the money. I wonder how much of it he earned and how much of it he stole. Over two and a half million dollars. Why would he need my one hundred and sixty thousand?"

"Like I said, some people never have enough. It could be he has an addiction to stealing too. Gets a thrill out of the game. Why don't you grab your money, and let's go. Are you done yet?"

"Almost."

Once she was done, she packed the laptop back into his suitcase, zipped, and locked it, then tucked it behind his shoes in the closet. She took one of his tennis shoes and shook it out. Then another.

"What are you looking for?" Tanner asked, glancing over his shoulder at her.

"Looking for his credit card." She found it and stuck it in her pocket. "He'll find it missing at some point and have to call it in to cancel it."

"Then he can't use it until they send him another."

"Exactly. He doesn't have another card and he never carries cash."

Tanner smiled at her. "Are you done?"

"Yep."

"Did you get your money?" he asked, hurrying her out of the cabana. They locked the door after them.

"Plus, a little extra to pay for the expense of us flying out here and the cost of the accommodations. That way it won't look like it was me just taking back my money. It would throw him off track. I changed his passwords on the accounts too. He'll have to prove he owns them to be able to change them himself."

Tanner smiled at her. "I had an idea, but was waiting until we learned if we could manage this."

"Yeah?" she asked as they returned to the rental car and got in.

"We're already here. We can't get a flight out to Colorado right away either. If we can get one, why don't we take one of those thirty-minute flights to one of the smaller islands? Cayman Brac or Little Cayman? They're quieter, but perfect for swimming, snorkeling, and running. Then we won't have to worry about running into Harold or his girlfriend. They haven't made any reservations to fly over there or stay there, have they?"

"No. He always has receipts for all his activities sent to his emails, and nothing's popped up. I like the idea."

"Okay, I'll make reservations. First, I need to call and make sure that my brothers and cousins don't come here."

When they arrived home, Tanner called Devlyn and put it on speaker so Serena could listen in. "Serena's got her money, but we can't get a flight out for a couple of days."

"She had no trouble getting it back at all?" Devlyn sounded surprised.

"She accessed his bank accounts. We're flying out to one of the smaller islands to stay out of the way until we can get a flight home. Just so we don't cross paths."

"You think you won't need your brothers? Or our cousins for backup?"

"We should be good."

Devlyn didn't say anything for a moment. Then he said, "I'm sending them anyway. A few days on the beach, watching your backs, and then you can all return home."

Tanner wanted to groan out loud. All his brothers and cousins were bachelor wolves, and he knew, though they would be eager to watch out for him and Serena, they would also be vying for her attention. She might have wanted to experiment with Tanner, but it didn't mean she had decided to mate him. Yet.

But Devlyn was right. Better to be safe than sorry, though Serena and he could leave about the time the others arrived. Maybe they'd hang around a little longer, then.

"All right."

"Everything else going all right?"

Tanner thought his cousin meant about how he was getting along with Serena. "We're doing great. I need to make reservations for the other island. We'll let you know how things are going a little later."

"Okay, stay safe."

When they ended the call, Tanner made reservations for a flight and accommodations to Cayman Brac. "Two hundred feet of sandy beachfront, four bedroom, three and a half bath villa. That will be enough room for the four guys, you, and me. We can enjoy the botanical gardens, Rum Point, blow holes, restaurants, and of course all the swimming we'd like." Tanner wished the guys could stay somewhere else but he knew they wouldn't.

How could they protect them if they were at some other location? Though Tanner really didn't believe they needed protection.

"Sounds great. I'm going up to pack. When are we leaving?"

"As soon as we get packed. We'll head on over to the airport."

"Do you have a pair of scissors?"

"For a credit card?" Tanner smiled at her. "He should never have messed with you. Here I thought you were going to need me."

"You never know when a little muscle can turn the tide."

After they packed up the car, they headed for the airport, turned in the rental car, and waited for their plane.

Tanner wrapped his arm around her shoulders as they sat next to each other in the airport. "I wonder how long it will take him to notice some of his money is gone. As much as he had, maybe he won't notice right away."

"He probably will notice. He's tight with his money."

"Do you feel better about everything now?"

"I do. Payback can cause some major heartburn—for him. I wonder if now that he's not as wealthy as before, his girlfriend will want to stick with him."

"I believe they might be mated," Tanner said.

"I agree."

"One hundred and sixty plus some change is only a drop in the bucket if Howard has that much money. Too bad we couldn't have made more of a statement." Tanner rubbed her back.

"If I'd known that he'd swindled others like me, I

would love to give the money back. But without know-ing that for certain, I won't be a thief like him."

"He swindled the wrong she-wolf."

———

An hour and a half later, they landed on Cayman Brac, grabbed their bags, rented a car, and headed to the villa. Serena loved the other island and would have enjoyed exploring some of the fun things they had to do there, but now that they'd finished the business she'd come for, she didn't want to chance running into Harold or his new girlfriend—and she was ready to have some fun.

"Did you want to keep the pretense that we're just friends?" Tanner asked as they entered the sunny villa.

"You mean as far as the bedrooms go? Nah. Not unless you're worried about what the other guys will think about us rooming together."

He laughed. "I would hope they would think they have no chance with the beautiful she-wolf."

"They don't. This is really nice. Not that the other place wasn't also. But it's nice to know we're here to just have fun now. Do you want to go swimming?"

"I'd love to. Then for lunch, I'm taking you to a res-taurant. Seafood sound good?"

"In the islands, absolutely. They have caves here we could explore too. Right now, the ocean is calling to me."

Tanner finished removing his clothes and pulled on his board shorts.

She pulled on her bikini bottoms, then pulled off her bra, but before she could fasten the bikini top, Tanner was doing it for her. "Are you worried he might figure out I did it and track us here?" she asked.

"Not here. If he believes we flew out of here, I'm sure he'll assume you went home with a wolf. He'll probably be looking for you on Grand Cayman for a while though. They have some flights back to the States, even if they didn't have the one we needed, so we could have been on any one of those. Did you ever tell him where you were from originally?" He grabbed a couple of beach towels and set them on loungers on the back patio.

"No. I never talked to anyone about it." They headed out into the tropical warmth, a sea breeze carrying the scent of fish, brine, seaweed, and salt water.

"If he finds us, I'll take care of him. As to whether he'd figure out you had a hand in this, maybe, since you had his email password. And he might realize you could have seen his bank passwords in the drawer."

"True." She dashed for the water. She smiled back at Tanner as he chased after her. "The sand is so white and so soft underfoot." She dug her feet into the warm sand, then reached the water's edge.

He swept her up in his arms and ran into the stirred-up surf, the waves cresting still higher than when they went swimming the first night. "Are you serious about not seeing any of the other wolves when we return?"

"After you stayed with me when I was in the woods, carried me to the house when I was injured, brought me here and helped me to break into his place, protected me during a tropical storm, let me beat you at dominoes, and now…this?"

"If you put it that way…" He smiled down at her, still

holding her in his arms, braving the impact of the waves as they rolled against his legs.

"But it's a lot more than that. I've never felt this way for another man. A wolf. With you, it goes a lot deeper. I love you and I didn't think I'd ever feel that way for someone."

"I fell in love with you the moment you showed up and I began to follow you as a wolf. I was ready to claim you for my own from the beginning. Wolves sense when they've found their mate. And I knew I had to convince you in any way I could that I was yours. I love you right back, Serena." He leaned down to kiss her, but just as his mouth touched hers, a rogue wave crashed into them, sweeping them off their feet, and they were pulled under.

He was out of the water first, grabbing her hand and pulling her from the water. She laughed and wrapped her arms around his neck, kissing him back.

The waves tugged back and forth at them, but they only broke free of the kiss when they were ready. Then they swam out beyond the breakers and floated together, loving sharing this time on the island before she met the rest of the pack and learned what her role would be.

She would no longer be on her own, but a contributing member of the pack. "I could create a small library, if you don't already have one," she suddenly said.

He smiled, and kissed her cheek. "I was thinking about returning to the villa and mating. You're thinking of going to work."

She chuckled. "Sorry. I know it's important to contribute to a pack."

"A library would be welcome."

After walking along the beach while holding hands, she said, "I want to come here again sometime. Not just to this island, but to Grand Cayman, to take the excursions Harold is going on with his mate."

"Anytime."

She wrapped her arm around his waist as they headed to the villa. "What do you want to do for the rest of the day?"

"I'm taking you to the seafood restaurant for dinner, but before that, we need to finish some other business."

"You're eager to be a mated wolf, I take it."

"Hell yeah."

She loved the way he wanted her, as if nothing could please him more. And she wanted him just as much—a new beginning, a return to her lands, and becoming close to her twin sister again.

They rinsed off outside under the shower and then dried off quickly. Then he opened the door, scooped her up, and carried her over the threshold. He paused to shut the door with his hip, and she reached down and locked it. Then he headed for their bedroom.

"Oh heavens, put me down," she said, as he reached the stairs.

He just leaned down, kissed her, and carried her up the stairs.

Tanner figured his brothers would ask him how he managed to convince Serena he was the right wolf for her. Loving the she-wolf came easy. Protecting her could be a challenge, but he would always be there for her no matter what.

He set her on the floor before helping her out of her

bikini. She reciprocated, pulling off his board shorts. Then he joined her in the bed, cupping her face and kissing her mouth, her hands wrapping around his waist, and pulling him closer. "I've waited for you all my life."

She smiled. "I feel the same for you."

Then they were kissing again, his hands molding to her breasts, feeling her nipples tighten. He rubbed his hard cock against her belly, a way of sharing his scent with her and carrying her scent with him. She was his and he was hers.

"You are one hot wolf," she breathed against his chest before she licked his nipple, sending shivers of pleasure to his core. She pulled gently on his nipple with her lips, then moved to the other.

She was breathing harder, her pheromones heating and triggering his own.

"Beautiful," he whispered as he trailed kisses down to her breast and licked one nipple, then tugged gently on it with his mouth, just as she had done to him.

She moaned softly, running her hands over his biceps.

He moved his mouth over her left breast to the right one and licked the nipple, his hand cupping the left, his thumb rubbing the nipple.

He couldn't believe how lucky he was.

He reached between them and began to stroke her, kissing her belly. He rubbed harder, more vigorously. She clutched at his arms, her face tight with concentration. He could see when the climax was about to hit, smell her sexy arousal, loved hearing her cry out with pleasure.

He began to kiss her mouth, and then she reached for his hips, grabbing hold, and pulled him closer.

"Do it," she said.

He slipped his cock into her, and once he was seated fully, he began to thrust. She was hot, wet, and tight, perfect for him. He hoped she felt he was just as perfect for her as she gyrated her hips and he thrust harder.

He paused to kiss her throat, her chin, her mouth, wanting desperately to prolong this. Then he drove his cock in deeply. Striving to make it last, he rubbed against her, but he couldn't hold off any longer and groaned with release.

She thrust her pelvis at him as he finished, then still joined with her, he pulled back enough to coax another climax out of her.

She clutched at his hair, tightening, then let go. "Oh. My. God."

He smiled, slipped out of her, and pulled her into his arms. "I love you, Serena."

"I love you right back, you beautiful, *big* wolf."

They were enjoying the afterglow of making love, of being mated wolves, when Serena's phone rang. Thinking Bella was calling, she rolled over to grab her phone off the bedside table and saw it was Harold. Her heartbeat quickened.

"Harold," she whispered, as if she had answered the call already and he could hear her.

"You want me to talk to him, or just hang up?"

She let out her breath. "I could block his calls, but I think it's important to hear what he has to say." She sat up, answered the phone, and put it on speaker.

"When I find you, you'll give me every cent back. Or you're dead."

Then he hung up on her.

# Chapter 7

Tanner was livid. No one threatened a pack member, let alone his very own mate, and got away with it. Harold might have just been mouthing off about deadly retribution, but Tanner assumed he wasn't. What made it so unbelievable was that Serena had only taken back what was hers.

The wolf had the chance to live, maybe a few thousand dollars poorer, but at least he had his life. Not now. Serena wasn't going to have to worry about looking over her shoulder all the time. Living in a pack, she'd most likely be perfectly safe, but all the bastard would need was one chance to get at her.

"I'm sorry," Serena said.

"Don't be. How much do you want to bet that he would have been just as much of a bastard if you'd taken only a fraction of your own money? You were able to access his accounts and make him feel vulnerable, yet you were gracious enough not to take his money too."

She frowned. "Right. Just like he violated my trust and my privacy by accessing my accounts."

"Correct. But I suspect he doesn't see it that way. He can do it to you, but no one gets away with doing it to him."

She let out her breath. "Okay, so we return to Colorado?"

"No. I suspect if he doesn't learn where we've gone, he'll be waiting at the airport, watching for us. We'll wait for my brothers and cousins to get here and make further plans then."

"He didn't say he was going to kill you also. Do you think he believes I'm alone?"

Tanner pondered that for a moment. "I think you're right. Which would make sense. How would you have found another wolf so quickly when you weren't seeing any and didn't know any in the area? He would have known about it. Everything happened so quickly, he most likely wouldn't suspect you'd be here with a male who would protect you with his life."

"I'm sorry I got you into this."

"This has all worked out for the best. I got you." Tanner grabbed his phone and called Devlyn. "We might have trouble. Harold discovered the money's missing and threatened to kill Serena. We're at a villa in Cayman Brac, and from the sound of it, he thinks she acted alone."

"Damn it. Okay, the guys are on their way. Vaughn and Brock got on a flight flying standby. They'll be in tomorrow morning. Your brothers are still waiting for a flight. Vaughn and Brock will help you put the guy out of his misery if it comes to it."

"Okay, thanks."

"You keep your heads low. Don't take any risks."

"We're going to be here. We're eating at a seafood restaurant, but otherwise, we're staying here." Tanner gave him the location of the villa.

Serena had quickly gotten on her cell phone, and he wondered what she was doing.

Devlyn responded, "All right. I'll let your brothers know what's going on. The other guys are on their flight, and we won't be able to reach them for a few hours. Anything else?"

"No. I'll call you if we learn anything further."

When he ended the call, Serena put her cell down on the bedside table. "Harold doesn't have any reservations for anything. Not for a flight out here either."

"He must know you used his computer to get into his bank accounts. Maybe he remembers you accessed his email for him before."

"Then he changed his email account and made up a new one so any reservations would go to that instead of just changing his password. That way he'd give us a false sense of security if he reserved a flight out here. Now we won't know about it."

"That's a good bet. We won't be able to monitor what he's up to. But he can't monitor us either. Brock and Vaughn are on their way. They should be here by tomorrow. Fisher and Shawn are stuck at the airport. They're still trying to get a flight out."

"Is Devlyn mad about it?"

"Hell yeah. No one threatens his pack members and gets away with it." Tanner pulled her into his arms and they snuggled together.

"I mean, that I got us in this predicament?"

"No, he respects you for what you did. Let's rest for a while, then go to eat."

They fell asleep for a while, then woke to go to the restaurant.

Serena so wanted to do this, but she was upset about

Harold. She was trying not to show it, but she worried he might discover she was here and try to kill both Tanner and her. She felt they needed to stay put and just wait for the guys to arrive.

"We're going out to eat," Tanner said, pulling her from the bed. "We'll deal with him if he shows up."

Tanner set up triggers that would reveal if anyone had come into the villa: sand left at the back door so that if anyone entered that way, they'd have to walk through it. Harold couldn't jump far enough to avoid it and if it was disturbed, they'd know. At the front door, he secured a strand of Serena's red hair at the bottom of the door with a little brown sugar and water solution. If anyone opened the door, it would pull loose.

They packed their laptops and her camera in the car and kept all their important documents with them. All they left were their suitcases and clothes, nothing they'd miss if Harold decided to take them.

They were off to the restaurant after that, ordering lobster tails and shrimp, her favorite food. In the islands, they were really fresh and tasty. "I think we need to take turns on guard duty tonight, don't you? Until your cousins get here?" She pulled another piece of lobster meat from its shell and dipped it in lemon butter sauce.

"I think it's a good idea, but we're staying together." He drank from his fruity rum drink.

"In the living room? We could set up the sofa bed."

"That's what we'll do."

"This was the nicest dinner I've ever had, the nicest company too."

He leaned over and kissed her. "It's been great. Ready to go back to the villa?"

"I am." She could tell he was tense too, not enjoying the meal as much as they would have liked. Not when they had to worry about Harold.

Tanner paid the bill and they returned to the villa. But he checked the front door, found her hair was still in place, indicating no one had been through the door, and she checked the back door. The sand hadn't been touched. No smell of Harold or the she-wolf either. They wouldn't have hunter concealment here, so Tanner was confident if they arrived, he'd smell them.

"Looks good. No problems yet, and we might not have any. Let's make up that sofa bed, we need to finish off this day right."

They quickly made the bed and fell into it, tearing off each other's clothes, half dressed and kissing. What a way to end their first day of mated bliss.

---

Tanner wanted Serena to pull first watch so he didn't have to wake her in the middle of the night. He assumed if Harold found where they were located, he would try to approach them in the middle of the night, figuring they'd be asleep. He had his gun nearby, but when he took out the wolf, he didn't want to show he'd shot the man. Better to have a wolf kill him; no one would be able to explain that.

Serena had shifted to be able to take him on if he showed up. Tanner told her if Harold did, he wanted her to come get him. They had no way of knowing if Harold's mate would take part in a fight or not.

An hour later, he heard Serena growl low. Tanner was out of bed in a flash, shifting, and joining her. He nuzzled her with his cheek against hers. And she turned and licked his face.

Then he heard movement outside the villa. Something moving quietly.

He stayed where he heard the movement while Serena headed to the back door.

The sounds moved away. They waited for a good half hour, then Serena shifted. "We need to see if it was them."

Tanner shifted. "We can't leave the villa. We're safer here. If they break in, we have the advantage. Besides, he won't want to kill you right away, if that was him out there. He'll have to force you to give up your money first. Why don't you try to sleep for now? I'll shift again and keep watch."

"All right. If someone comes again, tell me and I'll shift."

"Believe me, I will. If it is them, he might be regrouping, realizing you're not alone, not when a male wolf has left his scent here also."

"I hadn't thought of that. You're probably right." She shifted again and climbed on the sofa bed.

He smiled at her for shifting back into her wolf form, and while she curled up to sleep, he checked out the whole of the villa inside, listening for any indication someone might be trying to find a way in. He heard the wind and waves, but nothing else. As soon as it was light out, he'd check to see if the wolves had left their scent behind.

As soon as she heard a kitchen window break, Serena was off the sofa bed in a flash, not running for the kitchen as a wolf, but heading in the opposite direction to the front of the villa. She suspected the window was a diversion. She was right. Harold used his lock pick on the front door, but a chain lock prevented him from opening it. He used bolt cutters to cut the lock and then barged inside as a naked human. She lunged for him before he could shift, knowing she couldn't take on the heavier male wolf once he shifted. But Tanner slammed into him first, biting him hard in the arm, forcing him to drop the bolt cutters.

Harold shifted, growled, and struggled to get the aggressive wolf off him, snapping his jaws, unable to get to his feet. He'd made the tactical mistake of entering the house before he shifted, of thinking whoever was with her wasn't as powerful as him. His arrogance could be his downfall. She only hoped.

She was half watching the two wolves fight—though Tanner was winning the battle—and keeping a lookout for Harold's mate in case she tried to come in the back way. Serena couldn't believe Velvet wasn't already here. Maybe she wasn't as alpha as her mate.

Then Serena heard something crunching on glass, and she prayed Tanner would take care of Harold quickly, while she raced off to stop Velvet from helping Harold. The gray she-wolf was bigger than Serena, but what the gray had over her in size, Serena had in pure aggressive adrenaline. Like Tanner, she didn't hesitate to take the wolf on. Serena might not have fought with wolves for some time, she imagined neither did this she-wolf. But Serena had killed a couple of real wolves who hadn't liked that she'd crossed their territory. What could she have done? As much as she'd hated to kill the wolves, it was either that or be killed herself.

Thankfully, the two grays hadn't ganged up on her, so she fought one and then the other. So one gray she-wolf wouldn't be an issue.

She still heard growling in the front room when she tore into Velvet. The woman growled just as loudly back, which made Serena even angrier. She hadn't wanted Tanner to hear her fighting with a wolf. He needed to concentrate on his own fight and not worry about her.

The wolf came so close to her throat, Serena nearly panicked. She had to quit thinking about Tanner and concentrate on the menace before her. She lunged forward, snapping her jaws, tearing at the wolf. She didn't want to kill her, but if she left Serena no choice, she would do what she had to do.

She tasted Velvet's blood and the wolf squeaked and dodged away from her. Serena waited to see if the wolf would quit. It was quiet in the other room, and she glanced behind her to see Tanner standing there, panting, watching what the gray she-wolf would do.

A male gray and a smaller red female were too much for the gray she-wolf to handle. She jumped out through the kitchen window and tore off down the beach. She wouldn't report this to the police. She couldn't.

Serena licked her mate's face, and they both shifted. He took her in his arms and hugged her tight.

"Do you think she'll return?" Serena asked.

"She would be crazy to. I'm going to take a swim."

"I'll go with you."

"I'd rather you—"

She raised her brows at him.

He let out his breath. "—go with me and we'll take your ex-roommate swimming."

She thought of them bleeding—Tanner had suffered some bite marks, and the she-wolf had managed to claw Serena—but neither were badly wounded. Harold was bloodied too, and all she could think of was that sharks feed at night and they all would be bleeding in the water.

"There's a boat rental place not far from here. I'll get a boat and we'll take the body out," Tanner said, changing his mind.

"They have to be closed for now."

"Exactly. Will you be all right?"

"Yes. I doubt Velvet will stick around to see what we do next. While you're gone, I'll be a wolf."

Serena shifted as Tanner left, and it took him so long, she didn't think he'd ever return with the boat. Finally, he returned and brought a fishing net, too, and carried Harold's human body out to the boat.

"You can stay here."

"I'll help you." Wolves helped their mates out, always.

They went out as far as they could, where divers wouldn't be diving to see the coral reefs, and after weighing him down, they heaved Harold into the ocean. Once they were done, Tanner dropped Serena off at the villa beach. He'd been torn between taking her with him just in case Velvet visited again and dropping her at the villa in case he got caught returning the borrowed boat.

Serena had worried about the same thing, anxious that the she-wolf might come back. She'd shifted to wait and watch for her.

When Tanner finally returned, they locked the front door, and would call management in the morning about the vandalism to the window and security chain at the door. Which meant they had to keep up the guard watch until then in case Velvet snuck back.

But she didn't.

The next morning, Tanner called Devlyn with an update on what had happened. "We don't need my brothers' help, if they can't get a flight out."

"They got one earlier this morning. They're afraid they'll miss out on a chance to get to know Serena."

Tanner pulled Serena into his arms and said, "It's too late for that, unless they mean in a brotherly way."

Devlyn laughed. "Is this news I can share with the pack?"

Serena smiled and nodded.

"It sure is. It's a done deal. Hey, I've got an incoming call. Get back with you in a bit." Tanner took the call from Vaughn. "Are you arriving soon?"

"At the airport on Grand Cayman now. We're boarding the flight for Grand Brac, but we passed a woman—a gray wolf—with bags in hand, headed for a flight leaving for the States. She had light-brown hair and looked just like the picture you sent to us of the two of them when they were at the grocery store."

"Okay, that's Harold's mate, and he's dead."

"Hell, don't tell me we flew all the way out here just to miss out on all the action."

"You can help us celebrate the mating."

And that's just what they did. Tanner's brothers joined them several hours later, and while all of them sat on loungers on the beach, rum drinks in hand, they watched the sunset go down over the aqua waters.

"Next time a new she-wolf shows up, I want to be the one doing the protecting," Brock said, sipping from his rum and cola.

Tanner smiled. "The SEAL wolves always think *they* should get the girl."

Serena snuggled up to Tanner. "Not this time. An Army Ranger won out. Are you ready for bed?"

All the guys looked at Tanner and laughed.

"With the pretty she-wolf of my dreams?" Tanner swept her up in his arms and headed for the house. "You don't *ever* have to ask."

# Epilogue

DEVLYN DIDN'T TRUST THAT VELVET WOULDN'T TRY TO steal from another wolf, so Brock and Vaughn located her to see what she was up to after she'd left Grand Cayman Island. Ironically, she hadn't married the wolf and he'd never given her access to his accounts, so she was penniless. Which meant all that money was still sitting in a Grand Cayman account. She'd run off with another wolf and was living in Virginia and it seemed that was end of the story for her.

Serena couldn't wait for Bella to have her babies, though Bella hadn't wanted to know their sexes, so Serena was waiting for the babies to be born before she bought anything for them. They got together all the time, whenever Tanner was at work, or when she wasn't working hard to set up her lending library.

She and Tanner had set up housekeeping in her family's home and hoped to have their own children one day, while Heath was building a home behind the clinic. Fisher and Shawn were building a place of their own, though all of the brothers often came over for pizza parties once a week at Serena and Tanner's home. Serena enjoyed being part of a wolf pack again.

"It was way too many years for us to be apart," she told Bella, hugging her lightly, not wanting to squish the babies.

"Every day I can't believe our good fortune to have you home again."

Serena couldn't have been happier to be home with her sister again and to see her as a pack leader with her loving mate.

And Tanner had been the greatest, as if he'd been her red-hot lover for an eternity. She loved him for it.

Tanner was reminded daily that he had stolen the red wolf from his brothers just because he was the eldest. But he knew that no matter how it happened, in the end, he and Serena had been meant to be together.

And no one could have been more right for the vivacious and protective alpha red wolf he would cherish always.

*The End*

*Read on for a sneak peek at the next book
in Terry Spear's White Wolf series*

# FLIGHT
## OF THE
# WHITE WOLF

*Coming soon from Sourcebooks Casablanca*

## Prologue

*En Route to Big Lake, Alaska*

THE CASE JUST HAD TO INVOLVE FLYING.

On his first day as a private investigator in Seattle, Gavin Summerfield had gotten a case that made him want to string the thieves up. Stolen pets had become a lucrative market for criminals. In this case, two male, champion-sired Samoyed pups, worth nearly three thousand apiece, had been stolen from their owner's fenced-in backyard. The woman and her two teen daughters were in tears.

"I vow I'll find Kodi and Shiloh and bring them home safe," Gavin told the trio. He hoped he wouldn't fail them. Sometimes, pets ended up in lab experiments, or were sold to breeders or puppy mills. Sometimes, the criminals who stole them were looking to return them for a reward.

Soon after he left the family's home with pictures of the pups and their favorite fetch toys, he had discovered that a white van had been sighted at the owner's house and also in the vicinity of four other dognappings. One of the neighbors had captured a photograph of the Alaska license plate on the same van parked in a friend's driveway when the friend wasn't home.

Then Gavin had gotten a lead that the dogs had been flown to Alaska.

Now, he was trying to settle his stomach and pretend he wasn't flying high above the world on his way to see London Lanier, a retired police detective in Big Lake. Gavin's fear of crashing wasn't just a figment of his imagination. Six months earlier, while he was still a Seattle cop, he'd survived a plane crash after jewelry-store robbers had taken him hostage.

The Alaska-bound plane hit more turbulence, and his stomach dropped. He closed his eyes, telling himself he wasn't going to crash. Not this time. That wasn't the only reason he hated to fly. He liked to be in control, and flying left him with no control over anything.

At least he had a lead on the pups. He wanted more than anything to return them to the family, safe and sound. The Samoyeds' pictures reminded him of the dogs his family had raised when he was growing up. Their German shepherds had been as much family to him as his human family had been.

As soon as Gavin's plane landed, he picked up a rental car and drove to the town where his contact was located.

London Lanier was an animal rights activist, primarily concerned with the illegal hunting of wildlife in

Alaska. Gavin had called to tell him the pups had been flown to his neck of the woods, and London had begun to check into it.

When Gavin met London at his Big Lake home, he thought the retiree looked like Santa Claus, with the white beard and hair, though he was a trim version of jolly, old Saint Nick. He was tall, fit, and eager to take on hunters with his bare hands.

"You look like a cop," London said, shaking Gavin's hand.

Gavin took the remark as a compliment. Now that he was a PI, his hair wasn't as short as when he was on the force. Today, he looked more like a SWAT team member, with a black T-shirt, black cargo pants, and heavy-duty black boots. He was in a no-nonsense mood and ready to take the bastards down.

London served them both cups of coffee, and then he got down to business. "From what I've learned, a home near here has lots of dogs barking all day long, and then a few days later most of them are gone. Shortly after that, they have a new batch of dogs. Some of their neighbors are suspicious. Since I don't work on the police force anymore, you'll need to do some canvassing. If you learn anything that proves they really are involved in trafficking pets, let me know, and I'll call the police. I'm still friends with several on the force."

London handed Gavin a hand-drawn map, saying, "I talked to the locals, but everyone knows who I am. Maybe a new guy, just looking for his pups, could convince someone to share something they didn't tell me. Or maybe they've seen something new, or remembered something they hadn't thought of before. Good luck."

"Thanks, London. I'll let you know what happens. And I owe you."

London smiled. "Never know when I might need a PI. Besides, if you can help us take these bastards down, you've done me a favor."

Afterward, Gavin headed over to the Big Lake housing area with its high-income homes, lakefront property, trees all around, and large yards for hiding a slew of runs for stolen pets.

He pulled into the driveway of the home three doors down from the suspect's house, parked, and went to the door. When he knocked, a gray-haired woman with bright-blue eyes greeted him with a smile.

"Ma'am, I'm a private investigator, searching for these two missing pups. They were stolen from the backyard while they were outside playing. Have you seen them? Or know anyone who might have them?"

"Oh yes, of course." Her eyes were rounded, and she licked her lips. "She's my next-door neighbor."

He frowned and glanced at his map. That wasn't the correct house. At least, not according to London. "Are you sure?"

"Yes. She has dogs all the time. Not the same ones though. I see her out walking them along the road in the late spring, summer, early fall. Even in the winter when we're buried in snow. Always different dogs. I figured she fostered them or something. I saw her with two of the cutest little Samoyed pups earlier, maybe six months old? Not sure. They look exactly like yours."

"Do you know her name?"

"Amelia White. She lives alone. Well, except for the revolving door of dogs. I never considered that any of the dogs could have been stolen."

"What about the people at this place?" Gavin pointed to the house on the map that London had targeted.

"Oh yeah, sure. Did London send you? He already asked me."

"You didn't mention Amelia to him?"

"No. She's so sweet. I really didn't think she could be involved in anything so nefarious. But she does have two Samoyed puppies. And that's what you're looking for, right? I hadn't seen them with her before yesterday morning."

"And the other people?"

"Oh, the Michaelses? Asher and Mindy? Yes, I wouldn't be surprised at all about them. Not sure what he does. They don't seem to have a regular occupation, just… money and lots of dogs. They don't walk them. The dogs just bark most of the time, and I've seen all of them rushing to the chain-link fence when I've taken strolls past the place. Different dogs all the time."

"What does Miss White do?"

"She's a seaplane pilot. Her family owns the business."

"Thanks." It would be easy to move stolen pets around as a pilot, wouldn't it? No paperwork hassle. Just fly them where they needed to go. What were the chances that both people were involved in the illegal trade of pets? Maybe Amelia took care of the overflow and the transportation. It would be convenient, with her living so close to the Michaelses.

Gavin drove to Amelia's house first, since she apparently had dogs like the ones he was looking for. He'd start surveillance on the Michaelses after that.

He parked and headed for the large, blue-vinyl-sided home, where he climbed the porch stairs. No dogs barked as he approached, and the front door was slightly ajar. That's when two curious little Samoyed pups poked their noses out, probably hearing his footsteps.

Before Gavin could stop them, they nudged the door open, and one raced down the steps. *Hell!*

The second pup ran to join the first, and Gavin was led on a merry chase. He managed to scoop up the one closest to him, and finally reached the other, grabbing him up in his left arm. The puppies licked him as if this was just part of their playtime.

The problem was that Samoyed puppies all looked the same to him. These two were both white, identical to each other. And they looked just like the photos he had of Kodi and Shiloh.

One pup secure in each arm, he hurried back to the house, ran up the steps, and hollered through the open door, "Miss White? Your front door was open, and your pups ran off." If they weren't the right pups, he wasn't about to confiscate them and be accused of stealing *her* pets! On the other hand, he worried about foul play because the door was slightly ajar and no one was answering. What if something had happened to her?

Suddenly, a wet, naked woman streaked across the living room, glancing at him for a second as she ran, and disappeared down a hall. "Put them down, get out, and close the door," she called out.

Shocked, he just stood there, his mouth hanging agape, the image of the gorgeous blond in the raw still imprinted on his brain. She was in great shape, her hands covering her bouncing breasts as she'd dashed down the hall. He closed the front door so the puppies wouldn't run out of the house again, and set them down on the hardwood floor. "I'm leaving," he called. "Sorry... Your door was open, and I was worried something might be wrong."

He needed to question her about the pups...maybe later. He started to back away from them slowly, and had almost reached the door when they came bounding after him. He was trying to figure out how to keep them from dashing out again as soon as he opened the door, when suddenly the woman reappeared with a blue towel wrapped around her curvy body and a Taser in her hand—and shot him.

---

After taking down the man, who was unlawfully in her house, Arctic wolf shifter Amelia Marie White knew she recognized him—the uniformed, human cop from Seattle. The man who'd been taken hostage on the plane she'd been forced to fly as the getaway pilot. What angered her also was that the man in charge of the heist, Clayton Drummer, the gray wolf she'd been dating, had been a Seattle cop too. She knew now that he'd only been dating her because he wanted to use her to fly him out of Seattle after stealing the jewels.

Had the two men known each other?

Possibly. What if this one was really here to take

her down for killing Clayton? Not arrest her, as she'd thought initially.

"Stay there. Don't move a muscle. I have another Taser all ready and fired up to use on you. And the police are on their way."

Not that the guy was moving. He lay prone on her floor near the door, watching her, groaning. *In her home*. He was half-dazed and looked like he was having trouble focusing. Maybe he hadn't seen enough of her to recognize her as the pilot of the plane that day. But if not, why would he be here?

Confident he wasn't going anywhere, Amelia rushed back to her bedroom, her foster pups running after her. She pulled on a T-shirt and a pair of jeans, then grabbed her phone to call the police.

Wouldn't you know, of all the times her front door hadn't locked properly, she'd stripped to take a shower, and the faucet handle had fallen off in her hand— probably due to mineral water corrosion. She'd had to use the guest bathroom and remembered only after she showered that she'd washed all the towels in there. Which were still in the dryer. And she hadn't brought clothes with her because she normally just walked from her master bathroom to her dresser.

When she'd heard the deep-voiced male calling out her name inside her house, shocking her, she'd had a split-second decision to make. She could shift into her wolf and scare the guy off, but she worried she'd scare her foster pups too. Or she could dash through the house naked, grab a towel and her Taser from the master bathroom, and take care of the guy. Dashing through the house as a naked woman had seemed to throw him off guard, at least long enough for her to tase him.

She'd hoped he would be gone by the time she returned. When he hadn't been, she'd had to take action.

Once the police were on their way, she hurried back into the room where the guy was still lying on the floor, stunned. She wasn't sure if he was staying put because she told him to, or if he really was still incapacitated. Too bad he wasn't a wolf, as sexy as he was.

"Who are you, and why didn't you leave when I told you to?" She prayed he didn't say he was still a cop and investigating her leaving the scene of a crime.

"Gavin Summerfield," he managed to get out. "Former Seattle police, private investigator now, looking into the theft of a pair of Samoyeds in Seattle, which led me here to Big Lake. And your place."

Now that she could really observe him—unlike the first time she'd seen him when he'd been hustled into the back of the plane and she'd been forced into the cockpit, or when he was lying on the ground half-conscious after the crash—Amelia couldn't believe the hot-looking man she'd just tased was now a PI. Dazed green eyes, red hair, all dressed in black, his T-shirt showing off his nice muscles.

She'd really thought he'd been in on the heist, offering himself as a hostage as a cover. When Clayton had tried to kill him, she'd taken her boyfriend out, mainly for trying to kill the cop, but also because as a wolf, Clayton couldn't go to jail. And because Clayton had used her and would have killed her if she hadn't gone along with the program.

"Stolen Samoyeds?" What Gavin said wasn't registering because all she could think of were the jewelry heist and the downed plane. Sure, she was taking care of a couple of Samoyed puppies. She was fostering them, for heaven's sake. Just like she fostered tons of dogs until she could find them good homes.

Then she worried. What if Molly and Snowflake *were* the stolen pups he was searching for?

Two cop cars pulled into her driveway, and she met the uniformed men at the door. She prayed Gavin hadn't recognized her and wouldn't say anything about the Seattle business to them.

Brenham, one of the cops, began checking Gavin over and verifying his identity, ready to take him into custody.

"Call London Lanier, the retired police detective who worked in your department. He gave me the information about the pet theft ring in this area," Gavin gritted out.

The other cop called London to see if Gavin's story checked out.

"Do you want to press charges?" Brenham asked Amelia.

"No," she said. "He shouldn't have stayed in the house when I told him to leave, but he did return my pups when I could have lost them for good."

"I was working my way toward the door, and the pups were following me. I was afraid they'd dash out again," Gavin said.

She liked his deep, manly voice, though it was a little rough around the edges right now, different from when she'd first heard him talking to her from the foyer.

"*Was* your front door open?" Brenham asked Amelia, a black brow arched.

"Yeah, I'm having trouble getting it to seat properly, and though I locked it, apparently it wasn't shut all the way. I have a carpenter coming to check it this afternoon."

She couldn't believe Gavin hadn't told the cops who she was. Maybe he truly hadn't seen her face before, and he really was only here about the missing pups. If that was the case, she hoped he found them for the puppies' and the family's sake.

Brenham helped Gavin to his feet. Frowning, Gavin asked her, "Have we met before?"

Her heart pounded. The police waited for her to answer him. She quickly shook her head. "Everyone says that."

"You look familiar," Gavin insisted. "Have you ever been to Seattle?"

She felt light-headed all of a sudden and was afraid the color had drained from her face. "No." She hated to lie. Since she hadn't reported what had happened to her six months ago, she was afraid the police would believe she'd willingly been the robbers' getaway pilot. Especially if they learned she had been dating the dead wolf.

"Okay, my mistake. It's probably like you said. You just look like someone else." Gavin didn't sound like he truly believed that.

Which reminded her he was a former cop—like these two here who were watching her behavior. She was trying to look perfectly innocent. She wasn't sure Gavin was buying it.

Brenham began looking at the pups' photos that

Gavin had, and then he carefully considered Amelia's pups. "The ones in the photo and the ones you have look the same to me. Are you sure the pups you're fostering hadn't been stolen before they were taken to the shelter where you picked them up?"

The police were thorough, so one got in contact with the animal shelter to verify her story. Especially since her neighbor had told Gavin the pups had arrived about the same time he learned the Seattle pups had been stolen.

Fearing that they might be, Amelia took the photo from the officer and really studied it. The Samoyed pups did look very much like hers. Except for one thing. The ones in the photo were wearing blue leopard-print collars.

She frowned at Gavin, who was leaning against the wall, still looking like she'd just tased him. "Are the two puppies you're looking for males?"

---

Once Gavin was feeling more like himself—though still having visions of a beautiful, naked, blond female streaking across her living room—he set up surveillance to watch Asher and Mindy Michaels's home, the place London had originally steered him to check out. Gavin still swore he'd seen Amelia White before—in the commission of a crime. A flashback of the blond wearing a blue dress flitted across his brain for a couple of seconds. The experience was like when he'd see a bank teller at the grocery store. Because she wasn't where he normally saw her, he couldn't quite make the connection. Yet, due to having been both a cop and a private investigator, he was good at remembering faces.

Still, he needed to get his mind on his work and off the woman.

————♦♦♦————

Early in the evening three days later, a new vanload of dogs arrived. Gavin quickly made a call to coordinate with the police. Once they were on their way, he went to talk to Asher Michaels, the man getting out of the van, to delay him until the police arrived.

"Hey, excuse me. You're Asher Michaels, right?" Gavin asked, stalking up the driveway and getting close to the man. He was dark haired and clean shaven, his square jaw tight with a cleft in the center of the chin. His hard, gray eyes narrowed at Gavin.

Gavin knew Asher wanted to secure the dogs pronto before anyone began asking questions. He kept looking back at the house as if expecting someone to come out and help him.

"I've got work to take care of. I don't allow solicitors on my property," Asher said.

"I'm not trying to sell anything. I'm just looking for these two little fellas. Kodi and Shiloh. They got out on me, and I heard you took in dogs sometimes. Your neighbor fosters dogs, and she thought you did too. Our family has been devastated by the loss. Can you look at the picture and tell me if you've seen them? Or have them?"

"Look, I don't have your dogs. Now get off my property."

Asher refused to look at the picture. Gavin shoved it under his nose, trying to stall him, but also wanting to get a reaction. "*Please*, take a look."

Asher did, only because it was hard not to since the photo was so close to his face. His eyes widened fractionally. Either he had a couple of Samoyeds he'd stolen, or he'd already gotten rid of them.

"I'm an undercover cop," Asher said. "Get out of here before you blow my cover."

Gavin hesitated, processing that information. Then he assumed Asher was spinning a tale to serve as a cover for his illegal business. "If you know anything at all about them, I'm willing to pay a big reward for their return," Gavin told him.

Asher moved his jacket aside and reached for a holstered gun. *Ah, hell.*

Gavin hadn't expected the guy to pull a gun on him. He grappled with the man, hearing the cops pulling up street side. Gavin was glad for his police training as he struggled with Asher, trying to wrest the gun away before it went off. He hoped the police didn't think he was assaulting Asher for just suspecting he had stolen the dogs.

Gavin called out to the cops, "He's got a gun!"

The cops ran toward them, yelling at Asher to drop the weapon.

Gavin finally managed to trip Asher and take the perp down. When a shot fired, just missing Gavin's head, he was thinking this PI work could be damn dangerous. At the same time, a woman raced out of the house and began beating on Gavin with her fists, trying to free Asher. Gavin wouldn't let go for anything. He was just glad the woman hadn't gone for the gun.

The police finally reached them and arrested Asher

and Mindy, a petite brunette with catlike green eyes. Another couple of police vehicles arrived. The police officers hauled the couple off to jail. London even showed up with a list of dog thefts in Alaska to see if any of the dogs matched those that had been recently stolen.

"Hell, you need to come work for us," London told Gavin.

"I thought you were retired."

"Just got rehired to be on a special unit that deals with stolen pets and illegal hunting. Come on inside. Let's see if we can find those pups of yours."

"Asher said he was an undercover cop," Gavin told him as they found kennels full of dogs of every size and breed in the backyard. He would guess the Michaelses had well over a hundred, not including the ones in the van.

"Yeah, like I'm a strip-club dancer. He didn't fool you, did he?" London asked, smiling.

"No. I figured he thought I really was looking for my missing pups and he could convince me to go away. Then he must have realized I wasn't buying his story and thought a gun would change my mind."

Brenham, one of the officers who had gone to Amelia White's home to arrest Gavin, called out to him, "Hey, Summerfield. You might be interested in looking at a couple of Samoyed puppies in the bedroom up front." Brenham smiled. "They even have blue collars, just like the ones the pups in the picture were wearing."

Hoping they were the pups he was looking for, Gavin hurried into the house and found Kodi and Shiloh in a crate together. They were watching the other dogs being rounded up, excited, wanting to play. Gavin called their names, and they both turned, wagging their tails.

He checked them over. Their microchips had been removed, but he made sure they were both males. They were wearing the same blue leopard-print collars too. Thankfully, they were in good condition.

Gavin was glad to be going home with the two pups but found himself thinking about the naked woman who'd had two Samoyed pups. He hoped she'd hear that he'd broken up a pet theft ring so she knew he'd been completely honest with her.

After the terrifying plane ride back to Seattle and the return of the pups to their grateful family, Gavin went in to the PI agency, where his partners, all former police officers, were eager to hear how the agency's first case had gone.

He told his story, not leaving any detail out. Owen Nottingham whistled when Gavin mentioned the part about Amelia. David Davis laughed. Smiling, Cameron MacPherson slapped him on the back. "Hell, Gavin, you have all the luck."

# Chapter 1

*Nearly seven years later*
*Northern Minnesota*

GAVIN HATED ONE THING MORE THAN ANYTHING ELSE IN the world—flying. And that's just what he was going to have to do for this mission.

Eleanor Dylan was a cosmetic heiress, though she also had other kinds of businesses, and she was certain her husband was having an affair. She needed proof to start divorce proceedings and keep her inheritance intact. "Conrad is going on a fly-in company canoe trip to the Boundary Waters Canoe Area Wilderness, the BWCA, and your agency is the closest to that location. They'll be in the wilderness, so you'll have to take a seaplane to get there. Well, I guess you could just paddle in, but it would take you too long to catch up to them. Wouldn't it? I mean, if you only have a day and a half to get ready and be there?"

"Yes, ma'am." Gavin grimaced, glad they were speaking on the phone.

"I would have called sooner if I had thought of doing this earlier. But it's the perfect way to catch them at it, I think. They'll be there for nine days. The tour package includes food and all the equipment they need, so they won't be stopping for supplies anywhere. Can you do it?"

"Yes, ma'am. Our agency can definitely take care of it."

All of Gavin's PI partners and their mates were Arctic wolf shifters who had been turned a few years ago. As wolves, they had enhanced night vision, and their hearing was superior whether they were in their wolf coats or human form. They had settled in Minnesota and their PI business was booming, which meant Gavin was the only one available for this job. A trip to the Boundary Waters totally appealed. More so if he could have just paddled in.

"Not your agency. *You*. I've looked into your background already, and from everything I've seen, you've got an outstanding track record."

"Thanks. All of my partners are also well qualified." Gavin didn't want her to believe that they couldn't handle the case if one of them had to take over for him.

"You, or no deal."

"Yes, ma'am. I'll head up there and check it out." His pack had already reserved permits for him and two of his partners to go to the Boundary Waters later in the summer. He checked on his computer for the availability of a different entry point, and he found one. Some canoeists must have canceled their trip because of the bad weather expected over the next couple of days. Gavin was able to switch his time and port of entry without any trouble.

"Conrad gave me a copy of their trip itinerary in case anything happened," Eleanor said. "It shows their route and where they intend to set up camp. He'll never suspect a lone canoeist is doing surveillance on him, will he?"

"No, ma'am. Does he often give you the detailed

itinerary for his trips?" Gavin couldn't help but think that if her husband were having an affair, he'd keep his wife *out* of the loop.

"Always. I would have been suspicious if he hadn't."

Okay, that explained it. Though Gavin wondered if Conrad would have given her a fake itinerary if he thought his wife was having him watched.

"Have you been in the Boundary Waters before?" she asked.

"Yes, ma'am. Several times." Especially once they had more control over their shifting. The wilderness had been the perfect, close getaway for them.

"Oh good," she said with relief.

"How many are on this company trip?" As a wolf, he could get up close to the campsite, and Conrad and his party would never know he was there.

"Four executives from various departments. Lee Struthers, the CEO, likes to chill out with her executives on adventure tours a couple of times a year, instead of always conducting business in the boardroom. It's supposed to be a team-building trip. One of the executives is a woman. And the two sales associates going with them are women too."

"You suspect your husband is having an affair with someone in the group, then?"

"A top sales associate. She's in her late twenties. He's forty-five now. I know Orwell Johnston, who's also on this trip, is having an affair with the other sales associate. Conrad told me all about their antics. The long lunch hours at a nearby hotel. The gifts he gives her, even at work."

"How did you learn who would be going?" Gavin wondered why Conrad would tell his wife, if the guy was having an affair with someone at work.

"I asked. And Conrad told me."

That sounded like he was open about things with his wife. "Have you had other investigators checking into his activities?"

"Yes, before we were married eight years ago. I had inherited quite a large estate before I met him, and I wanted to make sure he wasn't marrying me just for my money."

"You must have learned he was a good prospect, since you married him."

"No skeletons in his closet. He worked his way up in the greeting-card business and is now one of their executives. I didn't suspect anything was wrong between us until he came home from the last trip. He acted distant and aloof, and he didn't seem to be his cheerful self for several weeks. I asked what was wrong, but he said nothing was. Which I knew was a lie. He wouldn't tell me what had happened."

"The sales associate had been with him that time too?"

"Yes. They seemed close when I attended the company Christmas party. She was sweet and got me refills on my drinks, and she was trying to be careful about not showing any overt affection toward Conrad. But there were coy smiles, and she patted his hand and ran it over his back in a way that led me to believe there was more intimacy going on between them."

"How did he react to her attentions?"

"Like he was used to it. He didn't make her stop. I didn't see him treat her in the same way, but that could just mean he was being more discreet at the party because I was there. After the way he acted following the last team-building trip, and with Cheryl part of the group again, I want to know what's really going on."

"Okay, so anything else that raises your suspicions? Like he's taking more care with his appearance? Staying away from home later, leaving home earlier? Evasiveness? Defensiveness?"

"He has been working later. If you must know, our sex life is nil. He's always taken care of his appearance. Evasiveness? Yes, especially after the last trip. And defensiveness, yes. He's received calls he's secretive about. I haven't smelled a woman's perfume on his clothes though—and I haven't seen any receipts that would make me suspicious. Of course, he could be using a separate account that I don't know about for more... personal business."

"You have a prenuptial agreement, right?"

"Yes. If he's having an affair and we divorce, he doesn't get a cent from me. To be fair, if I divorced him and he wasn't at fault, he'd receive a settlement. I do love him, and I was willing to make that concession."

"Okay. I'll get right on this." Gavin didn't know what to think. If Conrad was telling his wife about his coworker's affair, was he trying to get a reaction out of her? Maybe. One of the cops Gavin knew on the Seattle force had done that. His wife thought it was amusing, until she learned her husband was having an affair with a nurse at one of the local hospitals.

"Thank you. I'm emailing you pictures of Conrad and Cheryl. I trust you'll be inconspicuous."

"Guaranteed."

They finished the call, and Gavin studied the photos Eleanor had sent, apparently taken at the company Christmas party. There was a Christmas tree in the background, and both Conrad and Cheryl were holding glasses of champagne.

Conrad was dark-haired, dark-eyed, and had a mani-cured, pampered appearance. He didn't appear to be the type who was ready to rough it. Cheryl had dark roots, but the rest of her hair was pale blond, and she had light-green eyes. She looked like the girl next door, sweet and innocent.

Gavin called Faith MacPherson, one of his partner's mates, to let her know he had a job and would be leav-ing as soon as he could. She managed the calls for their business while taking care of her six-year-old triplets. Her husband, Cameron, and their other two partners were out on jobs of their own.

"Oh, Gavin, I'm so sorry you had to be the one to take this particular case," Faith said.

He wished no one knew about his fear of flying. Faith had learned the truth when Cameron had needed his help to locate their missing friends, and he'd had to fly from Seattle to Maine to aid them.

"No problem. I'll let you know what's going on when I locate the group and tell you if I learn anything."

"Be careful."

"I will."

# Acknowledgments

Thanks to Deb Werksman, who believed in the world I created and gave me the chance to share my story. And to my critique partners who have been there every step of the way—Rebel Romance Writers: Vonda, Judy, Pam, Randy, Tammy, Carol, Betty (may she rest in peace), and Darcy! Thanks to Sourcebooks for a decade of sharing my Heart of the Wolf world!

# About the Author

Bestselling and award-winning author Terry Spear has written over sixty paranormal romance novels and four medieval Highland historical romances. *Heart of the Wolf*, her first werewolf romance, was named a 2008 *Publishers Weekly* Best Book of the Year, and her subsequent titles have garnered high praise and hit the *USA Today* bestsellers list. A retired officer of the U.S. Army Reserves, Terry lives in Spring, Texas, where she is working on her next werewolf romance, continuing with her Highland medieval romances, and having fun with her young adult novels. When she's not writing, she's photographing everything that catches her eye, making teddy bears, and playing with her Havanese puppies. For more information, please visit terryspear.com or follow her on Twitter @TerrySpear. She is also on Facebook at facebook.com/terry.spear and on Wordpress at terryspear.wordpress.com.

# Also by Terry Spear

**Heart of the Wolf**
*Heart of the Wolf*
*To Tempt the Wolf*
*Legend of the White Wolf*
*Seduced by the Wolf*

**Silver Town Wolf**
*Destiny of the Wolf*
*Wolf Fever*
*Dreaming of the Wolf*
*Silence of the Wolf*
*A Silver Wolf Christmas*
*Alpha Wolf Need Not Apply*
*Between a Wolf and a
Hard Place*

**Highland Wolf**
*Heart of the Highland Wolf*
*A Howl for a Highlander*
*A Highland Werewolf
Wedding*
*Hero of a Highland Wolf*
*A Highland Wolf
Christmas*

**SEAL Wolf**
*A SEAL in Wolf's
Clothing*
*A SEAL Wolf Christmas*
*SEAL Wolf Hunting*
*SEAL Wolf In Too Deep*
*SEAL Wolf Undercover*

**Heart of the Jaguar**
*Savage Hunger*
*Jaguar Fever*
*Jaguar Hunt*
*Jaguar Pride*
*A Very Jaguar Christmas*

**Billionaire Wolf**
*Billionaire in
Wolf's Clothing*

**White Wolf**
*Dreaming of a White
Wolf Christmas*